I0846849

THE MOSTLY HAPPY LIFE OF TOSHI OZAWA

Kamaishi Heritage

Book 1

Copyright © 2024 by D. D. Davenport

ISBN 979-8-9905440-0-0 paperback

ISBN 979-8-9905440-1-7 eBook

ISBN 979-8-9943916-0-0 Large Print

This Book is Dedicated

to

readers of every age and culture who push forward with
integrity to overcome adversity.

This is a work of historical fiction. Three of the many characters in the story were real and living at the time of their appearance. All thoughts, conversations, and actions attributed to them are solely of my imagination. See Author's Notes following the story for more information about the story and the characters.

INTRODUCTION

For twenty-five generations leading up to the Meiji Revolution, Japan was sealed off from the rest of the world. *Upheaval* is not too strong a word to describe the changes that followed.

Feudal class systems were eliminated, a national army was formed, a national tax system was initiated, a national education system was launched, and Christianity was no longer banned.

The result was an industrial revolution that brought with it accelerated growth, opportunity, and profit for many—turmoil and hardship for others.

***

While Japanese culture refers to family name first, followed by the given name, this book refers to them in Western format, given name first, followed by family or surname. Admittedly, it is an example of why Japan was reluctant to interact with foreign countries back in 1864: the fear of losing their cultural heritage. Since most readers of this book will likely be Westerners, that is the format used here.

Regarding honorifics, *san* is used at times in the story to show respect for a stranger, age, or social standing. While there are many variations of honorifics, depending on who is being addressed, only *san* is used here.

CONTENTS

PART ONE

Kamaishi

Chapter 1
Toshi's First Job

TOKYO – 1873 – GRADUATION

Yuko turned to her husband with a frown and said, "Tell me again why Kotaro isn't here."

Isao was staring at the dignitaries sitting on the platform one row ahead. It never hurt to know important people, and if he had to be here, he might as well make the most of it. He sighed and turned to face his wife, about to respond, when she answered for him.

"Oh, I remember now...you said he was busy…too busy to watch his only brother graduate from university."

Isao shrugged. "Someone had to stay and run the factory."

"He didn't want to come; that's the real reason," she retorted.

"If both of us came, who would watch over the factory? Somebody has to be there."

"If my father still ran it, you can bet he would have taken the time to be here."

"It was different then. You could trust workers without watching them all the time."

Yuko studied the group of students arranging themselves to the left of the platform. Toshi was somewhere among them.

She turned to Isao and said, "Trust works in both directions, you know. When my father owned the factory, workers trusted him because they knew he cared about them as people, not just as workers. That seems to be something you didn't learn from him."

"Look how much the factory has grown since I took over. Are you telling me you don't like living in Shibamata? We wouldn't be able to live there if I let the workers push us around. Your father was too easy on them. That's why your father couldn't afford to move to a better neighborhood. We would still be living in his house, instead of Kotaro. In a few more years, Kotaro will be able to move to a better neighborhood, too. Besides, Kotaro doesn't believe in school. He thinks it's a waste of time; nothing more than a fancy place where young people go to keep from going to work."

"That is absurd," Yuko said. "He should be here to celebrate with his brother. The factory is always there. Graduation only comes once." She turned away from her husband and feigned a newly acquired interest in the other students as they walked across the platform.

Isao fidgeted through the rest of the program, watching them pass, one by one, until he spotted his youngest son approaching the platform. He nudged Yuko's arm to alert her, but she was well ahead of him and already leaning forward in her seat.

"Toshi Ozawa: mathematics and engineering," came the announcement a few minutes later. Yuko clapped her hands, then, unable to contain herself, stood up and waved when the distinguished man in a crimson robe handed Toshi his diploma. Turning to Isao, she said, "Isn't this exciting? The first person in our family to graduate."

Isao smiled at her and nodded lightly. But he did not look excited. He looked like he would rather be back at the furniture factory, dusting the inventory.

When Toshi joined his parents following the ceremony, he was smiling so big he could barely speak. He settled for a bow and held the certificate out for them to see.

"We're so proud of you, Toshi," his mother beamed.

"Yes, son, we are proud of you," his father added. "It shows that you have the discipline to do what you set out to do."

Just then, two young girls about Toshi's age walked by. Yuko clearly saw them steal a glance at her son. Toshi, however, either did not see them or was too excited about his diploma to notice.

"Won't it be nice when girls attend university?" Yuko murmured.

Isao turned his head away from following the two young girls to look at his wife. "What?" he blurted.

"Girls… I said, won't it be nice when they can graduate from university?"

"What on earth would girls do with a university education? They learn all they need to know from their mothers. That's what mothers are for. Where do you get these ideas?"

"From the emperor," she replied. "The emperor cares about educating girls. My friends told me all about it. He even set up a new ministry. The government is going to provide school for everyone—including girls. So, if girls can go to school when they're young, some are bound to keep going when they get older—just like the boys."

"What has happened to our country?" Isao stammered. "What is our country coming to?"

***

Isao gave Toshi the rest of the week off to celebrate his graduation, but was waiting for him at breakfast the following Monday morning. They walked together to the furniture factory at six thirty, arriving forty-five minutes later. The factory was well across town from Shibamata, in a seedier section of Tokyo, closer to where the workers lived.

The sun was above the horizon, even at this early hour. But a perpetual haze filtered the radiant sky above. Home to a million inhabitants, the largest city in the world seemed to create an environment all its own. At this time of day most residents were taking their morning meal, with puffs of gray and black smoke emitting from every chimney for as far as Toshi could see. The night soil workers had mostly returned home from their grisly work. Others passed without looking up, their telltale stench giving them away.

Isao walked with purpose. He had walked this route a thousand times. There was little to see along the way, and work to be done the minute he walked through the factory door. Over the years he had come to recognize familiar faces, mostly ones close to home—

this man sold Persian rugs, that one, fine silk garments. He smiled and bowed politely to each important face. A person could never have too many important contacts.

As they neared the factory, the street thinned almost entirely of human traffic, only to be replaced by traffic of a lesser breed. Rats and other rodents remained mostly underground and out of sight, but a few of the more adventurous could be seen sipping rainwater at the gutter, or nibbling the carcass of a fallen crow, beneath a pile of weathered rubbish.

It was Toshi's first visit to the factory in several years. "Do the rodents bother you?" he asked his father as they walked.

"Rodents? What rodents?" When he looked where Toshi was pointing, he seemed surprised by their presence. "Oh, the rats? No, you get used to them. They're nothing to worry about. If you're thinking about the day ahead and what you're going to accomplish, you don't even notice they are there."

Toshi's brother, Kotaro, lived with his wife and two small children near the factory. It was the house Yuko had inherited from her father ten years prior, along with the factory. He was waiting at the entrance when Toshi and their father arrived.

"Good morning, Father," he said. Then, almost as an afterthought, turned to Toshi. "Are you finally ready to go to work?"

Isao turned and headed for the sales area, leaving Toshi in the hands of his older brother. "I'll meet you here after work," he said as he left. "Then you can tell me what you learned today."

Kotaro led Toshi through the large production shop, making sure as they went, that all the workers had arrived and were busy at their designated tasks. Along the way, he pointed out to Toshi how he was able to increase production by assigning each worker small, specific duties. "They get very good at their job," he boasted, "but the best part is, they do it faster. That means we make more furniture in the same amount of time—and that means more profit for the factory." He smiled at Toshi at his demonstration of creativity.

Toshi followed his brother up one aisle and down the next as Kotaro made his daily assessment of workers and materials. "It is extremely important," he told Toshi, "that we think ahead at every station. Does it have enough material? An idle worker is money lost. There is no excuse for an idle worker. That will be one of your jobs: to make sure there are always enough materials, whether it be wood, glue, saws, whatever. We must never run short of equipment or materials."

"How do you ensure the supply?" Toshi asked, after thinking about it. Do you have control over the suppliers? Like the wood and glue. How can you tell if they are keeping up? Do you buy more than you need and maintain excess inventory?"

"Yes, that is precisely what we do. Always keep the warehouse filled to the roof with extra materials. That way, we're protected, in case one of them gets behind."

"But doesn't that waste a lot of our capital, by having unneeded materials?"

Kotaro responded with an agitated look. "We might have more of our capital invested in materials than necessary," he said with authority, "but at least we don't have to worry about running out, and workers sitting on their hands."

When they arrived at the second floor, he gazed through the large windows overlooking the production floor below and, waving an extended arm from one side to the other, proclaimed with pride, "This is what we've built, Father and I. With all the changes taking place in Japan, we will soon be part of the new frontier, like Germany, England, and America. Together, we're building an empire, right here in this small factory." Then he looked at Toshi with a face that suggested he could almost see the money rolling in.

"Welcome to my office," he announced as they walked a few steps down the hall. They stepped inside to reveal two magnificently carved tables, a plush oriental rug covering most of the floor, and a beautifully inlaid writing desk that consumed the center of the room. Shelves along the back wall were filled with leather-bound books of different sizes.

Then Kotaro led his younger brother out the door and farther down the hall. "This will be your office," he said as he opened the door and stepped inside.

Looking around, Toshi saw a table in the center of the room, behind which was a small wooden chair. There were no books in this office, not even shelves to hold them.

"Don't worry, little brother. I had a modest beginning, too. And after six years of hard work, you can see how it paid off. If you dedicate yourself to the factory as I did, Father will reward you as well. I'll be in my office, and you are welcome to enter unless I'm meeting with someone. If I'm busy, it will have to wait until later." Then Kotaro turned and left the room.

Not knowing what, exactly, his duties were, other than being the owner's second son, Toshi first searched his office for any documents, reports, or other information that might help him understand what made the factory succeed. Finding nothing, he sat for several minutes in the plain wooden chair.

The largest wall in his office, the one behind his chair, held a large and simple clock. He assumed it was meant to remind him that discipline and punctuality were the primary elements of a successful life. It did seem odd that such an important symbol would hang behind him and not in front, where he could see it throughout the day. He decided it must have fit the back wall better.

Having accomplished everything he could think of from the confines of his new office, Toshi decided to step next door and ask his brother for suggestions on how to begin taking the company to the exciting new future he had alluded to. Exiting his office, he took the dozen steps to his left and was just about to enter when he observed Kotaro bent low over his table with another man. They seemed deeply engrossed in papers spread across the top of his table, and the implication was, they were not to be disturbed.

Luckily, Toshi had not yet knocked or begun to open the closed door. He was able to turn quickly on his heels and keep walking toward the stairway. He went down the steps and continued across the floor, retracing the route he had only recently trod with his older brother.

He found himself stopping at every station, observing each step until he understood the sequence and the consequence. He had traversed only half the floor when a whistle sounded loudly, which in turn caused the workers to lay down their tools and hurry to a door leading to the alley behind. It was lunchtime. He could barely believe how fast the time had passed once he began to study the actual tasks of every worker. *Working here might be more interesting than I thought,* he decided.

Since all the workers left for lunch on their own, Toshi returned to the upper floor, but now his brother was conferring with someone different. Neither seemed concerned that the whistle had blown for lunch, or that all of the workers had left the floor.

Not wanting to enter uninvited, he entered his office instead, and opened the sack his mother had prepared for him early that morning. He sat at his desk and ate alone. While he ate, he searched through the single drawer for a pencil and paper. Then he wrote down all the questions and ideas he had collected throughout the morning.

When the whistle sounded a second time, Toshi grabbed the paper and started for the factory. He was about to exit through the door when he considered how the workers might react if they saw him observing them and then writing in his notes. *They might think I'm grading them or spying on them*, he thought. He returned the paper to his desk and headed for the door a second time. Still, the idea stuck with him. *Who better would know why they are doing something a certain way than the person doing it?* He would have to remember their answers and write them down later, back in his office.

Watching an obviously talented woodworker carving small birds on the face of a table leg, Toshi asked, "You are so precise with your carving that it must surely require a sharp tool to make the cuts. How often do you have to sharpen your tools?"

"It depends," the man replied solemnly. "Sometimes the wood is not as hard, and the blades last longer. I sharpen them at the end of the day, as your brother taught me. Sometimes, by after lunch, they get a little dull, but I always manage until the end of the day."

"How long does it take to sharpen the blades?"

"I usually spend fifteen minutes," he said. It doesn't take long."

Toshi's progress slowed in the afternoon, precisely because of his idea of asking questions as he went. At first, the workers were reluctant to respond and carefully selected their words in such a way as to avoid giving him a direct answer.

Realizing he was the one at a disadvantage, Toshi responded in the only way he knew, and the way that came naturally to him. He tried to get to know the worker.

"Have you been working here for a long time?" he asked in a neutral voice.

"Three years," came the reply.

"That is quite a long time. You must like what you do."

"Ah, well enough, I guess. I don't think about it too much."

"Is there anything I could do to make it better for you?"

The man laughed at first. "You could give me a raise."

Toshi laughed, too. "I suppose that would be nice," he replied. "But I don't have that much authority. I could use one myself, but since I'm a family member, I don't get paid. What about your tools? Do you have all the tools you need? I noticed the clamps on your workbench seem a little worn. Is that something that would help you?"

"Yes, that would help; sometimes the wood slips, and I have to re-clamp it."

"I'll ask my brother if it can be fixed," Toshi said. "Thank you for taking time with me."

Later, he talked with a worker who seemed unusually quiet, almost lethargic. "Are you feeling okay?" he asked.

"Huh? Oh, yes," he finally replied. Then Toshi heard his stomach growl.

"It sounds like you might be hungry."

When the man flushed red in the face, Toshi regretted his attempt at a lighthearted joke.

"I forgot to bring my lunch today," he stammered. "I'll be all right tomorrow."

"I'll be right back," Toshi told him. "I have some rice crackers and manju that my mother sent with me. I wasn't hungry, so I'm not going to eat them." Then he dashed toward the stairway before the worker could stop him.

"I'll be fine," the man said when Toshi returned. "It's my fault I forgot to bring my lunch."

"No, really," Toshi said. "I'm not going to eat them, and they will just go to waste. They should tide you over for the afternoon, at least."

"Thank you," the man said. He dropped his tool and stuffed a rice cracker in his mouth.

When the workers realized Toshi seemed genuinely interested in them, they began to open up and tell him what they thought.

By late in the afternoon Toshi found the opportunity he'd been waiting for—his brother was alone in his office. He knocked gently as he opened the door. His brother smiled when he entered.

"Well, little brother, how was your first day at a real job? Did you learn how to operate a factory?"

"It went better than I'd hoped," he replied. "At first, I was not sure how to proceed, but then I decided to walk the floor and observe each of the workers. It didn't occur to me until after lunch to ask the workers why they did things in a certain way, but when I did, they gradually opened up with their replies. I think there are several ways we could improve production if you give me the approval."

Kotaro looked back at him and Toshi saw the anger rising, simply by the color of his face. "You did what?" he blurted. "You asked the workers for advice on how to do their jobs? That is against every factory rule I ever heard of. It's *our* job to tell the worker how to do *his*. If we start asking their opinion on how to do the work, we have given away our right to lead. The next thing you know, they'll be wanting our jobs."

Kotaro inhaled deeply several times, which helped return his face to a normal color. "You are forgiven because you are new. But from now on, you are not to ask workers for their opinions. Your job is to make sure they are working hard every minute of the day—without slacking. Slacking is what costs money. If we let them think they're smart enough to run the factory, there will be no hope. Do I make myself clear?"

Toshi bowed to his brother and nodded. "I'm sorry," was all he could manage to say.

Walking home with his father, Toshi hesitated when asked how his first day had gone. When Isao asked a second time, Toshi had no choice but to relay the encounter with his brother. He was hoping to hear he had done the right thing by talking with the workers, but instead, his father reiterated the same position as Kotaro.

"It is not good to show weakness to the workers," he said. "They will begin to question your authority, and before you know it, they will expect more wages and shorter hours. Who knows where it might lead? Kotaro is correct. We must always keep them in their place. I'm sure you will agree now that it has been explained to you. You always have to think of the bigger picture, not just of the moment at hand."

The next morning, Toshi and his father again left the house precisely at six thirty, reaching the factory at seven fifteen, where Kotaro was waiting. Isao unlocked the door to the salesroom while Kotaro led Toshi through the factory floor. Toshi noticed that none of the workers looked up to acknowledge him when the two walked by. It seemed odd, he thought, considering how yesterday the workers had accepted his presence, some even smiling and joking when he walked through alone.

Climbing the stairs to the offices, Kotaro reminded Toshi of his obligation before entering his own large office. "Remember what we talked about yesterday," he said. "We are the owners. We tell them what to do. Your job is to make sure they do it." Then he disappeared into his office and closed the door.

Toshi walked to his office and sat down behind the table. After several minutes he stood and moved to his small window to view the workers. He watched them for half an hour, observing what each man was doing. Even from this distance, he thought many were simply going through memorized motions, doing what was required, but without a hint of enthusiasm. He gazed at their faces. Most reflected a face of boredom. One man at the far end of the floor struggled to keep his eyes open even at this early hour of the day. He watched as another man dropped his carving tool several times. Another man coughed and rubbed the dust from his eyes.

How am I to help build this factory into something bigger if I'm not allowed to improve the process? he wondered. He may not have studied management in school, but Toshi did learn about the process of building things. *All the management principles in the world surely would not help if they were not using sound procedures.*

He watched as the level of dust continued to increase, caused by any number of stations sawing, sanding, carving, and sweeping. Without thinking, and simply reacting to a common instinct, he walked down the steps to the floor and opened two windows, one on either side of the large enclosure.

The sun was shining, and a pleasant whiff of wind swayed through the trees outside. When he opened the second window, a light draft made its way across the floor from one side to the other, giving air above the stations an opportunity to escape. He inhaled deeply several times, just for the pleasure of fresh air in his lungs. When he looked around, several others were doing the same. One or two looked over at him and smiled.

That afternoon Toshi caught Kotaro with no one in his office. He was anxious to tell his brother about the small improvement he had given the workers that had cost absolutely nothing. "I noticed all the dust in the air above the workers and how some of them kept rubbing their eyes," he said. "I was tempted to ask one of them about ventilation, but after what you told me yesterday, I decided to make the decision on my own. I opened a window on each side of the factory. It helped immediately, and a few of the workers waved their approval."

"You did what?" his brother responded, much like the previous day. "We can't have the windows open. It's hard enough to heat the factory without letting warm air escape through open windows. And besides, it doesn't really get rid of the dust; it simply moves it around. It's hard enough to keep dust away from the painting area as it is, without having it blow around the room. You should have asked me before making such a decision. Is that what they taught you in math class? To open windows and stir dust throughout the building? Next time, ask me before you decide to make a change on your own."

Again, Toshi was silent during the nightly walk home with his father. When asked about his second day, he replied simply, "I can see I have a lot to learn about the furniture business."

For the next four days, Toshi mostly sat in his office and watched the hands on the antique clock behind his chair spin slowly through their orbit. He observed several of the workers from his office window, but in the end, could only find empathy for their boring and redundant activity. By Saturday he had reached a decision.

After work, he joined his father in the library for their usual cup of saké, and after taking a larger sip than he was accustomed, began. "Father, first, I want to thank you for the opportunity to follow in your footsteps at the furniture factory. You have made

Grandfather's business one of the most successful factories in Tokyo."

"You are welcome, my son," his father replied. "I am sorry it has not been easy for you. But your brother, as the oldest son, will someday become the owner. That's why he is in charge. He started working there when he was only fifteen. I taught him everything about the factory, and he was quick to learn.

"You must remember, a father always knows more than a son, in the same way that a grandfather always knows more than a father. We learn by experience, and the more experience we have, the more we know. It is folly for a son to try new things without first obtaining approval from the father. This is simply the way of things."

"I understand your reasoning," Toshi replied while looking at him from across the room. "But with that reasoning, how does a person learn anything new? Whether a son or a father. If all knowledge is based on past experience, aren't we then doomed to the limits we already know? How are we to develop new knowledge if we are limited to the old?"

Toshi wisely stopped at that point to assess the damage. And it was greater than he anticipated.

"Is that what they taught you at university? To question your elders? To question fundamental truths that have been relied upon for centuries? How dare you speak to your father in this manner! Have you lost all respect for your elders? Is that, too, what they taught you at school? Why I ever agreed to let you attend university is nothing but a regret. Not only have I wasted my money, but you have wasted your chance for a successful life, filled with foolish ideas about doing whatever comes to mind."

Then, totally out of character, Isao called Yuko to bring him a second cup of saké.

Chapter 2

Toshi Makes a Decision

TOKYO - 1873

Toshi bowed to his father through a sense of obedience and quietly left the room. He later asked to be excused from dinner, explaining he wanted to visit a friend he had not seen since starting at the factory. Leaving the house, he headed straight for the university. He did not have money for a rickshaw and the walk gave him time to think.

Happy to see lights were on in the engineering building, he entered the familiar doors and inhaled deeply. The scent brought back so many memories that he stood frozen for a time before moving on. The now empty corridor held a fragrance of its own: a blend of ancient tomes, smoke from popular *kiseru* pipes, and the stale, musty air of a normally crowded building.

At the far end of the hall, he let himself in through the single door. Once inside, he scanned the small room in search of his former professor. A dozen tables filled the space, each one stacked with files and papers of various shapes and sizes. On this Saturday night, only two men were present, seated at different tables. One was Professor Murata.

Relieved when he recognized his mentor, Toshi moved toward the table and waited to be recognized.

"Toshi Ozawa," Mr. Murata said when he looked up. "What a pleasant surprise to see you. And so soon after graduation. Have you decided to continue your studies? You were a gifted student. It would be a privilege to teach you again."

"Thank you, but no, I am not planning to return to school. I've just completed the first week at my father's factory, and I would like to talk to you about it."

"You were fortunate to have a job waiting for you at graduation. How was your first week?"

Toshi looked at the floor. "To be honest," he said, "it was terrible. Both my father and my brother made it clear I should have studied management instead of engineering, and they are reluctant to let me do or change anything, or even listen to my ideas. It is not how I want to spend my life."

"I'm sorry to hear that, Toshi. A lifetime of work will seem like two, unless you like what you do. Have you made other inquiries? Are you planning to leave the factory?"

"I haven't had time to search for something else, but I definitely have to leave. My family and I will all be miserable until I do."

"That is distressing, indeed. Perhaps I can help you find something." He began to rearrange the stacks of papers in front of him until finally, Toshi saw his eyes light up. "Here is a list of job opportunities posted several weeks before graduation. I don't know if any are still available, but let's look at the list and see if any of them catch your interest."

Together, they scanned the list, which was not very long, and Toshi tried not to get his hopes up. It was an old list to begin with, and he knew many of the jobs would likely be filled by now. There were postings for teachers, merchants, and government administrators, but only one entry captured his attention. It was listed as assistant foreman at an iron-smelting plant in the north. The only thing that gave Toshi hope was a requirement for logic and engineering skills. A brief description indicated the assistant would work closely with the foreman to improve current procedures, with an even briefer reference to two new furnaces currently under construction.

"Where is this place?" Toshi asked his former teacher.

"The posting says in a town called Kamaishi, on the northeast coast. It describes the area as primarily a fishing village, but that nearby mountains contain magnetite, which is used in the production of iron."

"Do you have a map we could look at?" Toshi asked.

"I think there is one around here somewhere," he replied.

Mr. Murata asked the man at the other table if he had a map of Japan, and a moment later, all three were searching for a fishing village by the name of Kamaishi.

"Here it is," the other man said, pointing at a small dot near the upper edge of the map. "Kamaishi. It doesn't look very big but it could be beautiful, with its location between the mountains and the sea. I suspect the job has already been taken by someone who loves the sea or the outdoors."

"Could we write to find out for sure?" Toshi asked. The job sounded interesting to him regardless of the terrain. Anything where he could contribute to increased production would be better than sitting in his office at the furniture factory. The more he thought about the job, the more interested he became. His hands trembled lightly when he and Mr. Murata sat down to compose a letter of application. He would worry about telling his father later, if anything came of it.

One week passed without a reply. Toshi continued at the factory, trying to hide the fact that he hated the job. By the end of the second week, he had developed a routine of his own, which seemed to satisfy his brother.

Each morning, as soon as his brother settled in his office to study papers or meet with important visitors, Toshi slipped back down through the production floor and out the door. Two blocks away, a young boy sold the *Yokohama Mainichi Shimbun* newspaper. It was a day-old copy, but even so, it provided the most reliable source of news available. That it had little to do with running a furniture factory did not diminish its appeal. Not only did it report the major stories near Yokohama, it also contained news beyond Japan, further evidence the Meiji revolution was alive and well. Further proof the emperor wanted his subjects to open their minds to new ideas and new ways of doing things. Events reported there were like drawing open the curtain to a new universe.

It was from the *Mainichi Shimbun* that Toshi first learned human slaves were bought and sold, in an article about Britain pressuring

Zanzibar to close its famous slave market, and from there that he read where a British naval officer, John Moresby, discovered a new port in a place called Papua, New Guinea, and named it after himself. There were so many things taking place away from Japan he could hardly wait for each new issue.

And whether his interest in American stories was in any way linked to the well-known tales of Admiral Perry's historic entry of Tokyo Harbor in 1854, Toshi did not know or consider, but he was drawn to any headline with the word 'America' in its title. He tried to understand the implications of a woman named Susan B. Anthony being fined one hundred dollars for attempting to vote in the last presidential election. He wondered if one hundred dollars was more or less than one hundred yen.

One name that appeared more frequently than others in the 'American' articles was a place called California. He presumed states were geographical areas like prefectures in Japan, and wondered if there were more states than prefectures. Several headlines from the newspaper caught his attention:

- The University of California opens its first medical school in San Francisco.

- Construction of the first cable-driven streetcar begins on Clay Street in San Francisco.

- Progress continues in California for Transcontinental Railway.

Some of the articles referenced the California gold rush of 1849. The rush was over by now, of course, but the effects of fortunes won and lost still captured the imagination of thousands of readers. Toshi, occasionally, was among them.

Sitting idly in his office above the factory, it was hard to overcome visions of adventure in a land of abundant wealth, far across the sea. After several days, and without his tacit permission, the seed was planted. *I'm going to America as soon as I can afford it.*

After reading the daily news, Toshi found himself drinking more and more tea, not because he was thirsty or because it tasted particularly good, but simply to pass the time. Some days, he found himself having three or four cups of tea before his first visit to the factory floor to check on the workers. He no longer stopped to ask about their families or their advice, and they no longer took time to acknowledge him with a smile.

At lunchtime, he ate alone in his spartan office, glancing at the clock several times over the following two hours until he repeated the tea regimen, and then a second patrol of the factory floor. On two occasions, he tried to solicit advice from his brother, but both times was told it could wait until later.

He dreaded the walks home after work with his father, afraid he might ask for details of his day. Though his father did not seem to notice, his mother began to ask why he was not hungry at the evening meal.

"You send me too much lunch," he explained one night, which did not explain why he was losing weight. He dared not tell her he shared most of his lunch with one of the workers who struggled to feed his four children.

***

A month passed, and Toshi decided to visit his friend at the university instead of joining his family for dinner. He pinned his hopes on an updated list of jobs available. Maybe he could even get a job teaching at the university. It would be far more rewarding to help develop young minds than to spend his days idle at the factory.

Following the predictable glass of saké when they arrived home from work, Toshi asked to be excused from dinner. "I haven't seen my friends for several weeks," he said. "I'm going to the university and see if anyone is there."

"Don't stay out too late," was all his father said.

When Toshi arrived at the office where he first found Mr. Murata, he was not there. Nor was the other professor who had been there on his previous visit. But a different man was there, working at a table that looked like most of the others, with papers stacked high and helter-skelter. The man was reviewing one paper with such intensity that he barely looked up when Toshi walked in. When Toshi failed to seat himself at any of the tables the man raised his eyes absent-mindedly, and only then realized Toshi was there in search of someone.

"May I help you?" he asked.

"I am looking for Mr. Murata," he replied. "I was hoping to find him here."

"I'm afraid you just missed him. He received a letter in today's post, which he seemed excited about, and shortly after, he headed out the door."

"Do you know where he was going?"

"I'm afraid I don't know. He only said his former student would be excited about the news."

"Do you know what news he referred to?"

"No, but he mentioned a job offer from somewhere in the north. Then he grabbed the letter, and out the door he went."

Toshi froze. *Could that be a letter for me?* It seemed too much to hope for after all this time, but surely that must be it. After all, he was a former student, and the job in Kamaishi was certainly in the north. Together, they had looked it up on the map, right here in this very office.

Then Toshi began to panic. *What if Mr. Murata went to his house and broke the news to his father?* It would be a disaster. Toshi had expected time to work out a plan for breaking the news. His mother would be disappointed, but his father would be furious.

"Thank you," Toshi said. "If he comes back, please tell him Toshi was here to see him. Thank you." Toshi was already headed for the door.

The walk to the university had been calm and peaceful, almost therapeutic. The walk home was not. He needed to intercept Mr. Murata before he reached his father. He walked at the fastest pace he could sustain. Twice, he had to apologize for bumping into pedestrians who were moving too slowly. Once, he was so intent on observing the traffic that he missed his turn and had to backtrack to the previous intersection. All the while, he scanned the crowds for the face of Mr. Murata.

At last, arriving at home, his heart lurched in his chest. Light filtered through windows by the front door and parlor. Lanterns were rarely lit in the Ozawa household unless someone occupied the room. Toshi quickly climbed the three steps leading to the door, and with a trembling hand, tried the handle. Small beads of sweat formed on the back of his neck and his pulse began to race. Then he closed his eyes for several long, deep breaths. A disaster was about to begin.

There were voices coming from the parlor, both of which he knew by heart. One voice was coming from his father, the other from Mr. Murata. He could not tell how much damage had already been done; whether Mr. Murata had shared the news or whether it was merely a prelude to the news. Toshi walked heavily on the wooden floor as he approached, hoping to announce his arrival in advance. When he walked through the parlor door, he saw the look of horror on Mr. Murata's face. It was mostly drained of its color as he peered sheepishly back at Toshi.

His father, on the other hand, seemed to have received all the color from Mr. Murata and added it to his own. His face was red to the point of almost purple, and his eyes were narrowed and squinting so tight that Toshi wondered how he was able to see.

"Mr. Murata tells me you have applied for work at an iron factory in some faraway place called Kamaishi. I tried to tell him he was mistaken, because my son is already employed in the family business here in Tokyo. Then he showed me a letter from an iron foundry that has your name on it. Can you please explain to me, as well as to Mr. Murata, how this obvious mix-up could have occurred?"

Toshi swallowed hard and looked pleadingly toward his mother for help. She acknowledged him briefly before turning her gaze to the floor.

"I am sorry, Father," he began. "I wanted to be the first to tell you, but I only just found out myself. It is true. I asked Mr. Murata to help me find a job that allowed me to use the things I learned in school. I do not believe I can contribute at the furniture factory in a way that suits you. And with all respect, I do not think I'm needed there. I have decided to create my own destiny, and not try to become another you. I am sorry, and I hope you will understand."

"Understand? I understand that I have paid for your frivolous dreams all these years. Do you think university is free? Do you think living here is free? For twenty years, I've paid everything for you. And now, as repayment, you want me to forget all of that and send you off to a remote fishing village?"

Then he turned his scorn on Mr. Murata. "Is this what we pay you to do at the university? Indoctrinate young minds to forget their history? Their culture? Make them think they can do anything they want, never mind their obligations? I cannot believe I let this happen. Worse, I cannot believe I *paid* to let this happen. I suppose you and your kind over at the university are still celebrating the Meiji Revolution and all that 'enlightened thinking' that goes with it. Well, we'll see where that gets us, won't we? Let's meet again in two years, or five, and then we'll see how 'enlightened' Japan has become. We'll be lucky if we still have a country in ten years. You mark my words."

Mr. Murata avoided looking at Toshi. Instead, he looked at Isao and said, "I accept your offer. I look forward to meeting with you again in two years, or five, if you prefer. It is possible we might both be surprised at the state of our great country in that length of time. One thing we do teach at the university is that there are many things we cannot control, but we are best prepared to deal with them when we retain an open mind. My humble apology to you both for interrupting your evening. I will see myself out."

Toshi could think of nothing meaningful to say as his friend exited the room. He looked at his father, still red in the face and breathing heavily, but his mind was made up. "I'm sorry you do not approve, but it is my life, and I need to make my own decisions about how to live it."

Isao glared at him before responding. "If you need to make your own decisions, then so be it. But let me remind you that making your own decisions requires paying your own way. Maybe you have somehow managed to save enough money to provide for your travels but if you haven't, rest assured it will not come from me, and do not ask your mother to provide it either." Then he stomped heavily from the parlor to his study and slammed the door behind.

Toshi had no money of his own. His father was fully aware of that. Working for his father was simply contributing to the family, in his father's eyes. Toshi had everything he needed while living at home, so had no need for an income of his own. And it was clear he was not to ask his mother for help.

He went to his room and calculated how long it would take to walk six hundred kilometers, and whether he could carry enough food to last the trip.

By Monday, he decided it was fruitless to continue going to the factory, so he went instead to the university, hoping to get advice from his friend. He arrived early, before Mr. Murata's first class.

Finding him standing by the table, with a book already under one arm, Toshi blurted out almost before reaching him. "Good morning, Mr. Murata. I am sorry for the way my father behaved on Saturday. It was kind of you to deliver the message, and you had no way of knowing my father would not be happy about it."

"Good morning, Toshi. Don't you worry. I should have been more considerate. Have you decided whether or not to accept the job?"

"I definitely want the job, but my father won't provide any travel money. I don't know how I'll get there. That's what I came to talk to you about. I calculated that walking twenty kilometers a day would take a month. I don't think that is very realistic. Do you have any ideas?"

"Is there anyone who could loan you the money to get started?" he asked.

"My friends are all like me, either still in school or newly graduated, so I don't think any of them have money to loan."

Mr. Murata sighed and looked around the crowded office, now bustling with professors and assistants gathering papers and notebooks, and heading off to classrooms.

"I don't have any ideas at the moment, but come back tomorrow. Maybe I can think of something. It would be a shame for you to miss out on the job only because you can't afford to get there."

Toshi bowed to his former teacher, who hurried off to his class amidst the throng of others.

Toshi, left alone in the office, walked to the library and searched for all the books he could find relating to the smelting of iron. Just as he was pulling one of the books from the shelf, someone cautiously called his name from behind. He turned to see one of his friends from math class. "Genkei," he said. "Genkei Shibata—it is good to see you again. What are you doing here?"

"I decided to continue my studies," Genkei replied. "I'm here looking for a reference book. What about you? I thought you were going to work at your father's company. Shouldn't you be at work?"

Toshi blushed with embarrassment. "I was," he replied. "But I hated it. Mr. Murata helped me find a new job at an iron foundry up north, but my father was so upset he won't loan me the money to get there. I'm not sure what will happen. I just spoke to Mr. Murata, and he said he would try to figure something out."

"Your father's factory must have been pretty bad," Genkei said. "Everyone was envious that you had a good job waiting for you at graduation. What happened?"

"It was a combination of things," Toshi replied. "Mostly, my father and my older brother wouldn't allow me to make even small decisions, and I felt like I was not contributing. It was so boring that after a few weeks, I realized I had to try something else."

Genkei's grin faded to a solemn grimace. "I am sorry to hear that," he said. Then, after a short delay, continued. "So how do you plan to get to the new job if you don't have the money?"

"That's the problem. Father won't cover me, and he forbade me to ask my mother. My friends from school are not in a position to help either. I don't know what to do."

Genkei was silent for a few moments, then lowered his voice and asked tentatively, "Have you ever considered Christianity?"

Toshi looked around to see who might have heard. "Christianity? Isn't that banned by the government?"

"It used to be, but not any longer," Genkei replied only slightly louder. "It became legal four years ago, the same year I started my studies here."

"Is that when you learned about Christianity, when you started here?"

"Not really," he replied with the trace of a smile. "My great-grandfather acquired a Bible when he was my age, and it's been in our family ever since. So, even though Christianity was outlawed, it was not completely suppressed, if you know what I mean."

Toshi stared at him in disbelief. "You mean you continued to follow it, even though it was banned?"

"Yes, that's the only way we could manage. But compared to the first Christians, we actually had it pretty easy. A lot of them were killed for their beliefs. Even the one who started it all was killed for his teachings. So we didn't have it so bad. And now that it's legal again, we can come out from the shadows."

Toshi continued to look at Genkei with a blank face. Finally, still using a quiet voice, he was able to say, "How would Christianity help me get to Kamaishi?"

"Well," Genkei said, "whenever I have a problem I can't solve, I pray to God. It doesn't always work, but often it does. Tonight, I'll ask Him to help you get to your new job. Where did you say it was? I think it might help my prayer if I am more specific than just 'up north'." Then he smiled, and Toshi smiled back at the logic of it.

"It's in a place called Kamaishi," he said. "It's a small village along the coast."

"Very well, then. I'll pray you find a way to get to the small village of Kamaishi along the coast, so you can report for work on time."

"Thank you, Genkei. I need all the help I can get."

"I have to go now," Genkei said. "I have an exam to study for. Good luck. It was good to see you again."

When Toshi returned the next day, Mr. Murata greeted him with a look of excitement. "Good news," he began. "I told your story to several of my colleagues, and they volunteered to pool enough money to pay for your passage from Tokyo to Kamaishi. It's a loan, Toshi, so it will need to be repaid as soon as you are settled and earning money at the iron foundry. But at least you will be able to accept the job and report for duty. I assured them you were a good risk."

Toshi bowed to Mr. Murata, and then to every other person in the office. Some of them didn't seem to know what he was thanking them for, but bowed in return just to keep him moving.

Chapter 3

Toshi Leaves Home

TOKYO - 1873

At the end of breakfast, Toshi turned to his father. "This is the day. I'm leaving on the *City of Tokyo* this afternoon. I'll write when I get there."

Isao looked at Toshi with a look he could not fully decipher. It was a cross between anger and sorrow. "Where did you find the money to get there?" he asked.

"Several friends from the university loaned me enough to get started," he replied.

Isao's face began to flush. "You borrowed money from strangers? What will people think of us? That we're too poor to take care of our own?"

"They are not strangers, and no one needs to know. They won't be telling anyone. You don't need to worry."

"I don't understand what is happening to our country. Families should stay together. I worked hard to provide a place for you, and just because you went to school, now you are too good for a factory. You move far away in search of something you think will be better. This is not the way of our heritage. Families should stay together."

"Times are changing, Father. Look around you. Look at what the emperor is doing. He wants everyone to learn new ways of doing things. The iron foundry is one example. Iron is important to the future of our country, which is why he wants to find better ways to make it. I want to be a part of it."

"The emperor! He should stick to his ceremonies and leave running the country to the shoguns. We prospered for generations under the shogunate. There was no reason to change. Suddenly, other cultures are superior to our own? They even changed the name of our city from Edo to Tokyo. How that makes us a better country, I would like to know. I only hope they return to their senses before it is too late."

Toshi waited before responding. "Time will tell," was all he could think to say without the risk of an unwinnable argument.

"I'll tell Kotaro you have gone," Isao said. Then he turned to Yuko and said, "I'll see you after work."

"You better get your trunk ready," Yuko said to Toshi as soon as Isao was out of sight. "The livery will be here soon."

Toshi looked at her with a blank face. "Livery?" he asked.

"You can't carry that trunk all the way to the dock. I've arranged for a livery to take you."

"But Father said you were not to give me any money."

"No, he didn't say I could not give you any money. He said you were not to ask me for money. There is a difference." She smiled at her youngest son. "Sometimes a mother knows best."

Toshi broke into a grin. Then he went to his room for one last look before dragging the trunk to the door. Expecting to be gone for an extended period, he packed everything he owned. It fit into a single trunk.

Thirty minutes later, the livery arrived. Toshi pulled the trunk through the door while his mother held it open. The driver, seeing the opportunity for a few extra sen, hurried to the door and helped Toshi carry it to the cart and hoist it up.

Toshi returned to the house expecting to bid his mother a final goodbye when she surprised him by coming to the livery instead.

"Is there room for both of us?" she asked the driver.

"Yes, plenty of room," he replied with a smile, seizing the opportunity for a few more sen.

"You're coming to the dock with me?" Toshi asked in surprise.

"Yes, why not? I won't be seeing you again for who knows how long. I want to see you for as long as possible."

Sitting beside his mother as the livery pulled away, Toshi drank in the sights of the city where he grew up. Edo in his early years,

Tokyo in his final five. Halfway to their destination, he realized he had never really *seen* many of the sights before, no matter how many times he had traveled this same route.

Not until he might never see them again, did he actually pay them attention. He closed his eyes and inhaled deeply to take in the city smells. The air was filled with smoke from cooking fires, factory chimneys, burning trash, and a dozen other pungent odors. When the stagnant blend filled his lungs, he struggled to suppress a cough. It was not only the sights he had taken for granted; it was the air as well.

They reached the shipping terminal in less time than any previous trip he could remember. The driver had to ask a second time if he wanted help unloading the trunk. Toshi nodded and helped his mother step down from the cart. She walked with him to the dock, and together they gazed at the ship. *City of Tokyo*, it proudly proclaimed in dark green letters across the bow.

"It's not as big as I expected," she murmured. "Are you sure it is safe?"

"The man told me it has made the trip many times," Toshi replied, "so it must be safe. I don't think they get very far from shore." Then he added, "I thought it would be a little bigger, too."

As they studied the ship, Toshi heard the captain shout orders to his crew. It was time to board. Toshi looked his mother in the eyes and bowed farewell. She stepped forward and pulled him close for a long embrace.

"I'm proud of you, Toshi," she said, looking him in the face. "Your father is, too. He just doesn't know how to show it." Then she slipped an envelope in his hand and took a short step back.

Toshi blinked several times, trying to clear the moisture from his eyes. He bowed a second time and turned to board the packet ship, too soon to see the tears running down his mother's cheeks.

Once on board, he found a place along the rail to wave, as the *City of Tokyo* slipped from its mooring and slowly pulled away. When he could no longer make out his mother's silhouette, he lowered his arm and turned to watch the skyline as it slowly disappeared.

From this distance, the city seemed shrouded by a large and ominous cloud. How it could have appeared during the short trip from the dock, Toshi could not guess, but it was there and plain to see. Black grime and smoke rose from every section of the city—more spires than he could count.

As they sailed into the Pacific and veered to the north, Toshi decided the cloud must have been there all along, and that residents were simply used to it. Then he remembered how he coughed on the way to the docks.

When the steamer reached its first stop at Kamogawa later that afternoon, Toshi noticed how clear the skyline was, compared to Tokyo. The next morning, with the ship tied securely at the wharf in Isumi, he inhaled deeply several times just to see if it would make him cough.

The third morning out, Toshi found several crew members gazing at the sky. "A storm is on the way," he heard one of them say.

"Red sky at morning; sailors take warning," another replied.

"That's just an old wives' tale," said a third.

"No," the second man said. "It's in the Bible. There's a verse in the Bible—Matthew, I think."

"You wait and see," said the first. "By noon, we'll be dropping sail and heaving to."

Toshi waited and watched. By midafternoon, the auxiliary sails were furled, and waves were flooding across the deck. This was his first time at sea, but it did not take experience to realize the ship was taking a beating. His natural inclination was to look for the crew and see if they were alarmed. When the wind paused for a few brief moments, he found two sailors taking shelter behind a stack of crates lashed firmly to the deck. "Time for a few prayers," he heard one of them say above the din.

Toshi turned and headed back to the main cabin. Just as he reached for the door, the bow of the vessel slammed down into a trough, and with it came the crest of a wave, sluicing across the deck to the depth of his ankles. He grabbed tight to the large metal handle on the door just as his feet washed out from under him, leaving him to flail first one way and then the other, as the heavy door swung repeatedly open and closed in the turbulence.

He yelled out to the crewmen for help, but they were too busy saving themselves. The same wave that swept Toshi's feet from under him had washed across the deck where the two men were hiding beside the crates. Unfortunately, neither of them had a heavy metal handle to grab hold of, and they were thrown to the deck with such force it was a wonder that Toshi didn't hear the sound of their muscle-toned bodies slamming against the wooden planks.

Once prostrate on the deck, with the ship rolling up and down in the turbulent sea, they slid from one side to the other in unison with the pitch of the boat. When the bow rose on the crest of a wave, the crewmen slid along the deck toward the stern. When it dipped down in the next wave, back they came again, desperately reaching for something, anything, along the deck, to keep from sliding over the side.

Finally, one of the men reached out for Toshi's foot as he slid across the deck and slammed into the cabin wall. Alarmed, Toshi had no idea what to do next. He hung onto the heavy door with both hands as it continued to swing on its rusted hinges, and now, with the crewman's arms wrapped tightly around one of his legs, it seemed for all the world they were doomed to die.

Toshi lost sight of the other crewman. *Did he go overboard? Did he find something to hang on to? Maybe the stack of crates or a ventilator tube?* But he was the least of Toshi's worries. For a moment, Toshi hoped the man clinging for dear life to his leg would let it go. Surely, he would find something else to hang on to, something more rigid than Toshi's leg. But just as quickly, a vision of the man sliding all the way across the deck and off into the sea gave Toshi strength to cling even harder to the heavy metal handle.

The door, Toshi's only chance at life, continued to swing. First, all the way open; then, when the ship rolled, almost all the way closed. *If only it would close all the way and latch,* he thought. At least then he might have a chance.

He strained to look up at the sky on one of his hapless swings of the door and shuddered at what he saw. The clouds were dark and menacing, swirling in all directions at once. Then rain came down. Lightly at first, then building to a torrent. For the next half hour Toshi could see nothing but the rain slashing his face. All he knew was that the crewman still clung tightly to his leg.

Then he began to worry about the crewman. *How much longer could he hang on?* His position was even more precarious than Toshi's. It reminded him of when he was a child, playing crack the whip with the neighbor boys. While the arc of Toshi's swing was bad enough, for the poor man on his leg, it was even greater.

Toshi's arms were burning and his fingers were numb. *How much longer can I hang on?* he wondered to himself. *But I can't give up. If I go, so does the man on my leg. We both have to hang on.* He tried calling out to the man, but the wind and the waves were too strong, and his strength, too weak. The words barely made it to the end of his flailing leg.

Time went by and the rain began to weaken. He could no longer feel either his arms or his hands. But he could feel the man still attached to his leg. He had to keep going. Another half hour passed, and the boat began to steady until, finally, the rain stopped.

The second crewman still clenched firmly to Toshi's leg when a third crewman came through the cabin, secured the heavy metal door, and helped Toshi to the deck. The *City of Tokyo* had settled enough that he could stand upright again. The other man was too battered, and simply sat where he was, while the third man went in search of the first crewman.

By evening the wind had calmed. They found the first crewman clinging to one of the lifeboats, still praying to his Christian God.

That was when Toshi recalled his conversation with Genkei in the library. He said he would ask his god that Toshi find a way to get to Kamaishi, and here he was. Today the sailor prayed for better weather, and now, the storm had passed. *I wonder if it was just a coincidence, or was there something to this Christian God?*

On the fourth day, when his stomach was no longer queasy from the endless motion, Toshi scanned the coastline for Kamaishi. He had no idea there were so many peninsulas along the coast. Each time he saw land approaching he felt certain they must be getting close, only to see the land give rise to another bay.

By afternoon, Toshi felt a shift in the way the waves washed the side of the boat. Looking up, he noticed the largest sail was not as tight as it was before. Then, looking back to the shoreline, he realized the landmarks had shifted positions. They were heading for shore. He tried to hide the smile that crossed his face as he moved closer to the bow for a better view.

Looking at the bay ahead, he panned the horizon. It was at least three kilometers wide and half again as long, protected on either side by high, rocky peninsulas. Off to the right were more fishing boats than he could count, bobbing at their moorings. White seagulls dotted the lazy sky above.

The *City of Tokyo* was headed directly for the wharf, now two kilometers away. Beyond the dock, the village was coming into view. One- and two-story buildings clustered the narrow valley, hugging a river that led west into the mountains. As they drew near, Toshi saw people moving here and there between the dock and the scattered buildings.

With the ship safely moored, Toshi half-carried, half-dragged his wooden trunk to the gangplank. Not for the first time, he silently wished he had left some of his meager possessions at home. Especially the books; they were heavy and might never be used. But he *had* brought them and this close to his destination, was not about to leave them behind.

He looked down at the water below as he crossed the gap between the deck and the dock, making sure not to lose his footing. When safely on the dock, with the trunk dragging along behind, he heard the song of an unfamiliar bird just above his head. Looking up to see what kind it was, he didn't notice the small puddle of water on the wooden plank at his feet.

Without the weight of a heavy trunk, Toshi might easily have recovered from the slip of his foot. But as it was, his right knee went quickly to the dock, followed by the weight of the trunk on his leg, and a loud thunk as the rest of his body fell to the ground beneath the heavy load.

Embarrassed, he looked around to see how many people had witnessed his clumsy fall. Only one man seemed to have noticed, who was making his way toward him. Toshi quickly rolled out from under the bulky wooden box and climbed to his feet. By now, the man was standing only two meters away, and when Toshi looked at him, the man smiled politely.

Toshi did the same, with the blush of embarrassment still on his face.

"Toshi Ozawa?" the man asked.

Toshi cringed and hoped it didn't show. "Yes, I am Toshi Ozawa." He bowed to the man, hoping to make amends.

"I am Haruki Yamamoto, from the Kamaishi Iron Works. Welcome to Kamaishi."

Toshi cringed a second time. *This must be my new boss. Of all the times to trip and fall, this is the absolute worst,* he thought.

"I came to help you get settled. It looks like you have quite a load. I'll help you carry it to the livery. We'll need a cart to get it to the boarding house." Then he lifted the front of the trunk and motioned for Toshi to lift the back. "It's not far," he said. "Follow me."

"Did you hurt yourself in the fall?" Haruki asked, after a few minutes.

"No, it was nothing," Toshi replied. "Just a little clumsy of me."

"Do you fall often?" Haruki asked.

"No," Toshi replied. He was starting to get an uneasy feeling this was more than simply an interest in his well-being.

"Do you remember when was the last time you fell?"

Toshi thought for a moment before responding. Now he was sure there was more to the questioning than mere curiosity. "Not exactly," he said. "Several years at least. I was just off balance from carrying the heavy load. Then, when I slipped on the water, I was not able to catch myself."

He tried not to act alarmed as he waited for a response.

After several more steps, Haruki confirmed his suspicion. "The smelting furnace is no place for someone who is clumsy," he said. "The furnace reaches over five hundred degrees in order to melt the ore. You can imagine what that would do to a man, were he to fall near the furnace. I won't have that kind of injury on my conscience."

Toshi considered the words carefully. *Does that mean I don't get the job?* he wondered. He remained quiet, hoping for something more from Haruki so that he did not misinterpret what he was trying to say.

"Here is the livery station," he said. "Let's find out if they have a cart we can rent for a few hours."

An hour later, they had ascended the steep path up the ridge and then to the boarding house. Haruki introduced him to the widow who owned the spartan house and rented out her two extra bedrooms. The man in the other room was older than Toshi and worked at a shop in the village.

Before he left, Haruki paid the widow for two weeks of lodging in advance, on the assumption that Toshi probably had very little money. "I will deduct it from your pay," he said. "It should help until you get on your feet."

Toshi smiled in relief and bowed. "Thank you." *I must still have the job,* he decided.

"Now, can you find your way back to the village to return the cart? If so, I'll be on my way. I live close by, which is why I made this arrangement. I'll pick you up at six thirty in the morning to take you to the foundry. Welcome to Kamaishi," he repeated. Then he was gone.

Chapter 4

Ayami

Ayami awoke with a start. Looking up at the ceiling and rubbing her eyes, she listened for movement. Hearing the figure next to her begin to stir, she patted her gently on the shoulder. No words were needed. The gesture was enough to say, 'Sleep a little longer, I'll help Mama with breakfast.' She rose slowly from the mat and stepped over her sleeping sister.

Three steps beyond the mat Ayami reached the bedroom wall, just as a rooster crowed outside in the predawn light. A slight draft made its way through a gap at the bottom of the window. *We'll need to stuff that with a rag before winter,* she thought to herself. Looking toward the doorway, small flickers of light from an oil lamp filtered through holes in the curtain. Her mother was already awake and working in the kitchen.

She pulled her tattered clothes from a peg on the wall and dressed. Turning toward her sister before leaving, she smiled at the sound of her softly reassuring snores. Then, slipping carefully through the curtain, she padded barefoot on the rough wooden flooring, down the hallway, and out toward the kitchen.

Passing by the bedroom of her three older brothers, she need not have tiptoed to hear their snores. They were loud and regular, like a trio of off-key singers, each one dreaming a different tune.

From the other side of the short hallway, snores of her father were louder still. The pattern was familiar. The more saké he consumed the day before, the louder he slept at night. *Yesterday must have been a thirsty day,* she concluded. *No wonder Mama is always up early. Who could sleep through that?*

"Good morning, Mama," she whispered when she reached the kitchen. "Did you sleep well?"

"As good as always," she replied, with the trace of a smile. "And you? Is Emiko still asleep?"

"Yes, Mama… and yes, she is still sleeping, in spite of the rooster outside."

Ayami moved close and instinctively held her young hands over the stove to test the heat. A kettle was warming, not yet hot enough for tea. "I'll go and gather the eggs," she said, pulling on a light jacket as she went out the door.

The sun was almost to the horizon, and she could see her way to the small shed some thirty meters away. Pulling the latch from its hook she swung open the wooden door. It creaked on its hinges as two chickens burst through the opening into the crisp morning air. Ten others remained, slumbering in their nests. Ayami entered slowly so as not to alarm the precious birds, then, one by one, gently slid a hand beneath each of the nesting hens, hoping for an egg.

Eight of the twelve nests revealed a treasure. Each family member would have an egg for breakfast, Papa would have two. Unless, of course, he was present when the rest of them ate. In that case, each of the men would have two eggs; the women, none.

Ayami placed the eggs into a bowl next to the stove and watched as her mother counted them. "If we hurry, we can each have an egg before Papa gets up," she said, trying not to show her feelings.

"We'll have to see how long your brothers sleep," Fujita replied. "They'll complain to your father if we eat without them, but if they aren't up in an hour, I'll have to call them. They were supposed to start clearing the paddies today.

"The Sasakis have already cleared their first paddy and are flooding it now. It's no secret why they have a better harvest. I don't know why your father can't keep up with our neighbors. Getting out of bed in the morning would do wonders."

She looked around the room from force of habit to see if any of the men were close enough to hear. She might end up with a new bruise if they were.

Ayami did not have to see her mother's face to know how frustrated she was with her father; the tone in her voice held meaning enough. In the dim light of the lantern, though, she did gaze at her mother's face for signs of bruising. It was not unusual to see blue or red coloring between her eye and cheek, or sometimes a swollen nose. Ayami scanned her arms and hands. She sighed in relief at spotting nothing new.

A slight and growing whistle from the stove caused them both to turn toward the kettle, now boiling and ready for tea. Fujita reached for it while Ayami pulled two tin cups from the shelf. "Let's sit and have some tea until we hear them stirring," she said to her mother.

Thirty minutes later, they heard a rustling noise from down the hallway. Expecting one of the boys to come out soon, Fujita put a kettle on the stove to boil the eggs. When the water began to bubble, she removed and covered the pot and let it cool. Just as she was removing the eggs, footsteps approached.

"Your timing was good, Mama," Ayami said. "At least one of the boys is up."

Just when she finished speaking, Emiko entered the kitchen. "Good morning," she said. "Are we the only ones up?"

Fujita's face fell momentarily when she realized it was Emiko and not one of the boys. "Good morning," she replied. "I was hoping to see your brothers. They should be headed for the paddy by now."

"Should I wake them?" Emiko asked.

Fujita sighed. "Let's give them another half hour. Otherwise, they'll be cross with us for the rest of the day. When the eggs are cool, the two of you can remove the shells. If they're not up by then, we'll have to bang a few pans."

The eggs cooled, and the rooster crowed several more times, to no avail. None of the men emerged from their beds. "Put the kettle back on the stove and we'll start the rice," Fujita finally said. "If they're not up when it's ready, they'll just have to eat it cold. Maybe it will teach them a lesson."

"But Mama," Ayami pleaded, "won't that just make them angry? What if Papa... punishes you again? I'll wake them if you want. That way, they will have me to blame, not you."

"Let me think about it while we cook the rice," she replied.

Ayami saw a slight tremble in her mother's arms as she lifted the kettle to the stove. Ayami had seen the result of her father's tantrums before. *I don't think I can stand to see her suffer again,* she thought to herself.

The water reached a boil and Fujita slowly stirred rice into the kettle. She watched absent-mindedly as the bubbles dissipated and began to simmer. Then she asked Ayami to hand her a lid from the nearby shelf.

Seizing the opportunity, Ayami pulled out the bottom lid, knowing full well it was too large for the pot of rice, but with it came an assortment of smaller lids and several tin cups, bouncing off the edge of the stove and crashing against the washbasin. The sound was not as loud as she had hoped, but it created a distinct and annoying noise. She hid her excitement as the rooster, now closer to the window, responded with annoyance of its own, even louder than before.

Fujita gave Ayami a stare at first, then looked away with a knowing look that said, *Thank you.* Emiko started to laugh, but seemed to think the better of it and pretended to look busy at the table.

The three women waited to see if the commotion had done its work.

Shortly, the sound of grumbling voices and labored movement commenced from down the hall. First to the kitchen was Shoji, the youngest son. He rubbed his eyes and stretched while he yawned and moved toward the stove. Opening the lid, he merely sighed as if expecting to find something else beneath it.

"Let the rice cool before removing the lid," his mother said. "You know it sets up better if you leave the lid on."

"I heard the noise and thought maybe someone had fallen," he replied. "Is everyone okay?"

"I'm sorry," Ayami said. "I was reaching for a cover for the rice, and a few others fell out on the stove."

After looking at the kettle of rice, Shoji scanned the room for something else to eat, and seeing the freshly boiled eggs, quickly grabbed the one closest to him and slipped it in his mouth.

He chewed once or twice, then tried hard to swallow before his brothers arrived. It was mostly down his throat when the twins, rarely far apart, lumbered down the hallway and into the kitchen. "Who was making all that racket?" Koichi complained in a loud voice. "How do you expect us to sleep through all the commotion?"

"How hard is it to boil a few eggs and a little rice without waking up everyone in the house?" his brother echoed.

"It was my fault," Ayami explained again. "I accidentally pulled too many lids from the shelf and they fell against the stove. I'm sorry it disturbed your sleep, but didn't Papa say today was the day you start preparing the paddy?"

"We can't work without sleep," Koji replied sharply.

The sun was fully up when the three brothers walked out the door and toward the barn. Ayami was certain she heard the twins grumbling about not having enough to eat for breakfast, and that besides, it was already cold by the time their mother served it. But she heard no criticism of their father, whose snores could still be heard from the bedroom to the kitchen.

The sisters watched through the window as two oxen plodded from the barn to the paddy, pulling a harrow. Ayami winced when she saw Shoji driving the team. The twins followed at some distance behind, talking between themselves as they shared a cigarette and periodically shouted instructions to their younger brother.

The girls could no longer see them once they reached the paddy, because of its location behind the barn. But it was already clear who would be doing the work. Ayami looked at her mother for some indication of her reaction, but all she saw was her mother staring at the last two eggs in the bowl.

The women ate a simple breakfast of rice, and after clearing the table and washing the dishes, set about their morning routine. Fujita washed clothing in a tub just outside the door while Ayami hung it out to dry. Emiko carried the table scraps and eggshells to the garden to help replenish the soil, then swept the wooden floors in the other bedrooms and the kitchen, careful not to disturb her still-sleeping father.

Catching a glimpse of movement as she hung a garment out to dry in the morning sun, Ayami peered up the road to discover two riders. Something about them was ominous from the start.

The riders turned off the main road and entered the lane toward their farm.

"Mama!" Ayami yelled across the yard to her mother. "Go get Papa. I think he needs to be here!"

Fujita viewed the scene in front of her and dashed into the house.

"Good morning," the first rider growled. "Is this the Matsumoto farm?"

"Yes," Ayami replied. "This is my father's farm. What do you want?"

"We are here to speak to Matsumoto. Is he here?"

"Yes, he is here. My mother just went to get him."

Ayami listened carefully for any signs of activity coming from the house. Hearing none, she waited as patiently as she could, trying not to betray her rising fear of the two unexpected intruders. Finally, she said, "I'll go and see what's keeping him. Who should I say is here?"

"Just tell him we need to talk," the rider replied.

Ayami hurried into the house, almost as afraid of what she would find inside, as of the two men she left behind in the yard. The kitchen was quiet.

Emiko was standing in a corner away from the door with a look of bewilderment still in her eyes. She tilted her head toward their father's bedroom and twitched it a few times to signal to her older sister where their mother had gone.

When Ayami walked down the hallway, she heard a series of foul words, which always caused her mother to wince. Announcing herself as she neared, partly to alert her father, but also her mother, who was likely taking abuse for waking him.

"Father, two men are here to see you. They wouldn't tell me what they want, only that they needed to speak with you. They look like government officials. What should I tell them?"

She waited outside his door for an answer. Then her mother stepped through and met Ayami's eyes. "He's getting dressed," she said. "He should be coming soon."

Not waiting for her father, Ayami turned and walked back through the kitchen and into the yard to relay the message. The two strangers were still sitting atop their large mounts.

"My father is not feeling well today," she stammered. "He was resting in bed, but he's getting dressed and will be out to see you shortly."

After what seemed far too long, Kunio finally emerged through the doorway wearing a faded gray kimono and loose-fitting sandals, his hair a tangled mess. In the late morning sunlight, he momentarily stopped to shield his eyes. Sizing up the visitors from a distance, he straightened his body to its full height and walked deliberately toward the two. His face was as grim as Ayami had ever seen it. When he stomped past, she saw the redness in his eyes and the trembling of his hands.

Fujita and Emiko, after following him through the door, remained standing near the house.

"What is so urgent that you must deny a weary farmer his rest?" Kunio said to the man who appeared to be in charge.

Without the hint of a smile, and with an unblinking face, the man replied, "Are you Kunio Matsumoto?"

"I am."

"And are you, Kunio Matsumoto, the owner of this farm on which we are presently standing?"

"I am."

The second man then held forth a parchment document and, leaning down, handed it to Kunio.

When Kunio accepted the document the first man said, "You are hereby duly notified that your farm, consisting of..." He hesitated, then looked over at the first man, who recited a number from the preceding document.

"Twenty hectares..." the first man said.

"Twenty hectares of land and..." looking briefly around the farmstead, continued, "one modern house plus two additional outbuildings... are hereby duly notified that you are in violation of the laws of the Emperor of Japan for failure to pay legal and just taxes, as required by law. Do you understand what that means?" he then asked.

Kunio stared blankly at the man.

"It means," the man said, "that you are behind on your taxes, and unless you pay them completely, we will have no choice but to claim your farm, consisting of some twenty hectares and three wooden structures, in the name of the emperor."

Kunio continued to stare at the men with a blank face, now draining of what little color it had when he left the house.

"You can't take my land," he finally managed to say. "It's not my fault we can't pay the tax. I can pay you in rice, like we used to. Take the rice. It's there in the shed. Take five barrels... take ten barrels if you need to. All we have is rice. Rice used to be good enough for paying the tax. What happened to that? Now the emperor wants currency. Where are we supposed to sell our rice for enough currency to pay twice the amount we used to pay in rice?"

"We don't make the laws. We are here to inform you of your responsibility. By the goodness of the emperor, you have until the end of this year to pay all taxes that you owe. That means you will have this year's harvest to help raise the money. If not paid in full by the end of this year, eighteen seventy-five, the emperor will be forced to claim your land, and you will not be permitted to remain."

"We can't grow enough rice to pay that much tax. That's what I'm trying to tell you. I could harvest two crops of rice and still be lucky to pay your filthy tax. The same for all the farmers. Just look around. Do you think we're living half as good as you, riding through the country on fancy horses and dressed in fancy silk uniforms? Think again if you do, because we barely make enough to feed our families, let alone pay your ridiculous tax."

The man on the first horse slowly and deliberately scanned the horizon surrounding Kunio's farm. Then he growled, "Is that your farm we saw coming in, with three young men working the field?"

"Yes, that is part of our farm. Those are my sons. They are out there working as we speak. See how hard they work, and what do we get for it? Harassment for payment of taxes so officials in Edo can live in fancy houses and wear fancy clothes. That's what we get for it!"

The man on the horse met Kunio's eyes as he continued in his unwavering voice, "First of all, it is Tokyo, not Edo. It has been for several years. Just because you live out here in the middle of nowhere is not a reason to remain ignorant. Secondly, why is it that on your farm, we have witnessed three workers... your sons, as you have stated, now in the process of preparing the paddy for its first sowing of rice, when any number of farms that we passed along the way have already sown the seeds, and the seedlings are now tall enough for replanting?"

Kunio stared at the man. Ayami almost felt sorry for him as his hands continued to shake and beads of sweat slowly broke across his forehead. But she knew the man was right. If only Kunio would stop wasting his days at the open end of a saké bottle and force her brothers to get up early like the neighbors, their nursery would be ready to plant as well.

Still looking at Kunio in the eyes, the man shot another arrow. "If you have trouble feeding your family, as you have just indicated, perhaps it would serve you well to rid yourself of any unnecessary members." Then he shifted his gaze first to Ayami and then to Emiko, still standing by her mother near the front door. "Women rarely contribute enough labor to justify the amount of food they consume in return."

Ayami was sure she saw a momentary sneer as he looked briefly at Fujita and hurled yet another spear. "Of course, if it is comfort you seek, then perhaps you need to decide which is more important, your farm or your comfort."

Kunio advanced two steps toward the man, but before he could reach him, the man prodded the large animal toward Kunio with such force that he had no choice but to retrace his steps.

Ayami watched as her father's face filled with anger and the veins on each side of his neck swelled almost to bursting. Then he looked around the yard as if looking for his sons to help, but realizing he was surrounded only by three helpless women, he simply stood his ground.

"Enough of you!" he shouted at the two riders. "Get off my property and don't come back! It's my land, and you can't take it! I don't care what the emperor says. It's my farm, and it always will be!"

Kunio watched the two men ride off in the direction they had come. When they were beyond the range of hearing his voice, he turned and stared at Fujita with a look that Ayami had seldom seen. He narrowed his eyes and raised his shoulders, looking even more intimidating than the two men who had just departed.

"It's your fault we can't pay the tax. If you and your *daughters* would pick up a little more of the work around here instead of slacking in the house all day, maybe we could grow a decent crop. You don't see my sons milling around the house, do you? No, they are out planting the crop, trying to make a living."

All three women stared at him in disbelief. Emiko almost laughed at the absurdity of his words but caught herself in time.

As Kunio walked toward the door, Ayami could no longer contain herself.

"If anyone is seen milling around the house, Father, it is you. Why are you still sleeping in the middle of the morning? Mother and I, and Emiko, were up long before you or any of your sons, fixing breakfast and doing chores. Those men were right about one thing. If we followed our neighbors' example, we would have enough money for the tax. Oh, and regarding feeding our family, how much extra rice would we have if you didn't use so much of it to make your beloved saké? Maybe you're the one who needs to face the truth."

Kunio had never been insulted in such a way. Ayami braced herself for what was sure to follow. He turned to face her directly and stared into her eyes until she thought she might wilt to the ground. But she had to take a stand, if not for herself, then for Emiko and her mother.

Kunio stared at her for a minute or more. She saw the small tremble in his hands increase to the point his entire body began to shake. Perspiration from his forehead covered his jaws and neck, and the front of his kimono was soaked with sweat.

Kunio had twelve centimeters of height advantage and more than thirty kilograms of weight advantage, but Ayami was prepared to take her punishment. She spread her feet wide enough to allow some degree of balance should he suddenly strike her across the face. Sweat began to form on her forehead as well, and she felt drops trickle down the back of her neck.

Then, to her amazement, her father turned back to the house and headed for her mother, who was standing near the door. He stopped less than a meter from her and waited patiently until she looked him in the eye.

"Your daughter is a disgrace. See to it she is gone from this house when I return for supper. I don't care where she goes. That is her problem. But she will not live here." With that, he launched a single slap to Fujita's left ear, nearly toppling her to the ground, and then he entered the house.

Moments later, he walked out, holding the two remaining eggs in one hand and his hat in the other, headed for the paddy.

Ayami and Emiko rushed to their mother as soon as Kunio passed them by. Ayami first hugged her, then held her face in both hands, sizing up what would soon become her latest bruise. "Can you see out of your eye?" she asked. "It's starting to swell already. It will turn black before long, certainly by the time he comes home from the fields."

"You have to leave, Mama," Ayami pleaded. "You can't stay here. Who knows what he'll do if you stay?"

"Yes, Mama, you have to go away with Ayami," Emiko added. "I'll stay and take care of them. He has never hurt me, and I don't think he will. I'm no threat to any of them. You go. I'll be alright."

"No," Fujita replied. "I have to stay. Where would I go? I have no money and no place to live. You two go; I'll manage. He only gets this way when he's worried. It was only because of the tax officials that he got so angry. He'll get over it soon. He always does. Emiko, you go with Ayami. I'll be okay here alone."

This time, it was Emiko who declined. "No, Mama, I won't leave you. I'm staying here with you." Then she looked at Ayami. "I don't think you can stay. Papa sounded really mad, like he meant it. What choice do we have?"

Chapter 5

Ayami Leaves Home

HANAMAKI - 1875

Fujita looked at Ayami and tried to smile. "Pack your things," she said. "We'll see if the Sasaki's can keep you until we find somewhere permanent. Emiko, help pack her things." Then she went back into the house to splash cold water on her face.

Twenty minutes later the girls stood before her in the kitchen, each carrying a cotton bag filled with the few possessions Ayami claimed as her own. Emiko was still sobbing, and Ayami's eyes were red from crying moments before.

"You have to come with me," Ayami pleaded again, to her mother and sister. "You know what happens when he drinks too much. And he keeps getting worse."

"Emiko is free to go if she wants but I can't leave, I'll just have to make the best of it."

Emiko looked at Ayami and the sobs returned. "I have to stay with Mama," she sputtered. "Please don't be mad at me."

Ayami hugged her sister and whispered, "Emi, I could never be mad at you. You are the nicest, bravest sister I could ever hope for. I'm sorry I have to leave. Maybe when this whole tax thing is over, he will be his old self again. I remember when he was a good father. Maybe he will be again."

Then the three of them, carrying nothing but two sacks of clothing, walked toward the road and turned in the direction opposite the fields, careful not to be seen by Kunio or the three brothers.

Two kilometers away, they knocked on the door of the Sasaki household and waited. Yuro soon answered. After one look at the trio standing at his door, he called back through the house to his wife. She showed no surprise when she saw Fujita and her daughters. The only surprise was that it had taken so long. Gyo Shin opened the door and motioned them in.

"You are welcome here for a few days," she told Ayami, "but I'm afraid your father would soon learn your whereabouts if you stayed longer. Put your things in that empty bedroom for now. We'll do our best to keep you safe."

Then Emiko thought of something. "Do you know the Ishii family?" she asked. "They live another five kilometers down the road. I met their daughter, Suki, last year at school. She was very nice, and I bet her parents would let Ayami stay with them. Maybe she could go there when she leaves here."

"I've heard of the family, but I don't know them," Gyo Shin replied. "That would certainly help us, if they are willing. Yuro will go tomorrow and ask for their help, won't you, Yuro?" she said, facing her husband. "We'll keep her hidden until we can get her moved."

Then Fujita turned to Yuro. "Would you write a letter for me? My sister lives in Kamaishi, over on the coast. I'm sure she would take Ayami in, if I ask her. But I never learned to write. Kunio didn't think girls needed to know." Then she looked at Gyo Shin with an embarrassed look, in case her husband felt the same.

"Yes, of course," Yuro replied. "Come and sit with me in the kitchen, and we'll do it now. Just tell me what you want to say."

An hour later, Ayami hugged her mother and sister one last time. Then the two of them walked out the door toward home.

***

The next morning, Emiko's mouth dropped when she heard her father's voice. She turned to her mother, standing in front of the stove. Together, they turned toward the voice coming from the bedroom hallway.

"Time to get up!" he called to his sons. "We have work to do."

Emiko recovered from her shock only in time to reach for more bowls from the cupboard when Kunio arrived in the kitchen.

"Good morning, Papa," she stammered.

"Good morning, Papa," Fujita echoed.

Kunio gazed at them briefly with a repentant look. "Good morning," he said. "Is breakfast ready?"

"We're making it now," Fujita stammered back. "We didn't expect… it took longer to heat the stove…" she corrected… "the wood was a little too wet… Emiko has already gathered the eggs, and the rice will be ready in a few minutes. Did I hear you calling the boys? Breakfast should be ready by the time they get here."

"Good. If we're going to catch up with the neighbors, we'll need an early start today."

Emiko tried not to stare at her father. It was the first time ever, that she'd heard him worry about the crops.

Fujita filled a bowl for each of the men. "The rice is ready," she said.

Emiko put six eggs in a bowl and placed them on the table. Then she poured tea in each of the six cups as her brothers stumbled in.

"Why are we starting so early?" Koichi complained.

"Yeah, what's the rush?" Koji asked.

"We have work to do," Kunio replied. "With Ayami gone, it's that much more to fall on us. The paddy won't get cleared by itself."

The table went quiet while they ate.

Ayami did a lot of work, but none of it in the rice fields, Emiko thought to herself. How her absence meant more work for the men seemed a mystery, but it didn't matter. What did matter was, they were finally going to get some work done.

After they left, Fujita said, "I think Ayami's words to your father had more impact than he wants to let on."

"I can't believe the change," Emiko replied. "I couldn't believe my ears when I heard him coming to the kitchen. We should have stood up to him a long time ago. I hope he learned his lesson. And if he has, maybe Ayami can come home again."

"I hope he has," Fujita replied, "but time will tell. The first test is whether he gives up his saké. Most men can't, once it gets a hold on them."

***

Three days later, several kilometers away, Yuro packed up Ayami's belongings, and the two of them trudged south to the Ishii farm. Emiko's friend Suki was watching for them at the end of the lane. When she saw Ayami coming, she ran out to greet her.

"Are you Emiko's sister? I was hoping Emiko would be with you. She is so much fun. I wish I had a sister like her. She always watched out for me at school."

"Yes, I am her sister," Ayami replied. "And I agree with you, she is fun to be around. I wish she could be with me today, but she had to stay home with our mother. She likes you, too—in fact, she is the reason I'm here. She will be happy to hear about you."

"Follow me," Suki said. "I'll introduce you to my parents."

"You may stay as long as you like," Miwa said, when Suki led her through the doorway. She looked at her husband, Rikuto, for confirmation.

"Yes, for as long as you need," he affirmed.

Ayami bowed to each of them with tears in her eyes. "Thank you," she managed. "You are very kind."

One month later, a letter arrived from Kamaishi.

Dearest Ayami,

We would be delighted to have you stay with us. Please come as soon as you can.
Your loving aunt,

Minako

Chapter 6

Toshi and the Mystery Girl

KAMAISHI - 1875

Walking home from work that day, Toshi was feeling good—even better than normal. Watching the raw chunks of rocky ore turn to molten lava and then into useable iron was fulfilling work. Some days he was so engrossed in the process that he forgot to eat the cold rice and fruit he brought for lunch.

And on his walks home at the end of the day, he often slowed his pace to enjoy the lush mountain foliage and listen for the ever-present songs of birds along the way. Today was even more rewarding because when he tallied up his savings the night before, it totaled more than one hundred and fifty yen. More than fifty yen for each year since coming to Kamaishi.

Only one thing stood in the way of total happiness, and it nagged at him frequently, if not constantly, no matter how hard he tried to suppress it… *America.* Why he had thrown those old copies of the *Mainichi Shimbun* into his luggage along with his university books, he did not know, but while the textbooks remained mostly untouched, he read and re-read the few copies of the newspaper almost every week. Especially the articles about America. Maybe it was because they sounded so exotic, so romantic, so filled with the promise of adventure and opportunity. And wealth.

Now, after three years of saving, he had the money to go. It would be hard to bid goodbye to Haruki, especially given how supportive he had been since the very beginning, but also the other workers. They had been good to him and he liked them. It would be hard to leave.

These were the thoughts in his mind when, partway home, he met three young pedestrians coming from the opposite direction. He was so preoccupied with America and how he would tell Haruki, that he nearly missed seeing them. He was just meters away when he glanced up from the path and instinctively moved to one side, giving them room to pass.

The oldest girl was about his age. The other two were younger. *They could be sisters*, was his first impression. They seemed to be enjoying their walk together, wherever they were going. All three wore smiles as they approached, and two of them were talking animatedly between themselves. The third girl, the older one, caught his attention just as they were meeting. She was walking at the edge of the path, on the same side as Toshi, and if he had not moved quickly to the side, he might have bumped her shoulder when they passed by. He stole a look at her face just as she glanced his way, and then she was gone.

A few steps later, Toshi stopped to collect his thoughts. The girl was attractive—very attractive. *I wish I had looked up sooner*, he thought to himself. He walked several more meters and stopped again. He turned around for another look, but they were gone. It happened so suddenly, and he was so absorbed by America and the one hundred and fifty yen in his special can, that he almost missed her entirely. For a fleeting moment, he considered turning back and trying to catch them up. Then came the realization that he would have nothing to say to her. It would make him look a fool.

Then, another realization. If she were on the path today, maybe she would be again tomorrow.

***

Ayami Matsumoto enjoyed being with her cousins. Hisa and Kanae were fun to be with. Slightly younger than Ayami, they looked up to her. And their younger sister, Saya, was impossible not to like. She looked up to her visiting cousin almost in awe. Coming from a remote farming village in the west, Ayami was sheltered from social life, yet somehow sophisticated when compared to her Kamaishi cousins. Perhaps it was merely her age that gave her an edge.

Returning from the village that day, they had walked three abreast, wherever the narrow path allowed.

"I think we should get Saya the blue and yellow fan with butterflies," Hisa had proclaimed. "Blue is her favorite color, and I know she likes butterflies."

"True, but she also likes dragons. And the red and black fan was larger. It would go nicely with any of her kimonos. And it would provide a perfect contrast to almost any color," Kanae interjected.

"Which one do you like, Ayami? You are the best at choosing colors," Hisa said.

"Well, since it is her twelfth birthday, I think she would prefer a more grown-up color, like the blue and yellow one. I like the pattern of the red and black, but I think it might be too bold for her. And butterflies are more uplifting than dragons, don't you think?"

Engrossed in their discussion about the perfect gift for her cousins' younger sister, Ayami could be forgiven for not paying attention to other pedestrians as they made their way home along the route. But she did look up just in time to see a young man approaching, and he was handsome, she thought, yet preoccupied. He was not watching where he walked.

She was proud of herself for not staring at him as she managed to continue in their conversation. Still, her heart had skipped a beat when he walked past. She was quite certain he hadn't caught her peeking, but admittedly, she *had* peeked, and she was taken by what she saw.

***

That night, Toshi had a dream that he met his wife for the very first time. Although most of her features were blurred in the dream, he remembered a face that smiled when it passed by on a path toward his home. The face was slender, with cheeks curved gracefully downward to a perfect chin. When she smiled, her ivory-white teeth glistened behind soft pink lips. She glowed with a natural, innocent beauty.

He awoke the next morning filled with anticipation. Hoping the dream had been an omen, and that the girl in the dream was, in fact, the girl on the path, he would be watching for her. He would bow politely and extend a greeting. He even rehearsed a plan, which was to ask if she could recommend a teahouse in the vicinity, since he was new to the area. He knew this was not entirely true because he had lived in Kamaishi for almost three years. But since he had not seen her before, he hoped she wouldn't know.

So, it was with great and growing excitement that Toshi headed up the path that morning, not particularly anxious to get to work at the foundry, but with hopes of meeting the mysterious young woman along the way. And since he didn't know where she began or ended her route, he decided it would behoove him to travel slowly, and maximize his time along the path. For that reason, he slowed his pace while trying to blend in with others who shared that same path to their various destinations.

The secret, he felt, was to pretend he was traveling at his usual gait, but not to cover as much distance. He tried walking at a normal pace, stopping frequently to observe a tree or flower, until it occurred to him that if he really was looking at one of the objects, he might miss his intended target.

His next idea was to continue walking the path without interruption and to keep his legs and feet moving at a pace consistent with other travelers, but taking shorter steps. This turned out to be a marching cadence, whereby his knees came up and down in a rhythmic pattern but with a shortened stride, causing his forward progress to be greatly diminished. It was a form of walking-in-place. He would try it.

And sure enough, he did seem to be in step with those around him, whose objective was most likely to consume the least amount of time between leaving home and arriving at work. The difference was that Toshi was not really going anywhere. At least not very fast. The advantage of this method was that it not only allowed him to maximize his time along the route, and thus the window of time during which he might spot his mystery girl, but it also gave him much more time to scan their faces. It was the perfect plan.

It was working so well that he continued the procedure for the remainder of the trip. He did begin to notice, as time went by, fewer and fewer travelers along the route. At first, he felt relief because it gave him more time to scan each traveler, whether coming or going. Until finally, it occurred to him he was not going to see her on the trail that particular morning.

He was almost at the foundry and had to concede—she was not on the path today. And then another thought came to mind, which was far more troubling than the first. For the first time in his life, Toshi Ozawa would be late for work.

***

"Ayami is quiet tonight," Minako said to Hisa in the kitchen. "Did something happen on your trip to the village?"

"No, we had a grand time together. She seemed fine all through the trip. She probably misses her family," Hisa replied. "It's the first time she's been away from home, and I'm sure she must be lonely for them by now."

"You're probably right," her mother said, "but all the same, stay close to her for a while and see if you can determine something more. It's not like her to be so quiet."

After their evening meal of rice and vegetables, Ayami helped clear and clean the dishes, then asked to be excused to the bedroom, which she shared with Hisa. She carefully removed her kimono and undergarments, and slipped into her favorite pajamas, which reminded her of home, her mother, and her beloved sister, Emiko.

Exhausted by the thoughts that filled her mind, she lay down on her mat. *This feels so good,* she thought, *I could lie here forever.*

After reliving the events of the day, the walk to the village, and the trip home, Ayami came to the last event of the trip, when they happened upon the stranger. She remembered the sudden pang of excitement when, from the corner of her eye, she noticed he was staring at her. That's what she would call it. His eyes were definitely fixed on her. She dared not return his gaze for fear of appearing forward. But she did try her best to form his image in her mind. Ayami was not accustomed to flirting with men. It was certainly beneath her upbringing. This was as bold as she could ever remember acting to a total stranger.

***

"Toshi, where have you been? I was worried about you. You've never been late before. Is something wrong at home?" The foreman was full of questions when Toshi finally showed himself that morning.

"No, everything is fine. I just..." Toshi wasn't sure how to respond. He really didn't want to tell the foreman he was watching for a girl along the path. He would never hear the end of it from his fellow workers if they thought he was distracted by a girl. "I just... I just... overslept this morning. I didn't sleep very well for some reason."

"I'll let it go this time, Toshi, because you have always been one of the first to arrive, and you always set a good example for the others while you're here. But don't be late again. It's not fair to the rest of us when you show up late."

"I understand. I am sorry, and I won't oversleep again." And Toshi had every intention of not letting it happen again.

When the furnace emptied and cooled at the end of the day, Toshi felt a new surge of energy flow into his tired and hungry body. Now was another chance to watch for the mystery girl. As he left the foundry and headed home, he felt the best way to accidentally run into her would be to walk just as he had the previous day. If she were on a daily schedule, that would be the most likely way to replicate their meeting. He started off at what he thought was his normal pace following a day of work. After a short while, though, he doubted himself. *Had he really walked this fast yesterday?* It seemed like he was moving too fast and would soon be home. He had better slow down a little; he was getting too close to home. *Why hadn't he paid more attention to where he'd seen her yesterday? Was it before or after the footbridge?*

And just as he had feared, he soon found himself at his own doorstep, with no sight, hint, or clue as to where the girl might be. The energy drained from his body as if someone had opened a hole in his foot. Or, more to the point, a hole in his heart, because that is where he felt the pain.

For the second night, Toshi went to bed and lay awake for what felt like half the night until he could no longer remember her face. When morning came, even though weary from two nights with little sleep, he soon became energized again in the hope that *this* morning would be the day he saw her again. He was so hopeful that he studied himself in the mirror before leaving. He made sure his hair was combed exactly right, his face cleanly shaven, and that he looked his best for the mystery girl, should they meet on the path this day.

To avoid the risk of being late a second time, Toshi adjusted his strategy. He still liked the idea of the 'slow walk,' but today he would pay more attention to the time. And he would leave home a little early, just to be safe.

And so it was, that Toshi began his second march to the foundry, taking pronounced steps with a high vertical movement of the knees but a decidedly shorter horizontal stride. After a little practice, he found he could alter his forward progress either faster or slower, depending on the other traffic. In stretches where there were not many other pedestrians, where he could easily identify their faces, he stretched out his steps and moved forward along the path at a normal pace. And when the traffic increased, he could shorten his steps and thus have time to scrutinize faces coming and going. Most of all, he was keeping track of the time, so as not to risk another day late for work.

When he saw the foundry coming up just ahead, he had to admit another failure. The girl was not to be seen.

"Good morning, Toshi. I am glad to see you are here early as usual this morning," Haruki greeted him. "I hope you're feeling well today."

"Thank you. I am well and ready to work. I'm sorry about my tardiness yesterday," replied Toshi.

But as the day wore on, Toshi struggled to keep his mind on his work. His co-workers were puzzled by this change of behavior. He was always the person they looked up to and admired for his total dedication.

It was mid-afternoon when Kenshin Maeda approached Toshi with a huge grin on his face. "Toshi, I've seen this before, and I know what's happened. You're in love, aren't you?" At this, all those around him fell silent and looked over to gauge his reaction.

Toshi turned red, as his face flushed and his mind went blank. He did not want to admit his preoccupation *was* about a girl he had seen only once, and that he had no idea who she was. "I just haven't been sleeping very well lately," he said. "I think I've been worrying too much about the foundry, and I can't get to sleep at night."

He said it with as much conviction as he could, but it didn't seem to convince his face, which felt as flushed as ever. He couldn't tell if the others were persuaded or not as he quickly renewed an interest in his work and tried to close the conversation.

***

Ayami was slow to awaken after finally falling sound asleep in the early hours of the morning. She began to stir when she heard activity in the kitchen and the sound of quiet voices greeting the day. Slowly, she rose from the mat, stretched, and opened her eyes. After washing her face and a quick comb of her hair, she joined the others in the kitchen. Her uncle was already at work, but Aunt Minako and the two older cousins were seated together, each with a fresh cup of tea in their hands.

"Good morning, Ayami," they greeted her, with a sympathetic look. "Did you have a good sleep last night?"

"Good morning," she replied. "I had trouble getting to sleep, and then I slept so soundly that I had trouble waking up. I'm sorry I was not here to help with breakfast."

"That's fine," Minako said. "We know you were not feeling your usual self yesterday. Are you sure you don't want to talk about it?"

"No, I'm feeling better today. I'm sorry I caused you to worry. It is nothing really, and I promise to do better from now on. I hope you know how much I appreciate your letting me stay with you, and I hope it doesn't have to be for too long. You have all been so good to me. I know it isn't fair when I don't at least do my share of the work."

And Ayami believed herself when she said she was feeling better today. She started by telling her aunt about the fans they had seen at the market, and which one they were thinking about getting for Saya's birthday.

"Are we going to have a party for her?" asked Kanae.

"We'll have to ask Papa about that," Minako replied. "But we'll wait a few days before we ask," she added with a smile on her face. "We don't want to give him too much time to think up an excuse."

For the next few days, Ayami tried her best to forget how much she missed her mother and sister, but eventually she realized it was the young man that distressed her most. Each night, as she tried to fall asleep, she tried to recapture his face in her mind. It was difficult since she had only seen him those few brief moments, and even more because she had dared not face him squarely, or meet his eyes. And finally, she would reprimand herself for becoming so enraptured by the chance meeting of a total stranger.

And so, as the next day came and went, followed by several more, she gradually became her old self again. The radiant smile that her aunt so enjoyed and the daily conversations with her cousins returned. Hisa and Kanae were especially happy again, as they made plans to go back to the village and make their final selection for Saya's birthday gift. They would go on Tuesday of next week.

***

For Toshi, the days at work slowly came back in focus. More than once, he lost concentration for a few brief moments as his thoughts drifted to the mystery girl.

"Hey Toshi," Kenshin shouted above the noise, "tell us about your new girlfriend."

Shichiro Sugawara added, "Yes, Toshi, tell us. She must be quite a woman. We can tell you're crazy about her."

Toshi tried to ignore their good-natured ribbing, but their taunts were too close for comfort, and it only made his face flush all the more. He was not used to denying the truth, simply because he had never had to. "I don't have a girlfriend," he replied, forcing a laugh. "You guys are trying to make something from nothing."

But Toshi had far from forgotten his mystery girl, and each day, morning and evening, he continued his 'extended window' search for the girl. His legs were getting accustomed to the additional effort required, with so many extra steps each day, and the pronounced cadence of his high knee extensions.

After six days of his continued protocol, it was understandable that he began to lose faith he would ever see her again. *Toshi,* he thought to himself, *you must be a fool to act this way. You have no reason to think she lives here or even anywhere near here. Your co-workers are making fun of you, and if you are honest with yourself, they are right to do so. You are acting like a schoolboy and a fool.*

On the seventh day, Toshi was able to sleep an extra thirty minutes before getting up to dress, eat, and be on his way. *That was a good night's sleep for a change,* he thought as he headed off to work. It felt good to be alive and useful again. He would be sure to update his journal at the end of the day, which was Tuesday.

Chapter 7
Second Sighting

KAMAISHI - 1875

This time, it was Ayami who saw Toshi as he crossed over the bridge. He seemed deep in thought, much like before. Hisa and Kanae continued their conversation as Ayami gazed at the approaching stranger. They were getting closer; only a few meters between them.

Finally, when Toshi was less than three meters away, he looked up and saw Ayami. Her coal-black hair swayed gently across her forehead as she walked along the rugged trail. Her large, hazel-colored eyes, for the one brief moment she looked at him, seemed to penetrate his very soul. When she drew close, the corners of her mouth turned up slightly in the beginning of a smile.

Toshi's eyes widened and his expression went blank. He did not have time to think or time to deploy his plan about the teahouse. He didn't even have time to slow his feet. They kept walking at their normal pace until they were beyond the three young women. What now? He could not turn around and yell after her, his first instinct. There was nothing he could do.

A few paces later he noticed the fragrance. Lavender. Or maybe wild rose. The bouquet filled his nostrils with an aroma he could not resist. A few steps further, he inhaled deeply to revive the heavenly scent, but instead of lavender and rose, it brought only the unpleasant tang of sweat and dirt. Unavoidable smells from a long hot day at the foundry. What must she think of him? Smelly, stinky, and covered in dirt.

After another hundred meters, it finally registered that he had seen her again. She must live somewhere near. Then he remembered that she was smiling. And what a smile it was. She was even more beautiful than he had remembered, especially when she smiled.

***

At mealtime, Ayami seemed lost in thought.

"Are you not feeling well, Ayami?" Minako asked. "You're very quiet."

"No, I'm fine, just a little tired from our trip to the village. If you don't mind, I think I'll retire early tonight."

"Of course, Ayami, if you're sure it's nothing more."

Ayami changed into her pajamas and lay on the mat alone, thinking back to the young man on the path. This time, she had a long enough glimpse to confirm her initial impression. He had a gentle face and soft brown eyes, and he was definitely handsome.

Later, Saya came into the room and sat on her sister's mat, next to Ayami.

"Do you like our village?" she asked quietly.

"Yes, very much," Ayami replied. "I was not able to visit my own village often. Papa said we had too much work to do at home to waste time in the village."

"It must be tiring for you to visit. I remember the last time you went; you came back very tired."

Ayami thought about her first trip. "You have a good memory. I didn't remember that. I guess it must be more tiring than I realized."

Hoping to change the subject, Ayami continued. "Have you thought about what you want for your birthday?"

"Not really," she replied. "But I am excited to be turning twelve. I'm starting to feel grown up, and I like how Mother and my sisters treat me more like a grownup than a little girl." She was quiet then, and the two of them sat on the edge of the mat, enjoying the silence together.

After a while, Saya looked up at Ayami and said, "When I get to be your age, I want to be just like you."

Ayami was taken aback. She turned to face her young cousin. "Thank you, Saya. That is the nicest thing anyone has ever said to me."

Silence filled the room again before either of them spoke. Finally, Ayami let down her guard and began to speak. "Saya, I'm sorry for causing so much concern for you and your family, after all you've done for me. I do love it here, and I especially like being with all of you. You've made me feel like I'm part of your family. I miss my mother, especially, and my sister, Emiko. This is the first time I've been away from them for more than a day. And I worry for… about them." Saya was too young to learn the reason she was worried.

After a few minutes, she continued. "But there is another reason, and one I've not told anyone because it might seem foolish; it even makes me think it's foolish at times. But I can't get it out of my mind no matter how hard I try. Last week, when your sisters and I went to the village, on the way home, we met a stranger on the path who I was attracted to, even though we've never met. After a few days I managed to put him out of my mind until today, when we went to the village. On the way home I saw him again. I don't think your sisters noticed, but I couldn't help but admire him when he passed us by. And now I think about him more than ever, and I'm sure I won't sleep again tonight.

"I have no idea who he is or where he lives, but I suspect he was on his way home from work somewhere. I'm pretty sure he was attracted to me as well, even though we didn't speak or even acknowledge one another. I could just see by his face that he was interested. This is such a childish whim that I can't share it with your sisters or your parents. I don't even know how I can be so childish myself."

After several minutes, Saya looked up at Ayami and said, "Have you ever kissed a boy?"

"What?" she replied, trying not to laugh.

"Have you ever kissed a boy, like, you know, on the mouth?"

Ayami realized she was serious. She had forgotten what thoughts ran through her mind at age twelve. It seemed long ago and far removed from sitting here on her cousin's mat in Kamaishi.

"No," she admitted. "I have never kissed a boy. I suppose it was because there weren't any boys around, on the farm. The only boys I ever saw were my brothers. Shoji was nice, but even so, I didn't want to kiss my brother on the lips."

"That would be funny," Saya replied. "I don't think it would be much fun to kiss a brother." She wrinkled her nose.

They both laughed at the thought of it.

"What do you think it tastes like?" Saya asked.

"I'm not sure," Ayami replied. "I suppose it depends on what he's had to eat. Or drink. I remember times when my father was angry and close to me, and his mouth did not smell good at all. I hope he never kissed my mother when he was like that." Then she went quiet and stared at something across the room that Saya couldn't see.

Saya remained quiet for several minutes and then she said, "Ayami, I just thought of what I really want for my birthday… I want you to find the man of your dreams and be happy."

A glisten from Ayami's dark eyes trickled slowly down her cheek.

***

After once more seeing his mystery girl along the path, Toshi was elated beyond words. He could not eat that night for thinking what he might have done differently. When he went to bed that night, the thoughts in his head were going around and around with ideas. For hours he lay in bed, turning first one way and then another. Finally, as dawn emerged above the Pacific, exhaustion overtook him, and he fell soundly asleep.

When he awoke he knew he was in trouble. He had overslept. The sun was already above the horizon and casting shadows outside his window. He leapt to his feet and dressed as quickly as he could. He didn't have time to eat. He washed himself, smoothed his hair with his fingers, and hurried out the door. The good news was that there was hardly any traffic at this time of the morning. Everyone else had already arrived at their destination.

Haruki was waiting at the furnace when Toshi walked in. "Toshi, how long have you worked at the foundry?"

"Almost three years."

"How many times in three years have you been late to work?"

"Two times, I think."

"That's what I think, too. How many times do you think you have been early for work?"

"I'm not sure, but probably most of the other days."

"That's what I think, too. For three years, you have provided an example for the rest of us, as surely as the rising sun. And now you arrive late, twice, in as many weeks. Something is obviously wrong, and whatever it is, you need to fix it." With that, he turned and walked away.

***

Haruki's shoulders slumped on the long walk home. It had been a trying day, beginning with Toshi arriving late. As he thought about it, that likely was the cause of his other worries. Daily production was a disappointment, particularly when compared to the day before. He thought it must be due to a lack of teamwork, but it was not something he could put his finger on.

His spirits rose the minute he entered his home. It was such a comfort to see Minako and their three daughters, each one happy to see him in return. And recently, the addition of his niece, whom he almost considered as his own. He was pleased to think Minako's sister would entrust them with a gift as precious as their eldest daughter. He knew they loved her, but for the present time, simply could not provide for her at home.

As he greeted his family and inquired about their day, he was disappointed and a little surprised that Ayami was not among them. "Where is Ayami?" he asked no one in particular.

"She's not feeling well again today and is in her room," Minako offered. "I think she's lonely."

"Maybe I should talk to her after supper," he said. "There must be something we can do to help her get over it. Do you really think she likes us? Or is she simply being polite when she tells us that?"

"Oh, I'm sure she likes us, and she likes living with us," Hisa said. "We have so much fun together, and she seems interested in everything we do."

Saya thought about her conversation with Ayami the previous night. She did agree that Ayami liked living with them. She had seen the sparkle in Ayami's eyes many times, and the laughter and the teasing that took place among all the girls. She knew it was not fake or forced.

After supper, when Ayami and her sisters were cleaning the kitchen and putting away the dishes, Saya found herself alone with her father. "I don't know if this is helpful, Papa, but last night I talked to Ayami in her room. She told me she met a stranger along the path when they were coming home from the village. She had seen him once before as well. That was a week ago, when they went to the village. I'm too young to know anything about love, but I think she is old enough. I wonder if that's what is troubling her."

Her father was quiet for several minutes, and Saya was not sure if he was shocked that she would refer to 'love' at her age, or whether he had not been paying attention to what she said, or if he was simply thinking about what she had relayed to him.

Finally, he broke the silence and replied, "Thank you, Saya; I'm glad you talked with her, and also that you told me. Maybe it does have something to do with her mood. Now, let's talk about your birthday. I think we should have a party to celebrate. Maybe that would cheer up Ayami as well. If you like, you may invite two or three friends from school, and we'll see if Ayami or your sisters will make something sweet, and we'll get some nice fruit at the market. How does that sound?"

"Oh Papa, that would be wonderful. I was hoping we could do that. Thank you so much. I love you." And she wrapped her young arms around his waist and told him again.

***

Toshi knew Haruki was not happy about his tardy behavior. He absolutely could not let it happen again. That night, he worked out a plan. Because his bedroom had a window on the east wall, he would roll up the course fabric which served as a curtain, and allow the rising sun to stream into his room as it made its way up from the Pacific horizon. Surely the bright light from the morning sun would coax his eyelids open, even should he still be sound asleep. Then he moved his mat to the opposite wall so the light would shine directly on him as he slept.

And then it occurred to him there might be clouds to hide the sun. The light, in that case, would not be bright enough to wake him. As he pondered the dilemma, he extended the idea one step further. He would leave the window partway open. That way, he could hear the sounds of the birds and other creatures waking up in the early morning. And he would surely hear any sounds of human activity, such as neighbors heading off to work. This precaution would provide one more layer of protection against oversleeping and being late for work. It seemed like a good plan.

The final feature of his strategy would be to avoid thinking about the girl at bedtime. This might be the most important part. If he could get to sleep at his usual time, he would be rested by morning and find the routine that had served him well until that fateful first meeting two weeks ago. From now on, Toshi would force himself to think about anything except the girl.

It was the perfect strategy, and he liked the new arrangement. He liked being able to view the sky as he lay in bed before dropping off to sleep. And he was anxious to view it again first thing in the morning.

But when he laid down, his thoughts were of the girl. *I wonder where she lives,* and *I wonder if she likes the trees and flowers as much as I do.* And then he caught himself. *I must not think of her. I must force my mind to think of other things.*

And with perseverance, that is what he did. Whenever his mind wandered there, he forced himself to think about work at the foundry. He must remember to keep his journal updated so he could impress Haruki with any ideas he might later ascertain from it.

Toshi's new plan worked exactly as he had hoped. When the sun peeked above the horizon, it brought an almost magical glow into his room. And just as he was beginning to stir himself awake he heard the melody of one, two, then several songbirds, just outside his window. *This is an amazing way to begin the day,* he thought. *It's like waking up to music.* He eagerly dressed and washed himself, had breakfast, and headed to the foundry. He was rested and ready for a new day.

Toshi had hardly entered the foundry when he heard Haruki's greeting. "Good morning, Toshi. I'm glad to see you're here early. This is more like the person I've come to respect."

"Thank you," replied Toshi. He didn't know what else to say, so he just waited to see if Haruki would speak again, which he did.

"I'm having a birthday party for my daughter, Saya, on Sunday afternoon. We would like you to come."

Toshi was completely taken aback. They had never socialized before, not even after work, as the other workers sometimes did. The invitation made Toshi uncomfortable. It was not that he didn't like Haruki, because he did. It was just so unexpected. *Yesterday he was reprimanding me, and now today he is inviting me to a party for a daughter I have never met.* But he had no time to deliberate with himself about a response. Haruki was standing there, waiting for his reply.

Toshi did not want to go. "Thank you. That is most kind of you. But I..."

With that, Haruki interjected, "Good, it's settled then. We'll see you at two o'clock on Sunday." Then he turned and started to walk away. After a few steps, he turned back again and said, "Saya will be twelve years old. And she likes kites." After which he turned, and this time, he did walk away.

Chapter 8

Birthday Party

KAMAISHI - 1875

Toshi trudged along the path to Haruki's house. Most of the way there, he tried to think of an excuse to leave early, but without success. Haruki would see through a feigned illness immediately. If Haruki caught him in a lie, his future at the foundry would be over.

He had managed to find a kite in the village, which he hoped would be acceptable as a gift. It cost one yen, which he could afford, although it still pained him, as he would rather have added it to his special savings can. Still, he had no idea what else a twelve-year-old would like, especially one that might be cheaper. And it would not do to arrive with a lesser gift than expected by his boss. He was anxious about why he was invited, whether Saya would like the gift, and how he would conduct himself in front of Haruki's family for the very first time.

Toshi inhaled deeply and held it for a moment before exhaling. Then he walked the final few steps to Haruki's doorway and knocked. A moment later, Haruki himself opened the door and greeted him. "Hello, Toshi, I'm glad you were able to come. Saya is excited about her birthday and has two of her friends here as well. Please come in. I see you've brought a gift."

Toshi entered the doorway and stiffened when he saw the room filled with people. He was not at ease with strangers. Somehow, though, he would put on his best face and try to act calm, even while his insides were turning in circles.

"Everyone… this is Toshi Ozawa from the foundry," announced Haruki to those in the room. "Toshi, this is my wife, Minako, our daughters, Hisa, Kanae, and the birthday girl, Saya. And these two girls are Saya's friends, Eiko and Mizuki.

He looked around. "Where is Ayami?"

"I think she's in the kitchen finishing up the birthday treats," Kanae replied. She hurried across the room and poked her head in the kitchen. "Ayami… can you come out and meet our guest?"

There was the sound of dishes rattling, and Ayami came into the room. She was looking down as she entered, and Haruki again made the introduction of their guest. "Ayami, this is Toshi from our foundry. Toshi, this is my niece, Ayami, who is staying with us for a while."

Toshi watched as the girl with coal-black hair and hazel-brown eyes stepped into the room. When he looked in her eyes, his mind went blank. Forgetting completely how rude it was to stare, he continued to gape as the color of her face changed from a healthy pink to a grayish white. For one brief moment, he thought she might collapse to the floor. He waited for the beautiful smile he felt sure would follow, but it didn't come. He saw her lips move slightly, as if about to speak, but if they did, he didn't hear it.

Meanwhile, Toshi, already on edge at the summons to be here, and now in the presence of Haruki and his family, felt the room close in around him. At first, he thought it was a dream. He pinched himself on the arm to see. *How could she be standing in front of me? I've told no one about her. How could Haruki have known I've been looking for her?* But it was her, and she was even more striking than he had remembered.

Then it was Toshi's turn to worry about collapsing to the floor, so taken was he by the shock of her presence. He felt his face flush red, and he wanted to speak, but he didn't know what to say.

Finally he burst out, "Hello, Ayami, I am pleased to meet you," at the very instant that Ayami said, "Hello, Toshi, I am pleased to meet you," which provoked a smile from Minako and the girls.

"I brought this for Saya." He stammered. "Happy birthday, Saya. I wasn't sure what you wanted, but I hope this is something you will like," and he handed her the gift.

"Oh! Thank you!" she exclaimed. "May I open it now, Mother?"

"Why don't we all get our treats from the kitchen and take them to the yard, since it's so nice out today? We can eat under the trees, and after, you may open the gift from Toshi and the one from Ayami and your sisters."

"Oh good," Saya said. "Come on, Eiko and Mizuki, let's go first. I hope you like cake. Ayami and my mother made it this morning, just for my birthday." Saya led her guests and family to the kitchen and then into the yard behind their house.

Minako sat next to Ayami beside the garden and invited Toshi and Haruki to sit next to them.

"Toshi, it was thoughtful of you to bring a gift for Saya. Do you have any sisters in your family?" Minako asked.

"No," he replied. "I have an older brother." Trying to think of something more to add, he said, "It would have been nice to have a sister, though."

"Ayami, you should tell Toshi about your sister," Minako continued, hoping to start a conversation between the two of them.

"I have a sister," she replied. "She is younger than me... the same age as Saya. Her name is Emiko. I wish she could be here to enjoy Saya's party today. They would have had a lot of fun together."

Toshi tried to ignore the fact that he dropped part of his cake on his lap, by continuing the conversation. "Do you miss her?" he asked. Then, realizing how foolish it must have sounded, quickly added, "How long has it been since you've seen her?"

"Yes, I miss her very much. It has only been a few weeks since I've seen her, but it seems like a year. It was kind of you to ask. Thank you. But Haruki and Minako have been so good to me that I feel like I'm in my second home. And, of course, I love being with my cousins."

That is when Saya burst upon them, saying, "Father, may I open my gifts now? I can't wait any longer." Her friends were right behind her.

"Can she?" They echoed.

"If you're finished with your cake, then I think it's a fine idea. Yes, open your gifts and let us see what..." And with that, she was off to retrieve the two packages, one from her family and one from Toshi.

She opened the one from her family first, carefully untying the ribbon and unwrapping the paper. As she lifted the last of the wrap, her eyes grew wide with a smile to match. "Oh, I love this fan," she beamed. "Especially the colors and the butterflies. It will keep me cool in grand style. It will make me look really grown-up. Thank you very much. I love it."

Then she reached for the package from Toshi. It was a little larger than the first gift and also a bit heavier. She once again carefully removed the ribbon and began to unwrap the package. When she saw colorful paper with a dragon design, she realized it was the making of a kite, and could not contain a squeal of delight. She loved to fly kites, and her old one was beginning to tatter at the corners. "Oh Toshi, thank you, thank you. This is the perfect birthday gift. How did you know I like to fly kites? I love this gift, too. And thank you again for it. Father, may we go try it out?"

"I'm sure Toshi would love to see you fly it. Why don't all of you go out to the point, where you can catch a good breeze and see how it works? Take some extra string and scraps of cloth to make a tail. Minako and I will stay here and clean up the party dishes. When you get back, we'll finish the cake with some fresh tea. How does that sound?"

Toshi didn't realize a twelve-year-old could move so fast. Saya rounded up the material for a tail and along with her two friends, headed toward the point. Hisa and Kanae were close behind, which left Ayami and Toshi to bring up the rear.

After they had walked several meters, Toshi gathered up his courage and opened the conversation. "I think I saw you on the path a couple of times, but I didn't know who you were."

Ayami hesitated before replying. "I think I saw you as well. But it was only for a moment until you were gone again." They continued to walk along behind Hisa and Kanae, leaving about six meters between them to ensure they were adequately chaperoned.

A few meters later, Ayami continued, "I think it was last Tuesday and the Tuesday before that."

Toshi's heart jumped to his throat. He could not believe she remembered their meeting. In fact, he was convinced she had not seen him at all, the first time. His feet felt like they were off the ground. He wanted to skip and shout to the world that Ayami had noticed him. He forced himself to wait several more paces until his pulse returned to normal and he hoped his voice had done the same.

"Yes, I am pretty sure it was," he squeaked. Then he cleared his throat, pretending it needed clearing for some unknown reason.

"Did you know I would be here when you came to Saya's party?" she asked.

"No, I didn't know you lived here. Haruki never mentioned you at work. He told me on Thursday their daughter was having a birthday party and that I was invited. To be honest, I didn't really want to come, but he made it clear that I should. He even told me Saya likes to fly kites, which I took to mean that is what I should bring her for a gift. Luckily, I guess that's what he meant. She seems to like it."

"How do you think Haruki knew about us? Was it just a huge coincidence?" Toshi continued. "I never told anyone about our meeting on the path or that I was hoping to meet you." He waited a few minutes more. When Ayami did not respond, he said, "I probably shouldn't tell you this, but I lingered along the path for the next few days, hoping to see you again. Eventually, I gave up and forced myself to think about work, and that's when we met the second time. I was trying to think of something to say to you as we passed, but I couldn't think fast enough."

"I thought about you as well." She replied. "I'm glad you noticed me."

Chapter 9

Emiko

"Shouldn't Papa be back from the paddy by now?" Emiko asked her mother. "How are we supposed to know when to make supper?"

Fujita gazed out the kitchen window to watch for them. "All we can do is prepare the table and have food ready for the stove the minute we see them coming."

"Things were going so well after Ayami left, but I'm afraid you were right." Emiko said.

"Right? Right about what?"

"You said when saké gets ahold of you, it is hard for it to let go."

"Did I say that? I've forgotten, but I'm afraid it's true. It was probably too much to hope for, that he could stay off it forever."

"Do you think the twins will get hooked, too?"

"I hope not. I don't know how they could get any work done with three of them drinking. I think Shoji is smart enough to avoid it. He already gets the brunt of the work."

"I feel sorry for him," Emiko said.

An hour later, Fujita spotted Shoji coming up the lane by himself. "They must be coming," she said. "Put the rice on the stove, and I'll heat water for tea."

"Where are the rest of them?" Fujita asked when Shoji came through the door. "Are they coming too?"

"I'm sorry, Mother. They went to the village for lunch. Papa said he needed to sell some of last year's crop. I thought they would be back by now. Something must have detained them."

"I can guess what it is," Fujita said.

"Me too," Emiko added. "I'm glad you're not like that, Shoji."

Shoji blushed at the encouragement from his little sister. "I don't plan to," he said. "I have to work with them every day. I don't know why they can't see how harmful it is."

"Who knows when they'll be coming?" Fujita said. "We already have supper on the stove; we may as well eat while it's hot."

Two hours later the others came. Fujita and Emiko hurried to start more rice and reheat the tea.

"Supper will be ready in a few minutes," she said when they walked in. "We would have waited if we had known what time you were coming."

"We had biznish to do in the villich," Kunio slurred. "We can't help it took longer than espected."

Koichi and Koji shot a look at one another and smirked.

"We couldn't help it," Koichi said. "They didn't want to give us a fair price for the rice."

"Papa had to haggle with them," Koji added. "If it weren't for Papa, they would have cheated us for sure."

"Thank you, boish. So you see, Miss High and Mighty, we had work to do. It snot like we were sitting round a kischen all day wunderink when to put water on the shtove."

I wonder what Ayami would do in this situation, Emiko thought to herself. *When she stood up to him that day, he finally seemed remorseful.*

Fujita had learned over the years the best way to respond was to ignore his behavior and carry on. When the rice was ready, she filled a bowl and set it on the table in front of him. She filled two other bowls and set them in front of the twins. When they began to eat, she filled each of their cups with tea and placed them on the table.

The room fell quiet as the men, apparently hungry from their long afternoon in the village, devoted their remaining energy to transferring the rice from the bowl to their mouths. The twins were mostly successful, but Kunio struggled.

He became increasingly frustrated the longer he fought to keep each bite of rice balanced between the top and bottom chopstick as it approached his mouth. Twice, the rice fell from his chopsticks onto his lap. Sensing that Fujita and Emiko were watching from across the room, he clutched the next bite firmer between the two sticks and watched as the rice crumbled across the front of his already-soiled kimono.

Emiko watched as the color in his face turned a deeper shade of red the longer he tried.

After several more unsuccessful attempts, Kunio slammed his chopsticks on the table and glared at Fujita.

"Can't you eban make r-r-rice? It won't stay on my shtics."

Kunio made an effort to stand, and raised an arm like he was preparing to use it on Fujita, but his foot slipped out from under him, and he slumped back to the mat in front of the table.

Emiko had seen enough. "It's not the rice, Papa; it is you. You should have come home when Shoji did. You could have had supper the first time we made it, and you wouldn't have trouble keeping it on your chopsticks. Don't blame Mama for your problems. Blame yourself."

Kunio turned to face his youngest daughter. The color in his face was even darker now, and his eyes glistened in the fading light.

Emiko looked him in the eyes as he sat at the table, his head wobbling slowly back and forth as he fought to maintain his equilibrium. She had not seen his eyes like this before, not even that day when Ayami left. This was not the father she knew. Someone else had taken his place. Her eyes, too, began to glisten as she gazed back at him, but unlike her father, hers were caused by tears.

Kunio had given up trying to stand; it was too much effort. But the wheels in his mind were not completely numb, and he was not yet willing to admit defeat.

Whether he could see her with his eyes glazed over, Emiko could not tell. And whether he would remember his words tomorrow, she did not know. But they were words she would not forget.

"You will regret thish," he said. "I'll teash you to t-t-talk back to me. You jush wait."

Chapter 10

The Proposal

Toshi was in love. His co-workers had been correct, and once they learned the truth, they stopped teasing him. If ever they were tempted to kid him about courting the boss's daughter they never followed through. Technically, she was his niece anyway, one of the men had said. But every Sunday following Saya's birthday, Toshi visited the Yamamoto household.

Because Ayami's parents lived far away, Toshi was unable to meet them personally, to ask permission to marry his beloved Ayami. And because he spent virtually every day with Ayami's uncle, he felt the next best thing would be to ask Haruki, and Minako, who was actually the blood relative of her niece. After several months of regular Sunday visits, Toshi asked if he could meet with them before returning home.

"Haruki-san, Minako-san," he began nervously, "I'm pretty sure you know how much I've come to care for your niece, Ayami. And I realize we've only known each other a few months. But I want you to know that in all of my life, I have not been tempted or distracted by the sight of a girl—except for Ayami."

Looking at Haruki, he continued, "I hope you have witnessed in my daily behavior, traits that would be suitable and appropriate for a prospective husband. I am careful to show respect for those I work with, and even those I meet casually on the path or in the shops. I bathe regularly, and I do not over-indulge in saké, and I assure you that I have never used opium or other similar herbs, which I consider harmful.

"I've been putting money aside since the first day I started at the foundry, and have accumulated enough for a deposit on a house of my own… our own, and I have lived frugally enough that my budget would accommodate a loan if necessary, for the remainder of the cost of a home of my… our own. I can show you the amount I have saved if you want to see it, and I just want you to know I would be a good husband, and that is why I'm asking your permission on behalf of her parents to marry Ayami in the near future so we may begin a life together, before we get too old.

"Did I mention that I have never loved or even courted anyone else? Ayami is all I can think about. Well, except for when I'm at work, and there I have to concentrate very hard to keep her out of my mind, at least until I begin the walk home after work, when she is all that I think about. Oh, and …"

"Toshi," both Haruki and Minako interrupted together. "We have been expecting this day for months. It is obvious you were meant for Ayami, and she for you. We would be happy to write to Ayami's father and share our belief in you. But the answer that counts is the one from Ayami. Have you asked her if she would like to be your wife?"

"No, I didn't think it would be appropriate without your permission. If you're giving me permission, I'll ask her today before I leave. I don't want to delay the letter even one more week if I can help it."

With that, Haruki called to Ayami, "Ayami, Toshi forgot something and is waiting in the garden. Can you see what he wants?"

"Of course. I'll be right there," she replied.

Minako grabbed Haruki by the arm and led him to a window. She called quietly for the girls to come and join them.

"We shouldn't be watching them," Haruki murmured.

"I know," Minako whispered back.

When Ayami entered the yard, Toshi was sitting under one of her favorite trees. It reminded her of the first day they met, when they sat under that very tree to share Saya's birthday cake.

She could see by his countenance he was not his usual self. For an instant, she began to worry. But she had seen him off only minutes before, and he seemed normal at the time. He told her he was going to say goodbye to Haruki and Minako before he left, and she wondered if something had gone wrong during their parting.

"What is it, Toshi? Haruki said you had forgotten something? Do you want me to help you look for it?"

He looked at her without responding for a minute, then his face relaxed in a cautious smile. His face began to flush. "Actually, yes, I would. Would you sit here beside me, and I'll tell you what it is." As she settled on a large rock under the tree, she turned her gaze to Toshi, who was now facing her intently.

"Ayami, I have just spoken to your aunt and uncle, whom I think you know I greatly admire and respect. I still don't know how Haruki arranged for me to meet you, but I'm sure that he did and I don't know what I'd have done if he hadn't. I have also come to love your cousins and I'm grateful to them for making me feel so welcome in your family.

"I want you to know I have always tried to be an honorable person and I try to be nice to everyone I know or meet in the shops and I try hard to do my best every day at the foundry and I want to make Haruki proud of me and also of my work and that is why I try so hard."

By now, Ayami was starting to relax. She thought she might have guessed why Toshi was talking so fast and out of character. Her pulse quickened just a little, but she did not want to get ahead of herself.

Gaining confidence, Toshi pushed on.

"I'm sorry your parents live so far from here and I wish my parents lived closer so you could meet them even though I have not met yours, of course. But I would truly love to and I hope that if we can, they do, if you know what I mean. And I also want to tell you that I have been working hard at the foundry for three years and have saved part of my earnings all during that time so I would have money set aside for someday in case I needed it, which of course I would, although I didn't know when. I admit that in the beginning I was planning to use it for America, but that was before you. Now I just want to be with you."

When he stopped to take a breath, the silence felt like music. Her smile broadened, and she said, "Toshi, there is nothing I want more than to marry you. Is that what you are asking me? But what about your dream of going to America? Have you given up on the dream? I don't want to be the one to keep you from going, if that is your dream."

Toshi was slow to respond. This was not an easy decision. "I haven't exactly given it up," he admitted. "But since that first day I saw you on the trail, you are all I can think about. At first, it was about how I could find you, and then after Saya's party, it was about being with you."

He paused and looked down at the ground before he continued. "Going to America can wait. You are the most important thing to me now. If I have to choose between America and you, then I choose you. Maybe after we've saved enough money, we could both go. Would you consider going to America?"

"It is a long way away, and I would hate to leave my family, but if it would make you happy, I would go. It is you I want. If it means going to America to make you happy, I would go."

Toshi looked at her. "Oh, Ayami, I know this may seem less than honorable, but would it be okay if I hugged you?" Her answer was to stand up from the rock and lean toward him with arms at her sides. It was the first time they dared display such physical affection, and the faces of Toshi and Ayami both turned red from the embrace.

Much too soon to suit him, Toshi relaxed his arms and retreated slightly. Together, they wanted to share their news, not only with Haruki and Minako, but also with her cousins. They hurried into the house.

"Quick, everybody, away from the window," Minako whispered loudly.

"Congratulations," Haruki said when they entered. "Of course we still need your father's permission. Sit down and we'll write to him. Minako and I can help."

As soon as they sat down to write, Ayami's joy turned to apprehension. Kunio had told her mother explicitly that he didn't care where Ayami went, but she was no longer welcome at home. Surely, he would welcome the chance to have her married off and never see her again. But what if he wanted to punish her a second time, as a stern reminder that he was the one in charge?

She remained quiet as Haruki and Minako penned the letter.

The days passed slowly as Toshi waited for a reply. He calculated in his mind when to expect the letter. Twelve days from Monday should be enough. He was not sure if he should count Monday as one of the days, but he thought so. In that case, the return might occur on Thursday of the following week. He had eleven more days to wait.

To help pass the time, Toshi forced himself to concentrate on work. He made mental notes throughout the day, carefully remembering the amounts of charcoal and ore, and the timing of the mixture as it was added to the furnace. He repeated all the items in his head as he worked, so as not to forget anything that might prove helpful when he recorded them in his journal at night. It gave him something to fill his days as well as his nights. Finally, it was Sunday, the day to visit Haruki's house, and Ayami.

"Papa, he's here!" Saya shouted when she saw him coming up the lane.

She ran to greet him even before he reached the door. "We're having cake in the back yard," she said, and led him around the house. Hisa and Kanae were already there, placing mats and bringing refreshments. Haruki and Minako soon followed, bringing Ayami with them.

Hardly had Kanae poured their tea when Saya spoke up. "Toshi and Ayami, will you take me to the kite-flying place? I would love to fly it again, like we did on my birthday. That was so much fun. I can't wait to go again."

"I would like that," Toshi replied. "I love the view from the plateau. You can see almost forever from there, and the breeze is perfect for flying a kite. Ayami, what do you say? Should we go?"

"Why don't we all go?" Ayami replied. "Let's take refreshments with us and have a picnic. We can take turns flying Saya's kite."

Toshi held Ayami's hand as they walked to the plateau. When they arrived, he helped her sit, then nudged down gently beside her. Together, they gazed out over Kamaishi Bay and to the open sea beyond. "What a beautiful place—I think I could stay here forever," he said.

"I know what you mean," Ayami replied. "It is so peaceful. Do you hear the birds singing? And the sound of the waves against the rocks below? Wouldn't this be the perfect place to live? Just think of the view every morning when the sun came up."

Together they watched Saya's kite as it soared above the trees.

"I have some money saved," Toshi said. "Probably not enough, but I have money saved. Maybe we could build a house up here. Haruki might know if it's possible. I bet he could help us."

Kanae passed a basket of grapes and cheese across the blanket as they watched Saya's kite. When she and Hisa stood for a turn with the kite, Toshi found an opening to change the subject.

"I can't wait to hear back from your father. Do you think he'll answer right away?

Ayami stared out to sea. She seemed preoccupied with a summer squall that was making its way toward the shore.

When she didn't answer, he continued. "Is he good about answering letters?"

"I don't really know," she replied. "He doesn't get many letters. I only saw him get an important message one time, and that was the day I left home. The men who wanted to see him came on horses."

"It must have been really important if they went to see him in person," Toshi said.

"Yes, I guess it must have been," she said, looking away from him.

"I wonder how long it would take to get there on horseback," Toshi said. "Maybe I should have borrowed a horse and gone in person."

Ayami fidgeted on the mat. She looked out over the ocean, still gazing at the squall. "It was probably best to ask him in a letter," she said. "Sometimes, when he's busy in the fields, he doesn't like to be interrupted."

"What is your father like?" Toshi asked. "Do you think he will like me?"

Instead of answering, she pointed to the heavy gray clouds not far away and said, "I think we should head back. It looks like it's going to rain."

Wednesday passed by without a letter from Kunio. Toshi had expected as much. Based on his calculation, Thursday should be the day. On Thursday, there was no letter. Friday and Saturday came and went—still with no reply.

Toshi began to fret. At first he thought it was only because of the slowness of the post, but after two weeks, he worried that it was something more.

Chapter 11

The Response

KAMAISHI – OCTOBER 1875

Following his day of work on Monday, Haruki walked down to the village. About halfway between the church and the wharf was a small shop with a sign out front. The sign read: *Properties for Sale - inquire within.* Two hours later, Haruki made his exit, the agent still talking as he closed the door behind him.

When Haruki arrived home, Ayami was waiting. "It came today! You got a letter from Father today! Can we open it now? I can't wait to see what he says about Toshi."

Haruki was outnumbered. Not only Ayami, but also Minako and his girls were all staring at him expectantly. "Can we, Father? We want to know what he said."

Haruki was not prepared for the arrival of the letter; he had been thinking only about the news he brought from the village. "First of all," he began, "I have good news from the land agent. He told me he felt sure that enough land to build a house with a garden could be purchased. I plan to tell Toshi about it first thing tomorrow morning.

"As for the letter. Don't you think we should wait until Toshi is here before we open it? After all, it was his request. I don't think it would be right for the rest of us to know before Toshi does. Do you agree, Ayami?"

She blushed for not considering it on her own. "Yes, you're right. Toshi should be here when we open it so we can all hear together. Besides, I like the idea of being next to him when we learn our fate. May we go and get him tonight?"

"It's already late because of my trip to the village. I'll ask him to come with me after work tomorrow so he can talk with you about the land. After he gets here, we'll tell him about the letter. Minako, would you make something special for dinner tomorrow night? We can celebrate together."

***

Toshi arrived at the foundry early, as usual.

"Good morning, Toshi. I talked to the land agent last night after work, and I have good news. He knows who owns that land, and he is almost sure he would sell you a portion of the plateau. Why don't you come home with me after work, and you can talk with Ayami about it? Minako is going to fix dinner for us. I'm sure she and the girls will want to hear your thoughts."

Toshi was so excited at the prospect of obtaining a plot of land for their house that he didn't think to ask if the letter from Kunio had arrived.

At the end of the day, they left the foundry and headed for Haruki's house.

"Did you have time to think about the land today?"

Toshi stammered slightly before he replied. "I have to admit there were a few times when I found myself thinking about the land. How much do you think it would cost to build a house?"

"I think you could build a nice house for three to four hundred yen. If you wanted, you could start with a smaller house and add to it later as your family grows. The important thing is to secure the land."

"Do you know a builder we could talk with, to find out more about the cost and how long it would take to build?"

"The man who built our house is no longer living, but maybe the land agent could recommend someone," he replied.

When they arrived, Minako was waiting for them along with the girls, and most of all, Ayami. Toshi was always happy to visit, but tonight it seemed they were particularly excited to see him.

Once inside, everyone spoke at once. "What do you think about the land?" The wording changed only a little from each of the girls.

"Are you going to buy it and build a nice house for Ayami? When will you start? How big will it be? Can we come to visit you when it's done?"

Toshi didn't have time to answer any of the questions; they came at him so fast. He was relieved when Haruki announced, "Let's all sit down to eat. Minako and the girls have made us something special to celebrate tonight while we hear about your plans for a house.

"But we also have other news. We received a letter from Ayami's father. I didn't tell you at work because I knew it would bring nothing but worry all day long. Why don't we have some of this delicious fish that Minako and the girls have prepared for us? Then we can open the letter together and see what Kunio has to say."

It was Saya who spoke up. "Why can't we read the letter now? I'm too excited to eat. Can't we read the letter first and then eat? That way, we can talk about how Toshi and Ayami are going to get married."

Haruki looked around the table at the anxious faces staring back. "You're right. How about if we ask Toshi and Ayami what they want to do? After all, it's their future the letter holds. He turned to face Toshi and Ayami. Should we read the letter before we eat, or after?"

While Toshi weighed the merits of whether to learn the news before or after their meal, Ayami spoke up with his reply. "I think we should open the letter now. It seems like an eternity already, since you wrote to him. Then we can do as Saya suggested and begin to make plans for our wedding."

Toshi smiled in agreement.

Haruki opened the letter and read it aloud for all to hear.

October 12, 1875

Dear Haruki,

Your letter was a great relief. We have been worried sick about Ayami ever since she ran away. Her mother and I begged for information from all the neighbors, but no one had seen her.

And now that we've found her, even better news. A factory agent promised her a job almost too good to be true. She will be working in one of the new silk factories, reeling silk into spools of thread. It is easy work, and they will pay me thirty yen the day I sign the contract and high wages to Ayami for the next three years. Not only that, but they provide meals and lodging. It is exactly what I need in order to pay the taxes on our farm.

As you can see, marriage is out of the question. Ayami needs to join her hard-working brothers in support of our family. I will approve a marriage at the end of her three-year contract at the silk factory. Until then, we need the extra income she can provide.

Tell Ayami all is forgiven, and we can't wait to see her again.

Kunio Matsumoto

Although there were no more words on the page, Haruki continued to stare at the letter. His head tilted slightly downward, as did his shoulders. His breathing slowed, and the excitement in his eyes faded away.

Toshi collected his thoughts as he grasped the reality of the words. He turned to Ayami and gazed longingly at the face he had fallen so in love with.

He moved to where she was seated on the mat and wrapped his arms gently around her shoulders. He did not care that he was showing affection in the presence of others. Holding Ayami close in his arms, he felt her tears begin to flow.

Slowly, Toshi unfurled his arms from Ayami and dared to look at her face. It was almost a surprise when he saw it was still the beautiful face he had come to love, even with her dark eyes surrounded by red, and streaks running down her cheeks. Together, they turned to face Haruki and Minako.

Haruki gazed at Ayami, sitting across from him. "Kunio's letter puzzles me. How could he not know where you were when Fujita wrote, asking if you could live with us?"

Ayami's face turned red, and she fought to hold back more tears. "I didn't run away," she whispered. "He made me leave. He is not the person he used to be. He drinks too much, and he is sometimes mean to my mother."

Minako tensed and leaned forward for a better look at Ayami's face.

"Kunio is mean to my sister?" She asked, in a growing voice.

Ayami looked toward her aunt. "Yes, when he is angry or has had too much saké, he sometimes slaps her. I pleaded with her and Emiko to come with me, but they both refused. I thought she told you about it in the letter."

"No, she only told me the farm would not support all of you and asked if you could live with us until things got better. She should have told me—you should have told me—is she in danger?"

"I'm sorry, I thought she told you in the letter," Ayami repeated. "I didn't want to remind you of it further. I should have told you anyway. I don't think she is in real danger, especially with Emiko there. The two of them should be okay. Father threw me out because I talked back to him."

Everyone fell silent. What had promised to be an evening of celebration had turned to a night of heartbreak.

Finally, Haruki spoke.

"You better stay home from the foundry tomorrow," he said to Toshi. "I don't want to risk an accident when you have so many other things on your mind. I've heard bad things about the thread factories, but I'm not sure if they are true. Tomorrow I'll ask at the foundry if anyone has information, and we can talk about it when I get home from work."

***

The next day began with a cloudy sky and light rain. The sun didn't penetrate Toshi's bedroom window to prod him awake, but thanks to his backup plan, the birds welcomed the day even without a sun. His body felt numb and his stomach felt sick. It was past noon when he forced himself up from the mat. He dressed and walked aimlessly in the forest until late afternoon, then headed for Haruki's house.

Haruki arrived home from work later than usual. When he entered, they could tell by his face he had news.

"I found a man whose daughter used to work at a silk factory, and he said they are not good places to work. They work from dawn to dark with little food and only a few short breaks. Cotton is worse than silk, but he recommended not letting family work in either of them," he continued. "I don't understand how Kunio could send you there."

"I thought about the letter over and over last night," Toshi said. "Kunio seemed willing to approve our marriage after receiving an income for three years. Do you think he would accept those payments from me? I could send him the money I was saving for our house. The house can wait."

Haruki looked at Ayami. "What do you think?" he asked. "Are you willing to disobey your father?"

Ayami did not have to think about it before she replied, "Yes, I'm willing to disobey him. He can send the twins if he needs the money so bad."

Together, they formulated a letter to Kunio.

October 20, 1875

Dear Kunio,

Thank you for your reply. We were disappointed that you have currently withheld approval of Ayami's marriage. As you explained in the letter, you do approve of the marriage in three years' time.

After discussing with Ayami, Toshi, and Fujita's sister, we believe we have a solution that satisfies everyone. Toshi has offered to send you thirty yen immediately, plus additional payments of thirty yen at the end of the next three years. That amount would be the equivalent of what Ayami could make at the silk factory.

This would be in exchange for your approval of her marriage to Toshi at any time following his initial payment.

I must also add that I have learned through trusted friends that silk factories are not good places to work, and their promises of good jobs and high wages are not true. I urge you not to allow your friends or loved ones to fall for their empty words.

Minako says to tell Fujita she misses her and to please write often, so that we know she and Emiko are well.

Haruki

After two weeks of waiting and disappointment, his method of getting to sleep failed Toshi for the first time. He lay in bed, afraid he was going to be sick. He tried lying on his back, then on one side, the other side, and then his stomach. Nothing worked. He could not force the letter from his mind. He tried to focus on work, but it held no interest.

Haruki walked him to work in the mornings and home again in the evenings. His co-workers, who knew Toshi was beside himself in love, kept him closely in their sight throughout the day.

Finally, in the third week, a different reception when they approached Haruki's house after work. All the family was waiting outside the door. The letter had arrived.

"Hurry up, you two!" Saya shouted excitedly. "We want to open the letter from Kunio. We don't have to eat first, do we?" She pleaded.

"No, little one. We are not going to wait. I can't stand it any longer, either. Hand me the letter."

Haruki opened it and began to read:

October 27, 1875

Dear Haruki,

Since Toshi is obviously a good worker and knows how to save his money, I will consider his offer. However, in spite of your doubts regarding the wages of silk factory workers, I am told by others, my sons included, that Ayami could easily make forty yen or more each year. Because of that, if Toshi will commit to paying us forty yen for the next three years, I will accept Toshi Ozawa as a member of our family. Thirty yen is acceptable as the first payment, since that is the amount promised by the factory agent.

Fujita says that she and Emiko are well and that she will write when she has time.

Kunio

Saya was the first to jump up from her mat. Haruki had only gotten as far as "…accept Toshi Ozawa as a member of our family" from his mouth when she was on her feet and moving toward him. She bent down to where they were seated and placed one arm around Toshi's neck, her other around Ayami's, who was seated next to him, and exclaimed. "Finally! You're going to get married. My birthday wish finally came true! I knew it would!"

Before Ayami or anyone else could grasp the 'birthday wish' statement, Minako, Hisa, and Kanae were also scrambling to rise and move around the mat toward Toshi and Ayami. Haruki was close behind.

Saya tried to lift Toshi and Ayami since she already had her arms around them both, which only made it more awkward for them to rise. When she realized it was not helping, she released her arms, which caused Toshi to tumble into Ayami. In an effort to catch himself, his right arm rubbed across the front of Ayami's chest and came to rest. Whether it was the touch of his arm, separated only by the thickness of a kimono from her breast, or the words he had waited so long to hear from Kunio, he did not know, but a tremor shot through his body. It was a jolt he could not find words to describe. Ayami looked up at him with a look of surprised alarm. Then she smiled.

By the time his thoughts had recovered, everyone was standing around them with arms outstretched. He heard Saya say, "When will it be, Toshi? Will it be soon? We've waited long enough. Will you be married soon?"

Before he or Ayami could answer, Hisa and Kanae repeated the same questions. "When will you get married, Ayami? I can't wait for your wedding. We'll have to shop for a new kimono."

Chapter 12

The Wedding

Eight months later, Toshi's parents arrived in Kamaishi. They came on the *City of Tokyo*, just as Toshi had done three years before. Fortunately, there was no storm on this voyage.

"Toshi, it is so good to see you," Yuko told him the minute they stepped off the boat. She stretched out her arms as Toshi drew near, and wrapped them soundly around his body. "My goodness," she exclaimed. "You are so strong. I can feel it just by holding you. Have you gained weight? You have grown up since I last saw you. I've missed you. It's so good to see you again."

"It is good to see you, too, Mother," Toshi said. His voice began to quiver.

When he approached his father, Isao seemed more interested in the village. "Don't you get bored in a place like this?" he asked.

"No, I like it here. Wait until you walk through the forest, then you'll know what I mean."

"How do people make a living?" Isao continued. Looking around at the small shops and street vendors, he added, "You don't have much to choose from when you shop. I could never live in a place like this."

Toshi smiled in reply. "It has everything I need," he said. "At first, I felt that way too, but not any longer." He signaled for the rickshaw driver to help with the luggage, and the three of them departed for their lodging. Toshi knew nothing in Kamaishi would match their standard, but he found the best place available, which was at the western edge of the village, and convenient to the wedding shrine.

The following day could hardly have been better for such an occasion. The usually rainy month was sunny, and the temperature a pleasant twenty-two degrees. Toshi splurged to secure one carriage for his family and one for Haruki's family even though the shrine was not much further west, in the mountains above the Kasshigawa River.

Ayami was dressed in several layers of kimono and topped with a pure white over-kimono, made of silk, a gift from Haruki and his family. Toshi would never have considered it on his own. The wedding itself was expensive enough, not to mention the payment to Ayami's father.

Toshi wore a simple black kimono. It suited his budget.

The Shinto shrine consisted of two wooden structures located in a small meadow, surrounded by several large outcroppings. The sanctuary, or *honden*, housed the Shinto spirits, while the *haiden* provided a space for weddings and other small ceremonies.

Their driver halted the carriage in the shade of a centuries-old cypress tree at the entrance. Toshi helped his mother step down from the livery, followed by Ayami. Isao took his time stepping down. He craned his neck from side to side, taking in the quiet setting. In the carriage behind, Haruki helped his family down and joined the others.

The shrine was located in a narrow meadow surrounded on three sides by rugged mountain bluffs, rising upward a hundred meters or more. Their protection sheltered the shrine from even the strongest winter winds, no doubt one reason for choosing the site many years before. Between the meadow and the nearby bluffs stood a copse of the surviving cypress trees. Rotting stumps revealed the source of timber used in building the small but beautiful shrine.

Most notable was the sacred gateway, the *torii*. Two cypress timbers, at least a hundred centimeters square, protruded upward from the rocky soil to a height of five or more meters. The twin posts carried two large beams across the top, completing the gate-like entrance.

Standing between the carriages, with the sun warming his face, a chorus of birds singing in the trees, and the sacred gate of the shrine looming large before him, Toshi stood in silence. He was motionless as he considered his good fortune. He reached over, took Ayami's hand, and squeezed it gently. Lifting his eyes to her face, he skipped a breath as she returned the squeeze and smiled, a tear forming on each of her cheeks.

Toshi looked away. He dared not cry in front of his father, and crying was sure to follow if he looked at Ayami a moment longer. Gathered together, he motioned for Haruki to lead the way, under the *torii* and along the sacred path to the ceremonial room, the *haiden*.

Inside, the Shinto priest was already waiting at a central table. He signaled for the guests to enter and stand at one of several smaller tables occupying the room. First, he purified the shrine and its guests by waving a special wand above their heads and around the room. Then he invoked the benevolent spirits, collectively known as *kami*. Toshi lost count of the kami being heralded, after twenty: the god of creation… the god of health… the god of wealth… Amaterasu… Izanami… Izanagi… *Why do we need so many gods?* He wondered. *It does not seem very efficient.*

Purification completed, the priest motioned for Toshi and Ayami to step forward for an exchange of vows. Toshi had spent countless hours in preparation for this moment, but now, when needed, his mind went blank. He stared first at the priest, then at Ayami, hoping for guidance. Finding none, Toshi tried discreetly to search the inside of his kimono sleeves for a copy of the vows. It soon escalated into a panic-driven scramble, which, to Saya, watching from one of the nearby tables, wondered if a bee had crawled inside his sleeve.

When Haruki saw what was happening, he came to the rescue by handing Toshi a spare copy of the vows. And in an attempt to make it look like part of the ceremony, handed Ayami a copy of her own.

With a noticeable sigh of relief, Toshi opened the page, took a deep breath, and began to recite the words.

"I want to thank Haruki," he began. "Without Haruki, we would not be here. Somehow, Haruki brought Ayami and me together, but I don't know how."

Then he turned and stated his vows to Ayami.

"You are my strength," he said. "You are my light. You are my hope and my joy. When the last breath leaves your chest, my life too, will end."

By the last few lines, he no longer needed the page. The words came rushing back.

"…I pledge my love to you for as long as I live. I promise to keep you well."

Then Ayami returned her vows to Toshi. She held the letter, but it was clear she already knew the words.

"I pledge my love to you, Toshi, for now and forever. You are my granite, the foundation of my life. Your love in return is the only thing I need for a happy life."

Following the vows came the only controversial portion of the wedding. The *san-san-ku-do* ceremony was a long-held Buddhist tradition. After the revolution, the emperor had ordered a separation of Buddhism and Shinto.

"I don't think we should do the *san-san-ku-do*," Toshi told his father prior to the wedding. "The emperor doesn't want it to be a part of Shinto practice, and besides, Ayami and I don't drink saké."

"The emperor wants to change everything," his father retorted. "Shinto and Buddhism worked fine together for generations. I don't know why he wants everything to change."

Isao held his scowl firm before adding, "And besides, your mother and I enjoy a cup of saké every night. After coming all this way, it's the least you could do for us."

Toshi gave in. "Yes, I suppose it is," he had replied.

Now it was time to perform the ritual. Toshi and Ayami each sipped three drinks of saké from three different cups. The symbolism of three sips from each of the three cups resulted in nine sips. Whether the long-standing ritual represented joy and sorrow, heaven and earth, or woman and man, it did not matter. It was a long-held tradition, and traditions mattered to Isao.

"Take small sips," Toshi cautioned Ayami. "We're not used to saké."

"I know," she replied, "but nine is a lucky number, so we have to take all nine."

Toshi's parents also participated in the *san-san-ku-do*, and because Ayami's parents could not be present, Haruki and Minako stood in their place and repeated the sequence.

Then Toshi and Ayami boarded the carriage. Toshi cleverly placed his arm around Ayami's back and pulled her close as the others climbed in behind. When she turned to face him with a look of surprise, he gave her another surprise by kissing her gently on the lips.

Looking around to see if anyone had witnessed it, Ayami saw Saya looking back. Saya touched two fingers to her lips and pointed them at Ayami and smiled a knowing smile. It reminded Ayami of the night she and her young cousin wondered what a kiss on the lips might taste like. She rolled her tongue across her lips and smiled back.

***

The next day, Toshi and Ayami led Isao and Yuko to look at the plot of land they wanted to buy for their future home. As they walked to the plateau, Toshi pointed out the beauty of this part of the island.

"It is so quiet in here," his mother said. "So peaceful... and just listen to the birds."

"Much too quiet for me," Isao replied. "What would you do all day? There is no one to talk to."

When they reached the plateau, Toshi proudly showed them the view of Kamaishi Bay, some twenty meters below, with fishing boats preparing for their nightly trip out to sea.

"Where would the house be situated?" Isao asked, as he gazed at all the space.

Toshi moved to a spot looking directly over the bay. "This is where the house would be. We could watch boats in the harbor without ever leaving home." He pointed several meters away to a grassy area. "I think we could make a garden over there. The soil looks better over there."

"I think it would be the perfect place for a home," Yuko said. "Don't you agree, Isao?"

"If you like to live away from everything, I suppose it would be a good place," he said. "It would not be a place for me, but if you're determined to live here, I suppose we could talk to the agent."

Isao accompanied Haruki and Toshi to see the land agent the following day after work. Toshi trusted his father's business judgment, but he also respected his position as his father.

***

"We got it!" Toshi proudly announced before they were even through the door. "We got enough land for a house and a garden. We bought the whole plateau!" he exclaimed.

Once they all sat down, Isao recounted their negotiation with the agent. Isao felt the land would eventually go up in value, so they made an offer on the entire plateau. They were able to purchase all the land for seventy-five yen. Toshi never dreamed his life could be so good.

The following Saturday, Toshi, Ayami, and all of Haruki's family walked to the village wharf to see Isao and Yuko to the packet ship, which would carry them home. Toshi was quiet as he wrapped his mother in his arms for a final goodbye hug.

When Isao stepped forward to say goodbye, his eyes began to moisten. "Your friend was right," he said.

"My friend?" Toshi replied.

"Yes, your friend from the university. He said in two or five years we would see how the 'new' ways would work out for Japan. It has only been three, but I can already see the country is advancing. The foundry is proof enough. I can see why you were drawn to it, but it doesn't mean I have to like it. I would prefer to have you home with us, in Tokyo."

"We'll come to visit when we can," Toshi said. "I'm sorry I won't be able to help you at the factory," he continued. "I don't think my heart would be there the way it should."

"Never forget your family," was all his father said in reply.

Chapter 13

Emiko

Emiko rose from her knees and stretched both arms high in the air. Then she looked up and down the rows of carrots and beans. She was only half-done weeding, but her back felt ready to break. She lowered her right arm and wiped the sweat from her forehead with the back of her hand. The morning sun was still far from its zenith, yet her face, neck, and back were drenched. She turned her body away from the sun and, with outstretched arms, closed her almond-colored eyes and silently dreamt of a steady, cooling breeze.

Hearing the whinny of an approaching horse, she quickly turned toward the lane and dropped her arms. She did not want to imagine how she must have looked in that position. And if word got back to her father she was dancing in the garden instead of weeding it, even her mother could not prevent a scolding.

When the approaching horseman drew closer, Emiko could see it was a stranger, roughly the age of her twin brothers. Her first thought was that he might be a friend of theirs, but where they could have met was a mystery. The twins rarely left the farm.

The stranger pulled up well short of Emiko and dismounted in a smooth and practiced motion. He walked toward Emiko, and as he neared, she found herself entranced by his handsome good looks. He was tall and stood erect, not slouched like many young men she had seen in the village. His eyes were almost as dark as his shoulder-length hair, and his smile came so easily that it seemed a permanent part of his face. Even at fifteen, Emiko recognized handsome when she saw it, and the stranger was handsome. But his unexpected presence kept her from returning his engaging smile.

The young man stopped several meters before reaching her and bowed. "Good morning," he said. Emiko was not accustomed to receiving bows from someone older, and it made her feel strangely important.

Emiko remembered the last time strangers on horseback had ridden into their yard. On that occasion, however, the government agents had not bothered to dismount. They simply reprimanded her father for getting behind with his tax payments. No pleasantries were spoken on that fateful day. *That was the day her father forced Ayami to leave*, she remembered with a hurtful pang.

Even with the striking contrast between that day and this, Emiko remained cautious.

"My humble apology for interrupting your work," the stranger continued. "I can see you have been busy in your garden. You must be good at your work; the plants appear to be doing well."

"Thank you," she replied warily.

"Is your father at home?" the young man asked, with the still-lingering smile. "I have a business proposition I think he will find appealing."

"I think he was working on the farm accounts after breakfast," she said. Covering for her father had gotten easier because it had also become more frequent. On the chance the stranger did have a business proposition, she did not want her father to miss out on it. "If you wait here, I'll see if he has time to see you."

Emiko hurried to the house. Fujita was at the stove making fresh tea. Not seeing her father at the table, she asked, "Is Papa up yet? There's a man here to see him about a business proposition. He didn't tell me what it was."

Fujita turned to her and said, "I heard him getting dressed a few minutes ago. That's when I started the tea. You know how angry he gets if he has to wait for his breakfast." She started for the bedroom. "I'll see if he is in any condition to talk business with a stranger."

Emiko knew what her mother meant. Kunio usually had a headache and an upset stomach after a night of saké. He would not be in a cordial state of mind for at least two hours after rising from his bed.

She heard their voices, quietly at first, then escalating, the longer that she waited.

Finally, her mother returned. "You can tell the visitor Papa is on his way."

Emiko returned to the yard where the stranger was patiently waiting, exactly where she left him.

"Father will be coming shortly," she said. Then she heard his footsteps behind her.

"Do I know you?" her father asked loudly. "What do you want?"

The stranger bowed again, this time to her father, and said, "Good morning; my name is Saburo Kondo. It is a pleasure to meet you. My apology for calling unannounced, but I have a business proposition I think you will find most favorable. You will thank me later if you listen to my proposal."

"What is the proposal?" Kunio asked.

The handsome stranger looked at Emiko and then back to Kunio. "With all respect, it is a proposal best discussed only between the two of us. I am not at liberty to discuss my proposal in the presence of others."

"You don't have to worry about my daughter. She's only a girl. She wouldn't understand a business proposition anyway."

Saburo laughed at the reply. "No, business deals are not meant for women," he said. "Nevertheless, my employer requires that I speak only with the head of the family. Can we take a walk?"

Kunio nodded.

Saburo tied the reins of his horse to a nearby shrub and began to walk in the direction of the barn. He hesitated long enough for Kunio to fall in step.

Kunio motioned with a twitch of his head for Emiko to go back to the house.

Emiko and her mother waited patiently in the kitchen for nearly an hour before Fujita began to pace the floor. On each trip past the window she peered out, looking for Kunio. "I wonder if he has saké hidden in the barn," she said, almost to herself. "They've been gone too long to only be talking business."

They waited another hour. Emiko and Fujita took turns looking out the window.

Finally, Fujita said, "If only one of your brothers were here, we could send them out to see what's going on. Today, of all days, they're all working in the paddy."

Emiko was just about to check on them herself, under the pretense of asking if they would like fresh tea and a biscuit, when she heard them returning from the barn. From the boisterous sound of their voices, she knew her mother was right. They had been into drink of some kind. She motioned to her mother, and the two of them sat down at the table to await news of the proposition.

Several minutes later, Kunio entered the kitchen with a smile on his face. "What are you looking at?" he asked. "Can't a man conduct business on his own farm?"

"What did he want?" Fujita asked.

"It was just like he said... a business proposition. A very good proposition, I might add. And just at the right time. Just in time to pay our taxes."

"Didn't Ayami and her husband already send money for taxes?" Fujita asked.

Kunio stared at her. "They sent money, but it wasn't enough. They never send enough. I don't know why you don't understand that. I guess because you're a woman. You don't understand how business works."

Fujita stared back at him. "So what was the proposition, then? Is the stranger going to pay our taxes?"

"In a manner of speaking, yes," he said.

Then he looked at Emiko.

"Actually, it is you," he said. "Remember the time you talked back to me when I was trying to eat? The time I said you would pay? Well, now is the time. I signed you up to work at a factory starting next week. Mr. Kondo will be coming for you on Monday. That should give you more than enough time to be ready."

Chapter 14

A Child is Born

At the ridgetop home of Toshi and Ayami, Toshi paced the room. His hair reflected a restless night, and his eyes were open wide. Even though the weather was cool, beads of perspiration formed on his forehead and down both sides of his drawn cheeks. Ayami was having labor pains; he was certain of it, but what should he do?

Do I dare leave her long enough to run and get Minako? he asked himself. There were no close neighbors on the ridge. *Who would hear if I called for help? Why did we build a house so far from neighbors? We should have stayed at Haruki's last night. Sometimes I am such an idiot.*

As Toshi tried to organize his thoughts into some kind of meaningful plan, Ayami screamed from a combination of fear and pain. *"AAA-YEE-AHH!"* she yelled, over and over. Toshi felt she surely must be dying. He had heard midwives talk of boiled water and clean blankets, but what could he possibly do with those? He tried to ask Ayami what to do.

"AAA-YEE!" she replied. Not once, but three times, in rapid succession.

"Should I run to get Minako?" he tried to ask.

She answered, "YAA-AHH-AAA"

Then Toshi remembered something else the midwife had said.

"Breathe… breathe… breathe…" he pleaded to Ayami in a loud voice. He could tell she was listening to his advice. She opened her mouth in a big circle, and her chest expanded noticeably as she inhaled deeply. Then she stopped, and her eyes became even wider.

"Push…" he implored in a loud voice. "Push…"

Toshi found his way to what seemed a reasonable sequence and began to shout, "Breathe… push… exhale… breathe… push… exhale…" Whether this was in fact helpful or even logical, he wasn't sure, but at least it gave Ayami something to focus on besides the horrible pain.

As it fell into a rhythm of sorts, in spite of the fear and panic of them both, Toshi eventually noticed how wet the mat beneath her had become. The source of the clear, watery liquid was beyond his train of thought at the moment because of more pressing concerns. But it finally occurred to him why there might be a need for clean, dry blankets. They were not just to wrap a new baby, but also to keep the mother dry with at least some degree of comfort.

Between his chants of "breathe… push… exhale…" he ran to the linen trunk, retrieved several clean blankets, and brought them to the mat.

Periodically, the pain would stop, and Ayami was able to lie back and catch her breath for several blissful minutes. During those pauses Toshi was able to remove the wet blanket from beneath her and replace it with one warm and dry. Toshi offered her sips of water, which she took because they did seem to soothe her throat, now raw from the screams she could not control.

It grieved Toshi to see Ayami in such pain during those extreme periods, and each time they subsided, he tried to console her with encouragement and occasional kisses on the forehead or cheek. He could not determine if they helped, but not knowing what else to do, decided to keep doing it, whenever she seemed compliant.

Toshi could tell by the strength of her screams she was wearing down. *Is this normal?* he wondered. He continued to perspire and he, too, became drenched in sweat as he tried to figure out what to do next. *If only we lived closer to Minako,* he thought. *She has been through this several times. She would know what to do.*

The pain and the screams went dormant for what seemed like half an hour. *Is there something wrong?* He wondered again. *Did the baby come, and I didn't know it? Surely, I would know if it had.* But his thoughts were so frantic and confused that his logic, or rather, the lack of it, did not occur to him. He could only think of ways to try and help his beloved Ayami.

When she remained quiet for several more minutes, Toshi looked at her eyes. They were closed. He bent down, only centimeters away from her wet and clammy cheek. Her chest was moving slowly—too slowly, he was certain.

His own pulse then ratcheted to a new level. *She is dying,* he thought.

"Ayami!" he pleaded loudly. He kissed her forehead and grabbed her hand, holding it tightly in his own. *Was it moving? Was there a pulse?* Yes, he felt a light rhythm at her wrist. She was breathing, but it felt ever so weak. He rose from the mat, ready to leave her and bolt for Minako's house. Then doubt overcame once more. *Maybe I could carry her to Minako's.* That would be faster because I wouldn't have to travel both directions. Just as he was about to run for the door, another scream.

"OHH-AHH-IEE!" She wailed again, but not as loud as before.

Is this good news or bad? he wondered. *At least she is alive, but was that her final plea?*

Toshi dropped to his knees beside her listless body. *How could he have done this to her?* he asked himself. He held her face carefully, one hand on either cheek, wiping away the tears and sweat with each of his thumbs. It was getting harder to see her face through a growing stream of tears that now clouded his own.

He closed his eyes and bowed his head in complete and total humility. "Please God, if you are there and if you can hear me, tell me what to do. Please let Ayami live. You know how much she means to me. She is a good person who always tries to do what is right."

Then he waited. He dared not leave her now. If she were dying, he would not let her die alone. He thought of blankets, and hot water, and tea, and even of bread and cake. But what good were any of those? He had no idea what more to do.

He held her hand again and checked her pulse. He felt a steady rhythm—no worse than before. He reached up and kissed her again, on the forehead and on her puffy, sweaty, rosy cheeks. He thought she was the most beautiful woman he had ever seen, even lying there motionless as she was.

The two of them were quiet and still until Toshi jerked upright and let out a shriek. It took a moment to realize what was happening.

He had been startled by the sound of his front door flying open, followed by the sound of several feet moving quickly across the floor to where he and Ayami formed a single bundle: she—stretched out on a mat across the floor, he—with arms wrapped tightly around her, hoping to keep her from slipping away forever.

Haruki grabbed Toshi by the shoulders and helped him to his feet while Minako and the physician studied the lifeless form before them. The physician placed a small bottle of hartshorn under Ayami's nose while Minako gently stroked each of her hands and spoke encouragement into her damp and lifeless ears. She looked back over her shoulder at Saya, who was close behind.

"Quick! Warm some water. When it's hot, bring several rags soaked in it. Also, fresh rags rinsed in cold water. Then heat some tea with honey and bring it as soon as you can."

Haruki helped Toshi out the door, and together they sat on a bench overlooking Ayami's garden. "Saya," he yelled over his shoulder and toward the house, "when the tea is ready, bring some out for Toshi, and if you can find something to eat, bring that, too."

Saya first made sure to get the hot and cold rags her mother had requested, then searched the kitchen for something to eat.

Inside the house, Minako and the physician continued to work on Ayami. The smelling salts had helped. They pulled her mat away from the wall and positioned themselves one on either side. Together, they removed her underclothing, which somehow had not occurred to Toshi in his state of excitement. They raised her knees up close to her chest and placed her feet flat on the mat beneath them, then spread her legs apart enough to give the physician room.

"I can see the top of his head. That's a good sign," he said. "If only we can keep it moving. Hand me the hartshorn again." He waved the smelling salt under her nose and watched as her eyes traveled to meet his.

"What beautiful eyes she has," he muttered to Minako. Followed by, "Ayami, where did you get such beautiful eyes? I can't wait to see if this baby has your eyes.

"You are doing great," he continued. "Minako will help you take a few sips of tea. Don't drink too much, but you have to stay hydrated. Can you do it?"

When she nodded her head, Minako gave her a few sips from the cup. It was late afternoon now, and it finally occurred to Ayami that she had not eaten since the day before. No wonder she was weak. The physician gave her one more sniff of hartshorn, which seemed to put new light in her eyes.

"I think I'm ready," she said.

"Great. Let's see who it is that's waiting to meet its parents. When the next contraction starts, take a long, deep breath, then push with all your strength while I count to ten. We're going to help this little fellow get out."

Ayami's eyes got bigger. "It's a boy?" she asked.

"I really can't tell yet, but only a few more pushes, and we'll find out together."

As Ayami inhaled deeply and began to push, the physician watched between her legs for progress. He could see a nose. The head was slowly pushing out.

"Excellent!" he proclaimed. "Only a few more times, and we'll have it."

Three more times Ayami took long, deep breaths, pushing as hard as she could between each one, while Minako counted to ten. She was turning pale and listless.

"You're getting so close, Ayami. You have to keep going."

"Do you think it's a boy?" Ayami whispered back.

"Two more good pushes, and we should know," the physician replied. "Ready? Here we go. Breathe…"

Ayami inhaled once more and pictured in her mind an infant version of Toshi. She pushed as long and hard as she could, until finally, she exhaled and her eyes fluttered, and then went closed. Her frail body relaxed on the mat, and her arms went limp beside her.

***

Just outside the house, Haruki took the tea and fruit that Saya brought, and helped Toshi drink a few sips of the honey-seasoned tea. It was almost harder for Haruki than it had been for Minako because Toshi was trembling so much. The first few times he tried to drink from the cup, more tea spilled over the edge than into his mouth. Haruki grabbed Toshi's wrist to help steady his hand so he could hold the cup.

Toshi was still shaking when Saya handed him half a banana. "Eat this," she said. "You must be starving. No wonder you're shaking so much. When did you eat last? It's nearly four o'clock," she continued.

Hoping to distract Toshi, she rambled on. "Do you think it's going to be a girl or a boy? I think it's going to be a girl, and she is going to look exactly like Ayami," she gabbled. "Wouldn't that be the best thing ever? Think about it. A tiny little person just like Ayami."

The tea and the banana helped Toshi, but still he continued to tremble. His eyes were dark and misty. "I should never have moved this far away from you," he wailed to Haruki. "What would I do without Ayami? I don't think I could live without her."

Saya darted a glance at her father.

Haruki looked back at her and shook his head with little more than a twitch. Then he looked back at Toshi.

Not knowing what to say, Saya moved close to Toshi and placed her young arm around his waist. She leaned close to him and held him tight, trying to provide some small bit of comfort, and hoping to quell the shaking. Presently, Haruki followed suit, moving close to Toshi's other side and extending his long and reassuring arm around Toshi's shoulder.

Together, the three of them stood, a dozen steps from the doorway, on a sunny afternoon in July.

No one spoke. They stood almost as one, the arms of each entwined with another. There was a strength in that. Eventually, Toshi became aware of a chorus of birds singing, blended with the whisper of a Pacific breeze flowing through the forest pines. Were they finch…? tit…? warbler…? "This is why we live up here," he said.

Haruki and Saya did not understand at first, what he was trying to say. "What?" asked Haruki.

"Can you hear the trees and the birds?" Toshi repeated. "This is why Ayami and I wanted to live up here: to hear the birds. Ayami loved to hear them sing, especially in the evenings. And the sound of the wind in the pines… it has a music of its own."

Then Haruki and Saya listened, too. "I think I heard a finch chirping," Saya said. And the others listened for that sound in particular, as it played through the chorus of several others. "Did you hear it?"

Toshi trembled as the three of them listened for the song of a nearby finch.

Then the three of them jumped, startled by a loud and distinguishable wail from inside Toshi's house. It was the song of a different sort. It was the cry from a baby's mouth, and it was loud and clear.

All three of them ran for the door. Inside stood Minako with the trace of a smile, almost like the bundle she held was her very own, with tears shining down her weary cheeks.

***

Toshi knew they had a healthy child simply by the way Minako was holding it. But he continued to shake as his eyes darted to the mat. The physician was turned away from him, preventing Toshi from reading his countenance for any clue about Ayami's health. He looked at her but could not see her face, hidden as it was, behind the physician. He studied her body for signs of movement. There were none.

"Ayami," he wailed, with a voice filled at once with love and despair. The physician turned to face Toshi in reaction to his mournful call. Then, rising from his place on the floor, stepped forward to meet Toshi. He extended his hand as a smile filled his usually somber face.

"Congratulations! You have a beautiful son and a healthy wife. Right now, Ayami is exhausted, as she has every right to be. But with rest and something to eat when she's ready, she should be back to her old self before long. You may be a good man and a good husband, but you are not a good doctor. Next time, have Minako or Saya stay with you two weeks before the baby is due. Are you ready to hold your new son?"

Minako brought over what looked like a blanket rolled into a bundle, and handed it carefully to Toshi. As soon as she placed it in his arms, the trembling stopped. He could not remember holding a newborn baby ever before, and was afraid of holding him the wrong way, or dropping him, or a hundred other things. But as soon as the baby was safely in his arms, all other thoughts disappeared. He looked down at the bundle, searching for the face hidden somewhere deep within. The first thing he saw was the eyes of Ayami looking back at him. "Thank you, God, whoever you are," he whispered to himself.

He carried the bundle over to Ayami, who was smiling up at him. He carefully knelt down beside her and placed the bundle in her arms. She pulled back the flaps of the blanket so they could both see the infant, still pink from his ordeal. He did have Ayami's eyes, but the rest of his face was an image of Toshi. "I almost can't believe it," he murmured.

The physician intervened once more, saying, "Ayami, you should eat and then get some rest. Minako and the others will take care of the baby while you get some sleep. In a few hours you should feed your son. He will let you know when he's ready, and I daresay he will be ready before you are, but that will be the way of your life from now on. I'll stop by in a few days to see how you're doing."

Minako and Saya found a clean mat for Ayami to sleep on and coaxed her to eat a small snack of bread and fruit. They gave her a cup of the special honey-flavored tea to drink, and one glass each of milk and water to help replenish the fluid she had lost since yesterday.

Toshi held on to their little bundle of blanket containing a baby as Ayami drifted off to sleep. He walked all through the house carrying the infant, looking down at its tiny face, fingering each of his fingers and toes, and rubbing his tummy as he went.

***

The following Sunday, Toshi and Ayami took their new son to Haruki's house.

"When are you going to choose a name for him?" asked Haruki. "We can't just keep referring to him as 'the baby'."

"We think he is going to be 'Kiyoshi'," replied Toshi. "It is similar to my name, yet different enough that people will know it's not me. The name means 'pure' or 'saintly,' which we hope he will become."

"A good choice," replied Haruki.

Toshi was quiet for several minutes. Then he asked, "Haruki, what made you and the others come to see us that day? Did you know we needed help?"

"When you didn't come to work that morning, I thought maybe the baby was coming early. But as the morning progressed, I got busy with the new molds we were trying to make, and I admit I forgot about it. When lunchtime came and you still weren't there, I began to worry again. About two o'clock, I had a feeling, almost like someone speaking to me. I knew the baby was not expected for at least another week, but the feeling worried me. After fifteen minutes of worry, I asked the others if they would cover for me, and that's when I headed for home.

"When I got to our house and Minako hadn't heard from you either, we began to worry in earnest. The three of us headed directly to your house and as we passed the fork in the path, we met the physician, who was heading back to the village. He'd been on the ridge seeing one of his patients.

"Can you believe our luck? It was almost like he was waiting there, just for us. Anyway, we told him Ayami was expecting her first child in another week, but we had a feeling something wasn't right. So he came with us the rest of the way, and there you were. I still can't believe how that all worked out like it did. But I'm glad."

Toshi was quiet. Haruki figured that was the end of it.

"Haruki, do you think there is a Christian God?" he asked.

Now it was Haruki's turn to pause. "I've known a few families who practiced an underground version of Christianity over the years," he replied. "But I really don't know much about it. Why do you ask?"

"I was just wondering," he replied.

Chapter 15

Called to the Office

KAMAISHI – 1879 - IRON FOUNDRY

When Kiyoshi reached his first birthday, in July of 1879, he was able to toddle about the house by himself, with only minimal crashes to the floor. He entertained his parents as well as Haruki's household with his continual attempts to throw a toy to anyone who would take the time to give it back. Between vocal transmissions and animated articulations, he was usually successful in communicating whatever it was he wanted to say. Most often, it translated to 'hold me' or 'hungry' or just plain 'no.' In other words, Kiyoshi was a lot like most little boys his age.

One October morning, after Toshi had gone to work at the foundry and Kiyoshi was just about to finish his breakfast bowl of rice, Ayami felt a wave of nausea overcome her. Thinking it was something about the aroma of the rice she was feeding Kiyoshi, or maybe that portion of it spread around his face mixed with the yolk of a half-eaten egg, she willed herself to get over the feeling. It worked for the moment. But when Kiyoshi finished the rice and announced with a flail of his arms and a squeal from his mouth that breakfast was over, Ayami was again overcome. This time she was not able to will it away and dashed to the cupboard for a bowl to empty her stomach. An hour later, it occurred to her this was not the flu. It was time to prepare for another Kiyoshi.

When Toshi arrived home from work that day, Ayami noticed the worried look on his face.

"Did something happen at work today? You don't seem yourself tonight," she said.

"I'm not sure," he replied. "But when I went to the charcoal warehouse today, the inventory was low. I asked the man in charge about it, and he shrugged and said they were making it as fast as they could, but admitted it was getting harder to keep up. He thinks we're using too much of it in our blending formula. I told him the current ratio of charcoal to ore gives the best production result, but he just shrugged and said there was nothing he could do about it."

"Have you talked to Haruki? Surely, he would know if there is a problem."

"Not yet, and that's what I was trying to decide—whether I should bother him with it. He knows more than me about running the foundry, and I don't want to look foolish. I'm going to study my journals tonight."

Then he looked at her with a mischievous grin and said, "Could you put Kiyoshi to bed early?"

"Yes, I can easily take care of Kiyoshi," and she returned his smile with a matching one of her own. "But there is something you should know," she continued. "We will need to get to bed early ourselves for the next few months, because after that we will only be able to sleep."

Toshi liked riddles, but this one took a while to solve.

"Are we going to have another baby?" he finally managed to sputter.

"Yes—we're going to have another baby."

The cloud lifted from Toshi's shoulders, and a smile formed across his face.

"Oh Ayami, when did you find out? Does Minako know? When will it arrive? You said in a few months; is that when you're due? I love you, Ayami. We have to tell Minako so she can come and stay with us. I love you so much, Ayami. We don't want to go through another birth on our own again. Not after Kiyoshi. I was scared to death that day. We don't want to be alone this time. Should I go tell Minako now?"

She laughed at his flurry of questions. "No, Toshi. We have plenty of time to tell Minako. I just realized it this morning. I got sick when I was feeding Kiyoshi his breakfast. I think it will be in

April or May of next year. And we will definitely have Minako or one of the girls come stay with us long before—I love you too, Toshi."

"When are you going to put Kiyoshi to bed?" Toshi asked with a grin.

****

The next day, Toshi arrived at the foundry even earlier than his usual time.

"Good morning," Haruki greeted him. "You are early today, even for you. Is something wrong?"

"I'm not sure, but that's what I wanted to talk to you about. Yesterday, when I went to the charcoal warehouse, the supply was running low. When I asked the foreman about it, he said they can't make it fast enough to keep up with the furnace. I reviewed my journals last night, and based on what I've recorded over the past three years, it looks like we might be running out of charcoal."

Haruki listened as Toshi told him about the charcoal. When he finished, Haruki considered the implications this could have for the foundry.

"Thank you for bringing it to my attention. I'll speak with the director to see if he's aware of the situation. Maybe they plan to bring charcoal in from another source and he hasn't told me. I'll speak with him today."

Later that afternoon, Haruki approached Toshi as he was adding charcoal to the furnace. "I spoke to the director, and he was concerned by what you told me. He plans to request a report from the charcoal manager. He seemed pleased that you reported it."

Walking home from work that day, Toshi felt proud to be complimented for his observation, but the feeling was overshadowed by the nagging thought they might run out of charcoal. *What would happen then? Smelting required a mixture of magnetite and charcoal. Two new furnaces were already under construction, scheduled for completion next year. How could those operate if they ran short of charcoal with only one furnace?*

When he arrived at home and found Ayami and Kiyoshi waiting at the door, his anxieties floated away. By holding on to Ayami's leg with one hand, Kiyoshi was able to balance himself just enough to wave his other arm wildly, and with an excited smile across his face, welcome Toshi home from work. Sounds came from his mouth in rapid bursts, louder than Toshi thought possible from such a tiny person, and though he was not exactly sure of the words, they made his heart run wild as he wrapped him with his hands and lifted him high into the air.

Later that evening, when Kiyoshi was safely tucked away for the night, Toshi turned to his journal. He recorded his conversation with Haruki. It definitely fell into the category of a significant event for the foundry. As he considered how best to summarize the day, Ayami watched his somber expression and asked. "Did everything go okay at work today? You look more serious than usual."

"I'm not sure," he replied. "I did talk to Haruki about the charcoal, and he reported it to the plant manager. It's probably nothing, but it worries me, especially with the new furnaces under construction."

"I'm sure whoever is in charge of the foundry would have thought of that. Maybe the new furnaces don't require as much charcoal. Aren't they supposed to be a new design from England or somewhere?"

Toshi considered her response. "That does make sense," he said. "I'm probably worried over nothing. I hope I haven't put Haruki in a bad position by causing him to go to the director. I need to learn to think before I speak." He made an abbreviated reference to the charcoal supply in his journal and closed the cover.

A week later, about three o'clock in the afternoon, Haruki approached Toshi as he was helping two other workers move a large cannon mold to the cooling area. It was a heavy mold, and all three of them were soaked in sweat from the heat of the furnace and the heavy load.

"The director sent a message for you to meet in his office tomorrow morning. I asked the messenger what it was about, but he either didn't know or wouldn't say. He only said for you to be there at eight o'clock. I know the director doesn't like to be kept waiting, but since you're always here early, I'm sure that won't happen. I wish I could tell you more about the meeting, but that's all I know. I'm sure you'll be fine, so don't worry about it. I'll be here for you if you need me."

With that, he walked away, but there was something about the tone of his voice, or maybe it was the profile of his back as he departed, that left a hollow spot in Toshi's stomach. *I must be in trouble,* he thought. *Why did I stick my nose where it doesn't belong? What will I do if I lose my job? How will I support Ayami and Kiyoshi, and now another baby?*

It was not until Haruki was falling asleep on his mat that night that he thought of it. Toshi had never been to the director's office before. *He forgot to tell him about the interpreter.*

***

Toshi was up early the next morning, leaving Ayami and Kiyoshi sleeping soundly as he left the house and headed toward the foundry. His mind was filled with images of what might come of his meeting with the director. The normal tranquility that came from the forest and songbirds was wasted on him today, as he marched along the familiar trail. It was earlier than normal and the trail was quiet. It gave him time to rehearse his answers to a dozen unknown questions.

When he arrived at the foundry, he forced his mind to clear his fears and his carefully thought-out responses, and simply accept whatever was to be his fate. As long as he had Ayami and Kiyoshi and a place to live, that was all that mattered. He thought back to the birth of little Kiyoshi and how he had been so terrified of losing Ayami.

Then he remembered calling out to God for help in saving Ayami. *Had the request been answered?* It was soon after his request that Haruki and the others had burst through the door, bringing the physician. *Was it a coincidence, or did God really hear and answer him? Maybe there is a God,* he thought as he considered his upcoming meeting with the director.

"God, if you're still there, and if you can hear me, please guide the director to be fair, and please allow me to provide for my family no matter what happens," he prayed to himself.

Chapter 16

The Waiting Room

KAMAISHI - 1879 – IRON FOUNDRY

The construction site was a short distance removed from the current foundry. In addition to the new blast furnaces currently taking shape, there was a small one-story building about one hundred meters to the west, which Toshi presumed was the director's office. As he approached, he noted that it was situated with a maximum view of the Aonoki River, which flowed beside and curved around behind the building. It was not as close to the new furnaces as Toshi would have placed it, but the German no doubt had his reasons for locating it where he did.

Toshi solemnly climbed the two steps leading up to the door. It was flanked by a window on either side, which provided a view of the new furnaces some distance away. Not sure what was expected, he knocked on the door lightly and waited for a response. The only sound came from a few early workers in the distance as they began their day of construction.

Toshi knocked again, this time with a note of confidence he tried to portray, though on the verge of trembling beneath the surface. Again, no one answered. He tried the door and found it unlocked, so he slowly swung it open as he announced himself to anyone within. "Good morning. Is anyone here?"

Toshi expected to find a small office like the one he had during his short stay at the furniture factory. What he found was something far different, more like his brother's office. In addition to the two front windows facing the foundry, large windows on both sides of the building helped bathe the room in natural light. In the center stood a western-style table with a large single chair behind, and two smaller ones in front. On the table lay a calendar, displaying each day of the month in squares of seven or eight millimeters. Most of the squares contained notations, which Toshi assumed were to identify important meetings for each day.

Along the wall to his right, between the two generous windows, stood a wood stove still warm from the day before. The view from the windows was clearly aimed at the river which flowed just beyond, with pine trees adding to the natural beauty. He watched birds flying freely among the trees, but with the window separating them he was unable to hear their songs, if any were being sung.

Not wanting to be caught snooping, he took a seat in one of the three chairs lined against the entrance wall. As he waited in silence admiring the table, he heard the sound of footsteps, followed by the door to his left swinging open.

Through the door walked a man of Japanese descent, shorter than Toshi and substantially older. He glanced at Toshi and after a momentary look of surprise, returned to his unhappy countenance and continued toward the table. Toshi tried not to stare directly at him, out of courtesy, but he did try to observe him from the corner of his eye, watching for a signal to approach the table. Obviously, this was not the German director. *Was this man sitting in the director's chair? Or did the director have a different office?*

He watched as the man carefully studied the calendar, much as he himself had done a few minutes before. Then he stole a direct look just as the man reached down and retrieved a watch from a pocket sewn into his western-style shirt. He looked once more at the calendar on the table and then at his watch. Then he abruptly rose from his seat at the table and walked toward the door behind his desk. *That must be the director's office*, he thought. *He's going to announce that I'm here.* His heart began to quicken. He licked his lips, which suddenly felt very dry. Impulsively, Toshi ran his hand through his hair and slicked down the front of his kimono with both hands, trying to make himself presentable.

The man knocked three times lightly on the door. Then he returned to his table and took a seat.

The director must not be in his office, Toshi concluded.

There was nothing to do but wait. Toshi sat quietly and attentively, and simply observed what he could from his seat along the front wall. He had a full view of the office, so he could watch all of it without being obvious.

Eventually, Toshi heard muted voices coming from behind the director's door. He watched the door and before long it began to open. Once more Toshi's heart began to race and he felt his body tense. He swallowed to clear his throat. For the second time, he licked his lips to remove the dryness.

But instead of the German director, out walked a young Japanese woman. Toshi blinked in surprise. Without knowing it, he momentarily stopped breathing. He turned his head, scanning the room to convince himself he was actually sitting in the foundry office. There, just ahead of him and to his left, sat the older Japanese man at his table. It was the office. But who was the woman?

Not until she reached the stove did Toshi notice the small metal pot she carried in her hand. Then he held back a quiet snort as he felt his face flush. *She is his servant,* he decided. *The director would certainly have a maidservant. But where did she come from? Does she live somewhere behind the door?*

Toshi watched as the woman placed the small pot on the stove and returned to the door from which she had come. She did not look at Toshi, nor did she look at the man at the desk. Apparently, she either expected them both to be there, or did not care, or possibly was instructed not to acknowledge anything beyond her specific duties.

Still nothing from the man at the desk. He continued to study pages from one of the folders. Toshi tried not to stare, but wondered if the man was actually studying his papers or merely working hard to mind his own business.

Several more minutes passed until the director's door slowly opened and the same girl as before entered the room, again headed for the stove. This time, she had a large ceramic cup in her hand. She poured a small quantity of dark brown granules from the cup into the pot on the stove, walked over to the man at the table, and spoke something in his ear. They both looked directly at Toshi for a moment and then she retreated back through the door.

By this time, Toshi was getting more and more anxious, and in spite of that, also becoming slightly bolder. When the two of them looked at him, he took the opportunity to return the gaze directly to his observers. Since he had already stolen a few studied glances at the man, this time he focused on the girl. To his surprise, she was older than he originally suspected. She still was beautiful, but instead of a young lady in her teens, Toshi now realized she must be twice that age, probably older than Toshi himself. Her face belied the wrinkles around her large brown eyes. But most of all, what Toshi noticed was the look of despondence. As she turned and walked back through the door, he could almost feel her unhappiness.

He thought of Ayami and how her eyes sparkled with a love for life. She would often smile at Toshi, or even a stranger, without a second thought. He felt sorry for whatever it was that caused this poor woman to be so forlorn.

Chapter 17

The German Director

KAMAISHI – 1879 - FOUNDRY DIRECTORS OFFICE

It was more than a little embarrassing when the man from the table had to ask Toshi for the second time to please follow him into the director's office.

As he followed the man through the door, Toshi's eyes widened in surprise. Not only was it much larger than he had imagined, but there were two additional doorways leading from the space. Much like the outer office, there were large windows along the right side wall, providing a commanding view of the river and the forest beyond. Along the left wall was one of the doors, and along the back wall, another door, similar to that which graced the outer office. In the center of the room was a table as in the outer room, but this one much larger, and the front and sides were skirted with beautifully carved and polished wood. His first thought was that it must have cost a fortune, followed closely by a second thought: could his father make one like it.

The director was seated behind the large table, dressed in a tan-colored, western-styled shirt, immaculately pressed, with white buttons that might have been pearl. The collar was crisp and pressed neatly down against the shirt surrounding his neck. Although he was seated, Toshi could presume the man was tall, particularly by Japanese standards. His posture was rigid to match his face.

Toshi tried to guess which of them least wanted to be at this meeting: he or the director. By outward appearances, it was a draw.

Toshi noticed the ceramic cup which the woman had filled and retrieved from the stove earlier. It was sitting on the director's table on the bare and polished wood, which he considered a rather careless gesture, given the cup must have been hot when first retrieved.

As he observed the director, trying not to make a hasty impression, he noted the thick, blonde hair and the neatly trimmed mustache. His blue eyes and angular profile were as different from Toshi's Japanese traits as day was from night.

If Toshi was surprised by all the strange appearances within the director's office, he was totally astounded when the director looked directly at Toshi and then uttered a greeting in a language he did not understand. Then, from his left and slightly behind came a greeting that he did understand. It came from the man at the front desk. Toshi was not sure whether to turn and face him or continue to look ahead at the director. Confused, he simply stood there at first, trying to collect his thoughts as to what was happening. Only then did he realize the director could not speak Japanese and that the man at the outer table was his interpreter. In what he hoped was a quick recovery, he glanced at the interpreter, then returned to the director with a painted smile of acknowledgement.

"Good morning," Toshi responded to the director.

"Please have a seat," was the reply, first from the director in German, then from the interpreter in Japanese.

Toshi sat in one of the two chairs placed on his side of the director's elegant table.

"I'm told you maintain a secret diary of everything that happens at the foundry," the director said, as he stared at Toshi.

When the interpreter repeated the statement, Toshi felt his face turn red, even without the ability to see it himself. He tried to force his muscles to relax but could see, even from the peripherals in his line of sight, that his arms and hands were beginning to tense. He forced himself to take two slow, deep breaths while he composed a response.

"Yes, it is true I keep a journal. But it does not include everything that goes on at the foundry, and it is not a secret journal. I have mentioned it many times to the people I work with."

He waited until the interpreter relayed his message to the director.

The director gave no hint of belief or disbelief in his reply. "What is the purpose of your journal?"

By now, Toshi was beginning to grow accustomed to the concept of an interpreter, and turned to face whoever was doing the talking. He watched the director as he spoke, even though he was actually talking to the interpreter. Then he turned to look at the interpreter while he relayed the message on to Toshi.

"I started the journal several years ago as a method of recording things that seemed important to a smooth operation at the foundry. For example, if we had a day when production was unusually low, I would try to summarize anything that happened during the day that might have contributed to lower production. And whenever we had a particularly good day, I did the same. My hope was that I might be able to identify a procedure or method that resulted in the outcome, and thereby enable us to improve our procedures over time."

Toshi waited as the interpreter relayed his response back to the director. He hoped the man would repeat his answer correctly and without bias in the use of his German words or inflections. It occurred to him he was at the mercy of this man, who only minutes earlier, Toshi had considered bored and generally noncommittal to a successful operation.

Presently, the director asked, "And during all these years of recording such information, did you find anything useful?"

"One thing that became clear early on was that the composition of the team was more important than the procedures or the rules. When everyone worked together as a team, they seemed to know instinctively what needed to be done, whether it was more charcoal or more air pressure, or to wait longer for the iron to heat. When even one of the members was missing or not paying attention, that's when we had more accidents or less production."

The man relayed his message to the director. Toshi could see the director was thinking about the message. He thought he noticed the slightest release of tension in the director's face. There was no hint of a smile, but it did seem possible his answer had resonated with the director.

"Anything else?" came the next question.

"We tried a number of things, trying to reduce the amount of charcoal for a cycle of producing iron. For example, we tried changing the ratio of charcoal to ore from the mine. And we tried adding charcoal at different times during the process to maintain the required smelting temperature. One thing we could not control to a great extent was the force of the air mixture generated by the water wheel. We could only use as much as the wheel provided. We did find that the greater the air pressure, the hotter the heat, but it also used the charcoal faster because of that."

He waited as his message was relayed to the director. He was surprised by an obvious facial reaction partway through the exchange. Apparently, the director was not happy about something he had said.

The director looked at Toshi as he spoke his words to the interpreter.

"You might be happy to know that our new furnaces are much more efficient than the outdated relic we are currently using. We will have complete control over the amount of air infused in the smelting process thanks to innovations from outside Japan. True, the furnaces will burn hotter, but because of their efficiency, they will actually produce more iron with less charcoal."

The director made what seemed a planned and well-orchestrated movement to retrieve the still-warm cup of coffee from his table and gaze out the windows as if in deep thought. Then Toshi remembered advice Haruki had once given him: *don't offer any more information than needed,* so he kept his mouth closed and waited for another question.

After several long sips from the cup, the director continued. "I've been told you think we are running short of charcoal. Is that true?"

So this is it after all, thought Toshi. *That's what this is about. Why didn't I keep my nose out of that from the beginning? And then to bring it up again here, as a concern.* He tried once more to remain calm and take several full breaths without being too conspicuous.

"Yes, it is true I worried about the foundry running low. I visit the charcoal building periodically to see how things are going, and there were a few times recently when I noticed the stockpiles were lower than normal. That's when I brought it up to Haruki-san. I was afraid there might be a problem over time, and I just wanted to make sure we would have enough. I'm sorry if I caused a problem for the manager of the charcoal warehouse."

Toshi waited for the interpreter to explain his message to the director. It was agonizing to wait for each question and answer to be relayed to the intended person.

Toshi watched intently for any facial or other signs from the director as the interpreter finished speaking his latest response. He saw nothing. At least he did not see noticeable tension as his answer was received. That was slight comfort. However, this being Toshi's first encounter with the director, maybe he simply didn't realize how good an actor the director was.

"Tell me about Haruki," said the director.

"Haruki-san knows more about the foundry than anyone I know," Toshi replied through the interpreter. "He is always the first person to arrive and the last to leave. He never takes shortcuts, and he always watches out for his workers."

No one spoke for a few minutes. Then the director looked at Toshi as he spoke to the interpreter.

"What is the value of *pi*?"

When the interpreter repeated the question a second time, Toshi could almost feel the blank stare on his face. He was temporarily dumbfounded, and he knew that it showed.

When he didn't answer, the interpreter repeated the same question once more. This time with a note of authority in his voice. "What is the value of *pi*?"

As out of place as it seemed, Toshi could think of only one interpretation of the question.

"Do you mean *pi*? As in the mathematics of geometry? *Pi*, the ratio of the circumference of a circle to its diameter? If that is the *pi* you are asking about, then the value is 3.1415926535 carried to ten places. The complete number, as I'm sure you would already know, is irrational and has a never-ending value. For most calculations, the value is usually truncated to 3.14159 or rounded to

3.1416. The reason I hesitated initially was because I didn't see a connection between *pi* and our foundry. But I could surely be mistaken."

Now is when Toshi was really paying attention to the interpreter because he was pretty sure the man had no idea what he was talking about, and even less confidence that he could remember the digits in their correct order.

After several short exchanges with the director, the interpreter turned to Toshi with some hesitance. "The director asked if you would be willing to write the value 'to ten places' on a sheet of paper."

"Yes, I will be happy to do that," replied Toshi, which he did on a small paper handed across the table by the director.

"One last question," came a summons relayed through the interpreter. "Do you know how charcoal is made?"

"I have never tried to make it myself. I know only that you need to burn the impurities out of the wood. The trick is to burn out the impurities without burning up the wood itself. I believe one way to do that is to place small pieces of wood in a container and then heat the container for several hours until the pieces inside have turned into little black lumps. I suppose it takes quite a lot of wood to make a small amount of charcoal."

"That is basically correct," the director responded. "However, it works best with hardwoods, such as oak."

Then the director stood from his table for the first time.

"I would like to see your secret journal," he said. "Please bring me your journal tomorrow."

With that, the interpreter stepped in front of Toshi, and with a clumsy arm gesture, made it clear the meeting was over.

After Toshi left, the director called out to the interpreter, now seated at his station in the outer room. "Bring me the book entitled *Mathematical Fundamentals* from the bookshelves."

The man did as requested and returned to his place at the table.

Toshi stood just beyond the doorway and gazed briefly at the progress of the two new furnaces across the way.

By coincidence, he had paused just outside the director's window, and curious about how the view looked from outside looking in, watched as the director thumbed through a large, bound book, and when he found the page he was looking for, compared something written there to what appeared to be the paper where Toshi had written down the value of *pi*, to ten significant digits.

During his short walk back to the foundry, Toshi replayed the entire encounter over in his mind, trying to make sense of it. *At least he didn't sack me,* he thought to himself. Although he kept coming back to one word the director had used, "You *might* be happy to know…" he had said, when talking about how efficient the new furnaces would be. Did that mean Toshi might not be there to see them in operation? Or was it just a figure of speech used by the foreigner?

Haruki was relieved to see him return, and the men gathered around to hear what Toshi had to say about his meeting. He tried to relay everything just as it had happened, but he was still beside himself with worry and not sure he had represented the meeting accurately. The men seemed particularly interested in the woman who served the coffee.

"How old do you think she was?" one of the men asked.

"Do you think she lives with him?" another added.

"I think I'd like to have the director's job," another man said.

Toshi hurried home after work that day to share his strange experience with Ayami. And most of all, to wrap his arms around her and simply hold her, until Kiyoshi protested at their feet. He wanted in on the hug. Toshi and Ayami got on their knees to be at his level, and the three of them hugged and laughed until Ayami broke away to prepare a meal for all of them.

After Kiyoshi was put in bed for the night, Toshi sat down beside her. "What if I lose my job?" he asked. "What if the director sacks me for asking about the charcoal? Would you be willing to move to Tokyo? I could probably go back to work at the furniture factory."

"Didn't you hate that job when you were there?"

"Yes, but I could get used to it. It probably wasn't as bad as I thought, and now I have a better idea what to expect."

"I could learn to be happy in Tokyo," she said. "But I'm not as sure about you. I don't think you would be happy there."

Chapter 18

Fr. Henri Lispard

OCTOBER 1879 – ON TRAIL TO THE FOUNDRY

It had been more than three weeks since Toshi met with the foundry director, and he had heard nothing since, about the meeting or even the reason for it. As each day passed, he began to shed another layer of anxiety that he was about to lose his job because of the 'charcoal fiasco,' as he now referred to it.

On this particular morning as he left home headed for the foundry, he once again replayed the conversations he had had with the director. *I wonder why he asked about the value of pi.* What a strange question to ask of a foundry worker. *Maybe he was testing to see if I really studied math or whether I was smart enough to learn about charcoal.*

As he pondered those events, he thought he heard a voice call out. He stopped to listen. *Did someone call me?* he wondered. *I thought I heard someone.*

The voice called out a second time. "Good morning."

Toshi looked to the trail ahead where he thought the voice was coming from. Staying in the shadows himself, he strained as he searched the trail. It was early morning and the sun was just beginning to quell the darkness of the night. He raised his hands to shield his face and stared into the distance. Standing in the middle of the trail a hundred meters away, he spotted a figure. He was dressed in black and blended with the shadows of the forest. For a moment, Toshi was alarmed.

"Good morning," the voice said a third time. It was a gentle voice and contained no hint of foul intent. But it came from a tall, dark figure, seemingly dressed to camouflage its owner among the familiar pines and other forest flora. "I am sorry to interrupt you on this beautiful morning," it continued, "but I wonder if you could guide me to the family of Hideji Abe. I was told he lives just off the trail between the village and the foundry."

"I do know of the family," Toshi replied timidly. "What is your business with them, if I may ask?"

"Thank you, kind sir. Their young child has been quite ill, and they sent for me, to offer prayers. I am Fr. Henri Lispard, a priest of the Jesuit Order. The authorities have been kind enough to allow me to share the teachings of our faith with the people on your magnificent island."

"I'm sorry to hear of their illness. Have they called for the physician?"

"Yes, the physician has been with them several times. They fear the girl may not live, and that is why they sent for me."

"I'm on my way to work at the foundry. I pass by the lane to their house and I can show you where it is. I hope the child recovers. I have a small boy of my own, and I can only imagine the agony they must be going through."

"Thank you for guiding me. It is most kind of you."

They walked together in silence for several paces. Then Fr. Lispard chuckled to himself before he turned to Toshi and said, "Most of the time, I'm the one called upon to guide others. Today, it is *you* who are guiding *me*. I think it's a reminder from God about who is really in charge."

There was something soothing in the way the priest spoke his words. Or maybe it was simply the timbre of his voice, or even the state of mind Toshi was in, as he pondered his job at the foundry. But he found himself immediately liking this stranger who had asked for help.

They continued to walk in silence for some distance as Toshi collected his thoughts.

"Fr. Lispard, I have not studied your beliefs or your God, but I admit that on two occasions I have called out to him, in case he was really there. The first was when Ayami, my wife, was having our child and we were alone, and I was certain she was about to die in my arms. The second time was not long ago, when I was summoned to see the director of the foundry, and I was afraid I was going to lose my job. Did your God answer my prayers? Does he hear those who are not of your faith? Or does he only listen to those like yourself?"

"May I ask your name, my son?"

"My name is Toshi… Toshi Ozawa. I live with my wife, Ayami, and our young son, Kiyoshi, at the end of the trail, above the bay."

"It is good to meet you, Toshi Ozawa. And I'm glad to hear that both your wife and your son survived his birth. Apparently, you still have your job at the foundry as well. But Toshi, here I am, awake less than one hour, and already you have challenged me with the most difficult question in the universe: 'Does God answer our prayers?'

"The truthful answer, Toshi, is that I don't know. But this much, I do know. First of all, He is not *my* God. For thousands of years, scholars far smarter than me have studied civilizations, cultures, and documents, as well as stories handed down through generations, and they have determined there is really only one God in all the universe. By definition, then, that one God belongs to all of us. Or, I should say, we all belong to Him. So, you have as much right to call on Him as I do, or any of the millions of followers of my faith.

"Then the question becomes not so much did God hear your plea, but did He answer it? This is the part I cannot answer. I would like to say that he did. In fact, I am pretty sure he did, although I don't really know the circumstance of your pleas. Another thing I'm certain of, is that there is no legitimate prayer he cannot answer. I have been a priest for more than twenty years, and during that time I have seen many reasonable prayers be answered and many others that were not. At least not answered in the manner I expected. Perhaps they were answered in a more appropriate way, or not as expedient as I had hoped. It is also likely that some of the prayers that I thought were perfectly well-founded, were not justified in the eyes of God.

"So, Toshi, as much as I would like to give you an absolute answer, you can see I'm not able to do that. Only God himself knows your answer. I would go out on a limb, however, and suggest that if you have turned to *OUR* God twice, and you have received the result you hoped for the same number of times, it is probably worth your while to remember Him in the future.

"But it might be even more important to think of Him at times when you are not in peril… when everything is going just the way you want. That's the perfect time to offer a simple 'thank you' for all the gifts in your life. For example, on your walk to work today you could thank him for your job at the foundry. And tonight when you get home, you could thank Him for the gift of your wife and child who wait there for you."

They walked on in silence. "Are we getting close to the Abe household yet?"

"Oh, I almost forgot. I was so interested in what you were telling me. Yes, we're getting close. The path leading to their house is coming up on the right. It will lead about two hundred meters until you see their house. I hope their little one is going to be okay. Do you think *OUR* God will hear your prayer? It seems to me it would be a legitimate plea."

"I just told you the answer to that question, Toshi," replied Fr. Lispard with a smile across his face. "But I will let you know the next time I see you. Please feel welcome to visit our church in the village any time. I would love to meet Ayami and your child."

***

"Ayami, you'll never guess who I met on the way to work this morning. It was the Catholic priest from the village. I was thinking about work like I usually do when I heard a voice call out to me from the trail up ahead. At first, I didn't hear him, or at least I didn't know it was someone calling me. Then he called again, and I could barely make out a person, but I couldn't tell who it was.

"Anyway, it turns out he was looking for Hideji's house. Their daughter must be very sick, and he was on his way there to offer prayers. We walked together as far as the turn-off to their house. Along the way, I told him how I had called out to his God when you were giving birth to Kiyoshi, and again the day I had to meet with the director. I asked him if he thought his God had answered my prayers. I expected him to say, 'Why yes, of course he did,' but he didn't say that. Do you know what he said?"

"No. What did he say?"

"He said he had only been awake for an hour, and already I'd asked him the most difficult question in the universe. Can you imagine that? I didn't know I was smart enough to ask the most difficult question in the whole universe. Then he said he honestly didn't know if God had answered me or whether it was just a coincidence. But he went on to say that two separate coincidences in a row made for a good argument, in his mind."

"Then he did think your prayers worked?"

"He said that over the many years he's been a priest, he has witnessed times that prayers were answered as well as prayers that were not, and he didn't always understand why that would be. But then he said one thing really important is to thank God for everything we enjoy and not just call on him when we need something. Oh, and he said as far as he's concerned, God belongs to all of us, so it's fine to call on Him whether we belong to his church or not.

"There was something about him that I liked. He was easy to talk to. I hadn't intended to ask him those questions at all, but they just popped out as we walked along. Wasn't it some coincidence that we met on my way to work, right out of nowhere?"

Ayami thought about his question for a while and then she smiled at him. "Didn't you say he called out to you from the trail?"

"Yes, he was up ahead, in the shadow of the forest when he called out to me."

"Does that seem like a coincidence?" She asked.

Toshi looked at her blankly for several moments. Then he smiled at her.

"Maybe not," he replied. "He invited us to visit his church sometime. Do you think we should go?"

"Would he pressure us to join if we only went to look?"

"I don't think so," Toshi replied. "He didn't put any pressure on me during our walk. There was just something about him that made me feel comfortable. Maybe it was his voice. He also had a kind face. It could have been that, too."

Chapter 19
Letters to Tokyo

KAMAISHI - 1879

November 1879

Dear Father and Mother,

Ayami and I have exciting news to share. We are expecting our second child in the spring of next year. So far, Ayami is feeling well and has not experienced the sickness as she did with Kiyoshi. You may be sure we will ask Minako or one of the girls to come and stay with us before the birth.

Kiyoshi is growing so fast we can hardly believe it. He has learned to walk, and he talks to us all the time. We can usually guess what he is trying to say. He will be almost two years old when the new baby arrives.

I am reluctant to admit that I made a mistake at the foundry by questioning whether we had enough charcoal to keep the furnace running. It seems to have angered someone high up at the foundry, and I was called in to meet with the director. I have a continuing feeling that something is not right and that I might eventually be asked to leave.

Ayami has agreed that we could move back to Tokyo, if necessary. Is it too late for me to come to work at the factory if my job at the foundry goes away?

A few weeks ago, I unexpectedly met a Catholic missionary who lives in the village. We were walking along the trail toward the foundry, and we talked about God, who he claimed belongs to everyone, not just

members of his church. We are planning to visit his church when we have the time.
Hoping you are well,

Toshi, Ayami, and Kiyoshi (and the new baby, too)

Several weeks later, the reply arrived. Ayami held up the letter as he approached from work. "I can't wait to hear their news," she said. "And I hope they are excited by our news of a new baby. Do you think they'll come to visit us?"

"I hope so," Toshi replied. "Let's open it right now and see what they said."

December 1879

Dear Toshi and Ayami,

Thank you for letting us know about the upcoming birth of a new baby. We are happy and excited for you. Write to us as soon as it is born so we know you are well.

We are disappointed to hear of your troubles at the foundry. Toshi, you must remember that you are not in charge of the foundry. You are merely a worker. You should never overstep your authority. Think about the lessons that Kotaro tried to teach you at the factory. Remember that our culture was founded on duty, honor, and discipline. From now on, you must make every effort to perform your assigned tasks to perfection and not question the responsibilities of others.

Kotaro hired a new assistant after you left, so there is nothing available for you at the factory.

Regarding the missionary, your mother and I agree it would be a mistake to affiliate with the Catholic religion. There are a few such followers here in Tokyo, and they have not been well received by the more solid families. From what we have heard, their ceremonies are carried out in a foreign language. Latin, I think it is. Many people think they are mostly after money to build more churches, in an effort to take over our country. Our Shinto teachings have provided moral guidance for generations. They will continue to do so for many more.

Your father,
Isao

Toshi stared at the letter in silence.

Ayami looked at his face, searching for a reaction.

Slowly his arms lowered to his lap and came to rest, still holding the letter.

Ayami wondered if he was reading it again. She watched his eyes. They didn't seem to be reading the words. Instead, they seemed to be meditating, trying to digest what they had already read. She remained quiet and glanced out the window, almost hoping to find an answer in the open sky beyond.

Even tiny Kiyoshi sensed something out of place. Only moments before, his favorite person in the world was laughing and jostling with him as he always did. Now he sat silent and still.

Eventually, Toshi turned to Ayami and asked. "Do you think it was wrong to ask about the charcoal?"

She thought for a minute before responding. "No, Toshi. I don't think it was wrong. If the foundry runs out of charcoal, wouldn't it have to shut down? Think of all the people who would be out of work. If you had reason to think the supply was in jeopardy, I think you were right to question it. And Haruki must have thought so too, or he would not have taken it to his supervisor."

"Do you think I was wrong to ask Fr. Lispard my questions about God?"

Again, Ayami paused as she formulated her thoughts. "No, I don't think it was wrong to ask for his opinion. After all, isn't that what the emperor wants us to do? Isn't this supposed to be a new period of enlightenment? I think enlightenment means being curious enough to search for different points of view. And that is what you did. You asked an outsider what he thought about a higher power for our world. Look at the foundry. Didn't they bring in a director from outside Japan, in hopes of learning better techniques?"

Toshi sat quietly, still holding the letter in his lap. Ayami watched the skin on his cheeks and the muscles in his throat tighten as he swallowed.

Kiyoshi shifted his gaze back and forth between his father and mother, as if asking how he could help. Ayami forced a smile, trying to convince him everything was okay, even though she knew it wasn't. Then she reached down and put her arms around his shoulders and drew him close.

Eventually, Toshi looked over at Ayami and Kiyoshi. Their two meek smiles reflected back at him until he could no longer help himself. His muscles relaxed, and the mist that had been forming in his eyes began to dry. He blinked twice and reached over to Kiyoshi in a playful stroke, and tickled his tummy until he heard the sound of laughter. "I'm hungry," he announced. "Who else in this room is hungry?"

Kiyoshi knew those words by heart, and by now was able to respond in his still limited vocabulary. "Hungry. Hungry," he said through his giggles.

That night, as they lay together on their mat, each remembering the unexpected response by Isao, Toshi spoke up through the darkness. "Ayami, sometimes you remind me of your uncle."

"Really? Why is that? We're not really related, you know. Except through marriage."

"I know. But you are both so smart. You always seem to understand what is most important. I don't know what I would do without you."

"I'm glad, Toshi, because I love you too. No matter what happens."

Chapter 20

Charcoal Delays

It was a crisp December morning when Toshi stoked the coals in their kitchen stove, added three logs, then took an admiring look at Ayami and Kiyoshi as they lay sleeping on their mats. Grabbing a warm coat from its peg on the wall, he slipped through the door and closed it gently as he headed up the trail to work.

Approaching the foundry, something seemed off. He realized what it was only when he saw the charcoal cart approaching from his left, the direction of the warehouse. Usually, it would have been there and gone by now. The staging bin was empty, other than a few remnants left over from the day before.

"Good morning!" Toshi yelled across to the cart driver.

"Good morning," came the reply. "Sorry to be late this morning. It took longer than normal to get the cart loaded."

"I'm glad you made it," Toshi responded. "We won't be starting the furnace for another hour. I'll let Haruki know. Then I'll come back and help you unload."

Toshi found Haruki inspecting the furnace as he did each morning, looking for cracks or leaks, or any other thing that might cause a problem for the daily smelt. He had already shoveled in a few scoops of charcoal from the bin in order to bring the smoldering coals back to life for another run. He knew from the near-empty bin that today's delivery had not yet arrived.

"Good morning," he said. "The delivery man is here, so I'm going to help him unload."

The two men worked in silence to offload the charcoal into the staging bin, located far enough from the furnace to keep it safe from the heat and wayward sparks.

"Do you think you'll be late again tomorrow? I'll get here early to help unload if you think you'll be late."

The cart driver hesitated before giving his answer. Toshi wondered if the man heard him and was about to repeat his question when the answer came. "I can't be sure one way or the other," he finally said. "The kilns where we make the charcoal are either not large enough, or it could be the wood hasn't cured enough. But lately, it's been a struggle. Some days a kiln produces more than other days, which must have something to do with the wood we're using. We've tried using wood from different parts of the forest, but so far we haven't been able to fix the problem."

Toshi's body tightened as he listened to the explanation, but he tried not to show his concern. After a few moments he replied. "I'll come early just in case."

The alarm bells were ringing in his head as he watched the delivery man disappear behind the foundry and back toward the charcoal barn. *It's obvious we're running out of charcoal,* he thought. *I need to let Haruki know right away. He'll know what to do.* He turned and headed toward the furnace where he'd left Haruki performing maintenance. He had taken only a few steps when the words from his father's letter came back to him. "Toshi, you... are not in charge of the foundry... you must perform your assigned tasks... and not question the responsibilities of others."

Luckily, he remembered his father's advice before approaching Haruki and once again crying 'wolf' because of the charcoal. He remembered the eerily distressing meeting with the director that followed the first time.

For five minutes or maybe longer, Toshi stood outside the furnace chamber and debated with himself. Should he alert Haruki that the foundry was surely running out of fuel? Or should he listen to his father and concentrate on doing his own job the best that he could.

***

Ayami knew as soon as she saw him coming down the trail at the end of the day. She picked Kiyoshi up in her arms, and together they hurried out to meet him.

"What's wrong?" she said, even without 'Hello.' "Did something happen at work today? You look worried."

"We are running out of charcoal; I'm almost sure of it," he replied. "The delivery was late today, and the man who brought it said they're having trouble keeping up."

"What did Haruki say? Does he think they'll find a solution? Everybody knows that without charcoal, the foundry would have to shut down."

"I didn't tell him."

Ayami stood silent. She knew Toshi well enough to know there was a reason for everything he did. Or didn't do.

"Was it because of your father's letter?"

Toshi nodded.

By now, Kiyoshi could contain himself no longer and was frantically reaching out, trying to transfer his young body over to the strong and loving shoulders of his father. Toshi could not resist his son. He pulled him close and ruffled his thick black hair. They laughed and frolicked together until it was time for bed.

The next morning, just as promised, he arrived at the foundry early, waiting to help unload the daily shipment of charcoal in case it was running late. He tried to avoid seeing Haruki so as not to raise suspicion. Much to his surprise, and even more to his relief, the charcoal bin was already filled. The delivery man had come and gone, just like always. *It's a good thing I didn't say anything to Haruki yesterday,* he thought, *it would have been another false alarm. I don't even want to think what the director would say about that.*

When Toshi came down the path that night, Ayami let go of Kiyoshi's hand and let him run out to meet his father well before he reached the door.

"Did they solve the problem today? You're obviously much happier tonight."

"The delivery was on time today, and the man was already gone when I got there. So they must have straightened out whatever the problem was."

"Do you think it's permanent? Or is it just postponing the inevitable?"

"I wish I knew. It's hard to believe they could solve the problem overnight. Maybe they're bringing it in from another location. But I'm glad I didn't send another false alarm to Haruki yesterday. I would almost certainly get sacked after a second time."

"Toshi, I know you. I've come to know your mind. Everything about you is based on logic. Most people are blind to what seems obvious to you. If you think the foundry is running out of charcoal, then it is probably running out of charcoal. If you get sacked for saying that, Kiyoshi and I will not love you any less than we already do. We may even love you more, for being truthful to yourself. If you are torn between what you believe and what your father believes, I think you will sleep better at night if you act on what you believe."

Then she looked at his bewildered face with her almond-colored eyes, smiled the smile she seemed to save only for him, and turned to enter the house. "I'll fix you something special to eat while you watch over your son. He's been waiting all day for you to get home from work. Maybe you can wear him out so he'll go to bed early."

***

Eager to get to work, Toshi left home early and hurried along the trail. When he drew close enough, he could not stop himself from looking over at the charcoal bin. After yesterday, he expected to see it filled with charcoal and the delivery wagon long since departed. But today there was no charcoal lapping over the sides. He walked over for a closer look. In spite of his newfound confidence and detached opinion regarding the foundry, his heart skipped a beat.

Now Toshi had three voices to consider: his own, his father's, and Ayami's. Luckily, it was only moments until he heard the wagon approaching from behind the foundry. He watched as it rounded the corner and backed up to the bin.

"Good morning!" Toshi shouted with relief. "I can help unload if you like."

"Good morning to you, as well. That would be appreciated. Thank you."

Together, they offloaded the charcoal into the storage bin. Neither man spoke as they rushed to empty the cart. When they finished, the delivery man said, "Sorry again, for the delay. The wood we're using seems to take longer to process. I don't know if it's coming from somewhere new, or if it is just too wet, or what the problem is. I'm sorry if it is causing a problem for the furnace."

"It's not your fault. Thank you for letting me know. You are doing a good job of bringing it to us as soon as you can."

When the delivery man slowly rounded the corner on his return to the warehouse, Toshi knew what he had to do. He found Haruki in his makeshift office next to the furnace.

"I'm sorry to interrupt, but I'm pretty sure we have a problem with the charcoal," Toshi began. "The delivery man just left. This was the second time this week he was late. He told me they have trouble keeping up. He didn't know if it was because of the wood they're using or what the problem was, but I'm pretty sure it's not going to go away. That's what really concerns me. If we can't keep up for one furnace, how will we ever keep up for two? The director says they will be more efficient, but I don't see how they can be that much better. The new steam-powered air supply might well increase the heat and reduce the smelt time, but I don't understand why it would reduce the amount of charcoal needed."

***

Walking home after work that day, Toshi saw Hideji coming up the trail toward him.

"Good afternoon. I haven't seen you for a while."

"Nor I, you. How have you been? Are you keeping the foundry running properly these days? I would hate to have any iron pigs running loose through the forest."

Toshi laughed at the joke. The iron produced from the smelt was sometimes referred to as 'pig iron' because some of the molds were shaped like a pig lying on its side. "We lost two last week, so if you find them in your garden, be sure to feed them some carrots or potatoes to fatten them up. Are you headed down to the wharf for a night's work?"

Hideji nodded and fell in step with Toshi. After they'd walked a few meters, Toshi found an opening.

"Not long ago, on my way to work, I met a stranger who told me his name was Fr. Lispard. Do you know of him?"

"Fr. Lispard? Oh yes, I know him well. A true servant of God, if you ask me. He came to visit when our Nori fell ill. We joined his church about two years ago, and it has brought us great peace."

"Oh, your daughter was ill?" He started to say… *'I didn't know that,'* but stopped himself in time. There was nothing to be gained by telling a lie.

"Yes, she was very sick. We thought she was going to die. It came on suddenly, and even the physician wasn't sure what was wrong with her. We asked Fr. Lispard to come and offer prayers, which he did. Two days later, Nori was fine. You can't tell me God doesn't hear our prayers. Fr. Henri was slow to take credit for the recovery. He said Nori might have recovered anyway, but I know better. Without the prayers, our Nori would be gone from us."

"I'm glad to know she recovered. One of the things I liked about the man was his honesty. I asked him if he thought God had answered two of my prayers, and he said he couldn't be sure, but he thought so. Then he told me to thank God for the things I already have. He thinks by doing that, God will be more likely to listen when I ask for something new. What do you think?"

"I'm sure of it, Toshi."

Toshi thought about it as they continued to walk. He was glad he bumped into Hideji today. Maybe this was not a coincidence either, as with Fr. Lispard that day.

"How is the foundry business, Toshi? Are you making lots of iron?"

"Yes, we're planning to start two new furnaces in the spring. If all goes well, they will produce three times as much iron as we do today. But sometimes I worry about getting enough charcoal to run them. It takes a lot of wood to provide that much heat. How about you? Is the fish market good? Are you catching a lot of fish?"

"Fishing has been good. We've been able to sell everything we catch, and usually at a fair price. It's hard work, and the worst part is being gone all night. But that's how we get out to deep water in time for a pre-dawn catch. We're home again by mid-morning, but it does cause us to be away from our families overnight. I sometimes go out every other night to give myself time at home. Life is not all about making money, you know."

"I like that idea, Hideji. Maybe I'll join you one day. Do you think I could learn to fish?"

"I could show you, if you like. It's not really difficult. It's mostly being willing to concentrate on the task. You do have to be careful with the nets and pay attention to the waves, and so on. A lot of the time you might be bored, like when you're heading out, or back to shore, but you always have to stay vigilant, or you could find yourself in trouble. I suppose it's a lot like your work at the foundry in that regard."

"I suppose it is," replied Toshi.

The sign just ahead pointed toward the village.

"This is where I get off," laughed Hideji. "Thanks for letting me ride along. I've enjoyed our visit. And let me know when you're ready to become a fisherman."

"Thank you, Hideji. I will."

Chapter 21

Two Week Vacation

KAMAISHI - DECEMBER 1879 – THE FOUNDRY

It was Friday morning, about nine o'clock, when a man cautiously entered the furnace chamber. At first, Toshi didn't notice because the man stayed as far from the noisy furnace as possible. Eventually, he looked up and saw him, wearing Western-style pants. It was the interpreter from the director's office.

"May we help you with something?" Toshi asked.

"I'm looking for Haruki Yamamoto. I have an important letter from the director."

"Come with me. Haruki is checking his reports for today's smelt," Toshi replied, and led him to the small chamber on the other side of the blasting furnace.

"Excuse me, Haruki-san. You have a message from the director's office." He turned to the visitor and announced, "This is Haruki-san." Then he bowed respectfully and left the chamber.

"The director has asked me to bring this message. He said to tell you it is extremely important and that you are to make sure all your workers are made aware of it today." With that, he also bowed lightly, and quickly found his way out of the chamber and away from the foundry.

Haruki opened the letter, wondering what could possibly be so urgent that everyone must be made aware of it today. When he opened it, he found the reason why.

IMPORTANT OFFICIAL ANNOUNCEMENT

In honor of the Emperor's birthday, old furnace number one will be shutting down at the end of normal operations today. It will remain closed until Monday, January fifth.

This declaration includes all workers who currently report for duty at furnace number one. All other workers will continue their normal schedule. That includes all charcoal and mining operations as well as construction workers for new furnace numbers one and two.

As a gesture of goodwill to the workers of old furnace number one, in the spirit of the Christian holiday of Christmas, workers will be compensated at one-half their normal wage during the period of the shutdown, in honor of the emperor.

Haruki walked out of his small chamber and into the furnace room. It was not hard to see the looks of curiosity reflected in the workers' faces. They were not very good at hiding their concern. Several were watching him with their backs to the roaring furnace, always a risky behavior. He needed to tell them right away.

"As you know, we had a visitor from the director's office," he began. "I received an announcement that I will read to you now." He then read the document just as it was written. "We will begin the shutdown at three o'clock. After that, I will answer any questions you might have. Until then, I'm asking you to stay vigilant. I don't want any accidents because someone was not paying attention to their work."

"What the…" one of the men muttered, almost under his breath.

"Two weeks?" another said, a bit louder.

The men who had been watching from near the furnace apparently heeded his plea to stay vigilant, and turned back to their work.

When three o'clock rolled around, the molds were complete and the furnace had started its cool-down. The workers milled around in small groups talking about the announcement among themselves until Haruki entered the room. Without the roar of the furnace, everyone could hear the questions.

"We've never shut down for the emperor's birthday before. Why are we doing it now?" was the first one, from Kenshin Maeda.

"I don't know," Haruki answered truthfully. "I was as surprised as you."

"How come it is just the furnace that is shutting down and not the charcoal kiln?" asked Kao Wada.

Haruki tried not to flinch. "That is a good question, Kao, but again, I don't know the answer. All I know is what the announcement said."

There was silence from the group until Shichiro Sugawara spoke up with the question others were afraid to ask. "How are we supposed to survive on half-pay for two weeks? Our living expenses don't drop by half just because the foundry is shutting down." Several heads nodded in agreement.

"I realize this will cause a hardship for some of you," Haruki replied. "Especially, coming without warning as it did. All I can say is, come and see me before you borrow money from a lender in the village. If they learn the foundry is closing for two weeks, they might try to take advantage of you."

"Why are we celebrating a Christian holiday?" Fumiya asked with a puzzled look on his face.

Finally, a question Haruki felt prepared to answer. "I can only assume it's because the director is from Germany, and probably Christian. It could be that he wants to travel home for the holiday," he said. Hoping they had covered the most burning issues, he ended the meeting. "Enjoy your time off. I will see you on January fifth."

It was not until Haruki walked home with Toshi that Toshi confirmed what Haruki had himself concluded. "This is all about a shortage of charcoal, isn't it?" he asked.

"That's what it looks like to me," Haruki replied. "Did any of the other workers mention that?"

"No. I was surprised, but I didn't hear anyone talk about it. Maybe they were thinking it and just didn't want me to hear them say anything. Are you worried about the new furnaces running short?"

"The director seems to think they will be okay," Haruki responded, "but I don't see how he can think that. From our experience on this furnace, it seemed that on days when the stream was running faster and we had more forced air, it burned hotter and used more charcoal. But it's possible the furnace design itself will provide more heat with less fuel. We can hope so, at least."

They walked on in silence.

"I don't know what to tell Ayami," Toshi confessed. "She already worries about the charcoal. What if the foundry shuts down for good?"

"I wish I knew," Haruki replied. "Surely they would not be building new furnaces if they thought we might run short of charcoal—that's what I tell myself."

Toshi thought about it. "That wouldn't make any sense, would it? You are probably right."

They walked another distance, and then Toshi spoke again.

"But I can't help seeing what seems to be staring us in the face."

***

Ayami was in the kitchen and did not see Toshi open the door, but Kiyoshi, who was trying to stack several wooden blocks into a tower, suddenly burst out with a garbled greeting and rose from the floor to hug his father's legs as he entered the room.

"Toshi, what are you doing home so early? I wasn't expecting you for another hour. Is everything all right? Did something happen?"

"I'm fine," he said. "The foundry closed early today in honor of the emperor's birthday."

She thought for a few moments before replying. "But *Tenchō-setsu* is not until December twenty-third. That's almost two weeks away. Why would they close early today?"

"That's what a lot of us were wondering. But the rest of it is that the foundry will be closed for two weeks, which includes the holiday. We don't go back to work until the fifth of January."

She stopped moving and stared into Toshi's face. "You won't be working for two weeks? Can we afford that?"

"The director said in a spirit of the Christian holy day of Christmas, the foundry will pay us half our usual wage, even while the foundry is closed, so we should be okay. I've never heard of such a thing, and most of us are not sure what to make of it."

"Why don't I make some tea for us and a snack for Kiyoshi? Then we can all sit down while you tell me everything that happened."

When the tea was ready, Kiyoshi mostly played with his rice crackers while Toshi told her about the memo, word for word, as best he could remember it.

"This is all about charcoal, isn't it?" she asked when he finished. "The foundry is running out of fuel, just like you thought."

"I'm afraid that's the real reason," he replied. "What if they have to close down the foundry completely? I'm worried the foundry might fail, and I won't be able to take care of you and Kiyoshi, and now a new baby besides. And after that letter from my father, I can't go back to Tokyo. And what if we're not able to send your father the money for taxes? It's not only our family in trouble, but your family as well. "You should never have married me, Ayami.""

Chapter 22

An Omen

The next morning Toshi was up early. His eyes were red from a restless night. Several times Ayami had to move his arm from her face or shoulder as he fought against an unknown foe in the deep recess of his mind. He could only remember parts of the dream, but they were enough to remind him what it was about.

In the dream, Toshi was the boss of a large factory, and although he never did see what kind of factory it was, it needed charcoal in order to run. In one corner of the factory was the largest mound of charcoal Toshi had ever seen. Fifty, maybe even a hundred workers ran from the mound to a small furnace at the opposite corner of the factory, carrying one lump of charcoal at a time.

Back and forth they ran throughout the day, each man carrying one small brick of charcoal to the furnace and then back to the mound for another. As boss of the factory, Toshi could see how inefficient the process was, and he set out almost at a run himself, to tell the workers to carry two bricks at a time, not just one. It seemed so obvious to anyone who watched the workers.

But Toshi could never quite reach the men. In his dream, he ran toward them, shouting as he got close, but the workers never heard his shouts or saw him running. The most frustrating part of all was that Toshi never got any closer, even though he kept running and running. The workers carrying the charcoal were always too far away to see him.

Then, near the end of the dream, he noticed one of the workers stop to light a cigarette. "You can't smoke here!" Toshi yelled at the man. But just as the men carrying the bricks could not hear, neither could the man smoking the cigarette. Toshi watched in dismay as the man took a long last puff from the cigarette and tossed what remained of it toward the mound of charcoal.

Toshi ran toward the mound. He had to retrieve the cigarette before it ignited the mound. But like before, no matter how much he ran, he never got closer to his destination. Finally, just as he knew it would, the mound began to smolder, a small wisp of smoke at first, then larger. A few minutes later it became a bright red glow, and then a flame, as the charcoal mound ignited.

He watched helplessly from a distance as the entire mountain went up in flames. It was odd, he thought to himself, that nothing around the factory caught fire, not even things that normally should. Only the mound was affected.

That was all he could remember.

Standing at his kitchen window and watching the sun peek up from the Pacific, the dream seemed only what it was—a dream. But last night, during the dream, it felt so real he could feel the sweat on his skin and the burn in his lungs from running so hard.

The meaning was easy for Toshi to grasp. He was concerned about the foundry and about having enough charcoal to keep it running. But how to prevent it was nowhere in the dream. In fact, even in the dream he was not able to warn the men, and that made the whole affair even more troubling.

Realizing he had probably disturbed Ayami's sleep by thrashing against her for much of the night, he wanted to make it up to her by quietly fixing a pot of tea and leaving her to sleep in peace for an extra hour. With Kiyoshi still sound asleep, he pulled on a jacket and went outside to watch the sunrise. He needed time to think.

An hour later, when he heard Kiyoshi calling for his mother, he rushed into the house to care for his son. He lifted him up in his arms, and when he did, something else happened. He forgot every worry that filled his mind.

"Are you hungry?" Toshi asked with a grin.

"Hungry," the toddler replied. "Hungry."

It wasn't easy to fix breakfast without making any noise. And probably more difficult because Toshi didn't know where Ayami kept his bowl, or how Kiyoshi liked his rice, or any of the other things that only a mother seemed to know. After opening and closing what must have been every door and drawer in the kitchen, Ayami padded in, rubbing the sleep from her eyes.

She looked at Kiyoshi first, who was nothing but smiles, held in the tender caress of his father. And when she shifted her gaze to Toshi, it was almost like the image of her son smiling timidly back at her.

"What have my two favorite men been up to in my kitchen?" she chided, with a mock frown on her face. "I heard lots of doors opening, but when I look around, I don't see much in the way of breakfast."

"Hungry," Kiyoshi repeated.

"Maybe I should teach your father how to fix breakfast, now that he doesn't have to go to work for two weeks."

Then Toshi's smile took a turn. He had forgotten about the closing as soon as he picked Kiyoshi up from his bed. But now it was real again. The foundry was closed. For two weeks, at least. Maybe for good.

Ayami saw his face tighten and his smile disappear. "Don't worry," she said. "You'll figure out something. You always do. Why don't you two sit down while I make breakfast?"

But the spark was gone. Even little Kiyoshi could not bring a smile back to his father's face. He tried to imitate something his father did that always caused them both to break into laughter, by clumsily reaching out to his father's tummy and scratching it. Today, it brought barely a smile.

He lifted his arms toward his father with his biggest smile, which normally would get him a ride off the floor, almost to the ceiling and back. Today, it got him only as far as his father's lap. From there, he was close enough to stretch his head up as far as he could, and kiss Toshi on the cheek. Then he leaned his head close and wrapped an arm around his father's wide back as far as it would reach.

Toshi responded by wrapping an arm around his son and holding him tight. But there was still no laughter on his face. If anything, it seemed more solemn than before.

Toshi stared blankly around the kitchen as Ayami set out their bowls and poured tea into their cups. When she looked over at him and their eyes locked, he blurted out, "Do you think we could go to America?"

"What?" she replied.

"Maybe we could go to America," he repeated. "Maybe this is an omen. It's our chance to go to America."

She answered with questions of her own. "Doesn't it cost a lot of money to get there? Do we have extra money saved? Where would we come up with that much money?"

Toshi heard the questions, but he also saw the skin on her face begin to tighten. Her eyes, usually with a smile of their own, now gazed back at him with a menacing look.

"We could sell the house," he said. "That, and what we have saved should be enough."

"This is because you think the foundry is going to close, right?"

"Yes," he replied. "That's what I'm afraid of."

"If the foundry closes, how many people do you think could afford to buy our house? Isn't it possible that a few others might need to sell their houses too, if the foundry closes? And wouldn't that make it even harder to sell ours?"

Toshi had already considered those questions, and she was right.

"That's why we should sell our house first," he said. "Maybe we could sell it before the foundry closes."

From the look on Ayami's face, Toshi realized his mistake.

Somehow, she kept her voice level when she answered. "Would you be able to live with yourself if you sold our house to someone who didn't know about the foundry?"

Toshi's face turned red before he could answer.

"What if someone from the foundry wanted to buy it? After all, it would be a desirable location for someone working there, just like it was for us. Could you sell it to one of your co-workers, knowing the plant was about to close?"

Toshi's face flushed even more at the thought of deceiving someone he knew. His shoulders slumped, and he turned to avoid her face. Finally, he said, "No, I couldn't do that." He paused and said, "I just don't know what else to do. When I look at you and Kiyoshi, I would do anything to take care of you. You're the only things that matter to me. But without the foundry, how can I support you? Without the foundry, Kamaishi is nothing but a fishing village. There is nothing else here for us. I guess I should have stayed in Tokyo. At least there, they have a lot of different businesses. I should have found a job there, where I could have used my university education."

Toshi expected her face to soften, at least a little, when he confessed the underlying reason for his anxiety. Instead, her face remained as solemn as before.

"Didn't you just say Kiyoshi and I are the two things most important to you?"

Relieved somewhat that she had heard his message, Toshi replied. "Yes, you are the most important things."

"We would not have met if you had stayed in Tokyo," she said flatly.

Toshi's face flushed again.

He looked down at Kiyoshi, still sitting in his lap.

Kiyoshi turned his head from his mother to his father, following the conversation from one mouth to the other as they spoke. His little face reflected the confusion of a dialogue he had not heard before and could not begin to understand.

On seeing his bewildered face, Toshi tightened his hold on his son and pulled him closer with just enough force to show Kiyoshi how much he loved him. Then he leaned down and kissed the top of his head.

But Ayami was not done.

"You just said that Kamaishi, without the foundry, is a fishing village."

Toshi looked at her and said, "Yes, aside from the foundry, that's all there is."

"Didn't you tell me once that Hideji invited you to go out fishing with him?"

"Yes, we met on the trail on his way to work, and he said if I ever wanted to go out with him to let him know."

"Maybe it's time to let him know," she said.

Chapter 23

Toshi Goes Fishing

Two days later, Toshi met Hideji at the junction that led to Kamaishi village and the harbor. Hideji was not sure it was Toshi at first, with all the clothing and bags he carried.

"Are you ready to catch some fish?" Hideji greeted him.

"I think so. I hope I didn't forget anything."

Hideji did not respond.

When they reached the harbor, Toshi followed as Hideji headed for a small dinghy tied at the end of the pier. Two young men stood beside it watching them approach. When they reached the dinghy, Hideji introduced Toshi to Eishun and Fujio. Eishun would ferry them to the boat, and Fujio would be their other crewmate for the night.

They threw their belongings into the dinghy and carefully stepped in as Eishun rowed them out into the bay.

It did not take long to offload their gear into the fishing boat, and Toshi stepped aboard for the very first time. The boat was smaller than he had envisioned; he guessed about seven meters long and two and a half meters wide at the center. It seemed big enough here in the bay, but the thought struck him it might not seem as large thirty kilometers offshore.

When they were settled, Fujio slipped the mooring line, and with a wave and a 'good luck,' Eishun made his way back to the pier to pick up another crew.

Fujio positioned himself on one side while Hideji sat across from him on the other. They each grabbed an oar from alongside their seats and rowed away from the harbor.

"Toshi, watch what I do, and pay attention to how I stay in rhythm with Fujio, so that we both pull on the oar at the same time and speed. When you think you get the picture, let me know and we'll trade places."

It looked easy, and after only five minutes Toshi announced he was ready to take his turn. After fifteen minutes of rowing, Toshi was sweating and his hands were tired, but he did not want to risk losing his grip or throwing off the rhythm, so he kept going. Finally, he dared to ask, "How long do we need to row? Do we row all the way out?"

"No, not all the way," Hideji replied with a chuckle. "We're almost ready to hoist the sail. It varies depending on the waves and the wind. We have to get far enough from shore to catch a steady wind before we raise the sail. You can stow your oar next to the seat so it won't slip overboard, then move to the front of the boat while Fujio and I set the sail."

Once Toshi had moved out of their way, Fujio slipped the lines and hoisted the upper yard by pulling on its lift. As the sail unfurled and began to catch the breeze, Toshi felt the boat initially balk, then twist in protest, then settle into a new rhythm, powering the boat steadily forward. As Hideji adjusted the sail to catch more of the wind and rotate it several degrees around the mast, Toshi forgot everything else in his life for a few glorious minutes, and simply enjoyed the thrill of the wind as it propelled their boat out to sea. Toshi wouldn't care if they caught a single fish that night. Sailing was worth the trip.

With the boat moving eagerly ahead, Hideji positioned himself at the stern and gently maneuvered the long wooden tiller to steer their course. At times, Toshi thought Hideji was not paying attention, he seemed so casual. But occasionally there was a sudden jerk on the sail and Toshi watched him respond with a quick movement of the tiller, either closer to him or away from him, depending on what the wind had done.

Toshi relaxed in the steady rhythm of the boat slipping through the waves, and hardly noticed the sun had moved below the horizon behind them. Darkness was about to overtake the entire ocean. His heartbeat quickened when he realized for the first time, how precarious they were. Fujio lit one of the lanterns on board and hung it from the yardarm above.

As the night wore on, Toshi's stomach became increasingly unsettled. Fujio, seated at the front of the boat, was eating something from his lunch sack, and Toshi wondered if hunger was what ailed his own stomach. He reached for his sack and pulled out one of the rice-noodle pancakes Ayami had made.

A lantern, shining down from the overhead yardarm, gave just enough light for Toshi to see his food. Ayami had outdone herself in preparing a nighttime lunch. *She must have felt guilty for making me come fishing with Hideji,* he thought. Each pancake was carefully made and small enough for Toshi to easily eat with one hand if he was too busy carrying out orders from the captain to use both hands. The rice noodles had been trimmed, and stirred with eggs and scallions using just enough sesame oil to bind them together. The golden-brown color, even in the near dark, caused Toshi's mouth to water. And it tasted even better than it looked.

Half an hour later, Toshi lurched to the side of the boat and emptied his rice-noodle pancake into the sea.

"Welcome to sea life, Toshi," shouted Hideji from his position at the helm. "There's not much we can do for you. Most fishermen get seasick when they first start. But it should go away eventually. Some people say you can convince yourself you don't have it and it will go away, but I don't think you can. Stay near the center of the boat so you don't feel the full travel of the waves. When daylight comes, keep your eyes on the horizon and not on the motion of the boat. We'll be changing direction again soon and maybe that will help."

Toshi was not in a talkative mood. He sat at his assigned station and tried to force himself to feel better. It did seem to help when Hideji altered course, heading into the wind from a different direction. Toshi was glad for the small bit of relief as they continued further out to sea. Now that the nausea had subsided, or at least stabilized, he could concentrate on the cold. His body was shivering and would not stop. He thought back to Hideji's words last Friday: "It will be like spending the night on Mt. Goyo." Toshi had never spent a night on that mountain, but now he had an idea what it must be like. And he was not at all sure fishing could be his new life.

Eventually, Hideji and Fujio moved from their seats and released the line holding the sail aloft. The boat slowed to a halt. The rhythm of the waves subsided, and the boat became surprisingly quiet. His stomach felt better almost as soon as the movement stopped. When he looked around for telltale lanterns, he was surprised to count fifteen other boats nearby.

Fujio retrieved two lanterns from a storage locker under the seats and placed one on the bow and one at the stern. Toshi watched as the other boats did the same. When all had finished, their little patch of ocean glowed enough that small, dark figures could be seen moving about on the boats. In the black of night, kilometers from shore, the ritual reminded Toshi they were not alone. They were members of a silent brotherhood.

Once the lanterns were lit, Hideji and Fujio returned to the storage locker and pulled out a large net. Hideji carefully unfurled it and, with a swirling, sweeping motion, launched it over the side.

Toshi watched as the net slowly sank from sight until he wondered if they had lost the net. Then Fujio began reeling in the line and hauling the net back toward the surface. When it drew close enough, Hideji also grabbed the rope, and together they pulled the net into the boat.

Toshi was overjoyed when he saw several fish flopping in the net. But his joy turned to bewilderment as he watched them retrieve first one fish, then another, and methodically throw them over the side. Toshi mentally counted thirteen fish that went back into the sea. Finally, Fujio picked up one that appeared larger than the others and tossed it up toward the bow, almost at Toshi's feet.

When the entire contents had been sorted, Toshi counted two fish at his feet. He tried to calculate the selling price for two fish.

An hour later it was Toshi's turn. He threw the net, waited, and then reeled in the line. As the net came closer to the boat Toshi was almost afraid to look. When he opened his eyes, the net was flopping at the bottom of the boat. He caught something. But his joy was short-lived as, one by one, Hideji grabbed a fish and threw it overboard. One, two, five, ten fish, over the side. They were too small. Toshi stared hopefully at the last fish in the net. Hideji pulled it out and threw it up to the bow. "You caught one," he beamed. "Congratulations. Your first catch of the night."

Toshi didn't realize he'd been holding his breath until, at last, he was able to let it out in a sigh of relief. He had caught a fish. Even if it was only one, he had proven he could do it. The fish was not very large he noticed, and it was even possible Hideji might have lowered his standard just enough to give Toshi his first small victory.

"Now you know the secret, Toshi. Let's try it again."

When Toshi brought up the net on his second try, it felt different from the start. He could tell right away that it was heavier. "I think this is going to be good!" he exclaimed. He pulled at the drawstring, and as it neared the surface, his hands began to slip. "It must be full!" he exclaimed. "I can barely lift the net."

Fujio leaned over the boat and grabbed hold of the rope. Hand over hand, he helped Toshi retrieve the net. But even before it reached the surface, he cursed just loud enough for Hideji to hear. "Must be sharks," he muttered.

Hearing the word 'sharks,' Toshi stopped pulling on the rope, and his chilled and trembling body suddenly stopped shaking. "What's wrong?" he shouted, trying to keep his voice under control.

"It feels like we've hit a school of sharks," Fujio said. "If we have, they will scare the other fish away."

"What's in the net?" Toshi asked, confused. "The net feels like it's full of fish."

"It is, but they're sharks," Fujio replied.

"The net is full of sharks?" Toshi said, with a voice louder than he wanted.

"Yes, that's what it feels like," Fujio said.

"How do we get them out?" Toshi asked, now even more concerned.

"They're little ones," Fujio said. "They won't bother us if we're careful. But that's the end of fishing for tonight, at least here. We'll see what the other boats do. Maybe we should move somewhere else and try again."

Toshi looked at the fish lying at the bottom of the boat, near the bow. He didn't need to count them; he remembered how many there were. Hideji caught five before turning over the net to Toshi.

Counting the smaller one, the one that Toshi caught but Hideji let him keep, they had six fish.

When the heavy net reached the surface and they opened it up, it was swarming with sharks, just as Fujio had predicted. Their slick gray skins glistened in the dim light of the lanterns, writhing in a frenzy.

Toshi stared down at the net, so filled with angry, squirming sharks that it danced across the flooring of the vessel. He took a step back away from the net and pulled his hands close to his body. "What do we do now?" he yelped.

"If they were bigger, we could keep them, but they're too small to sell at the market. They're only fifteen or twenty millimeters long."

Hideji looked around at the other lanterns. They didn't seem to be moving. "Maybe we're the only boat on top of the school," he said. "Fujio, let's try moving a hundred meters farther out and try again."

This time, when they dropped the net and pulled it up again, only a dozen fish flopped at the bottom. "Keep the little ones, and we'll try the hook line," Hideji said to Fujio. "Maybe we can find something down deep. It looks like the sharks have scared away most of the fish up close."

Fujio pulled the hook line from a locker and carefully baited each of the several hooks, using the smallest fish from the net. Then he held it over the side of the boat and let the rock tied at its end carry the hooks down into the deep. Toshi counted five hooks slowly sinking over the side of the boat, each one with a baited fish. When they were gone from sight, Fujio handed Toshi the heavy string.

"Hang on to this," he said. "When you feel something tugging on it, give it a quick jerk and then start pulling it up. With a little luck, there will be a big fish on one of the hooks. Hideji and I will keep trying with the net."

It was almost dawn and Toshi was hungry, but the cold was his biggest complaint. His toes were numb, and so were his fingers, and it was hard to hang on to the string. He thought again about a night on Mt. Goyo.

After an hour of holding the line, he was so tired and cold that he struggled to keep his eyes open. He was afraid he might fall asleep and let go of the precious line. Not willing to admit his discomfort to Hideji, he turned his body so they couldn't see and tied the end of the line to his overcoat. If he did fall asleep, at least he wouldn't lose the string.

Then, just as his eyes went closed, the line jerked from his grip with such force that he woke himself with his own yelp of surprise. Hideji and Fujio turned in his direction to see what was wrong. When he was still sitting at his station at the bow of the boat, they looked at each other and began to laugh.

"What's the matter, Toshi?" they chimed in together. "Are you afraid of the dark all of a sudden? We thought you fell overboard. Are you okay?"

But Toshi was too busy to answer. Hand-over-hand he pulled, creating a ball of tangled mess at the bottom of the boat. Finally, when the pile was as large as the line was long, he watched expectantly for something from below to tumble over the side and into the boat.

When a big fish reached the surface, Fujio and Hideji both stood and moved closer to help pull it in.

"*Uwa!*" Hideji shouted. "A sea bass... this will make the trip worthwhile. A sea bass that size should bring four or five yen."

He pulled a scoop net from its locker and, holding onto the gunwale with one hand, leaned out, and was just about to scoop the treasure into his net when it spit out the bait, along with the hook, and swam quietly away.

Toshi had completely forgotten the cold and hunger for almost six minutes while he pulled the string from the depths below. Now, with the realization it was all in vain, the cold returned. His stomach growled in search of food, and his hands hurt even more, from pulling on the cold, wet line.

"Let's call it a night," Hideji said, trying not to show his disappointment. "I'm sorry, Toshi. I was hoping to show you a better time than this. Usually, we have better luck. But that is the life of a fisherman. Sometimes we do well, and sometimes we don't."

The temperature had warmed by the time they reached the wharf, but Toshi still shivered from the cold. His teeth chattered as he re-checked the buttons on his several layers of coats.

    D.D. Davenport

"How did you like your first fishing trip?" Hideji asked, as Toshi fastened the last button on the last coat.

Toshi was shaking from the cold. He was hungry and his stomach was still unsettled from the trip. He thought about the sharks and the six fish and the long night in the dark.

"Well," he said, "I guess sailing was my favorite part."

"Most nights are better than this, so don't make a judgement based on a single night. You're welcome to come back with us anytime," Hideji said. Then he added, "It wouldn't be fair to Fujio to pay you the normal wage, which is one-third of the catch, but we'd like for you to take one of the fish. As you said, there aren't many to pick from."

When Toshi was some distance away, Fujio turned to Hideji and said, "With all those clothes on, I hope he doesn't fall down. He won't be able to get up again."

Chapter 24

A Simple Idea

The temperature was just above freezing by the time Toshi headed home from the wharf, but his body still trembled from a long night on the water. A few of those he met walking through the village stared at him longer than he thought necessary, as he passed them by, wearing his five layers of clothing. Flung across his back was the lunch sack with what little remained of its contents, and most importantly, his solitary fish.

When he left home the afternoon before, it was with the expectation of a sack filled with the nightly catch. Catching only one fish was a disappointment. With the memory fresh in his mind of their first real argument a few days earlier, Toshi did not want to disappoint Ayami a second time. He had a yen in one of his pockets, if he could find it. *I'll bring home some fresh rice,* he thought to himself. *Maybe she'll overlook the fish if I bring along some rice.*

It was mid-morning and most of the stalls were open for business. Several shops offered rice for sale, so he could be selective in deciding who had the best quality and price. He stopped at three different stalls but was not satisfied with any of them. The rice seemed old and musty. At one of the shops, he watched bugs crawl near the back of the display. He finally bought from a fourth shop further from the harbor, where quality was better but the price was higher as well.

Ayami and Kiyoshi were watching for him when he came into view along the trail.

"How did it go?" Ayami asked right away. "Was it cold?"

"Yes," he said, "very cold. And I got seasick on the way out. I felt better when we got there and started to fish. We caught a few and then the sharks came."

"Sharks!" she exclaimed. "There were sharks?"

"Little ones," Toshi replied. "It was a school of little ones and they scared all the other fish away. So we didn't catch much after that. Hideji said that's the way of a fisherman—sometimes you do well and sometimes you don't. He said he usually gives his crew a third of the catch, but tonight we didn't catch enough. He had to share most of it with Fujio. He gave me one fish."

She seemed surprised at his response and tried changing the subject. "Did you enjoy it?" She asked.

"The best part was sailing out—until I got seasick. But moving by sail was the best part. You should have been there. The sail takes you right where you want to go; you don't even have to row. And it's quiet. The only sound is the boat gliding through the water. When Kiyoshi gets older maybe Hideji would take him for a ride."

Then Ayami asked the only question that really mattered. "Do you think you could become a fisherman?"

Toshi thought about it. "I think so—but I don't know if we could make a living from it."

She grimaced. "After the baby is born, I could look for a job in the village. Or, I could take in laundry. Some wives do laundry. That way, I could still be here with the children."

"Would you have time for that?" Toshi replied. "Especially with a new baby."

"I'm just saying we might have to adjust if the foundry closes, but somehow, we could manage. We could raise more of our own food and cut down on other expenses."

Then, turning to the small bag of rice, she said, "Where did you get the rice?"

"Since I only brought back one fish, I stopped in the village and bought some rice to go with it."

"That was nice, thank you. I'll make us a nice meal while you get some sleep," she said. "You look like you could fall asleep standing up."

By mid-afternoon, Toshi roused himself and walked in the kitchen. "I'm sure glad I don't have to go out again tonight," he said. "It would be hard to get used to living an upside-down life." He lifted the lid and looked at the bubbling pot of rice.

"I had trouble finding good rice," he said. "I hope it turns out okay."

"Kamaishi has excellent fish, but the rice is disappointing," she replied. "It tastes like barley and it doesn't cook well. I wish we could get rice from my father's farm. The people around here would be amazed at how much better it is."

Toshi moved across the room to play with Kiyoshi and his wooden blocks. The unofficial rules of the game were that he and Kiyoshi would stack his wooden blocks as high as they could without them falling down. Then, just when they were about to add the last block, Kiyoshi would wave his arms in a wide, threatening circle until Toshi got a stern look on his face, then Kiyoshi would lower his small hand as it gathered speed and crashed into the wooden tower, sending blocks flying in every direction. Toshi would respond by pretending to cry with a sullen face and wails of anguish until Kiyoshi erupted in laughter.

After two or three rounds of the game, as Kiyoshi methodically began to build them up again, Toshi looked out to the kitchen, where Ayami was preparing the fish. He stared directly at her, but it was not Ayami that he saw. His gaze was one of concentration, not observation.

In a little while, Toshi's eyes glistened and he exclaimed, "Ayami! You're a genius!" He scrambled to his feet and out to the kitchen. "Do you know what you said?"

She had to think for a minute before replying. "I said Kamaishi has good fish. I didn't really think it took a lot of intelligence, but I'm glad you think so."

"The rice! It's not nearly as good as your rice back home! That's it! If the foundry shuts down, we could bring rice from your father's farm and sell it here."

"I don't think that's a good idea," Ayami replied in a vaguely defensive voice.

"Why not? You just said it is much better rice than what we get here."

"It's not that," she replied. "It's my father. I don't think you should do business with my father. He is not a nice person."

"Surely, he would be nice to us if we were trying to help him," Toshi replied. "It would help him at least as much as it would help us."

"You don't know my father," she said. "Think how he treated me. He made me leave home just because I spoke up to him. And who knows how he is treating Mama and Emiko?"

"If he were mean to them, I'm sure we would have heard about it. Your mother would have written to us."

"Mother never learned to read or write, so she couldn't write, even if she needed to."

"What about Emiko? She was in school when you were there. I'm sure she would be able to write by now. She would let us know if they were in any kind of trouble."

Ayami was quiet. She turned away from Toshi and stared out a window.

"I hope you're right," she said, "but I don't trust him. I'm not sorry he made me leave. I don't miss him. I miss Mama and Emiko—and Shoji. But I don't care if I ever see him again. Or the twins."

"Why don't we go talk to Haruki and Minako about it? Let's see what they think."

That afternoon, Toshi held Kiyoshi as the three of them walked to Haruki's house.

Halfway there, Ayami spoke up.

"How would we get rice from Hanamaki to Kamaishi? Wouldn't that cost a lot that we'd have to add to the selling price? And when we got it here, how would we go about selling it? Wouldn't we have to have a shop in the village?"

"I don't have the answers and that's why we need to talk to Haruki. He always has good ideas about things like this. And he knows a lot of people in the village who might be able to help."

By then, they had reached Haruki's house, and Toshi rapped on the door to announce their unexpected appearance. Saya opened the door and grinned as she reached down to pick up her favorite little boy.

"Come in!" She exclaimed. "Mother, look who's here to see us! It's Kiyoshi—and his parents, of course."

"Toshi has an idea he wants to talk with your father about. Does he have time to spend with us?" Ayami asked Saya, as she hugged her young cousin.

By then, Haruki and Minako had entered the room with Kanae close behind.

"This is a busy place this afternoon," Haruki said. "I've had visits from several of the workers. Some wanted to talk about the shutdown and I'm glad they came to see me. I hope I was able to calm their nerves a little. And a couple of them came to ask my advice about borrowing money, which I was happy to provide."

"Actually, Haruki provided more than just advice," Minako added. "They were concerned about getting by on reduced wages until they're back at work. I felt sorry for them, and I'm glad Haruki was able to help."

"They are both good workers, and one has a large family at home." He neglected to say anything about the other worker. "We loaned them a little money to get by, and although I had to charge interest, it was better for them than if they'd had to borrow from one of the lenders in the village. I'm sure they will perform even better at work until it's paid off. They both seemed grateful. Of course we'll do the same for you, if that's why you're here."

"Thank you, Haruki," Toshi said. "We don't need any money today, at least not at the moment. Maybe we will by the time we leave."

Haruki and his family looked at him with wondering faces.

"Ayami and I have been talking about an idea, and we'd like your advice. We were discussing how the rice here is not as good as what she was used to in Hanamaki. Our idea is to bring rice from there and sell it here."

Haruki looked over at Minako. "What do you think? You're the one who knows about rice."

"I would love to taste Hanamaki rice again. It's been so long since I've had any that I almost forgot what it tastes like."

Turning back to Toshi, he asked, "Have you figured out how to get it here? Do you think you could ship it here and still make a profit?"

"That's what I don't know. Yesterday, I paid seventy sen for a kilo in the village. We might be able to get a yen for better rice, but I don't know how to go about getting it here."

"Kazuo, from the foundry, has a few horses. We might be able to pay him to bring it. I could ask him how many kilos a horse can carry. I should think at least a hundred and fifty. The biggest problem is that there is not much of a road between here and Hanamaki. It would be slow going."

"Do you have any ideas on how to sell it once we got it here?" Toshi asked.

"I suppose we could sell it from our houses if we had to. Once word spread that we had Hanamaki rice, they might come to us. If we had a wagon or something like that, we could park it in the village and sell it from there. The current vendors might not like it, though."

"I went out fishing with Hideji yesterday," Toshi said. "Maybe he would have some ideas."

"Did you have a good trip?" Haruki asked.

"Not exactly. It was cold and we didn't catch many fish. Hideji said that happens sometimes." He decided not to mention the school of baby sharks.

"I wonder if the people in Hanamaki would be interested in some of our ocean fish," Haruki said. "It would make the trip more efficient if we had something to sell going in both directions."

"When I was young," Minako said, "a man came around every so often with a fish wagon. I don't know where he came from or where he caught the fish, but I remember how excited we were when he came around. The rest of the time we mostly had rice, so it was a treat when we got to eat fish for a change. I suppose it's all different now, but I can still remember how excited we were when the fish wagon stopped at our farm."

Haruki looked over at Toshi. "Could you ask Hideji what he thinks? Maybe we could buy his catch, if he has a good night. He might give us a discount if we bought it all. If nothing else, at least the same price as he sells it to the vendors."

Toshi turned to Ayami. "What do you think? Would we be able to sell a load of fish in Hanamaki?"

Ayami looked first at Minako, then back to Toshi. "I suppose it depends on what kind of mood my father is in, and how he is getting along with his neighbors. When I left, it was not so good..."

Toshi watched as her words trailed off.

Ayami led a busy life, with a husband she loved and a son she adored. She had a beautiful house overlooking the bay and friends who cared about her. Hanamaki had become a distant memory and she preferred to keep it there. But sometimes—at times like this, the few good memories seeped back in.

"I suppose we could ask the Sasakis for help," she said. "They're the neighbors who helped me—that day I had to leave."

"I'll stop and talk to Hideji on our way home," Toshi said. "Maybe he could tell us about the fish."

"I'll talk to Kazuo about his horses," Haruki replied.

"We don't have much time to decide," Toshi added. "We need to be back before the foundry starts up again."

Chapter 25

Shots In The Night

Two days later, Toshi arrived at Haruki's, carrying a pack over his back, accompanied by Hideji and a young boy, each carrying a similar pack filled with their catch from the night.

"I talked to Kazuo this morning," Haruki said, "and he'll furnish the horses for us. I told him we hoped to bring back two hundred kilos of rice, and he said it would take two horses to carry that much. I asked him to go with us, since we don't have any experience taking care of the animals. I hope that meets your approval."

Toshi nodded. "A man at the dock said we were lucky to be going in December, when the bears are hibernating. Otherwise, smoked fish would act like bait and bring them running."

"Kazuo has hunted before, and told me he has a new *Chassepot* rifle, which he'll bring along just in case, but I don't think we have anything to worry about from the bears," Haruki replied. "I *am* concerned about the weather, though. Our route will take us west all the way to the source of the Kasshigawa River. The worst part of our trip will be the twenty kilometers from there to Tōno. It's a forested wilderness across high ridges, and the trail will be hard to follow. If we run into snow, we could get stranded. We'll need to carry enough food and water to last several days, just in case. And bring your warmest clothes. It will be cold, even if it doesn't snow."

At the thought of this, Toshi was reminded of his night on the fishing boat. "Will we be crossing Mt. Goyo on the way?" He asked.

"We'll see it on the way by, but no, we won't be going over it," Haruki replied. "Why do you ask?"

"Because Hideji told me a winter night on the boat would be like spending a night on Mt. Goyo," he replied. "And I'd rather not do that again."

Hideji couldn't suppress a chuckle. "I'm glad to know you listen to what I have to say," he said.

"Well," Haruki said, "now starts the first real test. If we don't smoke these properly, the fish will spoil by the time we get to Hanamaki, and we'll have wasted a lot of time and money for nothing. A man at the wharf gave us an old piece of sailcloth. He said it should work as a makeshift tent to smoke them in."

"All you have to do is keep checking on the smoke," Hideji instructed. "Maybe once every hour. Keep the coals hot and the smoke thick. You should have a grand feast by the end of the day. I need to get back home. Tonight is another night on the water for me. Good luck on your journey. Oh, I almost forgot to tell you… I saw Fr. Lispard on my way to work last night, and he is excited about your rice project. He would like to host a New Year's Festival at the church, and he'll give you a booth to sell it there, if you want. So, make sure you get back in time."

The next morning, Toshi, Haruki, and Kazuo mounted three of Kazuo's horses. Kazuo rode his most prized, known as a 'blood bay' because of its deep red color. Haruki and Toshi each rode horses with brown coats. The fourth horse was chestnut in color. It carried their food and water and their camping gear. He brought two mules along to carry the fish and rice.

Down the trail they went, one by one, toward the village of Kamaishi. They followed Kazuo to the Kasshigawa River, then turned west and followed it upstream until it was nothing more than a trickle; they had reached its source. On they trudged, in the shadow of the two landmark mountains: Goyo on the left, and Takashozu on the right.

The trail, if it could be considered one, was little more than a natural clearing, from three to sometimes twenty meters wide, between the forested growth on either side. Where the clearing was narrow, it was also smoother, worn of its rougher edges by decades of occasional human feet, equestrian hooves, and the large, padded paws of bears.

Traveling as they were, through a forest of pines, everything looked the same. Toshi looked as far as he could to his right, then to his left, and the views were identical. Nothing but trees and rocks, wherever he looked. There was no horizon, and without a horizon he could not tell if they were climbing up or going down.

He called up ahead to Kazuo, "How do we know if we're climbing? Have we crossed over any ridges yet?"

"Ask your back," Kazuo shouted back to him.

Toshi followed along in silence, trying to interpret the reply. *Is this some kind of special outdoors language? Did he mean I should ask the person in back of me?* He looked back at Haruki, several meters behind. Haruki was plodding along on his horse, just like Toshi. Finding no answer coming from behind, he asked again.

"What?"

"Ask your back—if you're leaning back in the saddle, we're going down. If you're leaning forward in the saddle, we're going up."

"Oh," he yelled back. He was leaning forward in the saddle, and had been for some time. They were going up and his back was beginning to ache.

As the small band slowly made their way toward Tōno for the night, Kazuo turned in his saddle. "The sky is getting heavier," he shouted back to the others.

When no one responded, Kazuo continued. "The wind is picking up. We should start thinking about a place to camp if it starts to snow. If you see a cave or an outcrop, point it out."

"Good idea," replied Toshi, trying not to sound alarmed.

They were traveling on what seemed to be the crest of a ridge, although with so many trees it was difficult to know. Toshi felt the weight of his aching body shift. He was leaning back on the horse; they were going down. They had just started down the western slope of a ridge when flakes began to fall. At first, they were light and sparse. "This is beautiful!" Toshi yelled back to Haruki. Ten minutes later he could barely see Kazuo, only a few meters ahead.

Toshi was not afraid of storms, but here, on a horse in the middle of a forest and far from home, with darkness setting in, he was getting concerned.

He strained his eyes, first in one direction, then the other, and back again. *Was that a cave?* He looked again. No, just shadows on the side of a rock. "There are so many trees in the way, I can't see anything," he said. But no one was close enough to hear.

In the fading afternoon light with the blowing snow, Toshi could not see more than five meters in any direction. *How can Kazuo even see to stay on the trail,* he wondered. His back stiffened, and he tightened his grip on the reins as he strained in search of a hideaway.

The snowflakes, at first welcome and beautiful, accumulated on the branches and pine boughs as the group trudged westward through the forest. The flakes were coming faster and heavier. Toshi pulled the scarf tight across his face, leaving only room for his eyes to see out. Periodically, the horse stopped to shake his head crisply from side to side, trying to shake the unwelcome accumulation from his head and ears.

When the buildup grew to the depth of his hand, Toshi leaned forward in his saddle and fluffed the snow from the horse's mane, then stretched as far as he could to rake the snow from around its ears. The horse whinnied each time Toshi finished, but he didn't know if the horse was thanking him or simply showing his frustration for the storm.

Occasionally, Toshi looked down at the ground beneath him and shook his own head to free the buildup from his hat and shoulders. The tracks from Kazuo's horse were getting easier to see. No longer simple hoofprints in a white bed of snow, they had turned to furrows, deep and ragged, where the fetlocks of the bay plowed a path with each succeeding step.

Toshi remembered Haruki's words from the day before. "If we run into snow, we could get stranded." He looked ahead at Kazuo, barely visible through the falling snow. Then he looked around in all directions. Everything he saw was white. Some of the white seemed close and some seemed far away. But all of it was white. He was afraid to shift in his saddle to look back at Haruki. If he fell off, Haruki's horse might walk right over him. And if Haruki went past him, he would be lost for sure, maybe forever. He stared straight ahead and gripped the horn on the saddle as tight as his shaking hands would allow.

It seemed like hours until he felt himself sit straighter on the animal's back; they were on level ground again. The snowfall diminished and the wind relented from across his face, but the howling noise grew louder. He reached up and pulled the scarf away from his face to feel the wind.

The sound was real, but not the wind. He looked around to see if Kazuo or Haruki were puzzled by the paradox. When he peered ahead, Kazuo had halted his prized bay and, half-turned in the saddle, pointed off to the right with his arm outstretched. When Toshi looked in the direction he pointed, he spotted an outcropping large enough for three people, and possibly even the horses. Toshi signaled acknowledgement with a wave of his arm, then turned back to see if Haruki had seen his signal.

When Haruki responded with a wave, they followed Kazuo off the trail and toward the overhanging rock. Kazuo reached it first and dismounted in a graceful move. Toshi was next and tried to watch carefully as Kazuo put his weight in one stirrup and swung his other leg over the saddle to the ground. It looked easy enough, but Toshi was cold, and shaking so hard that just as he swung one foot up and over the saddle, his other foot slipped out from the stirrup and he fell to the ground.

Kazuo held Toshi in high regard at the foundry. All the workers did. Toshi was second only to Haruki in knowing how to do almost anything. But Kazuo could not contain himself. He laughed out loud when he saw Toshi lying on his back in the snow.

Haruki learned from Toshi's unfortunate miscalculation. He, too, was shaking from the cold, but not quite as bad as his friend. As an extra precaution, he grasped the horn of the saddle firmly in both hands before swinging his right foot up and over the saddle. The snow on his boot slipped in the snow of the stirrup and, just like Toshi, his body tumbled toward the ground. But, because of his solid grip on the saddle he was able to hold his torso upright, next to the horse, while his legs pivoted to the ground below. It was not a moment to remember, but at least Kazuo didn't laugh.

When all three men were on solid ground for the first time since early morning, they convened under the overhang. There, in the shelter of the mountain, Toshi discovered how the wind could howl without blowing. The raging noise was not the wind at all, but a mountain stream several meters away. They were at the bottom of a valley, and not only did they have shelter, they had fresh water besides.

"This looks like a good place to spend the night," Kazuo said. "It will be dark soon, and I don't see any chance of making Tōno for the night, especially if the snow continues. It's not as heavy down here, but when we head over the ridge, it will be hard to see again."

Haruki responded first. "I agree. What about you, Toshi?"

"This seems like a good place," he replied. In truth, he was simply overjoyed at the thought of stopping.

"See if you can find a ledge up in the rocks to store the fish," Kazuo said. "Even though the bears are sleeping, there are others out here who would love to find an easy meal. Storing it above the ground should help."

Then, eyeing the sailcloth they brought along, he continued, "Let's tie the corners of that canvas to four trees, as high up as we can reach, for a makeshift roof. It should keep us a little drier if the snow keeps falling. I'll scout around for wood and try to get a fire going. I don't mind cold rice, but I would sure like some hot tea. How about you guys?"

"Hot tea sounds good," Haruki replied, his body shaking from the cold.

"Do you think it would be a good idea to update the map as we travel?" Toshi asked. "It might prove useful on future trips if we could draw or write notes along the margins."

Haruki and Kazuo both grinned at him. "We can always count on you to keep your journals, Toshi. That's a great idea. Why don't you carry the map? That way, you can make your drawings as we go."

The three of them sat close to the fire and ate. They had barely finished when Kazuo said, "Even though it's early, I'm exhausted. Why don't we get some sleep? We'll start in the morning as soon as it gets light. Maybe we can make up lost time if the weather is good."

After one last check of everything in camp, Kazuo found a flat place under the tent where he could stretch out without being too exposed to the falling snow. He pulled his winter coat tight around himself, then slipped under a heavy wool blanket, and using his saddle as a pillow, closed his eyes and drifted off to sleep.

Toshi pulled the edges of his blanket close and tucked them under each arm. Then he closed his eyes and said a silent prayer. "God, if you can hear me," he said, "thank you for sending Kazuo with us."

Haruki found a place next to Toshi under the makeshift tent. He pulled his blanket as close as he could and tucked the edges under his body like the others. With the fire nothing but a small orange glow, he looked up at the canopy and watched large white flakes floating through the hole he had cut for the smoker. He lifted his head slightly to gaze at Toshi lying next to him and a little further over, at Kazuo. *We look like cocoons,* he thought, *wrapped in our gray blankets, with a frosting of snow.*

***

The makeshift camp was quiet. The wind had died. Only the snow continued, and it fell from the sky in massive flakes. Tree branches wilted under their weight. Here and there a branch gave up the fight, sending a mound of freshly fallen snow to the ground below. Those were the only sounds.

Then, sometime after midnight, the piercing discharge from a heavy rifle sounded up and down the valley, ricocheting off the rocky cliffs and the snow-laden boughs of pine. A pair of owls screeched in disapproval, as they carried out their nightly search for food. A murder of crows cawed loudly from a distance, in protest of an interrupted sleep.

Daylight would have masked the mix of orange and white flame erupting from the end of the long barrel, but in the dark of night, the light was bright enough to momentarily blind Kazuo as it lit their small encampment. Percussion from the blast reverberated overhead with such force that snow fell from every tree for meters around. Tufts of snow hit the ground with a thump, one after another. One of the mounds landed on Kazuo's shoulder. It made a different sound, but he was too busy to notice.

Toshi awoke with a start. He opened his eyes to a world of pure, white snow, dimly lit by a crescent moon. Before he could gather his wits, it sounded again, just meters away. Then came a blood-curdling scream, followed by a quartet of whinnies and neighs and intermittent snorts. Then, the sound of excited hooves clashing against rock and frozen ground.

He tried to get up, but was wrapped so tight that his arms and legs were pinned beneath him. Fully awake, he looked over to see if Haruki was still there, and then the other direction to look for Kazuo. Kazuo was not there. "Oh Lord," he pleaded, "don't let anything happen to Kazuo, or we'll die for sure."

Then he heard the scream again. He tried to sit up, but the blanket held him down. He tried to roll to his right, but Haruki was in the way. Filled with panic, he rolled to his left into one of the newly fallen mounds of snow, but it freed him from the blanket enough to rise to his knees.

"What happened?" he shouted, just as another blast and a stream of light erupted two meters away. The discharge set off the horses again, this time even louder than before. Their shrill whinnies reverberated off the trees and hillsides that only moments before, had provided a haven of peace.

Surprised by sudden gunshots, the horses reared in self-defense. The manila rope fence was never meant to contain the force of excited eight-hundred-kilo animals. Kazuo strung it through the trees as a makeshift pen for his normally docile horses. The fiery explosions from his Chassepot pushed the frightened equines in every direction, looking for escape. They pressed the rope on every side, bending the trees and stretching the rope almost to the point of breaking.

Haruki, by this time, had climbed from his blanket in time to see Toshi running to the makeshift corral.

"It's okay," Toshi said in a half-shout, trying to be heard above the chaos. "Easy, girl… Easy now… It's okay, big boy…" He could not remember which horses were male or female, and he wasn't sure it mattered anyway. All he knew was that he needed to somehow calm them before they broke through the small, single, spindly strand of rope. If the horses got loose, even Kazuo might not be able to save them.

Kazuo's favorite, the blood bay, seemed to be the leader. Toshi worked his way in the snowy light to the back of the corral, where she stood with eyes ablaze. "Easy, girl… It's okay, big girl… Easy now," he half-shouted again, trying not to add to the confusion.

The bay was beginning to calm. She stopped rearing and dipped her head to the oncoming figure. He called out again, "Easy, girl. It's going to be okay. It's all over now." He didn't truly know if it was or not, but he did not have time to investigate.

Just when he thought he had succeeded, Kazuo approached from behind with an outstretched hand, and the bay stood still. When Kazuo reached her, she lowered her head to accept his warm hand across her nose. Only then did Toshi realize it was Kazuo who had calmed her, not him.

Haruki was on his feet by now, but reluctant to make any movement or noises for fear of spooking the horses further. Finally, he could wait no longer. "What happened?" he asked in a quivering voice.

"We had a thief," replied Kazuo. "Our smoked fish was just a little too much temptation, it seems."

Oh no, thought Toshi, *he killed someone!* "This is terrible!" he exclaimed in disbelief.

"Oh, not so bad," replied Kazuo. "He had it coming and should have known better. Besides, now we'll have a meal of our own."

Toshi nearly fainted. His knees went limp, and he tried not to look conspicuous as he reached for a nearby tree to steady himself.

Haruki was silent, not quite sure himself what had happened. Finally, he asked Kazuo, "What was it?"

"A wild boar. They get aggressive sometimes. I guess he was pretty hungry, and he must have smelled our fish. I woke up when I heard the horses getting restless. I'm sorry if it frightened you, but I couldn't very well shout out a warning. He would have hidden behind the trees or somewhere, waiting for a better chance. This way, it's over with and we don't have to be on the lookout for him. I'll drain his blood and as soon as it's daylight, dress him and add to our food supply. Unfortunately, it will slow us down by another hour or two, but the meat will be worth it. He'll go well with all that fish."

Kazuo was already up and dressing the wild boar when Toshi and Haruki began to stir. It was too early to know if the day would be clear or stormy, but it was light enough to see Kazuo and the horses. When he saw them up and moving around, Kazuo put more wood on the fire.

Two hours later, they loaded up the mules, the chestnut, and saddled the three riding horses.

After one last drink at the stream, they found a narrow stretch less than a meter deep, and one by one, forded across to the western bank. They had only gone a few hundred meters when Toshi felt himself leaning forward in the saddle. They were climbing again.

They climbed three more peaks and descended three more valleys before the Hayase River came into distant view. According to Haruki's map, the worst was over. They should start seeing signs of habitation soon.

As the trio rode in silence, Toshi considered his assignment. So far, he'd had little opportunity to make notes or drawings on Haruki's map. When he studied the map, he realized it was not large enough to add meaningful sketches, such as the campsite they had just used. He could make notes near the location with an arrow pointing to it, but a better solution would be additional pages.

"Do we have anything I can use to write on, for updating the map?" he asked.

"We brought a lot of things, but I don't think anything for mapmaking," Kazuo laughed in reply.

"Maybe we'll pass by a village along the way," offered Haruki.

"I see some huts in the distance," Toshi said. "Could that be Kitakami?"

"It could be," replied Kazuo. "Maybe we can find something there."

Chapter 26

The Warrior Empress

Adjacent to the landing was a large wooden structure with a sign in front. It bore brightly colored letters that read *Warrior Empress Emporium.* Several horses were tied loosely at a rail near the front door, and several handcarts were scattered here and there a few meters away. Most were empty, but some held a variety of goods used in farming, a sign they must be getting close to Hanamaki.

Kazuo was surprised to see partially filled carts left untended. Being strangers as well as cautious, however, he decided that one of them should stay with the horses and their own precious cargo. He had already noticed how none of the other horses were remotely as handsome as the four of theirs. And not lost on him was how many passersby had cast their gaze on his animals as they rode by. This was not a situation he liked. In a not-so-subtle move, he reached down with his right hand and gently caressed the butt of his Chassepot.

"Toshi, why don't you and Haruki go inside and see if they have the drawing paper you need. I'll wait out here with the horses."

"I'll be as quick as I can," he replied. After their adventure in the middle of the night, Toshi was still on edge. "Is there anything you need?"

"No, I'm fine. But I'll feel better when we're on our way again."

Haruki slid off his horse, followed by Toshi. Neither man caused a spectacle by falling. Kazuo even grinned at them after seeing their improvement in just two days' time. They walked a little straighter as they entered the *Warrior Empress Emporium*.

"I wonder how it got its name," Toshi murmured.

Just then, a short woman with broad shoulders and a full head of grayish-white hair intercepted them before they could reach the counter. "What do you want?" she barked with a voice that sounded more like a man than a woman.

"We would like to buy some drawing paper, suitable for making a map," replied Toshi, with as much confidence as he could muster.

"Are you lost?" she replied.

"Um, no. We're not lost; we're on our way to Hanamaki, but we'd like to make a better map than the one we have."

"Why are you going to Hanamaki?"

"We're on our way to visit a relative," Toshi replied.

"Who is your relative?" she barked again.

Haruki was beginning to worry. *Why all the questions?* he wondered. *Was there something wrong in Hanamaki? Why would she care why we're going?*

He took one step forward. "My name is Haruki," he answered, "and we're going to visit my wife's sister." Tipping his head toward Toshi, he added, "And Toshi is going to visit his wife's parents. Their names are Kunio and Fujita Matsumoto. Do you know them?"

"Why would I know them? Are they samurai?"

"No, they are farmers. I just thought maybe you had heard of them. Or maybe they had been in your store. It's a very nice store, by the way. Are you the owner?"

"Who else would own a store with the name *Warrior Empress?* Why do you think I named the store *Warrior Empress?* See that *naginata* behind the counter? I learned how to use one like it long ago, and I used it until the samurai were pushed aside... until I was forced to become a merchant."

Toshi and Haruki both stared at the *naginata* resting on two pegs behind the counter. The long, curved sword attached at the end of a pole would provide all the leverage needed for a lethal blow. It didn't take much imagination to see the Empress swinging her *naginata* in a terrifying arc. As they gazed at it, it occurred to both that it was not fastened to the wall. One quick move, and the Empress could easily be wielding it at the two of them.

Haruki then bowed lightly out of respect before he continued.

"Were you by chance at Aizu? I have heard many stories about it."

The Empress winced noticeably at the words. Her voice was low but firm as steel when she replied, "I was there." She seemed to look over Haruki's shoulder at some imaginary spot on the wall for more than a minute. "Takeko inspired us all. She will not be forgotten."

"She was the leader of your corps?"

"Yes. She was our leader, and she was very brave. That is her *naginata* on the wall. She was like a sister to me."

Haruki bowed a second time, and looked down at the floor. "I am sorry," he said.

"She was only twenty-one," the Empress barely whispered back. "We fought with *naginatas* while the emperor's army fought with guns. We had no chance. Looking back, we should have simply given in to the revolution… the *Enlightenment,* as some have called it… we had no chance of winning."

Toshi and Haruki stood motionless, in the aisle between a row of battle gear on one side and food items on the other.

The Empress turned and gazed at the *naginata* on the wall. Then she turned back to the two strangers. "What was it you wanted?" she barked again, but this time in a slightly softer tone.

"We would like to buy writing paper," Haruki said, "in order to improve our map."

She led them to the rear of the store, where shelves contained paper, parchment, and a number of writing and drawing instruments.

"Were you caught in the storm?" she asked while they studied the selections.

"Yes, we had to spend the night in the mountains. Luckily, our partner found a sheltered valley next to a stream, so it turned out all right."

"There are more of you?"

"One more. He's outside with the horses. He loves his horses and didn't want to leave them untended."

"Well, why didn't you say so? Go out and bring him in. He has nothing to worry about at my store. Who would dare offend the Empress?" She turned and shouted to a boy of about twelve who was standing by the counter. "Go with one of these men and watch their horses," she commanded.

"And will the fish be safe as well?" asked Toshi, as he turned to fetch Kazuo.

"Fish?" asked the Empress.

"Yes," answered Haruki. "We're carrying a load of fish for our relatives."

"Is it good fish?"

"Well, we think it is," Haruki said. "It was caught two nights ago about thirty kilometers off Kamaishi, and we smoked it the next day. Would you like to try some? It would be our honor, to thank you for the hospitality."

"We don't get much ocean fish over here. Yes, I'd like to try it. In fact, why don't we just trade a bit of fish for your mapping supplies?"

"We might have a deal," Haruki replied. "Toshi, pick out what you need, and I'll get Kazuo and some fish." The boy followed Haruki as he went out to get Kazuo.

When Haruki and Kazuo returned, Haruki handed the Empress a sample of their fish. They were careful to select a small sample of sea bass.

She tore off a piece with her fingers and slipped it into her mouth. The three travelers tried not to stare while she closed her eyes and began to chew.

As she chewed, they pretended to engross themselves in Toshi's mapping papers, and then at merchandise on nearby shelves. Using their peripheral vision, they could see enough to know she quickly took a second bite, followed by several more.

"This *is* good fish!" she exclaimed. "I'm so sick of nothing but rice and a few river fish. This is like learning to live again. How much do you have?"

Haruki replied, "We have forty kilos with us, but I'm not sure how much we can spare. We're taking it to our relative to trade for rice, which we'll take back to Kamaishi. Toshi, what do you think? It's your expedition."

Realizing he was in a rather delicate situation, he wished he'd had time to consider the options, but everyone was looking at him, waiting for a response. "I suppose we could give up a few kilos. Are you able to pay in cash, or do you need to trade for merchandise?"

"There is not much currency in Kitakami, as you may know. Or anywhere around here, for that matter. But people always seem to have a little money for special treats. I would be taking a risk, of course, but I would be willing to pay you one yen per kilo."

"I'm afraid we can't accept one yen," Toshi replied. "We would be losing money at one yen per kilo. Like you, we have expenses to cover."

Haruki turned to Toshi. "Do you think we could spare half our shipment at three yen per kilo? That would be twenty kilos for a total of sixty yen. That would leave us with twenty kilos to trade to your father-in-law. It would be a much smaller load, but it would also mean we could travel faster."

"It would mean a change in our plans but I suppose we could adjust," Toshi began. He paused, trying to look like he was thinking through the implications, or possible alternative offers. Mostly, he was wondering what to say next.

"If I might suggest," Toshi continued, "we are planning to make this journey periodically in the future. If your experiment with our fish from this trip proves successful, perhaps we could continue our relationship on future visits."

The Empress responded, "Sixty *yen* is more than I can pay on short notice. Even if the fish turns out to be a customer delight, twenty kilos is too risky for me. And I couldn't possibly make a profit at three *yen* per kilo. What do you say to ten kilos for twenty *yen*? And if that sells, then of course, I would welcome your visits whenever you can come."

Toshi and Haruki could not hide their disappointment. This was less than they had anticipated and did not bode well for the success of the trip. They eyed one another about whether to accept her offer. When he felt he could wait no longer Toshi bowed slightly, as he'd watched Haruki do earlier, and said, "You are an honorable warrior, Empress. We accept your offer. Please come with us to select your fish."

When the four of them reached the horses, they found the boy standing dutifully on guard. He had allowed no one to get close to the animals, although everyone knew the boy worked for the Empress, and would not have risked her wrath by getting too close, anyway.

"*Uwa!*" The Empress exclaimed, when she saw Kazuo's four horses. "What beautiful animals! How I miss the horses from my days with the samurai. But none were as beautiful as these, especially that bay. I haven't seen a bay this red in years. Maybe ever." She moved slowly, close enough to stroke his face. When he responded with a low moan deep in his throat, she rubbed his mane, neck, and withers as she continued to admire him. "No wonder you were concerned about leaving them alone. Be careful on the rest of your journey. Not everyone in Japan has the honor of a samurai."

"Thank you, Empress. We'll be vigilant. You are very kind," Kazuo replied.

He led her to one of the mules, standing patiently in the cold, loaded with their cargo of fish, and now the wild boar.

"What is that other sack? Is that a pig? Are you taking a pig to your family?"

"Actually, it's a wild boar that invaded our camp last night," Kazuo replied. "I guess he was after the fish, but he caused a raucous for the horses. Would you be interested in trading something for half the pig?"

"Let me have a better look at him. Was he young? Is the meat tender? Once they get old, you know, they're very tough. About all they're good for then, is soup."

Kazuo lifted the sack containing the boar from the mule and laid it on the ground for her to see. She pulled at the meat with her fingers, trying to gauge how tough it was.

"From the size of him, he must have been about a year old. What did you have in mind for a trade?" She asked.

"We *could* use some feed for the horses, and maybe some apples or other fruit?" Kazuo replied.

"We might be able to find something nice for our family," Haruki added. "Toshi, you might even find something for Kiyoshi."

An hour later, they left the *Warrior Empress Emporium* with twenty-five *yen*, a journal for Toshi's map, five kilos of barley for the animals, a small sack of apples, four bottles of saké for Kunio and Fujita, and a toy cart for Kiyoshi.

Chapter 27

Toshi Meets His In-Laws

HANAMAKI – DECEMBER 26, 1879

When they reached Hanamaki six hours later, they had to ask for directions to the Matsumoto farm. Haruki had visited once, years before, but did not remember the way.

Toshi had been preoccupied with the travel until now, but with Kunio's farm just up ahead, he began to worry about their welcome. He had never met Ayami's parents, and the closer they got, the more worried he became. He remembered his letters asking for marriage and how Ayami's father only reluctantly agreed. The trip no longer seemed a good idea.

Haruki noticed that Toshi was quiet but decided not to interfere. Whatever relationship Toshi would develop with Ayami's parents had to happen between them. He did, however, maneuver himself and the chestnut to the front of the caravan, placing Toshi in the middle. Since he had met Kunio years ago, he could at least provide the introduction.

The trio turned right, onto the narrow dirt lane leading to a small house. The fields on either side were empty. The dwelling and two small outbuildings showed signs of neglect. Several overgrown bushes led to the door, and a group of chickens clucked noisily as they scurried away from the horses' hooves.

Kazuo stayed with the horses while Toshi followed Haruki to the door. Haruki looked briefly at Toshi before he knocked. When no one answered he knocked again, this time a little louder.

Still no answer.

He turned to Toshi with a puzzled look. They scanned the yard and outbuildings for signs of movement. Then, already filled with anxiety about meeting Ayami's father, Toshi sucked in a breath and knocked on the door himself. In his worked-up state of emotion, the knocks fell harder than he intended. Loose flakes of paint fluttered to the ground where his knuckles met the wood. But the knocks triggered a response.

"Go away!" a voice growled from behind the door.

Toshi looked over at Haruki with a bewildered look. "What should we do?" he whispered.

Unsure himself, Haruki stood and stared at the door. Then he looked at Toshi, shrugged his shoulders, and knocked on the door again.

"If you're here about the taxes, get off my land!" the voice boomed back at them.

Haruki, now beginning to understand why Kunio was reluctant to answer the door, called out. "We're not from the ministry. It's Toshi and Haruki."

Silence at first, then, "Who?"

"Haruki. Your brother-in-law. From Kamaishi. And Toshi, your son-in-law."

"What do you want?" the voice hammered back. "Did you bring money?"

Toshi darted a look at Haruki, then back to the door. "No, we brought fish."

"When are you bringing the money?"

Toshi was pale and his hands were shaking, but he answered in a loud voice. "I already sent you the money. It was last July, like always. I'll send you the next payment in six months."

This time, instead of a voice, they heard the rustling of movement somewhere behind the door. Then the sound of heavy footsteps, coming toward them. They both watched the door anxiously until it swung open with a start.

On the other side stood Kunio, his eyes red and his body trembling almost as much as Toshi's. "Fish!" he muttered. "Why are you bringing fish? We didn't ask for fish. I don't even like fish."

Toshi looked across at him through the open door, and then at Haruki, standing next to him. He was about to say they must be at the wrong house and return to his horse when Haruki spoke up again.

"Hello, Kunio. We're sorry to disturb you, but we came on short notice and didn't have time to let you know. We brought a load of fish, hoping we could either sell it in Hanamaki or trade it for rice."

Kunio gazed at the two visitors through bloodshot eyes and finally answered. "I thought you worked at a foundry. Where did you get fish?"

"We do work at the foundry, but we had a few days off and thought we might be able to either trade or buy a load of rice from you and take it back to Kamaishi. We're hoping to sell it there for a profit."

While Kunio was thinking about his answer, the twins approached behind him. They each carried a cup in one hand, but it was not clear what they contained. Their eyes were focused, but they wobbled slightly when they walked.

Kunio turned to them and said, "They want to buy rice from us."

"How much are they going to pay us?" one of them asked.

"Yeah, how much are you going to pay us?" Kunio echoed, as he turned back to the visitors.

Before Haruki could answer, a fourth person came to the door. It was Fujita—Kunio's wife, Haruki's sister-in-law.

"Kunio, where are your manners? Are you going to make them stand in the cold all night?" Then she stepped closer and said, "Haruki, it is good to see you again." She turned to the young man beside him and said, "You must be Toshi. It is good to finally meet you. Please come in from the cold."

Haruki turned to look at Kazuo, still standing with the horses a few meters away. He motioned with his arm for Kazuo to join, and the three of them entered. Toshi looked at the splotches of bare wood on the door as he passed through, hoping he would not be blamed for causing them. Inside, the windows were covered, which kept out the fading afternoon sun. A lamp rested on a small table at the side of the room, but it was not yet lit.

Haruki surveyed the room and then repeated his greeting. "We are sorry to interrupt your day without warning, but as I started to explain to Kunio, we left Kamaishi on short notice. The foundry shut down for a few days, and we decided to take advantage of the time and bring you a load of fish. We were hoping we could sell it or trade it for rice to take back to Kamaishi."

It was not how he wanted to announce their plan, but there it was.

"Sell us fish?" Kunio almost laughed. He turned to Toshi and said, "I thought you went to university."

Still shaking, Toshi gathered the strength to answer. "Yes," he said. "I did go to the university in Tokyo, before I moved to Kamaishi."

"If you're smart enough to attend university, you should be smart enough to figure out we don't have money to buy fish! If we don't have money to pay our taxes, why would we have money to pay for fish? Especially fish that we don't even want."

Haruki was beginning to sweat, even though it was not warm in the small house. "If you have time, we can answer all your questions." His eyes had adjusted enough that now he could see two other men sitting on a mat near the stove. The younger one stood and walked over to greet them.

"Hello, Haruki-san," he said. Then he bowed politely and turned to Toshi. "I am Shoji, the youngest. How is my sister, Ayami?"

"She's fine," Toshi struggled to reply. "She stayed at home because of the weather, but she is fine." He repeated.

Haruki introduced Kazuo to the family. "Kazuo is a friend from the foundry. He provided the horses and mules for our trip," he said.

Fujita stepped forward and said, "Could I heat you some tea? We don't have much food on short notice, but I could fix you some tea."

"Tea would be welcome if it's not too much trouble," Haruki said. He looked at Toshi and Kazuo, and they nodded.

As soon as she moved to the small kitchen area, Kunio started in. "You're not trying to renege on your promise to send money, are you? Because if you are, I'll have your marriage annulled so quick you won't know what hit you. You made a promise and that's the only reason I agreed to let her marry you."

"No, I am not trying to renege. This is just an additional way to make sure we can always make the payment." Toshi did not remind his father-in-law the payments were only promised for another year. This did not seem the time for that.

"Well, that's a good thing for you, then. I didn't want her to marry you in the first place, and you can bet I won't stand for you breaking a promise. Tell me about this 'trade' you came so far to make."

"We have thirty kilos of smoked fish. We would like to sell it for two yen per kilo, and then use the money to buy as much rice as possible, to take back with us." Toshi chose his words carefully so as not to offend his father-in-law. "We realize thirty kilos is more than any one family could use, so we would offer it to your neighbors as well. And if some of them are short on cash, we're prepared to trade our fish for rice, at a rate of four kilos of rice for one kilo of fish. Either way, when we get back to Kamaishi and sell the rice, we hope to make enough profit to make the trip worthwhile. Then I'll send you the tax money, as always. It just won't be from my foundry wages; it will be from selling the rice."

"What makes you think you can sell it for a profit?" Koichi, one of the twins, spoke up from another corner of the room. "Do you really think you can make the trip all the way out here and back again and still make a profit?"

"Yeah," Kunio said, still teetering close to Toshi, his breath sour from the smell of saké. "What makes you think you can do all that work and still make a profit? Even my son can see what a foolish plan it is. Do you think rice will go up in value just because it traveled from Hanamaki to Kamaishi?" Then he laughed at the thought of it. Brayed would be a better description.

"It is true; we're taking a risk," Toshi replied. "But we're doing it for you. If this works, it could provide a backup plan in case something should happen and I can't work at the foundry. Maybe it won't work, but I thought it was worth a try. And Haruki agreed, so here we are."

Fujita brought three cups of tea for their unexpected guests and then poured one for herself.

"Tell me about Ayami and little Kiyoshi, she said. "I miss Ayami so much, and I can't wait to meet Kiyoshi. Is he talking yet? Will he be walking soon?"

Toshi relaxed at the thought of his loved ones back home. He tried to wonder what it must be like for Fujita, trapped with three difficult men. Shoji, the fourth, seemed pleasant enough, but for the others, 'difficult' seemed too nice a word.

"I don't know why your idea wouldn't work," she said to her guests. After all, we don't get much opportunity for ocean fish this far away. It would be a nice change from the river fish we're used to. Most of the farms around here do make a little money, and I'm willing to bet they would part with some of it to buy your fish."

"Are you trying to say I'm not a good farmer?" Kunio glared at his wife. "…that most of the other farmers around here make money!"

"I'm only saying what is true. Most of the farmers are able to make it without help from their son-in-law. Whether that means you are not a good farmer, I don't know. It might be that other farmers apply themselves better; that is all."

Kunio took a long swallow from his near-empty cup. He stared at the stove across the room for a short time, and even Toshi could see the anger swelling in his face. His trembling arms, which had steadied since their arrival, now returned.

"I suppose you think it's easy to run a farm like this," he growled. "Of course you would; all you do is sit around the house all day. Well, I have news for you: running an operation like this requires a lot of work—a lot of work. Hard work. Just ask the boys."

"I'm sure it does," she replied evenly. "But what it requires and what it receives are not always in equal proportion."

Had Kunio not taken that last drink of saké, he might have gotten the meaning immediately. But as it was, he struggled to figure out what she meant. *Does it mean we work more than we need to? Or does it mean the farm requires more than we give it?* He looked over at the twins, hoping for an appropriate response, but they either had not been paying attention or didn't know the answer.

Toshi and the others, however, knew exactly what Fujita meant, and braced themselves for a confrontation.

When it didn't come, Toshi had a chance to ask about Emiko, who was not to be seen. Looking at Fujita, he asked, "Where is Emiko tonight? Ayami wanted to know all about her sister."

Fujita flashed a look at Kunio and then at the twins before turning back to Toshi. "Emiko is…" she started to say, but Kunio broke in.

"She's working," he murmured. "She's working. Where did you think she'd be? Unlike some others around here, who I won't mention, she contributes to the well-being of our farm."

"Oh," Toshi replied. "She is well, then? Ayami will be asking when I get back."

"Yes, she is well. Tell Ayami not to worry herself about her sister," Kunio said.

"That's good," Toshi replied. "Ayami will be glad to know that." But when he looked over at Fujita, something told him she was not well at all.

Sensing they had pushed their limit for tonight, Haruki downed the rest of his now-cooled tea and looked at the others, hoping they would follow his cue.

"We have taken enough of your time tonight," he said. "Do you think we could meet with some of your neighbors tomorrow to see if they're interested in our proposition? One way or the other, we need to start home by Sunday in order to get back to work at the foundry."

He looked first at Kunio, who was still fuming at his wife's biting remarks about their farm compared to the neighbors. He seemed unable to make a decision, and looked to the twins for direction.

Finally, Fujita spoke for them. "Thank you, Toshi. And Haruki—and Kazuo. You are kind and thoughtful to go to all this work, especially through the snow. We'll contact our neighbors tomorrow and see if they're interested."

Then Haruki had a sudden thought. "Kazuo shot a wild pig on the way here. What if we cooked it to feed your neighbors? Maybe that would give them a reason to come and listen to our proposal."

"I'm sure it would help," Fujita replied. "We don't see our neighbors much. That might be a good way to get them here." She looked at Kunio for confirmation, but he seemed to still be working out the meaning of her 'proportion' statement.

"I'm afraid we don't have room for you in the house," she continued. "But Shoji will be happy to help you set up camp by the river. I assume you have been camping on the way here, and that it won't be too inconvenient. I'll fix breakfast for you in the morning as soon as the others have gone."

Shoji led the three men outside and helped them set up a camp next to the barn. "It was good of you to come," he said, looking at Toshi. "Mother often talks about Ayami, and she would love to see Kiyoshi. It's lonely for her here, especially the way Father treats her sometimes. My brothers are not much better. They take after Father in that regard. Thank you for coming. I hope you get all the rice you need and that you make a profit when you get it to Kamaishi."

"Thank you, Shoji," Toshi replied. "I'm glad that we came. If we do make a profit on the rice, maybe we'll come back more often."

Shoji and the visitors had barely left the house when Kunio grabbed Fujita roughly by the arm and, with a low, menacing voice, snarled in her face. "How dare you! Who do you think you are? Talking back to me in front of your relatives! Maybe you don't think I understood all those fancy words about being a portion, but I understood every word!"

He tightened his grip with every syllable that spat from his mouth. "I don't have to take insults from the likes of you!" he growled, only inches from her face. Then he moved his other hand to her throat, and his eyes bore into hers with a look she knew too well.

Whether it was the unexpected visit by Haruki and Toshi, after all this time of being alone, or whether it was the reminder that Emiko was now also gone, or maybe she had finally had enough; even Fujita did not know. But she jerked her arm from Kunio's grasp so quick that he had no time to react. Then she stood back a half step and planted her feet for balance, and with her free arm, slapped Kunio as hard as she could across the side of his whisker-laden face.

Bracing for a swift response, she waited for it to come. When it did not, she stared at him almost in disbelief. He had not expected her to take a stand. He had abused her all this time because he could. Fujita thought back to the time when Ayami stood up to him and he had not retaliated. At least to her. He had taken it out on Fujita. Because he knew she would not respond.

Then, when Fujita realized her small success, she looked him directly in the eyes and said, "If you had half their ambition, we would not be dependent on Toshi in the first place. Look at them… they have a few days off from working hard at their regular jobs and what do they do? They risk their money and their lives to travel here through the winter snow, trying to help us out."

She turned to the twins. "And you should be ashamed as well. Here you sit all day long, doing nothing until spring. And when spring comes around, you make Shoji do all the work. You're no better than your father.

"Tomorrow morning, all four of you are going to call on our neighbors and see if they want to buy fish or trade for rice. If you want breakfast before you go, it will be on the table at seven-thirty. Otherwise, you can go without."

Then she stared at Kunio and her sons with a steely glare to make sure they understood.

Chapter 28

Letters From The Silk Factory

Toshi heard voices coming from the house as he pulled his blanket tight. It was still dark, but the sky in the east was beginning to glow. "God, if you're there, help us through this day," he whispered to himself. He closed his eyes and lay still, trying not to wake the others. When he opened them again, the sun was up.

"Kunio left the house an hour ago," Haruki said, "so I think it's safe for us to go for breakfast. You may as well come along."

"I'm awake," he stammered. "Why didn't you tell me? I was just waiting for you guys."

Haruki looked at Kazuo and laughed. "That's what we figured," he said.

They were almost to the house when Toshi remembered the gifts they brought from the *Warrior Empress Emporium*. "We forgot to bring the gifts," he said. "Maybe I should go back and get them."

"I don't think Kunio needs any more saké," Haruki replied. "Let's wait on all of them for now. They didn't seem very happy to see us. We might be going back to Kitakami with red faces and thirty kilos of fish."

The sun was warm when they knocked politely at the door. Fujita opened it wide and motioned them in. "The men have already eaten and gone to call on our neighbors," she said, unable to hide her excitement. "I have breakfast waiting. It's good to see you again."

The three of them sat down to a spartan breakfast of rice and two eggs to share among them. "I'm sorry we don't have enough eggs for everyone," she said. "The men insist on having at least one each, and I wasn't able to save up an extra on short notice."

"This is plenty for us," Haruki said. "We have eaten well enough on our trip. You needn't sacrifice on our account."

"It's our fault for not letting you know we were coming," Toshi added.

"Do you think your neighbors will be interested in either trading or buying our fish?" Haruki asked.

Fujita thought about her answer before replying. "Yes, I think they will be interested in your fish, but I'm not sure if they will trust Kunio or the boys. The truth is, we seldom see our neighbors, and I think they prefer it that way. You may not have noticed, but the other farms all look more prosperous than ours. There is a reason for that. I'm afraid Kunio prefers his saké to working. And it rubs off on the boys. Shoji is a good worker, though. He gets stuck doing most of the work."

They finished their breakfast in silence until Haruki could wait no longer. "Is there any reason we should worry about you when we leave?"

Fujita turned to him with a helpless look. "I'll be all right," she said. "I've managed for years. He never hurts me badly, just enough to remind me who's the boss. Then he regrets it when he sobers up again."

"If ever you need to, please come and stay with us. You can come the same way Ayami did. You will always be welcome," he said. "Minako would be thrilled to have you."

"Is Emiko still sleeping?" Toshi then asked. "Ayami will be anxious to hear about her little sister."

Fujita blinked to hold back her tears, but it didn't help. She darted a look toward the front door and then down the hallway, an instinctive reaction. She turned away from Toshi, trying to control her emotions, but they showed despite her effort.

Toshi sat silent.

Haruki looked first at Toshi and then at Fujita.

Looking down at the rough flooring at her feet, she croaked barely loud enough to hear. "Kunio… sent her away."

"He sent her away?" Toshi asked in a rising voice.

"Yes. He sent her to a silk factory."

Haruki winced. He started to speak but changed his mind.

"When did that happen?" Toshi asked with as neutral a voice as he could manage.

"It was a year ago, last May. An agent came through looking for workers. Kunio spent all the money you sent him and needed more to pay our taxes. The agent offered him a cash payment just for signing her up, and he took it."

"Do you know where she is?"

"No. If Kunio knows, he hasn't told me. I'm not sure he knows. He claims the agent wouldn't tell him exactly, only that he worked for several factories and that he would make sure to place Emiko with the best one. He was so excited by the money he couldn't think straight. I think it was somewhere down south."

She looked at Haruki. "I reminded him what you said about the silk factories, but he said it was too late to change anything now. He said he questioned the agent about their working conditions, and he told him the rumors weren't true."

"Do you know when her contract is up?" Toshi asked.

"I think it was for four years, so she would still have a year and a half to go."

"Did anyone else go with her?"

"Yes, a friend went with her. Suki Ishii. Kunio didn't tell me that, but I found out from Suki's mother. They farm several kilometers from here. It's the farm where Ayami stayed until you helped her get to Kamaishi. But I don't think they know, either."

"Have you heard from her?" Toshi asked.

"Yes, we've heard from her a few times. Someone from the factory wrote the letters for her, as she was still learning to read and write when she left. According to the letters, she is fine. Would you like to see them?"

"Are you sure you don't mind?" he asked. "They were meant for you and Kunio. I don't want to meddle in your relationship with your daughter."

"I'm sure she wouldn't mind," Fujita replied. "After all, Ayami is her sister, and you are part of our family."

It only took a moment for Fujita to retrieve the letters from a nearby cupboard. As she opened the first, Toshi could see, even from a distance, they had been opened many times. The single page had been folded and unfolded until Toshi thought it might soon become several smaller pages.

"Shoji has to read them for me," she admitted, "but I never get tired of hearing them."

She handed Toshi the first letter.

Dear Mother and Father,

I love and miss you both very much. I hope you are in good health and that without me you have plenty of extra food to share.
I have lots to eat here and a very nice sleeping room. I share my room with three other girls, who are very nice. We have fun after our work is complete, playing games or sometimes just talking.
Our employer provides schooling for us every night after the evening meal. I hope to be able to write letters on my own by the time my contract is completed. Our employer is kind to provide one of the older students to write for us until then.
Much love until I see you again.

Emiko M

Then she opened the second one and handed it to him.

Dear Family,

I love and miss you all. I hope you are doing well.
Time goes by fast and I'm sorry not to write more often. I've made a lot of good friends since arriving here and we find lots to do when our shift has finished for the day. I continue to attend the free schooling which I enjoy. Someday I'll be able to write to you myself without the help of a friend.
My supervisor says I'm one of her best workers and that if I continue to show progress I may qualify to become a supervisor myself one day.

Our factory is searching for good workers, so if the daughters of any of our neighbors are seeking employment please tell them what a generous place is our factory.
Much love until I see you again,

Emiko M

Toshi was struck by the greeting, and how Emiko missed all of them. From what Ayami had told him, there was not a lot of love for her father or brothers. The word 'all' seemed an odd choice. Maybe it was merely a shortcoming in the tutor's language or writing ability. Or maybe Emiko was just so lonely she had forgotten their strained relationship.

"And this is the last letter we received," said Fujita, as she handed it over.

Dear Father and Mother,

I love and miss you both. I hope you are well and taking good care of yourselves.
I'm glad to be working inside where it is warm at this time of year. It's so much nicer than going out in the cold to work in the fields. My supervisor is pleased with my work and encourages me to apply for section leader. It would mean an increase in my wages so I intend to apply at first opportunity.
My friends and I sometimes study our lessons together when the lecture period is over. Everyone is nice and it is fun to work here.
I like the food and especially the dessert of rice cakes with anko. They are almost as good as the ones from home.
Much love until I see you again.

Emiko M

"I'm so glad she is getting plenty to eat and that she has so many friends. And she doesn't have to go out in the cold, which is good. I'm glad she likes the dessert, but I don't think I ever tried it with anko." Fujita turned away to hide her feelings and headed for the kitchen.

Toshi watched as she put the letters away. Somehow, her comments did not seem very convincing. He wondered if Fujita also questioned their truthfulness.

"Yes," Toshi replied. "It's good to know she's doing so well. I'll be sure to tell Ayami every word of her letters. She'll be worried about her, as I know you are."

Chapter 29
Trading For Rice

HANAMAKI – DECEMBER 27, 1879

"Mother seemed pretty upset," Shoji said, as the four of them walked from one farm to the next.

The twins walked along in silence. Scowling looks mirrored their matching faces.

Unaccustomed to any form of physical effort, Kunio labored as they trudged one kilometer after another.

"We haven't seen much of you," was the usual response when Kunio knocked on their door. "Your son-in-law is here to buy rice? You're roasting a pig? Yes, we'll come."

By mid-afternoon, it seemed to Toshi that half of Hanamaki must have come. There were people everywhere he looked, but especially at the food table. He smiled at every person as they came through the line, helping themselves to a generous portion of roast pig. Toshi carefully added one piece of their precious smoked fish to each tray as it was held out before them.

Haruki opened the saké bottles from the Empress and circulated through the crowd, offering a cup to those who wanted, being careful to avoid Kunio whenever he could.

An hour later, when most of the guests had eaten their fill, Kunio stepped in the midst of a group and waved his arm in the air as a signal he wished to speak. Gradually, the guests interrupted or ended their conversations and turned their attention to Kunio.

"Happy New Year early," he began. His voice was shaking but he pushed on. "Thank you for coming to share this early celebration. It's a shame we don't get together like this more often. This time of year, especially, when we are not that busy in the fields.

"Toshi is my son-in-law from Kamaishi. He is married to our beloved Ayami, who many of you have known since she was a child. He, and Haruki, who is my brother-in-law, are acquiring rice to take back to Kamaishi in hopes of selling it at a better price than we can get here. Since Kamaishi is a large fishing village, they have brought a limited supply of fish, which they would like to trade for rice. Toshi will give you the details."

Toshi tried to hide his anxiety as he faced the crowd surrounding him. "We are grateful to Kunio for hosting this celebration and to all of you for coming on short notice," he began. "We're offering to trade one kilo of fish for four kilos of rice, which we feel is a fair trade. We are also offering to purchase rice at the rate of one yen for every two kilos of rice. We can carry up to one hundred and eighty kilos back to Kamaishi. When we reach that limit, we will have to close the offer. If we're successful in selling the rice we hope to return again in the future. If you are interested in either selling or trading, Haruki and I will be stationed at the table over there," and he pointed off to his left to a table where Haruki was standing.

A line soon formed, and Toshi recorded each name in his book, while Haruki confirmed the transaction. It all happened so fast that Toshi had no time to think about anything other than recording the transaction. When the line finally came to an end, one name caught his interest. He looked at his register and found the name *Ishii*. He had agreed to both a trade and a purchase, but Toshi could not remember what he looked like.

He called Haruki over and spoke softly, hoping no one else would overhear. "I need to speak to Mrs. Ishii, but I don't know who she is, and I can't ask Kunio or Fujita. Would you tell Kunio that I think I made a mistake with my record for Mr. Ishii, and could he point him out to you. If we're lucky, he'll be standing by his wife, and then I can approach her."

Haruki seemed to understand. But instead of going to Kunio, thought a better idea might be to approach one of the other farmers. *That would be innocent enough,* he thought, *to simply ask who a certain person was.* He approached a man and woman and a young daughter standing by themselves and asked if they knew the Ishii family.

"Better than anyone," the man replied. "I am Rikuto, and this is my wife, Miwa. This is our daughter Chiyo. We are the Ishiis."

"Toshi had a question about your transaction," was all he could think of to say. "He wasn't sure he recorded it correctly and just wanted to make sure." He led them to the table where Toshi was sitting and introduced them.

Toshi had been watching and deduced what had happened, so when they approached the table, was able to say, "I just needed to confirm that your name is Ishii, and that you wanted to trade for one kilo of fish, as well as sell ten kilos of rice for five yen. Is that correct?"

"That is correct," Rikuto replied. "We were just about to go and get the rice."

"Did you have some saké?" Haruki asked Rikuto. "We have a little left over; why don't we slip over to the shed and get a cup? I think there might be a little fish left as well. We can bring some back for your wife and daughter. Toshi, can we bring you anything from the food table?"

"No, thank you. I'll wait here with Mrs. Ishii."

As soon as they walked away, Toshi said, "Your name seems familiar. Was it your daughter who went with Emiko to work at the factory?"

Miwa was at once surprised and excited at hearing the name of her other daughter. She looked at Toshi and replied. "Yes. Our daughter, Suki, is working at a factory down south with Emiko. We miss her terribly but she writes when she can, and she likes her work, so we try not to worry about her."

"I'm glad to hear that. I know Fujita feels the same about Emiko. Emiko is my wife's little sister, so of course we're also concerned for her well-being." He paused, hoping to gain her trust and empathy before continuing. "Fujita showed me her letters from Emiko this morning. I got the impression she'd read them a hundred times before. Do you do that? Have you read Suki's letters over and over?"

Miwa smiled at the thought of being caught. "Yes," she said. "Rikuto has read them to me so many times I know them by heart. She said the food is good and that she likes her co-workers. She said she attends a free school provided for them after work, and she hopes to be able to write her own letters by the time her contract is up. And she said she's glad to be working indoors where it's warm, especially at this time of year."

Toshi tried to smile, but it may have looked more like a face of sympathy. "Did she happen to mention a favorite dessert they have there? Emiko talked about that in one of her letters."

"It's funny you would ask, but yes, she mentioned having rice cake with anko. Rikuto and I laughed about that since we couldn't remember ever using anko on our rice cakes. We sometimes grow azuki beans in our garden, but we thought it rather frivolous to sweeten the paste with sugar."

Chapter 30

Selling The Rice

HANAMAKI – DECEMBER 28, 1879

As he tightened the blanket around himself, Toshi watched with interest as Kazuo once again tucked the Chassepot next to his bedroll and crawled under. *I can't wait to get home to my own bed again,* he thought. His last thought before falling off to sleep was that they would not be able to sell a hundred and eighty kilos of rice.

The next morning, Fujita came out from the house to see them off. She thanked Kazuo for his help with the pig and other food. She thanked Haruki for coming to see them, and made him promise to come again, but next time with Minako and the girls.

When she came to Toshi, she thanked him for the surprise visit. Already, she had seen a spark come back to Kunio's eyes, which had left completely when Emiko did. "You've given him hope again," she said. "I can't thank you enough. Please come back soon and bring Ayami and your family."

The trio headed south under a threatening sky, waving goodbye until they were gone from sight. Two mules shared the cargo of rice.

Soon after they left, Toshi turned to Haruki, who was riding behind him. "I'm certain the letters from Emiko were phony. I think they send the same letter to everyone. Even if that was Emiko's signature, she probably had no idea what was in the letter. Suki's mother told me what her letters said, and it was exactly the same thing. They both talked about how much the rice cakes with anko reminded them of home, when neither Suki nor Emiko ever had them at home. Did you learn anything about where they are? The only thing I know is that the factory is somewhere in the south."

"Kunio did tell me the agent was a man named Saburo Kondo, who assured him Emiko would be well taken care of."

By late afternoon, they reached the *Warrior Empress Emporium*, where the two rivers met. Haruki and Toshi went inside while Kazuo stayed behind with the horses. They were walking toward the counter when they heard a loud greeting from behind.

"Haruki and Toshi! I've been watching for you."

They turned to see the formidable woman coming toward them.

"We were afraid you might not be open today," Haruki said.

"Open every day," she replied. "Travelers come every day. I'm here for them. I sold *all* the fish. As soon as word spread I had ocean fish, they came like bees to flowers. And since I didn't have an abundance, they were all afraid they'd be left out, and they bought as much as they could afford. You have to bring me more on your next trip."

"We will, if we can sell the rice. I'm glad it worked for you."

"How was your family? Were they surprised to see you?"

"Very surprised. And embarrassed, I think. They contracted their daughter to one of the thread factories and we're worried about her. We've heard the factories treat their workers like slaves."

"Which factory?"

"We don't know, which makes it even worse. All we know is that it's somewhere in the south. Do agents ever come through here?"

"Sometimes. Do you have a name?"

"Yes, Kunio said his name was Saburo Kondo. He would have been in Hanamaki around May or June, the year before last. A neighbor girl also went."

"Alas, I have no daughters—I suppose it's because I have no husband."

Haruki looked at Toshi, who looked back at him. They turned to the Empress. The corners of her eyes were just beginning to turn up in a smile. Then the corners of her mouth turned up, and she started to laugh.

"But I have friends who do," she continued. "Write down the names of the girls, and then write down your address. I will find them for you. And when I do, I'll let you know where they are."

Haruki and Toshi stared at her, trying to decide if she was serious. She was an intimidating figure, as they learned on their first encounter. But it did not seem possible she could locate two girls from another village, when all she knew about them was their name. And even if she could, why would she do that for strangers from yet a further village?

The Empress brought Toshi paper and a pencil. "Write on this," she said. "When I find them, you'll hear from me."

Then she marched down one of the aisles and soon returned with a sack for their journey. "Here's a little something for you to eat on your way home. You're probably getting tired of rice and you sold all your fish—just like a man, you didn't plan ahead." Again she laughed. And so did Toshi and Haruki.

"Is Kazuo outside with those beautiful horses?" she asked. "Because you can't leave until I have another look at them, especially the bay. I've never seen a more handsome horse. Let's go have another look," and she grabbed a few carrots on her way to the door.

The bay nickered a greeting when she saw them approach. "When are you coming back?" The Empress asked. She held out a large carrot to each of the horses. "I'll take all the smoked fish you can spare. That's the easiest money I've made since I opened the store five years ago. If I could do that every week, I'd retire and travel the country like you guys."

They stood with blank faces until she broke out in laughter. This was not like any other woman they had ever met, and they fell completely under her spell.

"Now, you'd better get on home to your wives before I decide to steal one of you for my own." Her laughter changed to a devilish grin.

Toshi thought back to Thursday, when they first entered her store and were almost too afraid to speak. Now they were talking to a woman who seemed to thrive on a smile and a joke, not one who made her living wielding a *naginata* in mortal combat.

It was Tuesday when the banks of the Kasshigawa River finally spread out before them, widening in the distance to form Kamaishi Bay. "Let's stop by the church and see if the festival is still set for Thursday," Toshi said.

An hour later, Toshi knocked on the church door, not knowing where Fr. Lispard lived. When no one answered, he gingerly opened it and peered inside. No lights were on, and even with windows on either side, shadows lingered across the benches. When his eyes began to adjust, he spotted movement near the front of the church.

"Hello," he ventured. "I'm looking for Fr. Lispard. Is he here?"

"Hello, Toshi,' came the reply. "This is your lucky day—does that mean God has answered your prayer?" He chuckled. "Because he will have answered mine if you're here with a mountain of rice."

This time it was Toshi who laughed. "Well, not exactly a mountain, more like two mule loads. But yes, here we are. Have you thought of a way to sell it?"

"Indeed, we have. We'll set up two large tables in front of the church where everyone can see them when they walk by." Then he explained how parishioners would make a recipe using the Hanamaki rice and offer it for sale at a food table. Toshi and Haruki would have a different table close by with their uncooked rice. When people tasted how good it was from the food table, they could buy an uncooked bag from their table. To get even more exposure, they would sell some of the prepared food using vending carts around the village.

He paused. "What do you think?"

Toshi thought about their trip, especially the first night out, when the snow fell so hard he could not see Kazuo a few meters away. "What if the weather is bad?"

The priest pointed out the window. "It must be ten degrees and the sun is shining. It's been nice every day since you left. Look at all the people out and about. They're used to January weather."

Toshi was so anxious to be back in Kamaishi and figure out how to sell the rice that he hadn't noticed the bustle of people along the street. "We've been through a lot of snow," Toshi replied. "I guess it's still fresh in my mind. What would happen if the weather is bad and no one shows up?"

"It's been warmer than usual, like I said, but that's a valid question." He paused to think about an answer. He could not think of a large enough building in the village to accommodate that many people. "I'll ask our Lord for good weather," he finally said.

Toshi remembered his own prayers, and how they had all been answered. "That's a good idea," he replied.

Then, getting back to the plan, he asked, "How much rice will you need for the recipe table?"

"Can you spare ten kilos?"

"We can spare fifteen if you need it," Toshi answered. "Where do you want it? Do you have a place to keep the rest until Thursday, or should we take it with us?"

"We can make a space behind the altar to store it. I have a pet tiger to keep the mice away—here Tiger," he called. "Come here, Tiger."

From out of the shadows a small cat walked a few steps before stopping to stretch from his nap. His color did resemble that of a tiger, but at that moment he did not appear much of a threat, even to a mouse.

"He doesn't look very ferocious," Toshi said.

"Oh, he's tougher than he looks," the priest replied. "They say cats have nine lives. If that's true, Tiger only has two left. He lives a rather reckless life, I'm afraid." Then he laughed.

"If you show us where to put the rice, we'll carry it in," Toshi said. "I'm so tired I can't stop to rest, or I'll never get up again. We've been sleeping on the ground for over a week, and I can't wait to get back to my regular bed."

Two hours later, the three travelers split up for the first time in a week and a half, and headed for home.

***

"How was my mother?" was the first question Ayami asked.

"Your mother was good. She seemed happy to see us. I think she found some extra courage after we arrived."

"What do you mean, extra courage? Was she okay?"

"She told Kunio he needed to pay more attention to the farm."

"What did Father do? Did he retaliate?"

"No, I think he was so surprised he just glared at her. Then she told all of them to go invite their neighbors to come and hear about our offer. They were up and gone by the time we came for breakfast, so he must have gotten the message. Haruki told her she could come and live with them if she ever needed to."

"I can't believe it. What about Emiko?"

"Emiko wasn't there. Your father sent her away to a silk factory."

"What? After Haruki warned him?"

"I'm sorry," he replied. "Fujita said your father spent the money we sent him and had to find a way to get more. They paid him a bonus for signing her up."

"Have they heard from her? How is she?"

"Yes, they've gotten several letters from her, and she claims to be doing fine. Our new friend in Kitakami said she would try to locate her, but I don't know how she could. Try not to worry about her. What we do need to worry about is selling the rice. If we don't, our savings will be gone."

On Wednesday, the eve of the New Year, the three of them collected Haruki and his family, and together headed to Fr. Lispard's church. Hideji and his family were already there, assembling two booths, one large, the other even larger. Hideji beamed as he showed them off to his visitors.

"This one will be filled with more kinds of rice recipes than you thought existed. We're making it with a large table space so customers can easily see each item. Off on either side will be space to pay for the item. That way, we can accommodate two customers at once, and they won't have to wait very long, even when we have many customers. We'll be sure to tell every customer the recipe was made using Hanamaki rice and that it's only available at the other booth.

"Over here will be your booth," he continued, walking a few meters away and spreading his arm to indicate the location. "You can use the space behind the altar for storage and bring sacks out to the booth whenever you're running low. I hope you have plenty of help, because I predict you will be very busy and sell lots of rice."

***

The next morning, the first day of 1880, Toshi and his family met Haruki and his family at the junction and headed for the church. The sky was overcast with heavy gray clouds. The temperature hovered at zero degrees.

"I don't like the looks of it," Haruki said.

Toshi looked at the sky for assurance. "Fr. Lispard said he would pray for good weather. The clouds should lift by the time people start coming."

"Happy New Year, by the way," Haruki said as they started down the slope. "It's hard to get used to it as the first day of January."

"I wonder if my father is still using the *Tenpō* calendar," Toshi replied. "I don't think he adjusted very well to the new way of things."

Flakes started to fall just when they reached the bottom of the trail. "It won't last long," Toshi said. "Fr. Lispard's prayers are sure to kick in before long. This might just be a test of his faith."

The flakes kept getting heavier.

"I prayed last night, too," he admitted. "Surely God heard at least one of us."

Walking east toward the church, they met a dozen other people going about their business. "See," Toshi said, "they're not afraid to come out in a few flakes of snow. Especially on New Year's Day."

Haruki looked at Minako and then at Ayami but didn't speak. He panned the village as they walked on, avoiding Toshi's face. A few blocks later they brushed the snow off their clothing and opened the door to the church. Toshi stomped lightly on the floor, trying to dust off the snow before walking in.

Fr. Lispard waited at the entrance beside Hideji and Teruko. None of them smiled when the group walked in. It was the first time Toshi had seen anything but a smile on the priest's handsome face. It was not a look of anger, but easily qualified as a look of frustration.

"Good morning," he finally said. "Not what I was hoping for."

"Maybe God just hasn't heard you yet," Toshi said. "Maybe it will blow over before anyone shows up."

"I would like to think so, Toshi, but I'm afraid it's getting worse." He pointed to the window off to his right. Snow was building on the lower sill.

"What am I going to do with all this rice?" Toshi asked.

"The rice will keep," Hideji responded. "It is safe behind the altar."

"I'm more worried about the recipes," Teruko said. "All those women have been hard at work making food. Some of it won't keep very well. Some will keep, but it won't taste as good after a day or two."

Just then, three women walked in with their recipes, still warm from the stove. "What are we going to do?" one of them asked. "We already put the posters out. It's too late to take them down."

Toshi looked at Hideji for an answer. Then he turned to Fr. Lispard—they were the ones who worked out the plan. They each looked back at Toshi with empty faces. Fr. Lispard looked ready to speak when the door opened again. It was another recipe dish. She set it down on one of the benches at the back of the church. It was wrapped in a towel to keep it warm. "This won't taste nearly as good tomorrow," she uttered.

"That settles it," Fr. Lispard said. "We'll keep everything inside the church and sell as much as we can. We can't let all this good food go to waste."

He looked over at Hideji. "Do you think that small table would fit inside the church? We could put all the food dishes on it, just like we'd planned."

"I think if we turn it on its side, we might be able to get through the door. Haruki, can you help me? Let's try. In the meantime, we can set them on the benches. At least they'll be warm and dry."

Ayami turned to Minako and the girls. "We can take turns watching for customers from the front step and send them in. They might not know we're open for business if they're just walking by."

The four ladies with food dishes looked at each other and without a word, grabbed hold of the very last bench, two on each end, and dragged it forward as far as it would go. Then they moved to the opposite side of the church and did the same.

Fr. Lispard seemed on the verge of scolding them until he saw the amount of extra space it provided for the food table. "What if we moved two rows forward?" he said. "That would give us even more room to work." Then he grabbed one of the benches and motioned for Toshi to get the other end. When all four of the back benches were butted up against the third row, he looked around. "That's more like it," he said.

Saya held the church door open for Hideji and her father. By laying the newly constructed table on its side they were able to walk it through the entryway with the legs barely scraping one of the several layers of paint off the interior wall.

"I'll get a sack of rice from behind the altar," Toshi said. "We can stack a few over here away from the food table where they won't be in the way." A few minutes later, they heard a yelp from behind the altar, but Toshi did not come back.

The ladies carefully arranged their favorite food dishes on the table, first bunched together, then spread out, then back together. With a table space of three square meters and a current total of four dishes, it didn't make much difference either way.

Finally, with the dishes perfectly arranged, attention turned to the uncooked bags of rice. Toshi had still not returned from behind the altar.

"I'll go see what's keeping him," Fr. Lispard said. "I'm sure he knows where it is. He helped store it there on Tuesday."

When Fr. Lispard reached the altar and stepped behind, there stood Toshi, some distance from the rice. He peered past Toshi for something amiss. There it was, the obstacle, standing tall on all four legs with its tail standing up behind and waving menacingly. Tiger's mouth was open wide, and his teeth were showing. Toshi held his ground but did not advance.

"Oh, oh," he said. It looks like someone interrupted Tiger's nap. "I told you he was tougher than he looked. I'll get the first bag. He'll follow me out and you can bring another."

Every person in the church watched bemused, when Fr. Lispard came back up the aisle carrying five kilos of rice, followed by Tiger the cat, followed by Toshi with another five kilos.

"What happened?" Hideji asked.

"Nothing," Toshi replied. "I wasn't sure which of the sacks to bring out."

Just then the door of the church opened and a customer walked in. "Are you still having the festival?" he asked. "My wife wanted me to bring home a dish so she wouldn't have to cook today."

Toshi's heart jumped. Their first sale. Maybe this was going to work after all.

The man looked over the four dishes carefully displayed on the table. Each lady who brought one held their breath from a short distance away. A woman had her pride, after all, even within the confines of a church. The customer bent down close for a better look. Then he inhaled deeply just a few centimeters above each dish, testing the aroma.

Ayami was standing across the table from him. They had no chairs to sit on, due to the hasty reconfiguration of the display table. She smiled her best smile, which should have been enough to encourage any man, and said, "These delicious recipes were all made using our special rice, brought from Hanamaki for the festival. Your wife could make any of these with our special rice." She pointed to Toshi along the outside aisle, standing beside the two bags of rice. "It is only one yen per kilo."

The customer looked over at her and smiled back. When he looked at her eyes, he seemed to lose his train of thought. He meant to steady himself with one hand against the table as he held her gaze. But instead, he placed his hand directly in the middle of Mrs. Ono's favorite recipe of Takikomi Gohan. He jerked it back so fast he lost his balance and fell to the floor.

Haruki was standing near and moved to quickly grab the man's arm and help him to his feet. For a moment, their heads neared one another, and Haruki rolled his eyes. The man's motive was most probably an appeasement for spending a long New Year's Eve somewhere he should not have been.

Mrs. Ono's Gohan was damaged goods no matter what the reason for the man's apparent interest, and could not be sold to someone else. Trying to salvage what little they could from the situation, Haruki stepped in.

"I'm sure your wife will be thrilled with Mrs. Ono's delicious Takikomi Gohan. You have made an excellent choice. The price is two yen. If you really want to make your wife happy, you should take her a sack of rice to go with the Gohan. Like the lady said, it is only five yen. Once she's tasted the Gohan, she'll be glad to have Hanamaki rice so she can make it herself anytime she wants."

The man looked at Haruki and then stole another glance at Ayami's smile and her beautiful brown eyes. He reached in the pocket of his rather wrinkled kimono and fished inside for money. Pulling his eyes away from Ayami, he looked down at his hand and counted the treasure. One yen note and a small pile of sen. He laid the yen on the table and began to count the coins.

"I can help you," Kanae said, stepping forward. He handed her half the coins and she counted them out, ten at a time, and placed the stack on the table beside the yen. Ten, twenty, thirty… "I'll take some more, she said."

The man laid each sen down as he counted, but not in piles of ten. When he stopped to give Kanae more coins, he lost track of his count and started over.

Kanae used all her coins and counted the piles. Eight piles. Eighty sen. She looked over at the man. He had followed her example and had one pile of ten. He had a few still to count. Then he reached in his pocket again to see if he had missed any.

"That's close enough," Ayami said. "We hope your wife enjoys the meal." She smiled again as he picked up the dish and moved to the door.

As he was leaving, two young men came in from the street. The one in front seemed a little older. "Is the festival still on?" he asked. "We're supposed to sell food from our carts. There were more of us, but I don't think any of the others are coming. It's snowing too hard."

The door opened again, and this time it was a group of women bringing more recipe dishes. "We already had them made," one of them said. "We didn't know what to do. It wasn't snowing when we started making them."

Hideji looked at Fr. Lispard and then at Toshi and Haruki. Toshi spoke up. He was sure that God would hear their prayer and answer it. And he was desperate to sell the rice. "I think it will stop snowing soon. Let's keep going."

The lady looked at Fr. Lispard. She held him in her highest esteem. The other ladies turned to face him, holding him in equally high esteem.

"Since you have already prepared your dishes, I think we should move forward as best we can. I am not as optimistic as Toshi about the weather, but the weather is out of our hands. I vote we keep going."

He turned to the two young men. "If you are willing, why don't you each take two dishes and stay close to the church. See how it goes. If you sell them, you can always come back for more. And that way, people will at least know we're open for business. Be sure to tell them about Toshi's rice, even if they don't buy a dish."

Five more ladies arrived with their favorite recipes. Every dish reflected the painstaking effort of its maker. Each dish a work of art and a different taste…kamameshi, chahan, omurice, onigiri, something for everyone.

But no one came.

Two hours later, the two young men returned. They were cold and wet from the falling snow. They carried the four unsold dishes with them. "I'm sorry," the older one said. "There wasn't anyone to sell them to."

Toshi nearly wept. He walked to the back of the altar and stared at the bags of rice, hardly noticing the yellow cat dozing peacefully atop the pile. He had to pay Kazuo for use of the horses and for half the pig they roasted to feed Kunio's neighbors. He still owed Hideji for the fish, and he should pay Haruki for all his help. After giving Fr. Lispard's parishioners fifteen kilos of rice for their recipes, he was down to one hundred and sixty-five. He had paid ninety yen for the rice and twenty for the fish. And today, not a sale. Not even one bag.

Toshi walked back to the front of the church and gazed at the recipes, then at the women who brought them. He looked briefly at Ayami but could not bear to hold her gaze. Finally, he looked at Fr. Lispard and said, "I don't think it's going to clear off after all." It was an effort to control his voice, but he turned back to the women and continued. "Thank you for all your work making these recipes. They look and smell delicious."

"Let's give it another hour," Hideji offered. "We don't have anything to lose by waiting. Maybe people are just slow getting started today. Maybe they were up late last night for the New Year. If nothing happens in an hour, we can close up and go home."

"I agree," Fr. Lispard said. "We can try again next week."

Toshi stood along the wall next to his two bags of rice. When no one was watching, he closed his eyes and asked God a second time.

Whether it was the result of Toshi's prayer or simply coincidence, a customer came through the door: an older woman, slight of frame and stooped as she walked. She dusted the snow from her hat and shoulders, leaving an imprint of her feet on the floor. "If I'm not too late, I would like to buy a bag of rice. I heard it came from Hanamaki. It has to be better than what my husband brings home from the market."

Toshi's eyes lit up. He grabbed a five-kilo bag like it was light as a feather and hurried to the front of the church. Ayami smiled at the woman and said the price was five yen, but would she also like one of the recipe dishes for just two yen more?

She looked in her purse before responding. "Yes, I would love to, but I don't think I can carry two things at once." She looked carefully at the eight remaining dishes displayed on the table. "They all look delicious," she said. "Maybe I should just take a dish for two yen. It would be a lot easier to carry than a bag of rice."

Before Toshi could catch himself, he called across the table to the woman, "Where do you live? I'll carry the rice for you."

She looked at him and smiled. "You are such a nice young man. Would you really carry it for me?"

Toshi had no choice. "Yes," he said, "if it's not too far."

When Toshi returned to the church an hour later, no other customers had appeared. Fr. Lispard looked at the women and said, "I think we might as well close down for today. Would you be willing to try again a week from Sunday? We can put out new signs during the week."

Then he turned to Toshi. "I'm afraid we would need more rice to do that. These dishes won't stay fresh until then, and we want them to be their best if they're going to sell your rice."

Again, Toshi had little choice. "Yes," he said, "maybe ten kilos this time?"

Chapter 31

Back To Work

Even after three days to rest, following the failed rice festival, Toshi could barely lift one foot in front of the other as he walked to the factory. His shoulders felt like lead and every breath was a labored effort. The thought of facing Haruki made it even worse. He had led his boss on a fool's mission through the snow and far from home, and for what? Only to end up with nothing to show but a few rewarding memories along the way. Seeing his sister-in-law again—meeting the Empress, little else.

Ayami tried her best to console him. She said it would all work out. But with a hundred and fifty kilos of rice still stored behind the altar at St. Mary's church, it was difficult to see how. The rice festival had been a disaster. Not only did they not sell all the rice as he had hoped, he now had to invest another ten kilos, maybe even fifteen, to remake the recipes and try again. What if the weather was bad again this time? He felt so bad about keeping Ayami awake half the night from his tossing and turning that he moved his mat to the kitchen. At least she could get a decent sleep.

The walk to work, which lifted his spirits so many days, was simply one more burden to carry. Adding to his already sizeable load, he could not reconcile why God had let him down. Not just him, but Fr. Lispard as well. Surely, with both men seeking his help, He must have heard their prayers. And if trying to help Hideji sell more fish, helping Kunio and all his neighbors sell more rice, helping Toshi meet his promise to pay the tax for his father-in-law, were not worthwhile and honorable requests, then what more did God expect?

His mind was churning when he arrived at the factory. He went straight to the changing room and pulled on his protective coat. Only when he stepped into the heavy boots did he realize he hadn't looked at the charcoal bin. He was not himself and it was a dangerous state of mind.

When the workers arrived, Haruki called them together to begin the day. "Welcome back, all of you," he began. "I hope you were able to put your time to good use. Today is different than a normal day. After three weeks away, I don't expect everyone to be as sharp as we were three weeks ago. So today we'll load a sixty-percent production run. Tomorrow, we'll bump to eighty-five percent. On Wednesday we'll get back to one hundred."

Toshi wondered if the speech was meant for him.

The day passed smoothly.

Tuesday, production increased to eighty-five percent. It also went smoothly.

When Toshi arrived at work on Wednesday, Haruki was waiting for him. "We've been requested to meet with the director at four o'clock this afternoon," he said. "Your guess is as good as mine what it's about. In case he wants to know why production was down on Monday and Tuesday, you can put the blame on me. I'll explain that I thought it was the right thing to do, since we'd been off for so long."

A few minutes before four o'clock, Haruki tapped him on the shoulder. It was time to go. He fell in step with Haruki and they headed for the director's office.

Toshi's confidence dwindled with every step. The only thing he could think about was his previous meeting: how the interpreter ignored him and the director kept him waiting. Then he thought of the servant girl, and his attitude shifted from defiant to belligerent. He prepared himself for a contentious meeting.

On this visit however, the interpreter was sitting at his table when the two approached. "Hello, I am Haruki Yamamoto, and this is Toshi Ozawa. We have an appointment with the director," Haruki offered.

To Toshi's surprise the man replied, "Yes, he is expecting you. Take a seat and I'll tell him you are here."

They took a seat by the front windows, just where Toshi had been rudely left to wait on his prior visit.

"Follow me," the interpreter said, just as they settled on the wooden chairs.

They followed him to the director's office.

"I was about to have a cup of coffee. I prefer it to tea. I guess it's my German heritage. Can I get you a cup of tea? Or a coffee? We have both." He then reached for a small bell on the edge of his table and rang it twice. He was looking at the two of them as he spoke, although they had no idea what he said until the interpreter relayed the message.

"I would take coffee if it's not a lot of trouble," replied Toshi. He had never tasted coffee. The words came out of his mouth almost as a reflex rather than a thought. Maybe he was becoming a different person after his previous three weeks of new adventures. This was not the Toshi of four weeks ago.

"I prefer tea," Haruki added.

The familiar, older-than-she-looked servant girl entered from the door to their left at the sound of the bell and walked obediently to the director. She looked at the interpreter and awaited his instructions.

While the attendant was on her mission, the director continued.

"As you are probably aware, the new furnaces are nearing completion. I am pleased to announce they will be ready by the first week of March. We intend to have a preview for all workers and their families at the end of February. This is a monumental achievement, not just for our foundry, but for all of Japan. We are hoping Emperor Meiji might attend."

He waited for the interpreter to catch up while the servant girl handed Toshi and Haruki their drinks.

"Haruki, I'm told you are conscientious and that you treat your workers fairly. I've watched your production results with a close eye for many months. For these reasons, you will become the Chief Foundry Manager for furnace number one when it begins production. I can hardly wait to see how well you make it perform, once you fully understand the new design."

Neither man was particularly surprised at the announcement, since Haruki was already the foreman of the current furnace.

Toshi took a few sample sips from his first-ever cup of coffee, wary about too much at once, not sure of its taste. At first, he was skeptical. But after several sips, letting it cool enough not to burn his tongue, the liquid warmed him, as the unfamiliar substance permeated his body. It felt good on this January afternoon.

The director continued. "Toshi, you are not only a knowledgeable mathematician, but a keen observer and a disciplined engineer. Your concerns about the supply of charcoal turned out to be correct, unfortunately. That is why we had to shut down the furnace these last few weeks—to let the supply build up again. But I suppose you figured that out on your own."

The director sipped from his cup while the interpreter passed forward the message to Toshi. Mimicking the motion of the director, Toshi brought his cup to his mouth for another sip. His initial reservation regarding the substance was now dismissed, clearing the way for a full sip, and he let the warmth fill his mouth as he waited for the interpreter to speak.

"For these reasons," he continued, "Toshi, you will be the Chief Foundry Manager for furnace number two when it begins production."

And so it was, that in the midst of his first long and tasty drink of coffee, the words of the interpreter reached his ears. Any aspiration he might have had to act dignified was lost completely, as he choked on the swallow of coffee now finding its way down his throat.

He was beyond embarrassed when he momentarily choked, but found some consolation in that he managed not to spit it back into the cup. Having nowhere to place the cup, he lowered it to his lap with both hands shaking noticeably, and pretended nothing unusual had taken place.

"I'm told the two of you are related by marriage and are uncle and nephew. Is that correct? It will be interesting to see which of you can produce the most iron with the fewest mistakes. In fact, it will be so interesting that, in addition to a twenty-yen increase in your monthly wage, I'm offering a one hundred yen bonus for the furnace that finishes the year with the best performance. We can talk about the details at a later time. Good luck to you both."

With that, he rang his bell twice to call the servant while the interpreter reached for their respective cups and extended his hand toward the door. The meeting was over.

They followed him from the director's office to the interpreter's outer office. The interpreter stopped at his table while Haruki and Toshi continued to the front door. Toshi's heart was pounding so hard he failed to admire the miniature library that had captivated him so, on his first visit.

Toshi followed Haruki through the door and down the steps. He was so surprised by the outcome of the short meeting that he caught his heel on the tread of the second step, and had Haruki not been a half-step ahead, would have fallen forward to the ground, right there in full view of the director's office. As it was, he grabbed Haruki's shoulder just in time to regain his balance and spare himself the humiliation.

"*Uwa*! Did you hear *that*?" he said, trying hard not to be loud enough for anyone in the building to hear.

Haruki instinctively looked over at the site of the furnace construction, looking for a source of noise. Seeing none, he looked around in both directions before answering. "No, I didn't hear anything. What did it sound like?"

"The director," he replied. "Did you hear what he said?"

"You mean about the bonus?"

"No. He said I was right about the charcoal. I have to write my father as soon as I get home and tell him I was right."

Haruki could not think of any good way to respond. Looking back on it, he should have realized how much it hurt Toshi to have his father pull away for what he considered a lack of respect for authority. "I'm sure he will be pleased to hear from you," he said.

They continued back to the foundry, each lost in their own thoughts. Finally, the financial implication sunk in to Toshi. The monthly increase would be more than enough to send money to Kunio. He would not have to make another rice trip to Hanamaki. Now if he could only sell the rice they already had.

Haruki was thinking ahead about what to tell the workers. Should he tell them about Toshi becoming the manager for one of the new furnaces? Should he tell them about the competition between the two furnaces? He never liked to withhold information from his co-workers, but it did not seem a good idea to tell them everything. Not yet, at least.

When they reached the furnace, the day's production was almost complete. A few of the men were moving molds to the cooling area while others were picking up scraps and cleaning the discharge tubes. They stopped and looked up at Haruki as he approached, eager to hear about the meeting.

"The director said the new furnaces will be ready by early March," he began. "He is planning for a preview during the last week of February, and our families are all invited. He said it's possible the emperor might come. It will be a big event, not just for us, but for all of Japan, and he said the new foundry will be one of the best in the world."

***

At the end of the week, worries about the rice festival returned. "Do you think they put out enough signs?" Toshi asked Haruki as they walked home from work. "They need to put out a lot of signs. Otherwise, everyone will think it was last week and won't bother to come."

"Hideji said they have been putting out a lot of signs."

"What about the recipes? Do you think the women will really make all those recipes again?"

"Fr. Lispard assured Hideji they would make them all again. He said they might even be better this time, since they had practice a few days ago."

"What if the weather turns bad again? We can't go through this again. We don't have enough rice for more recipes."

"Fr. Lispard told Hideji the women were going to check with him early Sunday morning, before they start making their recipes. If the weather is bad, we'll wait another week."

"Is Minako planning to be there? And the girls? If it gets busy, we'll need a lot of help at the table."

"Yes, they will all be there, ready to help."

"I wonder if I should pray again. It didn't seem to help last time."

"You will have to decide that, but I don't see what it could hurt. You can ask Fr. Lispard when you see him."

On Sunday morning, Haruki and his family met Toshi and his family at the junction. Toshi was quiet all the way from there to the church. Haruki left him to his thoughts. The snow from a week ago had melted away, and the sun broke through a few scattered clouds. Toshi did not say if he had prayed again, but if he had, this time it seemed to work.

Mass was over and Hideji already had the tables set up. There were thirty or more recipe dishes on the food table, including an even bigger pan of Mrs. Ono's Takikomi Gohan. The larger table was placed in the sun not far away. Other parishioners had carried several sacks of rice from behind the altar, ready for sale. Tiger dozed on the top sack with the sun warming his back and face.

By four o'clock that afternoon all the sacks were gone, all the food was gone, and the tables taken down and stored away. Toshi calculated the results in his head even before they reached the junction on his way home. After paying Hideji for the fish, Kazuo for the horses, the mules, and the pig they roasted at Kunio's, and the cost of the rice, he ended up with twenty-eight yen. Twelve yen short of the upcoming payment to Kunio. Ten days of work and nothing left for himself. It was the first time he resented the promise made to Kunio two years before. Especially after what he had done to Emiko.

Chapter 32

Foundry Open House

KAMAISHI – March 1, 1880 – IRON FOUNDRY

The first day of March brought sunny skies for the grand opening celebration. Spring flowers burst open along the banks of the Aonoki River, a perfect backdrop for dignitaries and visitors alike. It seemed the stars had aligned to show off their long-awaited event. Even the birds played their part, singing loudly in nearby pines and budding birches. The director was only mildly disappointed when the emperor could not attend. In truth, he had not expected him. But to emphasize the importance of the modern foundry, he sent Yamagata Aritomo, the Minister of War, as his personal emissary. The minister, the director, and a handful of less important dignitaries began the celebration with official welcomes and oratories. The most meaningful, of course, was that of the Minister of War, who relished a state-of-the-art foundry, able to produce a new generation of munitions. He remembered only too vividly the humiliating episode some thirty years before, when Admiral Perry from the United States entered Tokyo Harbor and forced Japan to capitulate their ports to foreign trade.

"…mark my words," he ended, "within your lifetime, Kamaishi will shine like a beacon to the rest of the world for its role in making Japan a military power, equal to any other country you can name. We won't have to kowtow to the United States of America ever again, because of what you have accomplished here today."

Then the music sprang to life, but not loud enough to drown out exuberant cheers and applause from the two hundred and ninety-nine other guests present there.

Hideji had solved Toshi's problem of how to feed that many guests by recruiting Fr. Lispard's parishioners to make a variety of their now popular rice recipes. A few of them contained what little leftover Hanamaki rice they could find in their pantries. Fr. Lispard was an invited guest for the ceremony, so no one gave a second thought when he strolled here or there during the celebration. He was careful not to mill about the food table, however, other than to add a few carefully chosen items to his plate.

Ayami was just about to sample one of the selections herself when an unexpected pain pierced her stomach. It was sharp, and her gasp caught the attention of Toshi and those around her. After a moment, she straightened herself and took a small bite of rice cake. "They said this has anko sauce on it. Have you ever tried anko, Toshi?" she asked. "It gives the cake a nice, sweet flavor. I should try this at home sometime."

Toshi was thrown into silence by the sound of her gasp. But before he could ask about it, she had asked about anko, which reminded him of the letter from Emiko. It was almost a minute before he could respond.

"No, I don't think I've ever had anko, but if you like it, let's try it at home. Are you alright? Are you having labor pains? If you are, we need to find somebody."

"I'm not sure," she replied. "We can wait and see if it happens again. I shouldn't be having labor for at least two more weeks." She paused. "Find somebody? We're surrounded by people. And Minako is right here, along with Saya and Kanae. I'm sure I'll be fine."

"I think we should go now. I don't need to see any more of the foundry. I'll be seeing it almost every day from now on. Can we go? I don't think it would interest you that much, anyway." Turning, he continued, "What do you think, Haruki? Is it okay if we leave early? I don't want to make the same mistake as last time."

"We can leave anytime you're ready," he replied.

"I'm feeling fine, Toshi. Let's stay a little longer. I want to see the new furnace you'll be in charge of. I want to be able to think about you while I'm at home with our family. It will be easier if I can picture what you're doing here. Let's go see it."

They walked from the food tables over to the new furnace. With so many guests for the event, they had to weave their way through the crowd to get to furnace number two. The furnace itself was housed within walls of stone, with large open windows to allow circulation during the hot summer months. Off to one side of the furnace was a large room with fewer windows. It contained the steam boiler, which Toshi explained was the latest technology from England, and it powered the fan, which forced air into the furnace. From now on, they could control the force of the air by regulating the amount of steam.

Along one side of the room was a worktable where Toshi could maintain his records, organize their schedules, and receive orders for each day's production. There was a doorway leading out to a toilet, which was especially helpful during the open house, because one of the furnace toilets had been designated for women while the other was designated for men. This was the first time Toshi had ever seen a woman at the foundry, so they had not needed the distinction until today.

Toshi hardly noticed when Ayami and Minako slipped away to use the toilet, but after several minutes, he began to worry. "What's taking them so long?" he asked Haruki. "Shouldn't they be back by now?"

"I'm sure they're fine," Haruki replied. "And Minako is with her. She'll let us know if anything is wrong."

Another ten minutes passed. "Saya, would you go check on them?" Haruki finally said.

Shortly they all returned, with Ayami looking slightly flushed.

"Ayami had another short pain," Minako explained. "It might be best if we headed home."

Toshi carried Kiyoshi and walked next to Ayami as they headed down the trail. After some distance, Ayami's pace began to slow. Instinctively, he shifted Kiyoshi to his left arm and shoulder and slipped his right arm through Ayami's in case she stumbled. Seeing this, Haruki stepped along her right side and slipped his left arm under her right. When they had traveled another few hundred meters, she spoke up.

"I think I need to rest for a few minutes. I'm sorry to be a nuisance."

"Nonsense," they both replied at once.

"Let's stop at that big rock, and you can sit there for a while," continued Toshi.

"Saya, do you know where the physician lives?" Haruki asked.

"Yes, I think so. Doesn't he live in the big house just past Fr. Lispard's church?"

"Yes, it's bigger than the others around it. I think there is even a sign at the door. You can ask when you get there if you need to. Go on ahead and ask him to come to our house. We'll take Ayami there after she's rested. Be sure to tell him who she is and everything that's happened today so he can be thinking about how to treat her when he arrives."

***

The others were pacing back and forth about the living room when they heard the neighing of a horse, followed by a commotion and heavy footfalls. When Kanae opened the door to look out, it was the physician. She had never seen him on a horse before. "It's the physician," she exclaimed. "He's here already. He came on a horse!"

"I'm glad you decided not to play doctor this time around, Toshi," he said when he entered the house. He examined Ayami in the bedroom while the rest of them remained out front. Minako periodically went to the stove to make sure there was plenty of hot water in case he called for it. Kanae tried to entertain Kiyoshi, although nothing seemed to interest him other than his mother.

Not long after, Saya returned on foot, still running when she reached the front yard. She burst in the house, asking for news of Ayami. "Did she have the baby?" she asked. "Is she alright?"

"No baby yet, and Ayami seems to be fine."

After several minutes with Ayami, the physician returned from the bedroom. "Her pulse is good, and she's not had any contractions. I think it will be a few days before the baby comes. You really should consider moving down to the village where you could reach me easier." He was still huffing from his excursion on horseback.

"It would be safer for all of you to live in the village where there are neighbors to watch after you. I don't know why you want to live up here all alone," he scolded. "Not to mention the inconvenience for me to rush up here every time you need a physician."

"I'm sorry to cause you the inconvenience," Toshi replied.

"Make sure she gets plenty of rest. She is not to do any work in the kitchen or in the yard until the baby arrives. Is there someone who can watch over her day and night?" he asked.

"Yes, we'll make sure Minako is here with her, and at least one of the girls," Haruki replied.

"Good. At the first sign of contractions or any unexpected pain or other symptoms, send Saya down to get me. We'll just have to hope I'm not called off to the hinterlands on some other emergency," he grumbled. "If I haven't heard from you within the week, I'll try to schedule a special trip up here, just to check on her."

Then he walked out the door to where the horse was peacefully grazing a little too close to Minako's flower garden. When he got to the horse, he turned to Toshi, who, along with Haruki, had followed him out. "Can one of you help me get back on the horse?" he asked. "I'm not particularly good at it."

After the physician left and the others had moved to the kitchen, Toshi motioned for Haruki to follow him outside. Standing on the porch where no one else could hear, he said, "Did you hear Ayami ask about anko at the foundry?"

"No, I guess I wasn't paying attention. What did she say?"

"She asked if I had ever tasted it. It reminded me of those letters from Emiko and Suki. I don't like to mention it around Ayami, but I'm worried about them."

"I worry too, but I don't know what we can do. Even if we knew where they were, Kunio signed a contract. I don't think we could get Emiko out of it even if Kunio agreed to let us try."

"I'm afraid you're right," Toshi said. "I don't know what we can do."

Chapter 33

Two New Furnaces

Dawn was breaking when Toshi left home and headed up the familiar trail to the foundry. It was a surprise when, as he approached the fork to Haruki's house, a figure emerged. It was Haruki.

"Good morning," he called out.

"Good morning, Toshi. You're up early today," came the reply.

"How is Ayami? Any change?" Toshi asked.

"She's doing fine, but no change. The girls are taking good care of her. You don't need to worry."

"I didn't sleep very well, worrying about her, so I decided to get started early today. Now we can worry about the foundry instead."

"Today will go fine, too. It's just a break-in day, so we'll do everything at half-speed. I'm sure the director will be there to walk us through the correct procedures."

"Do you think he'll be upset with us for leaving the open house early?"

"If he has children of his own, he'll understand why we had to leave. Besides, he was probably too busy with the dignitaries to even notice that we left."

"I hope so. I'd hate to start our new positions having him upset with us. He doesn't seem the sympathetic type. Do you think he could retract the bonus he promised?"

"I suppose he can do whatever he wants, but I really doubt he would be that upset with us. After all, the open house was not mandatory. And we did attend for as long as possible, under the circumstances." They walked in silence for several hundred meters before Haruki continued.

"I don't think we need to worry about that. If we concentrate on learning the new procedures, we'll both be fine. Imagine yourself in the director's place. Today is the first time he'll ever fire the furnace on a project he's been working on for over two years. If you think we're nervous, I bet he is twice that. He won't be thinking about us. He'll only be interested in whether his project is going to work. Today we should give him all the support we can, even if he is a little short with us."

When they arrived at the new foundry, not surprisingly, they were the first two workers there. Both men walked slowly around the new facility while they waited for others to arrive. It gave them another chance to familiarize themselves with the furnaces and consider how this or that feature worked and how it compared to the old furnace, a few hundred meters away.

They almost jumped when they rounded the corner of one of the boilers to find the director approaching from the other side.

"*Konnichiwa,*" (Good morning) said the director, using probably the only Japanese word he knew. He gave them a forced smile.

"*Konnichiwa,*" both men replied in unison. They also forced a smile, but Toshi felt theirs were better than the one they had received.

Not knowing what to do next, both men just stood and alternated between looking at the steam boiler and then at the director.

The director must have felt the same, as he mimicked their movements. Finally, he gestured for them to follow him back to his quarters. He raised his hand up to his mouth to simulate drinking tea, as they moved toward the building.

Haruki nodded his head to indicate their acceptance.

Toshi remembered the director drank coffee on their previous visit, so he was prepared when the director pointed to two different jars, as if asking whether they preferred coffee or tea. He thought it easier to ask for coffee, which he did, and Haruki nodded his agreement.

They were both surprised to see the director making it on his own instead of the attractive woman who seemed to always do his bidding on previous occasions. They watched his actions for signs he might be unfamiliar with the process, but he seemed very much at ease doing it himself. After a few minutes, he poured and handed each of them a hot cup of coffee, and even more surprisingly, his face reflected a natural smile as he did so.

Toshi was starting to feel more at ease. But it was still awkward until the front door opened and the interpreter walked in. On seeing the three of them already there, he quickly acknowledged the director as he managed an apologetic greeting.

"Good morning, sir. I didn't realize you were planning to start early this morning. I'm sorry if I've kept you waiting," he sputtered in German.

"It's quite all right," was the reply. "I didn't plan to be up this early when you left yesterday. I couldn't sleep, so I decided to get up. Help yourself to tea if you like, then we'll head to the furnace and get ready for the big day."

An hour later, the director was leading the entire furnace workforce from station to station, carefully explaining the required process for extracting iron from the ore brought from the adjacent mines. The explanation was like Toshi's previous experience. The director spoke in short bursts, carefully explaining the task at hand, and the interpreter repeated his words as closely as possible. This was repeated several times until the director asked, through the interpreter, if there were questions.

It was just after noon when the director announced they were done. Tomorrow, they would fire the furnace for the first time. It was too late in the day to run even a small test. Haruki sensed a reluctance by the director to fire his long-developing project. It would be an unbearable humiliation if it didn't work.

The director waited until the others were gone before he told the two foremen, "When we fire the furnace tomorrow, I would appreciate it if you took notice of anything that needs to be changed or improved. However, please keep it to yourselves until we're done for the day and the workers are gone. Then we can discuss in private, without causing confusion among the men." He paused again. "And Toshi, I know you are good at keeping a journal. Please keep a journal starting tomorrow, so that we'll have a good record of what we've done and what works. We'll meet after the first month and review the journal to see if together we can find improvements."

***

Early the next morning, with the charcoal fully ignited and heat from the steam chamber beginning to vent, it was time to add the magnetite. The men alternated adding charcoal and ore to the chamber as air flowing from the steam engine continued to increase. Sooner than they expected, iron began to flow. It was working.

The director stood back from the men and watched the first-ever fruits of his years of labor. The molds for today called for iron wheels, something simple for the first day's run. He watched as a dozen molds filled with molten liquid.

Haruki stood among his crew as they filled one mold, turned off the spigot, and quickly replaced the mold with an empty one. Other men quickly pulled the hot mold away to the cooling area and out of the way. It was a familiar process.

At first, Haruki was smiling almost as much as the director. But as the molds were filled and moved away, his smile began to fade. He stole a glance at Toshi to see if he showed any sign of concern.

Toshi smiled at him and continued with another mold.

Haruki glanced at the director to see if he noticed anything unusual.

The director had a smile on his face. He seemed pleased with the process.

They filled several more molds as Haruki watched. The molds were filling faster now as the furnace continued to heat. When forty-five minutes had passed, Haruki noted sweat dripping from all their faces. The men seemed to be moving increasingly faster with every mold that filled. *Can they continue the pace?* Haruki wondered to himself. *This is a lot faster than the old furnace.*

He looked again at Toshi, who was too busy running the spigot to look back at Haruki. The cadence was short and simple: close the spigot—position the empty mold—open the spigot—fill the mold—close the spigot—move the filled mold out of the way—replace with an empty mold, and repeat the process.

It was nothing the men had not done a thousand times before, but because it was the very first time coming from the new furnace, after two years of construction, every man who watched was mesmerized by the process. Even the men who were handling the molds were so engrossed in the operation they paid little attention to anything else.

When another fifteen minutes had passed, Haruki could see the men beginning to tire. These were men who had worked at the foundry for years, and not once had he seen them so fatigued in this amount of time. He looked again at Toshi, who was running the spigot, and watched him wipe the sweat from his eyes with the back of his heavy sleeve.

Toshi did not return the look. He was too busy watching the molds. If he opened the spigot before the men were ready, molten iron would flow not into the molds, but onto their arms, hands, and legs. If he closed the spigot for too long, allowing them time to catch up, the furnace would fill with iron, and they would only get further behind.

Sensing a disaster in the making, Haruki looked again at the director. His smile was gone and he was looking around at the men, but he made no indication that he was about to provide any kind of instruction.

Becoming more alarmed by the minute, Haruki broke away from his men and hurried over to the director.

Looking at the interpreter, who was standing next to the director, he shouted, "I don't think we can keep up with the furnace! It's running too fast! Someone is going to get hurt!"

Haruki waited anxiously while the interpreter relayed his message.

The director looked directly at the interpreter before he answered. He was so intrigued by how well the furnace was working that he had tuned out the possibility of something going awry.

"What did you say?" he shouted back to the interpreter.

"He doesn't think they can keep up!" he repeated. "He said someone is going to get hurt."

This time, when the director looked around at the men, he observed with the eyes of a foreman and not those of a designer. This time, he saw sweat dripping from the foreheads of every worker, running into their eyes, blurring their vision. He watched as they tried in vain to wipe the perspiration away using their bulky clothing, and finally he looked over at Toshi, who was trying desperately to time the spigot opening to avoid a tragic accident.

The director shot a look at Haruki and motioned for him to follow, then rushed to the boiler room next door and yelled frantically to the interpreter, "Tell him to lower the pressure!"

The interpreter turned and shouted the message to Haruki.

Haruki scanned the room looking for the boilerman, to relay the message. But when he looked around, no one was there. He ran behind the boiler, thinking he must be there. No one there. He came back to the front, but he was not there, either.

"Maybe he went to get more wood for the boiler," he shouted to the interpreter. Then he looked up above his head at the large, round dial that indicated pressure. From where he stood, it looked like the black needle was pointing at one hundred and twenty. On the face of the dial, behind the needle, the background color changed from white to yellow, he noted, beginning at a pressure of one hundred. Above one hundred and twenty, the background color was red.

Haruki shouted to the interpreter. "How much pressure?" Then he started up the short ladder, making his way to the valve.

The interpreter, though not always presenting himself as a dedicated employee, seemed to understand the danger of the situation and shouted to the director, then back to Haruki with his reply.

"Eighty pounds!" he shouted. "Eighty pounds," he repeated again, to make sure.

Haruki quickly turned the valve in a clockwise motion to lower the pressure. When he saw the needle move slowly to the left, he looked down at the interpreter and shouted, "Eighty pounds!" as a confirmation of his instruction. It took several minutes for the needle to reach eighty. When it did, and stabilized at that reading, Haruki climbed down the ladder.

He looked at the director when he reached the floor and pointed a finger at himself. "I should have been watching the boilerman," he told the interpreter. "I will have a talk with him."

When the three men went back to the furnace room, they could see the result of the pressure change. Toshi had already slowed his spigot procedure, and the other men were able to catch their breath between each fill of the mold.

Haruki found the man who was supposed to be watching the boiler. He was so enamored by the efficiency of the new furnace that he completely forgot his primary duty.

"We were lucky," Haruki told him when he talked to him in private. "We both heard the interpreter tell us only yesterday how important the pressure is for this new furnace. I am not going to sack you, because I should have made sure you were at your station. I accept part of the blame. But I am assigning Kenshin to be the new boilerman from now on. You knew your assignment, and you should have been there, even without my checking on you."

The remainder of the shortened day passed quickly. When the director surveyed the molds at the end of the shift, he could barely contain his smile. "Well done, men," he relayed to everyone present. "Tomorrow, Haruki will lead his crew here at furnace number one. Toshi and the rest of us will move on to furnace number two and repeat the process we started today. If we have as good a day tomorrow, you will have done your emperor proud."

Toshi thought back to his short career at the furniture factory. This was the reason he had to leave. This was a milestone in history. And he was a part of it. It was a proud moment.

When Haruki and Toshi walked home together the next day, they could hardly believe their luck. A few months earlier they had worried about their futures. Toshi even thought he might be sacked. And here they were today, each of them in charge of a furnace, with the furnaces performing better than they dared to hope.

They were sharing stories about their day when a familiar voice interrupted their thoughts.

"Toshi! Come quick! Ayami is having her baby!" It was Saya. "Hurry! I've already been to the village for the physician. He should be there by now."

Chapter 34

A New Baby

KAMAISHI – MARCH 1880

Toshi dropped his conversation in mid-sentence and began to run. Haruki was close behind, but not as fast. They quickly caught up to Saya, who turned around and ran with them toward Haruki's house.

They were a kilometer away when they met, and even though both men were strong and healthy from their work at the foundry, they were not accustomed to running. When Toshi reached the house, he bent over with both hands on his knees to catch his breath and sucked in several long breaths before he opened the door.

"Ayami," he called. "Are you alright?"

Kiyoshi rushed over to greet his father. He and Kanae were in the kitchen making sure there was hot water and whatever else the physician called for.

"Mother and the physician are with her. I think it may be over," Kanae said. I haven't heard Ayami scream for a while."

"Over?" Toshi exclaimed. "What do you mean, over? Did she die?"

Just as Kanae was about to reply, a baby cried in the next room.

Toshi's face turned red from embarrassment and then he grinned. "Oh," he said. He dashed to the bedroom to see his wife.

Minako was cleaning the newborn with a warm cloth when he approached.

The physician looked up when Toshi walked in. "You have a healthy new son," he said, then turned back to his patient.

Minako wrapped the infant in a soft blanket and carried him over to Toshi, placing the bundle in his arms. "Congratulations," she murmured. "He is beautiful."

Toshi's arms trembled as she lifted the baby to him. He'd forgotten how tiny a newborn could be. Then his eyes began to mist. He bent his head down and gave the baby a light kiss on his soft forehead. When he looked up, he was surrounded by Kanae, and Saya, who was holding Kiyoshi up so he could also see.

The physician stood and cleared his throat to get their attention. "This is not a festival. Everybody out except Minako and the baby. We'll let you know when we're done in here." Then he turned and knelt down next to Ayami.

Toshi noticed the physician was holding Ayami's hand with his left, and seemed to be massaging the top of her hand and her forearm with his right. It seemed an odd thing to do as part of the birthing process, but maybe he was simply trying to calm her. At any rate, he was too preoccupied to worry about it now.

Everyone was so excited about the tiny little boy that they overlooked the gruff disposition of the physician. It seemed to be his nature. And there was no other choice, anyway; he was the only physician in the region. Toshi handed the baby back to Minako and followed the rest of them from the room.

An hour later, the physician came out. "We're finished now and you may see her. Ayami is tired and should rest for twenty-four hours. Make sure someone is close by at all times. The baby is fine, too."

Then he turned to Toshi and said, "Before you go in, I want to talk."

The others were all rushing in to see Ayami and the baby while Toshi remained.

"You are lucky that Saya is a swift runner. Also, that I was available when she came to get me. If you're going to have more babies, you need to move to the village where I can care for you better. I'm nearly sixty years old. It's hard for me to climb up the ridge to your house. The trail is too steep for a rickshaw and I don't like horses. It would be much safer for you and your family if you lived in the village.

"You have two sons to think about in addition to Ayami. What if something happened to one of them and I couldn't get here in time?" He waited a moment or two, as if about to leave, then continued. "The charge for delivering your baby is ten yen. I have to charge more because of the distance. It takes me away from other patients when I come all the way up here."

***

The following Sunday, Toshi woke early. Ayami and the boys were coming home today. They had remained at Haruki's since before the birth, and today was their homecoming. He was so excited he barely heard the birds singing just outside the windows when he opened them to air out the house. He straightened all the mats in the bedroom, swept the floor in the kitchen until it nearly shined, and washed the few dishes he had used in her absence.

Satisfied their house was ready for its newest member, he headed out the door and up the trail toward Haruki's. As he walked, he gradually began to notice the songbirds. It had been a long time since he'd taken time to listen. Less than a kilometer from Haruki's house, he heard oncoming sounds of conversation and occasional laughter. Stopping to make out the voices, he recognized those of Haruki and their families.

This time, he turned the tables on Kiyoshi and hid behind a small bush until he saw them coming. Kiyoshi was out in front, walking hand-in-hand with Saya. Toshi smiled as he watched Kiyoshi stop to look at a brightly colored leaf that caught his eye. He would grow up to appreciate the beauty of his surroundings, just like his father.

Then, when he was just a few meters away, Toshi jumped out in front of Kiyoshi and said, "Boo," with a big smile on his face.

Kiyoshi jumped back and his eyes grew round, and his face contorted into a frown, until he realized who it was. Then the frown turned to a smile, and from a smile to a giggle, as he burst free from Saya's hand and headed straight for his father. "Papa," he exclaimed.

"Baby," he beamed, pointing to Minako, who was carrying his new little brother.

"I see him," replied Toshi, as he lifted Kiyoshi in his arms. "Let's have a look at him, shall we?"

They walked over to Minako and lifted the blanket to see his tiny face. Even with his eyes closed the infant was beautiful.

"We think he looks like you," Minako said. "He has your eyes and nose, even your mouth. He is going to look just like you when he grows up."

"What could be better?" Toshi replied. "We have one child who looks like his mother, and one like his father." He paused. "Kiyoshi, I guess you're the lucky one."

"What shall we name him?" Toshi asked. "We haven't even thought of a name yet."

Ayami chimed in. "The girls and I have been talking about it, and I'd like to name him Isamu. What do you think of that name? Isamu. It means 'courage.'

"Isamu," Toshi repeated. He played it again in his mind. "Isamu is a good name," he replied. "We'll name him Isamu. Now let's show Isamu his new home. And even if his home is up on the ridge instead of down in the village, I know he's going to be safe."

It took the rest of them a few minutes to understand what he was referring to. When they remembered the physician's admonition, they began to laugh. "We'll help you keep him safe," they agreed.

Chapter 35

New Production Record

KAMAISHI – LATE 1880 - IRON FOUNDRY

On his way to work that Monday morning, Toshi bent down to pick one of the scattered autumn flowers that lined the trail. This particular one was a special treat because it, like the other examples of *Tricyrtis affinis* along the path, were relegated by their size to the bottom of the forest. At forty centimeters, they struggled in the shadows of the towering pines for whatever slivers of leftover sunlight the trees would allow. No wonder, then, the delicate, polka-dotted lilies could last only two days until shriveling away for another year. This plant was clearly in its second day, and its flowers would likely be gone before Toshi's return trip home. He gently pinched the flower from its leafy stem and held it to his nose. If it ever held a fragrance, it was no longer present.

The different seasons each brought forth new favorites. He could just as easily admire a spring wildflower as a summer berry bush or the red and gold leaves of a powerful oak. He remembered walking to work in the spring, and now he pulled his jacket tighter as an autumn chill claimed his attention.

Isamu was six months old and, along with Kiyoshi, the delight of their household. The new blast furnaces had exceeded even the director's expectation. Every month saw a new record for iron produced. The railway could hardly keep up with deliveries to the waiting ships, bound for Tokyo. Overall, it had been a good year for Toshi Ozawa.

Although it was not uppermost in his mind, Toshi did, on occasion, dream about the bonus the director had promised to either him or Haruki. By the end of November, they were essentially in a tie, by his calculation. What if it ended that way? *Would the director give both of them the prize? Or maybe he would say there was no winner, and neither man would get the bonus.* He decided to talk with Haruki about that possibility. It might be safer to have a clear-cut winner. Surely, with the success of the furnaces, the director would be in a generous mood, but he could not be sure.

On the third Wednesday of December, in the early afternoon, Toshi was surprised by a visit from the interpreter. He rarely left the comfort of the director's building to visit the furnaces, because they were too loud and too hot.

The interpreter pulled Toshi off to one side and said, "The director wishes to see you at the end of the day today."

"Do you know what it's about?" Toshi asked.

"He only said that you and Haruki are to meet with him at the end of the day." As soon as he delivered the message, he turned and left.

For the remainder of the afternoon, Toshi struggled to keep his mind on the furnace. *Was the meeting about their bonus? What if it is something else? Are we doing something wrong? November was our best month ever. Surely, he's not disappointed with our work.*

Finally, the last of the molds were filled and the men were cleaning up for the next day's run. When the last man removed his protective apron and headed home, Toshi made one last sweep of the area to make sure everything was ready for the early crew. Then he walked over to Haruki's furnace.

"What did we do wrong now?" he asked.

Haruki knew from the smile on his face he was mostly joking. But he shared the same feeling; something could be wrong. It was rare they were called to see the director once both crews had found their rhythm.

"I wish I knew," Haruki replied. "I thought everything was going better than expected. Do you think it could be about the bonus? It's almost the end of the year." As he hung his apron on a peg near the door, he added, "I guess we might as well get it over with." And together, they headed to the director's office.

When the interpreter offered them each a coffee or tea, they relaxed slightly. It was not like him to offer a refreshment for a meeting of reprimand. Haruki asked for tea, but Toshi was beginning to acquire a taste for the German's coffee.

Before he could even bring it to them, the director opened his door and invited the two into his office. Both strained to decipher the lines on his face. He was showing a smile that looked authentic, yet it seemed to cover a deeper tension.

He waited for the interpreter to deliver tea and coffee to the visitors, then signaled for a fresh cup for himself. It was an awkward silence as they waited for the interpreter to return. They busied themselves by letting their cups cool and sipping lightly to fill the silence.

The meeting began. Through the lengthy process they had become accustomed to, the interpreter relayed his boss's conversation back and forth to Toshi and Haruki.

"We'll start with the good news," began the interpreter. "With your help, the new furnaces have produced beyond our expectations. The owners are grateful for that. I also, am grateful. I have reviewed the production from both operations since we began, and you are probably not surprised to learn the amount of iron produced by each furnace is nearly identical. I trust you have not conspired to make it so. At any rate, regarding the bonus arrangement we talked about last February, I have reached a decision. Since both of you have contributed essentially equal results, you will each be rewarded with one hundred yen as a measure of our appreciation."

Toshi and Haruki could not restrain a smile when the interpreter spoke the words. They smiled first at each other, then at the director, who smiled back at them.

"You will each receive an envelope when you leave today," the interpreter relayed.

"Now for the disappointing news. In spite of the efficiency of our new furnaces and the additional manpower we added to the charcoal division, we are not able to keep up with the demand. For that reason, both furnaces will shut down at the end of the day on Saturday, until Monday, January third, of 1881. We are hopeful that by not using charcoal for two weeks we'll build up a stockpile for use when we resume the furnaces. As with last year, only the furnaces will be dark; both the miners and the charcoal burners will continue to work. We will again pay half-wages to the furnace crews during the period, which we believe is more than generous."

There was a lull in the conversation to allow Toshi and Haruki to absorb the news. This caught them both by surprise since they had experienced no interruptions throughout the year.

"What about in the long run?" Toshi dared to ask. "Do you think we'll have enough charcoal to keep going next year? Will two weeks be enough for the charcoal division to catch up for the whole year? We've only been in operation for nine months with the new furnaces, and if we run short now, do you think we'll run out again in September?"

The interpreter relayed his questions to the director, and both managers could tell by the look on his face the answer would not be good.

"Those are the very questions I've been working on for the last two months. The truth is, I don't know. But I am concerned about running out on a regular basis. We are exploring the use of coal or some other fuel in place of charcoal, but as of today we have no clear resolution." He paused for a minute, then resumed. "This news is meant only for the two of you. It is not to be shared with the workers. We do not want to upset them needlessly. We're still hopeful that a solution will be found to keep the furnaces running."

So, this was the reason for his underlying tension when the meeting began, thought Toshi. *This could be devastating. How can we keep this secret from the men?* The one hundred yen bonus suddenly lost its luster.

Not wanting to prolong the meeting longer than necessary, the director asked if either man had more questions. They were so deflated they could only shake their heads and head for the door.

"Wait for your envelopes," the interpreter said as he pulled them from a drawer in his desk and offered one to each of them.

"Thank you," they responded.

Toshi was usually talkative on the walk home with Haruki. If it had been a good day of production, he would replay for Haruki every highlight and detail until Haruki could only pretend to listen. And if it had been a bad day, he would theorize on all the possible reasons production had been low. But on this day, Toshi was silent.

He looked mostly at the ground as they walked for a hundred meters or more.

Haruki watched as Toshi removed the envelope from his pocket and counted the contents. After getting to one hundred, he placed it back in the envelope and then back in his pocket.

"Have you decided what to do with your bonus?" Haruki asked, hoping to pull Toshi from his shell.

"Not yet," he replied. "I didn't want to think about it until I knew it was really going to happen. I didn't want to be disappointed if I had it all planned out, what to do, and then had to give it up."

"Have you thought about using it to pay off your house? That's always a safe decision. Especially if there's a chance the foundry might close later on," he continued. He immediately regretted the words. It was likely the probability of the foundry closing was precisely what was going through Toshi's mind.

"That does seem like a good choice," Toshi replied. "I'll talk to Ayami about it."

Hearing Haruki's voice, filled with concern about his well-being, very nearly caused Toshi to disclose his actual thoughts. One hundred yen was the most money he'd had since before the wedding. Chances were good he would not have this much again for several years, if ever.

This was his second chance to convince Ayami. With the one hundred yen bonus, they could get by without selling the house. Combined with the twenty-five yen he had saved since the wedding, they could travel to America. And this time it was even more compelling because the foundry would be lucky to last another year. The director as much as admitted it.

He and Ayami were still young. The boys were too young to miss what few friends they had. Neither he nor Ayami had immediate family members nearby. They rarely saw his parents, and Ayami did not carry much love for her father or brothers. If ever there was a time to go, now was surely the time.

It was Haruki that held him back. And his family. It would be hard to tell them they were leaving. Especially when he thought back to that very first day they met—the day he stumbled and fell getting off the boat.

It was a long walk home that Wednesday afternoon, as the wind picked up and darkness settled in.

When they reached Haruki's house, Haruki said, "Tomorrow we need to make sure we stay positive for the men. I think they'll be okay with the two-week shutdown, but we can't let them know our long-term concern. Maybe the director is right and they'll come up with a solution."

That night, after eating supper and putting the boys to bed, Toshi invited Ayami to sit down next to him. Once settled on their favorite mat, Toshi looked at her with a solemn look and began his proposal. He had been rehearsing its key points since leaving Haruki three hours earlier. They were the same points he so carefully articulated while walking home with Haruki, but this time he would actually say them out loud.

"Who knows when we'll ever have this much money again?" he said to Ayami. "It's like the hundred yen was given to us for a purpose. The boys are young and they won't miss their friends. Just think how much they would learn by traveling to a new country and how many opportunities there would be for us.

"America is a huge country, with so much land it's hard to imagine. I think it's at least ten times bigger than Japan, maybe more. And a lot of it has not even been settled yet. Maybe we could start our own village—and just a few years ago, they discovered gold in California; that's where we would be going, California. And not long after that, they found silver not far away in Nevada. Who knows what else is there, just waiting to be discovered?"

"What about Haruki and Minako? Wouldn't you miss them? And their girls?"

"Yes, I would definitely miss them. They have been like family to us since our wedding, but we could always write to them. After we got settled, they might even come to visit. Or, better yet, to live with us. We could help them settle there, too."

"What about all the workers at the foundry? Wouldn't you miss them? After all, they are almost like your family. I saw how they looked up to you at the open house last year. I'm sure they would hate for you to leave them."

It was proving a little more difficult to convince Ayami than he anticipated. Then he remembered another important point he'd planned to make. "The thing is," he said, "who knows how long the foundry will be operating? Even the director said they don't have a solution to the charcoal problem."

"I tried fishing," he reminded her. "How many fish did I bring home after all night on the boat? Do you remember?"

"I remember," she admitted. "It was only one fish. But Hideji said that was a bad night and most of the time they did a lot better."

"He did say that," Toshi said, "but remember how cold I was, and how I got seasick for much of the trip? I don't think I could do that every night even if I did catch more fish. The best part of the whole night was the sailing. I liked the sailing part."

Then Toshi thought of something else. "We wouldn't have to sell the house," he said. "We could rent it to Hisa and Hajime. They would probably love to live up on the ridge where they could be close to Haruki and Minako. We could rent it to them for a discount since they are family. I'm sure Minako would be happy to have Eito close by. She might even want to take care of him, and that way Hisa could get a job if she wanted to."

Ayami thought about his several arguments before responding. Then she said, "I suppose you're right. I love you, Toshi, and I've told you before I would go anywhere with you."

A moment later she added, "But I would rather stay here and take our chances along with our friends."

It sounded enough like an approval that Toshi gave Ayami a heartfelt embrace. Then, as his longtime dream became a possibility, he began planning a list of all the things he needed to do. The first item on the list was a visit to the wharf to find out how to get passage for himself and his family. It seemed likely they would have to take the packet ship to Tokyo, but how often ships sailed to America from there, he didn't know.

Two hours later, Ayami had to ask Toshi for the second time if he was coming to bed. "You still have to get up and go to work tomorrow, even if you do plan to leave the foundry. I know you won't want to let the other workers down by being late." She leaned down with a gentle hand on his shoulder and kissed him on the cheek. Then she turned and went to bed.

After she left, Toshi pulled out the envelope, still in his pocket, and counted the money. One hundred yen. It brought a sense of comfort he could not explain. Then he went to the special cupboard in the kitchen and retrieved the jar that held their savings. He emptied the jar and counted the money. Twenty-seven yen. It had taken three years to save that much. It was an easy calculation to figure how long it would take to save a hundred. Yet here he was, with an extra one hundred yen, already available, already in his pocket, waiting to fulfill his dream.

Then, by candlelight, he walked through their dream house, room by room, the one he and Ayami had so eagerly built when they were married. It would be hard to leave. They had dreamt of it together. He remembered how his father and Haruki had helped with the negotiations.

When Toshi went to bed sometime later, he tried not to wake Ayami as he slipped quietly onto the mat beside her. Some nights the heat from her body was enough to keep him warm, just by lying next to her. But this night was cold, and he pulled a cover over his torso for extra warmth. He tried to lie still and not wake his sleeping wife, but after what seemed more than an hour, he changed position and tried again to fall asleep. He could not stop thinking about America. *Could he find gold? Could he get a job at an iron factory? In a country with boundless opportunities, he could surely be successful, whatever line of work he might pursue.*

Then he thought about Haruki. *How will I tell Haruki, after what he's done for Ayami and me? After all, we would not have met if not for Haruki.* Then he wondered how he would tell the men at his furnace. *They did everything they could to make the new furnace succeed.* He thought about the extra hours they had worked through the heat and the cold, without complaint, because they cared about Toshi and the foundry. He was still thinking about them when he finally drifted off.

Ayami had to wake him the next morning, or he would surely have been late for work. He dressed quickly and skipped breakfast, then hurried up the path. He was surprised to find Haruki on the trail. Haruki had not slept well either, worried about what to tell the workers. Toshi gingerly shared his newest plan. It had somehow formed during the last few hours of his restless sleep.

Reaching the foundry, the two foremen headed directly to their stations. The early-shift workers were already on the job, firing the furnace and heating the boiler. The rest of the shift began to trickle in.

Toshi rehearsed over and over in his head the message he needed to give. *Tell the truth. Keep them motivated instead of worried. Live prudently.* He was worried about his men. He was worried about saying the right thing. And deep down, he was worried about his own future and what he would do if the plant shut down for good.

He took several long, deep breaths and then resorted to what had become his desperation strategy. He called on Fr. Lispard's God for help. How easy it was to forget his promise to himself only weeks ago, with so many things to worry about. His prayer today was a simple one. *God, if you can hear me, help me know what to say to them.*

Then, all too soon, the boiler tender knocked on his door to announce the men were ready.

He could tell by their faces they had been anticipating some kind of news. The decision to give it to them early seemed a good one.

"Good morning, everyone. You may have seen the interpreter stop by yesterday. Haruki and I were summoned to a meeting with the director after work. He told us that both he and the owners were very happy with how quickly you learned to operate the new furnace, and with your production throughout the year." He paused, trying to remember what he was going to say next. "He also said we will be shutting down for two weeks, just as we did last year at this time. We'll shut down at the end of day on Saturday, December eighteenth, and resume on Tuesday, January fourth. That gives everyone the opportunity to celebrate the New Year. As before, all workers will receive one-half their normal pay during that period."

He paused again, giving them time to digest the news.

Then he pushed forward with the plan that came to him almost as from a dream. "We have three working days left before the shutdown, including today. Haruki and I have arranged for a contest of sorts, which could result in a bonus for each of you, if you are interested." He paused, this time for them to start thinking about the possibilities.

"Here is the contest, but you must vote 'yea' or 'nay' as a group. There will be a one-yen bonus for each man, for each of the three days that we set a new daily production record… *without an accident.* For example, if today is a new record for us, each man gets an extra yen. If tomorrow you beat today's production, you each get another yen, then if we set another daily record on Saturday, you each get another yen. Each day starts anew, so if you miss today, for example, you could still qualify on Friday or Saturday."

Then he added, "However, if there is even one accident during a day, that day no longer qualifies. I hope the reason is obvious. I don't want any of you to get injured simply for the sake of an extra yen. It might be easy to take careless shortcuts in a contest like this, but we want to avoid that.

"We have broken the daily record almost on a regular basis since the furnace began, so it's a challenge I think we can achieve with only a little extra effort. But if you decide to accept the challenge, I want you to know it will take all of us together to succeed. I've already implemented my ideas, so we're going to need yours if we're going to improve.

"If we accept this challenge and if we're able to set new records, it will help in making up our shortfall during the shutdown. This is a good reminder that we all need to make sure our family budgets are sustainable and that we should always set something aside for emergencies.

"Our current daily production total is eighty-four pigs. Do you want to accept the challenge? Raise your hand if you want to set a new record."

Toshi watched as five hands went up immediately, four more soon after, and as the excitement caught, all fifteen hands went in the air. Toshi finalized the count by raising his own high in the air. It trembled slightly, but it was from how proud he was of his men.

"Eighty-five or bust!" he heard one of the workers exclaim. "Eighty-five or bust!" came a chorus of replies. And off to their stations they went.

Toshi headed back to his planning room. *Thank you, God, for watching over me,* he prayed silently to himself.

***

Ayami and Kiyoshi were watching at the door when they saw his lantern bobbing along the path. They were getting anxious, as it was later than normal for him to arrive.

"How was your day? Did you tell them about the closing?"

"Haruki and I decided to share our bonus with the others. We came up with a contest where we will pay them each one yen if they set a new production record. If we set a new record every day, that would be forty-five yen we would share with them. Do you think we did the right thing?"

"Of course you did," she replied without hesitation. "After all, don't they work as hard as you and Haruki? But what about going to America? I thought you were going to use the bonus to move us to America. How can we afford to go if you give forty-five yen to the workers?"

Toshi exhaled slowly and looked down at the floor. "Something changed overnight," he said. "I don't know what it was, exactly. I remember that, going to sleep, I was thinking about all the things I needed to do in order to make the trip. Then I remembered thinking about Haruki and all the men at work and how good they've treated me since I got here. And when I woke up this morning, I realized I could not run out on them, especially if the foundry shuts down.

"On the way into work this morning, I met Haruki on the trail, and by the time we got to work, we had worked out a plan for the workers. It seemed like the right thing to do, so we told them about it first thing this morning."

"Did they like the idea?" she asked. "Did it start today?"

"Yes, it started today, and they set a record. I guess I'm fifteen yen short already. I hope you don't mind."

Ayami picked up Kiyoshi with one arm, put her other around Toshi's shoulder, and pulled them both tight. "How could I mind?" she said. "I'm proud of you. Does this mean we're staying in Kamaishi?"

Toshi turned to face her directly and watched as she blinked away the mist in her eyes. "Yes, I suppose it does," he murmured. "At least for now."

***

The next day, both furnaces set new production records. *Fifteen more yen out of his pocket and into the pockets of his men,* thought Toshi as they walked. Thirty yen for the two days. That left him with seventy, or more likely, fifty-five, after tomorrow. Could they possibly hit another record again tomorrow? As the men were leaving today, they were determined to break one hundred on their last day.

He was excited for his men even at the financial cost to himself. *Why didn't we make a deal with the director when we had the chance, instead of from our own pockets?* But the contest had worked. The entire crew was focused on producing as much iron as they could, during a shift. Not one man had mentioned charcoal or the shutdown.

Then he considered how the men would feel if they eventually found out he and Haruki received a hundred-yen bonus and they got nothing. They would be lucky to produce fifty 'pigs' on any day after that.

Walking home that day, he said to Haruki, "Maybe we should double the bonus. If they manage to set another record tomorrow, that would be six yen per man, for a total of ninety yen from us. That leaves us with ten each, compared to their six. I think I'd sleep better with that arrangement than with three for each of them and fifty-five for me."

When they reached Haruki's house, he said, "I like the idea. I'll see you in the morning. Then he added, "Don't blow the rest of our bonus until you check with me."

***

On Saturday, the early shift for both furnaces arrived even before Toshi and Haruki. Both teams were gunning to break the one hundred 'pig' barrier. The director was nearly beside himself with excitement. It did not occur to him his two foremen were behind the recent surge. This was the first day either team could remember when the director made several personal visits to each furnace. By late afternoon he was seen walking around the cooling room with pencil in hand, counting pigs for another potential record.

Toshi could not have known that Haruki authorized his boiler team to bump the pressure by fifteen pounds. But on the other hand, it did not occur to Haruki that Toshi had done the same. Both teams were bent on crossing the hundred-pig threshold. Both were keeping a close eye on the equipment. A failure would result in disappointment for all of them, financial as well as emotional.

The director counted ninety-eight in Haruki's cooling room, with a half-hour still to go. He walked over to Toshi's furnace and began his latest count. Toshi was afraid to follow him to the cooling room; his stomach was already tied in knots. *What if something goes wrong at the last minute?* And just as he feared, when he looked up near the top of the furnace, he saw long strands of the drive belt whipping around and around the pulleys. It was beginning to shred.

Rushing over to the boiler tender, he shouted, "Decrease the pressure by twenty pounds. The belt is separating." He pointed up to where the belt was spinning.

The man turned the valve until the gauge steadied at eighty pounds.

Toshi worried it might be too late. The damage was already done. If the belt snapped, there was nothing they could do until the furnace cooled completely down. It was so hot up there it would be impossible to repair. If it failed, there would be no more air forced into the furnace, and it would reduce production to a snail's pace. *Will it last another thirty minutes?* he worried. *That's all we need to break the record.*

From there, he headed for the cooling room to check the latest count. The director was just leaving, but Toshi gestured with his hands and what he hoped was a quizzical look on his face to indicate, *What's the count?* The director walked over to him and held his paper out. Pencil marks grouped in clusters of ten revealed nine clusters for a total of ninety pigs. A tenth cluster showed eight additional marks. Ninety-eight total pigs. The record should be a certainty, given there was still iron in the furnace waiting to come out. The question now was whether they would break one hundred. Toshi smiled at the director, who returned one of his own. This time it seemed one of complete sincerity.

Toshi fought hard to suppress breaking into laughter right then and there. As the lines in his cheeks shifted from tense to round, and his mouth cracked into the trace of a smile, he noticed the director doing the same. They tried not to look at each other, which only made it worse. Finally, they both gave in and broke out in a deep relief of laughter. They did not say anything because they did not speak the same language. But for that one moment, they understood each other completely.

Months and even years of work, stress, and frustration now melted away with the excitement of a milestone achievement. Both men knew they would exceed one hundred pigs. This was far above the director's early predictions. He could not wait to tell the owners. He decided at that moment to personally shake each worker's hand at the end of the day. Then he ran back to his office to get the interpreter. He suddenly had an idea. *"Feier!"* he cried as he ran.

Toshi was puzzled by his sudden exit and wondered what it was he had yelled as he left. He'd seemed pleased, even excited by their achievement. But Toshi needed to help complete the operation. He first went back to check on the drive belt. At this point, even if it failed, they would finish up what iron remained in the furnace. It would simply take longer.

He wondered how best to explain its sudden deterioration to the director. He probably needed to tell him while the director was in a good mood. Hopefully, he would return this afternoon. He would have to tell him now, as they would need to find a replacement prior to the re-opening in two weeks.

Half an hour later, the furnace was empty and beginning to cool. The men were moving the last two pigs to the cooling area and clearing away the slag and spattered iron from around the furnace.

When he looked up, Toshi saw the director approaching. This time, the interpreter was with him and they were both carrying something, but he could not tell what it was. Their arms were filled with something that looked like bottles. The director had three under one arm and two in the other, while the interpreter held two in one hand and a sack in his other hand. When they were within earshot, Toshi heard that word again: *"Feier! Feier!"* He looked happy, but it was puzzling behavior, particularly for the director, who rarely let show even a simple smile.

When the two men reached the furnace, the interpreter spoke up. "The director wants to celebrate what he calls this extraordinary achievement." He reached into his sack and began to hand every worker a tin cup. "These are all we could find on short notice," he explained. "Not exactly fitting for the occasion, but they will have to do."

The director, by this time, had set his bottles on a workbench in the changing room where all the men had gathered. He opened the first bottle and reached out to pour its contents into the cup of the man standing nearest him. With a smile spread widely across his face, the director repeated, *"Feier,"* and lifted the bottle into the air, with a gesture that suggested the man do the same with his cup. After a second, then a third attempt by the director, the man finally understood. He lifted his cup in the air and repeated, as best he could make it out, *"Feier."* At that, the director beamed his approval and began to pour what turned out to be saké, into every cup extended out to him. Before long, every worker had received his cup of saké. They looked at one another, then at Toshi, then at the director, and spontaneously, as if it were the most natural thing in the world, they all raised their cups to the furnace and yelled in unison, *"Feier! Feier!"*

"Celebrate! Celebrate!" the interpreter shouted to the men.

Then the director said something to the interpreter, who quickly put down his sack and disappeared in the direction of Haruki's furnace.

The director held a cup of his own in one hand as he topped off the cups of the workers with the other. Some of the men were unaccustomed to drinking saké and drank it sparingly, while others relished the opportunity to drink what was obviously of better quality than they were accustomed to at home. Between re-fillings of the cups presented to him, the director managed a few sips from his own. After topping himself off a second time, Toshi noticed that his smile became even bigger and more relaxed.

Shortly, the interpreter returned, followed close behind by Haruki and the men from furnace number one. The director wanted to make sure they were in on the celebration. The interpreter quickly retrieved his sack and handed each of Haruki's men a cup. The director turned his attention to filling them, as he gave further instructions to the interpreter.

Nodding, the interpreter quickly opened another bottle and assisted the director in filling and re-filling the more than thirty cups that seemed to continuously extend themselves toward an open bottle. Before long, the task had been transitioned entirely to the interpreter, as the director made his way from man to man, shaking the free hand of each worker while trying overtly to make his smile speak the words he wanted to say, but which he knew they would not understand.

The combined effects of a long, hard day by the workers, hours since they'd eaten, and the culmination of years of hard work, apprehension, and stress by the director came together that late December afternoon. It displayed itself in smiles, laughter, handshakes, backslaps, and even a few short hugs.

"I've never seen the director this happy!" exclaimed the interpreter. "I've worked for him three years and can count on one hand the number of times I've seen him smile. I hope there's nothing wrong with him. It is certainly not like him to act like this. He must have been under more pressure than I realized."

Toshi and Haruki considered his words. *Maybe he is human after all*, they thought. It had not occurred to either of them the stress this foreigner must have felt, with no one to confide in for years, not even family. Possibly they had misjudged him.

When the count was complete, Toshi's furnace produced one hundred and two pigs, while Haruki's had one hundred and one, a virtual tie. Both furnaces had set new daily records for each of the three days. Each worker qualified for the three-yen bonus they had been promised.

As the celebration wore down and the men headed for home, Toshi and Haruki handed each man their pay envelope. In addition to their pay, they discreetly slipped not three, but six yen into each man's envelope. A few of the men noticed the difference and quickly met the eyes of their foreman. In return, they received a heartfelt smile.

It was later than usual when Toshi and Haruki arrived home that night. Minako and Ayami were watching for them at the door. But the bigger surprise was that they walked through their respective doors smelling of saké and acting giddy.

Chapter 36

A Walk In The Woods

KAMAISHI - DECEMBER 1880

On the following Thursday, Toshi picked up Haruki, and together they headed to Hideji's house. The day was cold but sunny, a good day to show Hideji how charcoal was made. They both liked his suggestion, as they were curious themselves and glad for a reason to explore the process.

As they walked toward the foundry, Toshi and Haruki took turns telling Hideji about the impromptu celebration they'd had on Saturday. He was interested to hear about the excitement of the director. They talked about what it must be like, away from home for months at a time, in a land where he could not speak the language, with no friends or confidants.

After reaching the foundry they continued around to the back to an entirely different compound of buildings and equipment. In addition to a warehouse where the charcoal was stored, there were a dozen sawing platforms and four large kilns.

Haruki asked one of the sawmen where the trees came from, and he pointed to a rugged trail leading off in the west, toward the mountains.

As they walked, they could see from the trail that a number of trees had already been harvested, leaving empty spaces with weathered stumps poking up from the rocky earth. Only pine trees remained alive.

They continued three or four kilometers until they met a wagon coming toward them, pulled by a team of four horses. The wagon carried six logs, each about twenty meters long with a diameter of about forty centimeters.

"How much farther to where you cut the logs?" asked Haruki when they met.

"Not far," was the reply. "About another kilometer."

They were relieved to be getting close. "Let's stop and have some lunch," Toshi said. "I'm getting hungry."

"Me too," replied Hideji. "Let's eat."

They found a fallen log to use as a bench, and sat down to enjoy lunch in the December sun. Toshi had never been to this area of the mountains before and listened for the sound of familiar birds. He watched absent-mindedly as Haruki and Hideji enjoyed the quiet.

"How far have we walked since we last saw an oak tree?" Hideji finally asked.

They thought for a while before Haruki answered. "I haven't seen any," he replied.

The other two men remained silent.

Haruki pondered the question. The foundry depended on charcoal to survive. What evidently started as an easy supply of charcoal close to the furnace now required bringing the only ingredient needed for charcoal from a further and further distance.

As the three men sat, lost with their individual thoughts, a second wagon came into view from the trail up ahead. As it drew close, they were surprised to find it did not carry logs, and was a normal wagon but with taller sideboards. It was drawn by a team of two horses, indicating the load was not as heavy.

They stood from their log, and Haruki waved at the driver as he slowed to a halt.

"Hello," he called. "I expected to see a load of trees. Are you going to the foundry?"

"Yes," came the reply. "I'm bringing a load of charcoal. Seems they can't get enough of this stuff. We're making it as fast as we can but they're never happy."

"You're making it out here?" asked Haruki.

"Yes, we have everything set up in the woods. Our camp is about ten kilometers up the road if you want to see it. They decided it would be easier to make charcoal where the trees are instead of taking the trees to where the kilns are. I guess they've used up all the trees that are close to the foundry."

The three men looked at one another.

"The last tree harvest is just up the road. That's where you saw the load of trees coming from. Everything beyond that, we make the charcoal first, then bring it in. It's a lot easier to haul after it's been made. This wagon here… it's the equivalent of probably six or eight loads of trees, so it saves a lot of trips."

Toshi thought for a minute before he asked, "Are there a lot of trees where your camp is? Will you be there for a long time?"

"Hard to say how long. I guess it depends on how much they need. The last few days have been especially busy. I don't know what they're doing at the foundry, but they've sure been using a lot of charcoal. There is a nice cluster of hardwoods where we're working now. We've been there for two or three months. Probably half the trees are left."

"Thank you for stopping to talk," said Haruki. "We'll let you be on your way. I wouldn't want you to get in trouble with your boss."

They waved to each other as he nudged the team forward again.

The three men turned and slowly followed in the direction of the wagon.

No one spoke for a long while. Finally, Toshi asked, "This doesn't look good for the foundry, does it?"

"It sounds like our record-breaking runs had an impact on the supply. If we keep that up, it will only make it worse," Haruki replied.

They continued in silence until Haruki offered, "It's a good thing we shared that bonus with the men. I'm afraid they'll need everything they can get before long."

"What will they do if the foundry closes down?" asked Toshi. His voice was strained. "How will they provide for their families? This is awful."

"I know of a fishing boat that might be for sale if you decide to become fishermen," Hideji offered. "I don't know if that would be of interest, but it's something you can think about."

By then, they were approaching Hideji's house. As he turned off the trail, he offered, almost as an afterthought, "By the way, tomorrow night we're going to midnight mass in the village in case you'd like to join us. You could walk with us or meet us at the church if you decide to go. I'm sure Fr. Lispard would be happy to see you again." With that, he waved and headed down the path to home.

"Sounds like we could use some spiritual guidance about now," Toshi said. "Do you have any interest in going?"

"We might," Haruki replied. "I'll talk to Minako when I get home. We could all walk together."

Chapter 37

Midnight Mass

KAMAISHI - DECEMBER 24, 1880

"Are you sure we need to go with Hideji and his family tonight?" Toshi asked Ayami, as she laid out clothing for the boys to wear. "When he asked us, it seemed like a good idea, but now that it's here, I'm not so sure. It will throw the boys' routine upside down, staying up that late."

"We told him we would go, and it would be rude to back out at the last minute. Besides, Haruki and his family are going. I wouldn't be able to face any of them if we didn't show up. And if you are even thinking it, the answer is no, neither of the boys came down sick at the last minute."

Toshi looked at her with a blank face and then laughed when he saw the corners of her mouth begin to twitch.

"Besides, I think we should go. You talk about Fr. Lispard all the time. It's time we find out what his religion is all about. The best way to do that is to attend his mass and see what we think. Besides, it will be fun to see Hideji's family and Haruki's family all dressed up. We have never been anywhere together before, and it should be fun."

Toshi laid out a fresh kimono and his best *obi* belt, the one with silk trim. Since he was going, he might as well look nice.

The day had been overcast from the start but not particularly cold. In fact, the temperature was above freezing, even at this late hour. The group of them made quite a column, with Hideji, his wife and daughter, Haruki, with Minako and their three daughters, and Hisa's husband, Hajime, plus Toshi, Ayami, and their two little ones.

Ayami held Isamu, warmly bundled in her arms. Toshi carried Kiyoshi most of the way. He wanted to walk by himself but could not keep up for very long. The adults conversed among themselves about a dozen different things, and laughter rang out with regularity. If Toshi still felt a reluctance to go, it was rapidly slipping away. It was a happy group that made its way from the ridge down to Fr. Lispard's little church.

They heard the sound of singing voices from a hundred meters distant. Even with the doors and windows of the church closed to keep heat in, the soothing sound of hymns escaped to the streets beyond. Conversations died as the group, one by one, heard the strains of music just ahead.

Heads turned when their long procession entered the church. Luckily, Hideji had insisted they leave home early in order to find a seat. Already, the church was filling. Hideji, being a regular at the church, acted as impromptu usher, and made sure he found a bench for Haruki's family, which was the largest. Then he found a bench immediately ahead that would accommodate Toshi's family, in addition to his own.

For the next several minutes they enjoyed the hymns being sung by the congregation. The hymns were sung in Japanese so they understood the words, but being Christmas hymns, they were not familiar with the music. They listened with interest, however, to the lyrics announcing the birth of Jesus and praises for his mother, Mary.

When Fr. Lispard spotted the contingent sitting near the rear of his church, he made his way from the small room beside the altar out to greet them.

"Hideji. Teruko. Nori. How good to see you," he said. "Merry Christmas. It looks like you brought a few friends." He turned his smile toward Toshi and his family. "Toshi, it's good to see you again. Are you ready for another rice fest? Ayami, thank you all for coming." He looked down at Kiyoshi and the sleeping Isamu. "Hello, young man," he said to Kiyoshi. "You are getting so big. Are you helping your mother take care of your little brother?"

Kiyoshi nodded his head and smiled back at the man in the strange black robe.

"As you can see, our parish has been growing," Fr. Lispard said. He gestured around as the church continued to fill. "Tonight will be standing room only, because it's such an important day in the church. It's a good thing you got here early." He nodded in the direction of Hideji. "We've been talking about adding on. Every Sunday it gets harder to find a seat. I don't want anyone to stay home just because they're afraid they'll have to stand through the service.

"People are hungry for spiritual help. We never know when our time on earth will come to an end. The most important thing on this earth is to be prepared to leave it. That's why I'm here. To help whoever I can, be ready." He turned back toward the altar. "I have to prepare for mass now, but thank you for coming. If you have time after mass, we can visit again. Merry Christmas."

Presently, the hymn ended, followed by a short pause. Then, from the small anteroom to the right of the altar, two young boys emerged, followed by Fr. Lispard. They proceeded to the base of the altar, bowed, then ascended two steps to the upper level of the ornately carved structure.

Making the sign of the cross as he faced the altar, with back to his congregation, he began the mass. *"In nomine Patris, et Filii, et Spiritus Sancti. Amen."*

As an engineering student, history classes were not required for Toshi, but he did take one class entitled World History Fundamentals. Hearing these words, recited in Latin, reminded him how ancient was their origin. They were first spoken about the time Japan first learned to plant and harvest rice. *Christianity has survived for a long time*, he thought. *It must have some merit.*

Following several Latin prayers, Fr. Lispard turned to face his congregation. He moved to a small lectern located to his right on the raised platform and opened a large book. Even from where Toshi was seated he could see it was special, bound in red, with gold lettering he could not make out. He opened the tome to a predetermined page marked by a red ribbon and began to read. *Fortunately*, thought Toshi, *this part is in Japanese.*

It recalled the story of how an angel had approached Mary when she was barely sixteen years old and asked her to become the mother of Jesus, even though she was not married. The angel went on to tell her it could be so, even without a husband, because for God, all things were possible.

Following that, he recited another short prayer in Latin and then turned to another ribbon in his big red missal.

This time, the story told how Mary, who by now was married to a man named Joseph, traveled to a distant village just at the time she was about to give birth. The village was crowded with visitors when they arrived, leaving them no place to spend the night. Not being a wealthy couple, they were forced to sleep in a small barn. The next day they were surprised by three visitors from a foreign country, who had followed a star in the sky that led them to the barn. When it came time for Joseph and Mary to return home, an angel again visited, warning them not to go home but instead to flee from the country because a jealous king wanted to do them harm.

Finally, he read a third story, this one short, from what he called the Gospel of St. John. "In the beginning was the word… The word was made flesh…" he read.

These stories caught Toshi's imagination, but he held a shadow of doubt about their authenticity. *Do angels really exist?* He wondered. *Why would a king be jealous of a newborn baby? And could a young girl really become pregnant without a man?* That part seemed extremely unlikely.

Following the readings, Fr. Lispard then put the tome aside and began to talk directly to the congregation.

"God bless you, believers and friends," he began. "Bless you for coming out on this cold winter night to celebrate the birth of our Savior. Just think of it. A girl of sixteen, away from home, away from family, except for her husband of a few short months… hardly enough time to get to know the man… her first child… no mother or sister to support and console her. Imagine the anxiety Mary must have felt."

Toshi found himself imagining her situation as Fr. Lispard continued. Then he thought back to the birth of Kiyoshi and how terrified he was that Ayami was going to die. It had not occurred to him until now, how Ayami must have felt.

When his thoughts turned back to Fr. Lispard, he tried to focus on the words.

"…The birth of Jesus set in motion a redemption of the world. He was sent here by God, Himself, to rescue people from their sins. It began with the birth of Jesus. It ended with his crucifixion, death, and resurrection thirty-three years later. He performed many miracles to convince us he was the son of God: he raised Lazarus from the dead, he healed many sick, blind, and lame, and he rose from his own death after three days. But don't take my word for it…"

He raised up a different book, which he retrieved from a shelf in the lectern. "It is all recorded in this book. It was written by those who were there, those who saw. You can believe what I've told you because I've told you stories from this book, the Bible. It is the primary source for our knowledge of God."

Fr. Lispard could be forgiven for hoping they could not see well enough in the dimly lit church that night to realize the Bible he was holding was written in French.

Then, as he stood at the foot of the altar, the congregation took up one last hymn, one particularly suited to Christmas, Fr. Lispard announced. He had obtained a copy from his home station in France, who in turn had received it from America, where it was written a dozen years before. Fr. Lispard said it reflected the birth of Jesus better than any other hymn he knew, and although the translation to Japanese lost some of the rhythm of the song, he still loved to sing and hear it.

There were several handwritten copies among the benches which the congregants studied as they began to sing.

"Oh, little town of Bethlehem, how still we see thee lie; above thy deep and dreamless sleep, the silent stars go by…"

When they reached the end of the hymn, the priest and his two helpers made one final bow in front of the altar and proceeded to the anteroom and out of sight.

Presently, he re-appeared, dressed in the black robe they were accustomed to. He approached the group with another broad smile as he thanked them again for attending at this late hour. By now, it was several minutes past one o'clock in the morning.

"Did you enjoy the service?" he asked, looking primarily at Toshi and Haruki.

"Yes, very much," they both replied.

"Although I still didn't understand most of the prayers, since they're in Latin," added Toshi. But I was very interested in the stories, and also your talk that followed them.

"How does one go about becoming a member of your church?" Toshi continued.

"There is a booklet that tells the fundamental teachings of the Catholic Church, which I can give you, if you like. Then, if you're still interested, I can provide personal instruction about the teachings. We would do that in several visits together. After that, you would receive the sacrament of Baptism, which formally makes you a member of the faith."

He paused there and studied the faces of not only Toshi but also Ayami, Haruki, and Minako, as well as the rest of his family.

"Baptism is available to all, if you decide to accept it, but it must be your decision. Once you become baptized, you become one of God's children, since he is our Father. And since he is father to all Christians, it follows that we all become brothers—and sisters—to one another. It is not a covenant to be taken lightly, or one that can be reversed simply because you change your mind later on."

By the look on their faces, Fr. Lispard concluded they were still interested enough to take the first step.

"I have two copies of the booklet in the sacristy; let me get them, and you may take them with you. Read them when you have time, and let me know if you want to schedule a session." With that, he turned and quickly headed to the anteroom to retrieve the booklets, hoping they would not change their minds in the interim.

When he walked away, Ayami noticed Kanae and Saya talking quite animatedly with Hisa and Minako. She moved closer to hear what they were talking about just in time to catch the trailing end of a question from Kanae. "Is it true they can't get married?"

"Who can't get married?" Ayami broke in.

"Priests," replied Hisa. "Is it true they don't marry?"

"Yes, I believe that is one of their vows," replied Ayami.

"What a waste!" replied Kanae. "He's too handsome to be living alone."

That brought giggles from the other girls. "Yes, he is quite charming," she continued. "He makes my face get warm when he smiles at me. Tell him we want to take the lessons from him and we might be really slow learners. It could take months of teaching to get it right." Then all the girls laughed, but mostly in agreement.

Fr. Lispard soon returned with two copies of a booklet entitled *My Catholic Faith – What I Believe*. He flipped through a few of the pages to demonstrate how easy it would be to read the book and understand the basics of his teachings.

"I'd be happy to meet with you. And don't worry, it will be very informal and I won't press you to join. It has to be something you believe in. If you want to keep going after that, we'll schedule more teachings to follow." His soothing baritone voice was enough to put them at ease; he didn't need to add the spontaneous smile for each of them. Saya wondered if he could see her cheeks turn red when he looked at her. Unbeknownst to her, Kanae wondered the same thing about herself.

They exchanged good nights and Merry Christmases and pulled their coats a little tighter as they headed out the door for the walk home. When they opened the door to leave, they were surprised to see fresh snow on the ground, with more falling gently from the sky.

"We'd better hurry," Haruki said, "before it gets worse."

He and Toshi carried lanterns to light the way. It seemed to reflect upward from the newly fallen snow even as it highlighted the flakes falling down around them. Toshi, Haruki, and some of the others were filled with thoughts of what Fr. Lispard said during his talk at the mass, while Saya and Kanae were filled with thoughts of how he smiled at them and warmed their faces. The walk home seemed shorter than the walk to arrive.

Chapter 38

End Of The Foundry

KAMAISHI - JANUARY 1881

On the following Monday morning, Toshi and Haruki discussed the foundry as they walked toward Hideji's house. They both agreed; the future looked bleak. Closure of the foundry was almost a certainty. Only the timing was open for debate. They each had ten yen left over from their production bonus. They could pool that to buy one of the fishing boats. How much more it would take they did not know, but Hideji might have an idea how much a boat would cost.

"Good morning, my friends," he greeted them. "Join me for a cup of hot tea?"

"Good morning," they both replied. "Tea is just what we need. Thank you."

As they reclined on mats around the table, Hideji jumped right in with his questions. "What have you concluded about the charcoal? Do you think there will be enough to keep it running?"

"Unfortunately, no," Haruki answered, "it does not seem likely. We don't see how the foundry can continue for any length of time. In fact, that is what we wanted to talk with you about. Did you say there might be a fishing boat coming up for sale? We wondered how much you think it would sell for, and whether we could make a living from fishing, if we bought it."

Hideji considered his questions before answering. "Yes, I believe there is at least one fishing boat that might be available. I have not spoken to the owner as I was not sure of your intentions, but the last time a boat was sold, I believe it brought around seventy-five yen. Of course, the condition of the boat would make a difference. The one I'm thinking of has been carefully maintained and is in very good condition. The owner is getting old and doesn't go out regular anymore. Fishing is in his blood, though, and he's reluctant to give it up entirely. I think he might be persuaded to sell his boat, especially if you offered to take him with you on occasion. That way, he could still enjoy his passion without the burden of caring for a boat."

He paused with a pensive demeanor spread across his face. "Regarding whether you could make a living from the boat is a more difficult question. Based on the time Toshi went out with me, I have no doubt that he is more than capable. I'm sure the same is true for you, Haruki. Would it be as fruitful as your job at the foundry? That I can't say. The townspeople seem to think foundry workers are better paid than most fishermen or shopkeepers. But fishing has provided a modest livelihood for a lot of families in Kamaishi for many generations. Most of us grew up as fishermen and had few other choices. But it's been a way of life we loved and would not have traded for another, even if we'd had the chance."

He paused again, noting how both men seemed to hang on his every word. "Are you thinking about becoming partners for one boat? It's possible there is another boat for sale in case you each wanted a boat. As Toshi knows, it takes at least two people to man a boat, but most captains hire a young seaman for a share of the profit. If you split the proceeds of your catch evenly, it might be a stretch to maintain two households. It would be more profitable if you each bought a boat and hired a mate. But that is something you would need to decide for yourselves."

"We would like to talk to both owners, if possible," Toshi offered. "We'd like to see both boats and learn how much it would take to buy one of them. Do you think you could arrange that?"

Hideji replied, "It's still early; we could go today. I'm sure Dai has not gone out. I'm not sure about Iwao. If his boat is in, you could see them both in the harbor. And I know where they live, if you want to talk with them."

"I'm ready," Toshi said. He looked at Haruki for reassurance. He was surprised to see a solemn and pensive face on Haruki. On the way over he thought Haruki was as committed as himself. It seemed to him the sooner they made a deal the better it would be.

"I'm not sure we should be making the trip just yet," Haruki replied. "What if word of this gets back to the director? What is he going to think if his two foremen are shopping for a fishing boat?" He let it sink in for a minute before continuing. "Worse yet, what will the men think if we're both looking for a different way to support our families? And not just the foundry workers; what about all the miners and the charcoal workers? If they thought we were bailing out from a sinking ship, what's left for them? They can't all become fishermen. A third of the village will be out of work.

"Even if it does come to that, I don't want to be the one to start the rumor, when we don't really know for sure what the foundry has in mind. Maybe they *will* come up with a solution. This is a tricky situation. We can't very well ask the director if they're going to close the foundry. He's already told us he is concerned, and that they're working on a solution."

Toshi's smile turned to a reflection of Haruki's solemn face as he thought about the truth in his words.

"I didn't think of that," he replied. "Of course, you're right. If they thought we knew the foundry was closing and looked out for ourselves first, we wouldn't have many friends left."

The three men were silent for several minutes. The reality of the situation was sinking in. It was worse than they had initially considered. At first, they were concerned about two families with the possibility of less income. Now, as they considered the bigger picture, there might be dozens of families without work.

"If we're going to increase the number of fishermen, and really, even if we don't, it looks like we're going to need to increase the number of customers if we're going to survive as a village. That's what we need to be thinking about," Hideji said, with sadness in his voice. "We need to find more customers away from Kamaishi. We need to branch out."

It was quiet again as the three of them considered the situation.

It was Haruki who broke the silence. "Hideji, I think it is still important to talk to the two owners you told us about. If you could contact them alone and only inquire as to their interest and price without ever mentioning the foundry or what we've discussed, they could be thinking about a selling price. After thinking this through, I'm not even sure Toshi or I should be allowed to buy one. After all, we do have information about the foundry that hardly anyone else would know. I'm not sure I could face my men if I secretly bought a boat right now. The men should have an equal chance to buy one of the boats."

"What do you think, Toshi?" he asked.

"You're right," Toshi replied, softly. "The only reason we're talking to Hideji is because we know about the charcoal. The symptoms are there for everyone to see, but still, the men rely on us for their jobs."

"Do you mind if I ask Fr. Lispard for guidance?" asked Hideji. "I have often found him to have a creative mind."

"I don't mind," replied Haruki, "as long as our concerns about the foundry are held in confidence. If even a rumor slips out the foundry is going to close, it would be a disaster."

***

Toshi and Haruki walked to work early on the morning of January third, 1881. It was their first day back since the shutdown. Neither slept well the night before. "What do we tell the men if they ask about the charcoal or a possible closing?" Toshi asked Haruki.

"All we can say is that the owners are aware of the situation and searching for a solution. In the meantime, the more productive we are, the better our prospects for keeping the foundry open. It's truthful, and it's really all that we can say with any certainty."

They walked most of the way in silence, each man lost in imaginary debates about a hundred different possibilities that might lie ahead.

Soon, the workers began to arrive. So far, everyone was too busy welcoming one another back or exchanging stories of their long hiatus from work to ask Toshi about their futures.

Later in the morning, the interpreter entered Toshi's makeshift office to announce the director wished to see Haruki and him in one hour.

What seemed like hours later, Haruki appeared at his doorway. His normal calm demeanor was replaced by a face filled with tension, the skin on his cheeks, taut. Toshi didn't bother to force his usual smile in greeting, but joined him as they walked out the door together to the director's office.

By now, they could usually glean some idea of what was in store from the behavior of the interpreter. On this visit, he asked if they would like tea or coffee, which helped set them at ease. The interpreter returned a light smile when Toshi chose coffee and Haruki chose tea. "Next time, I'll simply ask if you want *the usual*," he quipped. This put the two of them even more at ease. It appeared there would be another time.

Before their cups had time to arrive, the director appeared from his office and invited them in. He was smiling, and both men thought it was one of his sincere faces, not like the forced ones of their earlier visits.

"Good morning, gentlemen," he began, through the interpreter. "Did you enjoy your time away from the furnaces?"

They did not want to betray their deep anxiety by responding incorrectly. If they enjoyed the time away too much, the director might think they didn't like their jobs, but if they said they didn't enjoy it, he might not offer it again.

Haruki answered first and tried to cover both sides of the question. "Yes, it was very nice to have time with our families, but it also feels good to be back at work." He looked over at Toshi, who hoped a smile and nod would confirm his agreement.

"I have received rumors about a matter that interests me very much," the director continued, "and I would like for you to tell me if it's true."

Neither man could stop the color from draining from their cheeks, and they both knew without doubt the director could see it happen. Somehow, he had learned of their interest in the fishing boats.

"Is it true you paid each of your men a bonus for each new record they could set?"

The color slowly returned to their faces. Toshi tried to make eye contact with Haruki without turning to face him. While he was trying to think how to respond, Haruki spoke up. "Yes, it is true," he said. "We offered them an incentive for each of our last three days before the break."

"Whose idea was this? To reward the workers for their extra effort," asked the director.

"We both discussed it and agreed to do it," replied Haruki. He looked over at Toshi, hoping he had not included him in a reprimand. At this point, Haruki could not tell if the director considered the action as favorable or unfavorable. But the truth of it was, they had agreed beforehand, so there it was.

"And where did you get the money to pay all those workers?" came the next question.

This time, Toshi responded. He felt it necessary to affirm he was as guilty as Haruki if that was the verdict to come. "We used the bonus money you paid to us. We felt the men deserved to share in it as much as we did, since they work just as hard as we do every day. We also thought that by challenging them to new production records, it might keep their minds off the possibility we could be running out of charcoal. We were hoping they wouldn't question us about that, if they spent all their energy trying to set a new record."

"We also made it clear to them that if there were any accidents, the challenge would be discontinued," added Haruki. "It was important that no one get injured by trying to meet a production record. We were also concerned that two weeks with half-pay… although very generous," he added at the last minute, hoping it did not seem too obvious, "…might be a hardship on those with a large family or other obligations."

Then something welled up from deep in Toshi's memory, which he thought came as advice from Haruki. "Don't say anything more than necessary. Answer truthfully, but succinctly." So, he made simple eye contact with the director and proceeded to sip his coffee, as if it were the best drink of anything in his life.

Haruki seemed to follow the cue and sipped his tea while they waited for another question. They were willing to drink from their cups for as long as they needed. Eventually, the director spoke again. When it came to them from the interpreter, it was all they could do to refrain from choking on their respective drinks.

"That was a very creative idea, and I wish I had thought of it myself. Your motives were sound. I'm sure your men appreciate all you've done for them. And I'm sure your generosity will be returned to you in loyalty by the men."

A few moments later, he went on, "I commend you for your decision, and since I don't believe you should have to pay their bonus from out of your own, you will each receive an additional twenty yen. That, of course, does not replace all you have given, but since it was your decision to make the payments, the foundry can't be held responsible. At least you will be better off than before."

The director was quiet then, but motioned for the interpreter to refill his coffee. He pointed at the cups of Toshi and Haruki and nodded. Apparently, the meeting was not yet over.

The interpreter gathered their three cups and left the room. The attractive woman was nowhere in sight.

At first, it felt comfortable for Toshi and Haruki. But after a minute or two they realized they could not communicate without the interpreter, and it was beginning to get awkward. The director continued to gaze out the window with a faraway look.

Toshi tried his best to look casually down at the floor, then to the window, then back to the desk, and finally, at the hands resting in his lap. He glanced out the corner of his eye at the director to see where he was looking, and each time the image was the same. The director was staring at some invisible object beyond the window.

At last, the interpreter returned through the door carrying two cups of coffee and one cup of tea, which he handed to the three men. Trying not to show their relief, Toshi and Haruki each reached for their cup and smiled their approval at the delivery man. They tried to watch the director without appearing to do so, and followed his pace as he slowly took a sip and returned the cup to his desk.

When the interpreter was again seated at his station the director began to speak. "The problem is not a shortage of charcoal," he said.

When the interpreter relayed the message, Toshi and Haruki responded by staring blankly, first at the interpreter and then at the director.

"The problem is not a shortage of charcoal," he repeated. "The problem is a shortage of wood. A shortage of hardwood, to be precise."

When the interpreter relayed this portion of the message, they both remained motionless as the words sank in. On the outside they appeared calm, almost as if they had expected this, but on the inside, every muscle tightened. This conversation was heading to a harsh reality which they both seemed to know intuitively, but could not willingly admit.

"I tried to tell them early on there were not enough trees in the vicinity to support even the existing furnace, let alone two new ones." He paused for them to consider this revelation. "Do you know what they said to me?" he asked.

Both Toshi and Haruki merely shook their heads. It seemed obvious they wouldn't know the answer. They considered it a rhetorical question, at any rate.

"They told me it didn't matter. They said the important thing was that we produce enough iron to show the rest of the world we would no longer be a doormat for their navies. They said if we produced an average of one hundred and sixty pigs through the end of the year, it would provide enough steel to build an arsenal adequate to prove the point. In the meantime, they would try to figure out a more permanent solution."

He then paused to take a few sips from his cup as the interpreter passed the message forward to Toshi and Haruki.

"When I was recruited to come here, I thought this would be my chance to make history. Japan was far behind the industrialized world and I had the training to help catch them up, at least in making iron. We've made great strides in this first year. But a single year is nothing compared to the rest of the world. We have to get better every year if Japan is ever going to reach the level of Germany, or England, or America." He paused again.

"Now here we are, about to run out of charcoal because we have to travel kilometers inland, in search of suitable wood. It has reached the point where it is no longer feasible. We've tried mixing charcoal made from pine wood, which is everywhere, but thanks to Toshi's journal, it was clear that production fell even with a mixture of ten percent pine. If you check back to your journal, Toshi, you will find several random days where you could not figure out why production fell that day. The answer is that on those days, we tried to slip in the pinewood charcoal. We didn't tell anyone because we didn't want them to know. In the scientific world it is what we call a 'blind test,' but you are probably familiar with the concept.

"When I first came here, I received a letter from my wife at least once or twice every week. As time went on, they came less often. The last letter I received was six months ago. I don't know if that means she left me for someone else, or if she is ill, or if she just doesn't care anymore. I still write to her at least once every week.

"Helping Japan become a strong and independent country would easily be worth the failure of one man's marriage, but I'm afraid I have failed at helping your country as well as my marriage."

The director paused to drink from his cup. Toshi stared at his face as he swallowed. His face had changed since that happy day not long ago when they celebrated at Toshi's furnace with impromptu cups of saké. Today, it reflected the burden of an entire village in its tired and wrinkled skin. He took another sip of coffee and carried on.

"We expect to run out of charcoal by the first of March. Both furnaces will be shutting down at that time, along with the charcoal and mining operations. They have not found a suitable remedy as had been hoped. I plan to return to Germany and pick up my life as best I can, once I find out what remains there for me. I want to thank both of you for everything you have done to make these furnaces succeed. If not for you, we would never have achieved what we have. I am personally sorry that so many good lives will be turned upside down. I will leave it to the two of you to decide when to break the news to your men. I need to add that there is a small glimmer of hope. They plan to experiment by using coal as a fuel instead of charcoal. From what I've read, it does not blend well with magnetite. If it does work, the coal will have to be shipped here from China. So, there is a chance the plant might continue, but I've made a personal decision not to count on it. I had hoped to become a part of history, but instead, my name will be just another forgotten footnote."

The director turned then, to look out the window once more. Toshi wondered if he was leaving something out or whether he was just trying to make sure he had said all he wanted to say. The four men sat in silence for several minutes, until the director said, "Let's talk again a week from today. In the meantime, produce as much as you can, but at a comfortable level, and keep the men safe." Then he added, "By the way, our production for the year averaged one hundred sixty-one pigs per day. If you hadn't broken the record those last three days, we would not have made it."

The director stood, followed by the interpreter. It was the signal for Toshi and Haruki to leave the room. They walked out, too stunned to speak.

The silence continued as they returned to their respective furnaces. When they parted, Haruki said, "Try to act as normal as possible for the rest of the day. We'll figure out how to tell the men on our way home tonight."

It was one of the longest afternoons Toshi could ever remember. When he was sure no one was watching, he closed his eyes and prayed for help to get him through the day. When it finally arrived and he was alone with Haruki, he blurted out, "We have to tell them tomorrow. I can't make it through another day keeping this from them."

"I agree," Haruki replied. "It's like we're lying to them by not telling them what we know. And the director said it was up to us. I think we simply tell them everything the director told us, so they can start making plans of their own. But maybe we should ask them not to spread the word outside their families on account of the charcoal and mine workers. I'd hate for them to hear of it from us, instead of their bosses."

"Deep down, I knew this was a possibility, which is why I went out on the boat with Hideji in the first place. But now that it's real, I feel sick in my stomach." Toshi's hands were shaking as he spoke. "It's like a part of me has died."

"Most of us feel the same way," Haruki replied. "It's going to be a very hard blow to everyone in Kamaishi."

***

Shortly after seven, when all the men had arrived and begun their day, Toshi called them together in the changing room. He had to get it over with as soon as possible.

"Good morning," he began. "Haruki and I were called to a meeting with the director. He had important news. The charcoal shortage that has plagued us in the past has reached a critical stage.

They've had to go further and further inland in search of suitable wood to make the charcoal, and it is no longer feasible to continue. The director thinks the furnace will shut down around the first of March. He is not sure if it will start again after that. He said they might import coal from China to see if it will work in place of charcoal, but he himself is not optimistic. He is planning to return to Germany when the furnaces close down in March."

The solemn looks on their faces made it even harder to continue, and his voice wavered as he sought to finish. "The director did tell us he was proud of the work you have done and especially thanked us for the record-making production before the December shutdown. Thank you for everything you have done for me and for the foundry. I am truly sorry to see it come to this. For the record, it is worth mentioning that the director has also made great sacrifices trying to make the foundry a success. He has not seen his family since coming here three years ago. He is not sure what lies in store for him when he returns home again."

With that, he left the room and headed for the steam boiler, needing somewhere private to go.

The following weeks sped by like a winter wind. The truth of it was that no one, Haruki and Toshi included, could really believe the foundry would close. Twice, the closing date had been postponed by a week. Surely that was evidence they were finding a solution and the foundry would remain open.

On Saturday morning, March fifth, when the interpreter came down to the furnaces, Toshi, Haruki, and both their crews were hopeful this was yet another reprieve—that he had come to tell them they would be open for another two weeks, or better yet, they would stay open indefinitely. The workers tried not to be obvious as they eavesdropped when the interpreter talked briefly to each foreman. Those not close enough to hear could tell by the reaction from Toshi, and later from Haruki. This was the day.

Toshi felt moisture in his eyes and had to keep moving to keep his composure. He found himself staring blankly at the steam engine, the belt that drove the fan, the empty ingots waiting for their last fill of iron.

At one o'clock they stopped feeding the furnace. Now it was a matter of waiting for the last load of ore to change into iron and fill the last of the waiting molds. The men began to cluster together as they waited for the process to complete. Gradually they began to talk, asking what one or another of them planned to do after today. Most had no plan because they had not believed it would actually happen.

Finally, the last of the iron flowed from the furnace. The men changed from their protective aprons and gathered in the changing room, waiting for Toshi to lead them to Haruki's furnace.

At four o'clock, the director, followed closely by the interpreter, entered the changing room at furnace number one. All thirty workers, plus Toshi and Haruki, awaited their final envelope.

The director was solemn as he and the interpreter found a small stool to stand on. Through the interpreter, the director addressed them. "Thank you for all you have done to try and keep this foundry alive. We tried our best, and I am sorry it has not worked out. I wish you well in the future and hope you quickly find other work. I am going home to Germany next week. I don't expect to come back, but if I do, I hope to find you well. Each of you has an extra pay envelope today. I wish it could be more, but it is the best I could arrange." He stepped down from the stool, handed all the envelopes to Toshi and Haruki for distribution, and headed to his office.

The workers watched him go. He did not look back. His gait was steady and his back was straight. No one could see the mist in his eyes or weigh the pain inside his heart. The director walked away as if from his greatest triumph. Not until he was safely in his quarters, through the door behind his office, two doors behind the interpreter's office, did he sit with his head in his hands and weep.

Chapter 39

Foundry Fishing Fleet

After Haruki handed out his envelopes he took his turn on the little stool. "We have been placed in a difficult situation," he began. "There is nothing more any of us could have done to prevent the closing, so do not blame yourselves."

He noticed a few smiles when the workers opened their envelopes as they showed one another the contents. The director had placed an extra ten yen in each one. Haruki suspected it had come from the director's pocket, not from the foundry, and it put an extra lump in his throat.

"When the announcement was made last January, I asked Hideji, known to some of you, for advice, and whether there might be any openings in the fishing fleet. He explained that the guild controls the number of boats, but he located two existing boats that might be available. The price of each of the boats is one hundred yen." There were a few quiet sighs at the sound of that. No one had a hundred yen available to buy a boat.

"I see two problems with that. First, a hundred yen is probably not within the reach of any of us, and second, assuming a crew of two, even if we could find a third boat, would only provide for six families." He waited for a moment before continuing, as a new idea began to form. Without time to think it through, he pushed forward. "But the boats might still offer an opportunity. Thanks to the generosity of the director, we each have ten yen that we didn't expect. If we pooled our money, we could easily buy the two boats."

"Here's an example. Ten of us join together. Each of us contributes ten yen. That gives us the required one hundred yen to purchase a boat. Ten of us now own the boat. We split up into five teams of two men. Then each team uses the boat for one day each week. When you get back from the day, you split the catch evenly between the two of you. With your share, you can either sell it, trade it for rice or other things, or keep the fish to take home to your family."

He paused to let the concept settle. "If the weather is bad, or you are sick, or for some reason can't go out on your appointed day, you could switch with another team or go out on the sixth or seventh day, which would otherwise be idle. Or you could take turns going out on the idle days and sell that day's catch at the market and share the earnings as a bonus."

This was a total departure from anything the men might have thought about, as indeed, it was for Haruki. He was not sure where the idea came from, but it popped into his head just when he needed it. And the more he thought about it the better he liked it himself.

"This is not meant to be a new livelihood. It is a way to ensure that you have enough food to feed your family. Think about it overnight, and whoever is interested should meet at the docks tomorrow afternoon at four o'clock. I'll ask Hideji to be there with the two boat owners and tell you about the life of a fisherman."

Toshi watched the men as they listened to Haruki. Several of them stood a little taller as the opportunity was presented.

"Haruki, when did you come up with that idea?" Toshi asked, when they were alone. "We talked about buying fishing boats several times, but I didn't know you were thinking about sharing the ownership with everyone else."

"I was as surprised as you," he replied. "It never occurred to me at all until I started to speak. I was going to tell the men that Hideji found two boats for sale, but that's really all I had in mind. But when I got on the stool, the words just tumbled out. I've never had that happen before. I hope it has your approval. It just came out of nowhere."

"Did you see the reaction it brought? I was watching the men, and it transformed them. I could not believe how much it brought them back to life. They were still talking among themselves when they left the foundry. They were talking about who to partner with and how they would split up their daily catch. I didn't hear one word about closing the foundry."

Haruki smiled, but the thought foremost in his mind was that the men were still losing their means of support. Fishing might provide food for the table, but it would hardly replace their incomes.

By four o'clock on Sunday, twenty-five men had arrived, most with their wives, many with small children. The men, and even their wives, displayed a demeanor of excitement and hope. Haruki was encouraged by the turnout and, sensing the anxiety of the men, thanked them for coming and asked Hideji to tell them about 'a day in the life of a fisherman.'

Hideji explained to the men how they left port in the late afternoon in order to get to the deep-water trench before dawn and fish for three to four hours before heading back to port a little after sunup. He told them about the clothing to wear, food to take, the potential for storms, and the summer heat and winter cold. He did not depict the work with a coating of sugar.

The two boats for sale were brought from their moorings to the dock so each man and his family could have a look. Hideji encouraged them to get in the boats, which the children loved. The mothers among them stayed close enough to latch on to an arm or leg if a child got too close to the gunwale. The men were drawn to the stern, where the rudder was located. Some pretended to steer the boat out of the harbor and toward the fishing grounds. The atmosphere resembled a festival, with conversations, laughter, and several howls of delight from the children.

After almost two hours of listening, questions, answers, climb-aboards, and general information, Haruki turned a water bucket upside down and stepped up on it.

"Hideji and I have discussed and agree, that for those of you still interested in becoming a part-owner for either of the two boats, no one will be approved until you have completed at least one day of training. Telling you what to expect as a fisherman is one thing. To do it might be totally different from what you imagine it to be. That is the reason you will be required to join one of the boats for a day. Hideji will provide his boat in addition to the two that are for sale. Each of the three boats has agreed to take two apprentices, along with their regular crewman, so that you can decide as soon as possible if you want to become a fisherman. Hideji will take your name and assign a boat and a day if you wish to participate. Good luck to each of you, and we'll meet here next Sunday at four o'clock."

***

Some did not have to wait until the following Sunday to decide, however. On Wednesday, soon after the fleet left port, the weather turned bad. At five o'clock, when they rowed out through modest breakers, the horizon looked like any other day. The sun was low in the west, and the sky was mostly blue. By midnight, although they could not see it, the sky had filled with heavy, swirling clouds. By two o'clock, when they were almost to the trench, the wind changed from moderate to heavy, and the ocean swells began to foam. The three 'foundry' boats were most susceptible; they each held two extra crew members who knew nothing about sailing a boat.

Hideji, veteran fisherman that he was, foresaw the building storm in time to reposition his two guests to a spot at the bow, one on either side. "Lie down on the floor where you can't fall out and hang on," he warned. "We might take on water, but don't be afraid. Just hold your breath until it drains away. It *will* drain away and we won't sink, so don't be alarmed. Whatever happens, just stay out of our way. We know what to do in a storm. We'll be okay."

The captain on one of the other two foundry boats took further action. "Secure a line to each of their life jackets," he shouted to his mate. "If they go over, at least they won't get lost."

But the third boat was caught unaware until it was too late. The visitors were sitting at midship, trying to listen to instructions from the captain when the first of the heavy waves pounded over the bow and into the boat. The two men laughed at first, it was dark and they were unable to see the turbulence that surrounded them. When the bow slammed hard against the foaming water, their brief laughter changed first to concern, and then to horror, in quick progression. After two more punishing waves, they grabbed at the first thing they could find that seemed secure. The only thing they could find was the heavy wooden mast that held the sail.

When the captain shouted for his mate to furl the sail, the two frightened men only clung tighter to the mast. Afraid to let go, they crowded the small space precisely where the mate needed to perform his task. The mate had furled the sail a dozen times in seas like this, but never before with two horrified passengers standing in his way. Too much sail remained aloft to catch the howling wind. Before he could release the rope to lower the yardarm, the force of the wind snapped the wooden cleat that held it secure. The rope ran free and the sail flung away from the wind with a violent crash. Without its sail, the vessel stalled. The captain looked up through the dark to see if the mast had toppled with the sail, but it was too dark to tell.

With no forward progress, the boat turned to starboard between the towering waves. The wind came directly across the side of the wounded vessel, pushing it downwind with all its powerful force. Even life jackets seemed trivial as water from the sea gushed over the leeward gunwale and covered the planking at the bottom of the boat.

For half an hour or more, the fishing boat held its own against the sea. The captain began to hope the worst was over; he had survived worse. The first mate had also survived worse, but the two men from the foundry were stricken helpless. The man on the leeward side of the boat, the side leaning deeper into the sea, closed his eyes and held on. He opened them once to find himself looking up at the surrounding sea and quickly closing them again, so tight that his eyelids hurt from the pressure.

The other man, the one on the upper side, between moments of panic reassured himself that at least he was on the upper side, not like his friend, almost two meters below him as the boat continued to heel over on its side.

Then the wind subsided and the boat righted itself in a trough. Both men relaxed momentarily, thinking the storm was over. But when the next wave caught the boat, it lurched back on its side with such force that the man on the upper side was thrown across the center of the boat to the gunwale on the opposite side. Stunned by the unexpected turn of events, as well as by the force of the solid oak railing that struck the side of his head, he tumbled over the gunwale and out of the boat.

The captain lunged to grab an arm, a leg, or anything he could reach, but to no avail. The man was overboard. In daylight, because of his life jacket, there was a reasonable chance. But in the dark, in the roiling ocean waves, there was barely any hope.

Without the sail and with no way of controlling the boat, they could only continue to drift. The captain shouted for the first mate to watch for the man. Then he shouted to the man still clinging to the mast from the lower side of the boat to hang on, no matter what. He strained his eyes into the foamy mist, hoping for a miracle. But in the dark, there was nothing to see.

The captain scanned the surrounding area, looking for other boats that might be able to help. He counted two lanterns, dimly glowing across the misty waves. At least he was not alone.

"We have to stay here until daylight," he shouted to the first mate. "Then maybe we can see something. If you can reach a flare, send it off. Maybe the others will see it and stay close."

By five o'clock that morning the wind had abated. But more importantly, the sun began to rise. In daylight, the captain scanned the mast for damage. It looked secure. But the rope that controlled the sail had wrapped itself around the mast during the turbulent night.

"See if you can untangle the halyard!" he shouted to the mate. "Maybe we can get the sail up." Then he shouted to the foundry man, "Hang on to one of those heavy cleats and look for your friend. You look close to the boat. I'll look further away."

By six o'clock the waves had settled enough to signal the two nearby boats, and with their own rigging now restored, they sailed back and forth across the mellowing waves. After two hours, someone from a different boat shouted over to them.

"I see something!" he shouted. "Over there!" and he pointed to a spot thirty meters away.

Both boats closed toward the object.

"It's a life jacket!" The other boat shouted. "I can tell by the color."

The man in the life jacket seemed lifeless at first, but when he saw the boat coming toward him, he raised one arm as high as he could and tried to swim toward it. The first mate stood in the bow and shouted back to the man. "Stay where you are!" he shouted. "We'll come to you!"

Ten minutes later they pulled him into the boat. He was shivering so much he couldn't speak. His words came out only as a rapid series of staccato noises. The captain pulled off his own coat and wrapped it around the man. The first mate pulled his off and draped it atop the captain's coat. Then he took hold of the man's hands and began to rub them between his own.

The captain looked at the other foundry man, who was watching it all from the other side of the boat. "Rub his hands," he ordered. "We have to sail the boat." Then he pulled hard on the tiller and headed the vessel home.

The other boat sailed close enough alongside to shout across, "We'll tell the others!" the captain yelled. "See you at the dock!" Then they turned back out to the open sea to find the fleet.

Not one boat brought back a single fish, but they cheered when the still shivering man was helped from the boat to a waiting rickshaw at the dock.

When Haruki, Toshi, and Hideji met with the foundry workers on the following Sunday, eighteen men had passed the test. Some, including Kazuo, had gotten so seasick they could not participate. Others, like the unfortunate men caught in the storm, decided it was not a career for them, even as a part-time job. The remaining count was short by two members.

Haruki looked at Toshi, who, without a word being said, nodded his head. They offered the two remaining shares to anyone who wanted, and when no one did, they bought them for themselves. They would sell the fish they didn't need.

***

"I don't like it," Ayami said. "Are you sure it's safe? What would the boys and I do if something happened?"

"The boats are not any more dangerous than the foundry," Toshi replied. "I could have fallen close to the furnace or one of the molds. And look at Hideji. He's been fishing all his life. That night with the others was a fluke. It probably won't happen again."

Ayami was silent.

Toshi looked her in the face from a meter away. "Is something else troubling you? You didn't seem to worry when I was working at the foundry."

She turned to him with mist forming in her eyes. "Maybe it's just everything. The foundry, fishing, the boys. And Emiko."

"Emiko?"

"Yes. I'm worried about her. I don't know how Father could send her away like that."

He moved closer and put an arm around her shoulder. "She is probably fine and we are worrying for nothing. Her letters said she is doing well."

"I don't trust the letters," she replied. "Do you?"

Toshi was silent.

PART TWO

The Silk Factory

Chapter 40

News From The Empress

KAMAISHI - APRIL 1881

Tuesday was warm with white fluffy clouds drifting overhead. Toshi was stepping off additional garden space when a messenger from the village approached. He had a letter for Toshi Ozawa. It was sent from Kitakami, the messenger said. It took Toshi a few minutes to think who could be sending him news from Kitakami. Ayami's parents lived beyond Kitakami, in Hanamaki. Surely, they would have sent a letter from there, not from Kitakami. Then he remembered the Empress. *Why would the Empress be sending me a letter?* he wondered. He ran to the house to get Ayami.

"I just got a letter from Kitakami!" he shouted. "It must be from the Empress!"

April 12, 1881

Dear Toshi,
I have news regarding the sister of your wife. She is working at a small thread factory near Osaki. It is a hundred kilometers south of here. I have not seen her, but one of my samurai sisters talked to a girl who worked with her. She said Emiko is in better health than most but has lost weight and is sad and lonely. As with all the girls, she is forced to work as many as sixteen hours a day in poor conditions.
Should I retrieve the girl? What about her friend?
When are you going to bring another shipment of fish? Customers have been asking for it since your last trip.

Please reply soon regarding the girls and the fish.

Mei – my real name

Ayami's eyes began to water at the mention of her sister. "Thank goodness she's all right," she stammered. "But we have to get her back."

"Grab what you need for the baby, and let's go see Haruki," Toshi said. "Haruki and I can write a letter to the Empress and take it to the village this afternoon. I'm glad today was not our day to fish."

When they arrived, Kanae answered the door.

"We got a letter from the Empress," Ayami exclaimed. "She found Emiko!"

Kanae turned around and shouted, "It's Ayami. They found Emiko!" Then she turned to the visitors and motioned them in.

Minako came running. "Where is she? Is she okay?"

Haruki and Saya were close behind.

Toshi held out the letter. "It came today," he said. "We just got it!" He read it aloud, word-for-word. "What do you think? Should we get her? Can we go?"

Haruki extended an arm and invited them all to sit. "What about Kunio?" he asked. "He won't be happy if we go behind his back to bring Emiko home. And what about Suki's parents? Are you sure they want her to leave?"

"I don't care what they think," Ayami declared. "Emiko can stay with us if she needs to—and so can Suki." She looked at Toshi. "She can, can't she? They can both stay with us. Maybe they can find work here." She turned to Minako for reassurance.

"I agree," she said. "They can stay with us, too. I don't care what Kunio thinks. He has already proven we can't trust him—and Suki probably only went because of Emiko."

They wrote to the Empress and then to Ayami's mother. As soon as they were finished writing the letters, Toshi and Haruki hurried off to the village.

"Since we're making the trip again, what do you think about another load of fish?" Toshi asked.

"We could use a little extra income," Haruki replied. "Now that we don't have the foundry to think about, we don't have much to lose. At least this time we wouldn't have to pay for the fish. We can catch our own."

"This all happened so fast I'm not sure where to begin," Toshi said as they walked. "Do you remember how to smoke the fish? I don't know if I can repeat it again. What if the fish turns out bad? What if we don't have a good catch?"

Haruki knew if he remained quiet Toshi would work through all the questions in his mind, and more likely than not, the answers as well. "Let's stop at the church and see if Fr. Lispard is interested in another rice festival. If we bring back rice like the last time, we'll need a place to sell it."

"Good idea," Toshi replied.

It was four o'clock when they gently opened the door and looked around for Fr. Lispard.

"Good afternoon, my friends. What a pleasant surprise to see you," came a greeting from the front of the church. "What brings you to the village this fine spring day?"

The tall and slender priest walked to the back of the church to meet his friends.

"How are the workers from the foundry? Have they found other jobs? When Hideji told me about the foundry closing, I worried about them. I prayed that God would help them find new jobs, but most of all, that they would find a way to feed their families."

Toshi smiled. It was as plain to him as the black frock adorning the priest; God had answered his prayer. It was God who planted the idea in Haruki's head that day. He darted a look at Haruki to see if he'd made the connection, but if he had, it didn't show.

"A few of the workers who hadn't worked there very long went back to their previous jobs. So far, I don't think any of the others have found new jobs, but thanks to Haruki, most of them will at least have enough to live on. He figured out a way to let twenty of us buy shares in two fishing boats. Every man gets to fish at least one day each week, which should be enough to feed his family for the week," Toshi explained.

"Actually, that's part of the reason we're here," he continued. "We received a letter from our friend in Kitakami, and she wants us to bring a load of smoked fish. We're hoping to bring back a load of rice like we did last year. Would you be interested in another festival, to help us sell it?"

He answered without hesitation. "Of course we would. Especially now that spring is here. We won't have to worry about a snowstorm. People still tell me how much they liked your rice."

Then Toshi thought about Kazuo, the most important piece of the puzzle. *Did he still own the horses? Would he be available to make the trip?* He tried not to worry as he and Haruki made their way west to the small acreage where Kazuo lived.

No one answered when Toshi and Haruki knocked. They peeked through a partly covered window but the sun was low in the west, and they could only make out a few empty shadows, splayed across the opposite wall. They knocked a second time.

Then they walked to the rear of the house, where they found a larger building some twenty meters farther back. The building was not only larger, but built with obviously more care. Even as they drew close, they could find no gaps between the wooden slats of its siding. There were two large windows on each side, providing light and ventilation.

"This must be his *new* house," Toshi said, almost to himself. "No wonder he didn't answer at the old one."

They walked past what seemed to be the front, although it had no door, to the south side of the building. There they found a door and once again, knocked lightly and waited. A minute later Toshi knocked a second time, this time louder. Toshi was sure he heard noises, but there was no response. It being April, and the sun mostly down for the day, all the windows were closed to keep the house as warm as possible.

Toshi timidly put his face to the window nearest him and placed his hands on either side of his head to shield the last reflecting rays of the sun. Just as his face touched the glazed fabric that formed the window, he saw a large white face staring back at him through the same glazed material.

Too startled to move or make a sound, he tried to make out who it was, looking back at him. Then, just as he was about to duck under the window and run, he heard a familiar sound. It was a low, guttural, gurgling sound, which reminded him of a cat when it purrs, but a thousand times louder. It was Kazuo's chestnut mare. She remembered Toshi, and was telling him hello.

While the two were admiring the barn and the meticulous way Kazuo cared for his animals, the whinnying sound of a different horse caught their attention. It came from the opposite side of the barn and approached through a cluster of towering pines. They turned and walked toward the sound, and when they rounded the front corner of the barn, there was Kazuo, riding his blood bay and carrying two large rabbits next to the saddle.

When Kazuo saw them, the heavy lines in his young face disappeared. The transformation almost brought a tear to Toshi when he realized how distressed Kazuo must have been at leaving the foundry.

Kazuo jumped down from the horse and hurried to meet them with hands outstretched. It seemed like months, not weeks, since he had seen his friends.

When Toshi told him about the letter from the Empress, his face lit up. "This is exactly what I've been wishing for," he said. "When do we go? I'll have the horses ready. How many do we need?"

"We plan to leave next Friday and be back on Wednesday," Toshi replied. "We'll need six horses this time. We're planning to bring Emiko and Suki home from the thread mill."

"I thought they had another year to go," Kazuo said. "Are they coming home early?"

"We hope so," Toshi replied.

Kazuo looked at him. "Does the factory know that?"

"I don't think so," Toshi replied.

Kazuo raised his eyes. "Does Kunio know that?"

"I don't think so," Toshi replied.

"How are you going to get them out early?"

"I don't know," Toshi replied.

Kazuo stared at him.

"Oh," he said.

Chapter 41

Emiko

The shrill of a nearby whistle blared in her ears. *It must be five-thirty,* Emiko thought, and rolled over to see if Suki heard it as well.

The tatami mat was lumpy from age, and cold from an unheated floor below. She unwrapped herself from the thin blanket and tiptoed lightly over her bunkmates to retrieve her uniform from its peg on the wall. *If I could only write, I would ask Mama to send a warmer blanket,* she thought. *I wonder when they're going to provide the schooling they promised.*

She looked down at the crowded floor to see if Suki was awake. Her friend from Hanamaki slowly stirred, then lifted her head and coughed several times.

"You should see the nurse," Emiko said. "I think your cough is getting worse."

"I know, but I don't want to get punished. I'm afraid they'll hold it against me if I take time out to see the nurse. Maybe it will get better if I give it time."

"I hope so...hurry and dress so we can get to breakfast. It will help keep your strength up."

They scrambled to the washroom and then the dining hall.

Emiko looked across the room for a place to sit. "At least we have our choice of tables," she said. "It looks like a lot of girls would rather sleep than eat."

"Who can blame them?" Suki replied. She stirred her spoon in circles around the wooden bowl. "It's mostly water, anyway. Hardly worth getting up early for."

"I know," Emiko replied. "I probably should have let you sleep. But we have to eat when we can, or we'll get sick for sure. Hurry. It's almost time to go."

Just then, the whistle sounded.

"Forget the spoon," Emiko said. She lifted her bowl with both hands and drank down the last of the watery broth.

Emiko headed for her station and, with practiced efficiency, reached for a filament and carefully threaded it on the reel. Then with a pump of the pedal, she started the wheel in motion and began the day.

***

For some of the girls, the lucky ones, the constant rhythm of the spinning wheel took them to a magical place. It was somewhere between a land of sleep and a state of trance. Emiko was relieved whenever she entered that surreal condition. Time no longer mattered. She could forget her aching back, her sore arms, and her weary legs. Sometimes she could even dream of home while letting her body process the reel, almost without mindful intervention. It was her saving grace. It helped pass the time through the long and tedious days.

Whenever a supervisor approached, reelers could sense it, simply by the sound in the room. It was hard to describe because it was not a sound like the beginning or ending of something. Certainly not from a change in the sound of conversations. Reelers seldom talked while they worked. Yet somehow a reeler could sense, just by their presence, that a supervisor was in the area. Once there, he might linger just far enough away, and stare at a particular worker until she became so nervous that she pumped the reel too fast or too slow, and broke the delicate web.

Of all the supervisors at the Osaki Silk Factory, Orochi Mizuno was the worst. Today he made his way slowly down aisle one, toward Emiko. He stopped one station short, the one assigned to Kame Shimizu. Kame was from a rural village in the south. She was two years older than Emiko, big for her age, and not attractive.

Adding to the unfortunate hand she was dealt, her face bore traces of a childhood pox. Kame was the last person Orochi would take romantic interest in, but that was where he stopped.

While in one of her workday trances, Emiko was subconsciously dreaming about a favorite tree she and Ayami liked to climb when they were young. She did not see Orochi standing at Kame's station a few meters away. It was not until she heard a familiar cough from the station one aisle over that she turned her attention to the factory floor. She looked up just in time to see Orochi staring at her with a sordid grin. It was one of his favorite tactics: pretending to watch one person while staring at another.

Chapter 42

Nightmare

Hair on the back of Emiko's neck stood straight. Orochi had been leering at her from one aisle over, just moments ago. Now he was nowhere in sight. He had been watching her for days, a pattern she knew meant only one thing.

Suddenly, a hand formed at the base of her neck, right where the hairs were standing at high alert. The hand was large, warm, and sweating. A second hand then found its way to Emiko's thigh, well above her knee. Wearing her tattered uniform, she could not tell if the second hand was also sweating. Then it was her own hands that began to sweat, and not from the heat of the cocoons. All the muscles in her fragile body began to tighten.

Orochi bent down, his mouth next to her left ear, close enough to her nose that she could smell his unwelcome breath. As he began to speak, four of her five senses sounded alarm. It was a low, raspy voice, meant for her ears only.

"If you treat me nice, I can make your life easier," it taunted. "On the other hand, if you're *not* nice to me, I can make your life m-u-u-u-c-h more difficult." He raised his head slightly away to let her absorb the words. Then he slipped his right hand from her neck and shifted it slowly down her back, rubbing from side to side as far as he could reach, with her seated at the machine, him standing close beside.

He bent down once more, next to her ear, and with his left hand now free, pointed loosely in the direction of Suki, whose machine was adjacent to Emiko, but one row over. "And keep in mind that I can also make life much…*much* harder on your little sister, if you aren't nice to me. I noticed that she coughs a lot. Longer hours and less food would probably not be good for her health, do you think?" He laughed at his little joke as he squeezed Emiko's shoulder. "Something for you to think about until we talk again."

Then Orochi walked away, as quickly and quietly as when he arrived.

Emiko wanted to yell out to someone but could not get the words to leave her mouth. They formed in her head, but her voice could not get them out. She began to tremble and felt herself falling from the stool. She flailed her arms in an effort to regain her balance. Then she felt a hand on her shoulder. This time it was smaller. And gentle. She could hear someone coughing, maybe in the distance. Her mind was confused. When she felt the hand again, it was shaking her lightly. She heard her name a second time and opened her eyes.

"Emiko. Emiko. It's time to get up. Everyone else has gone to breakfast."

Suki paused to release several more coughs before she continued. "You were tossing and turning all night, so I thought you would like a little extra sleep this morning. If you dress quickly, I'll save you a place in the cafeteria. I think we still have time to get a bowl of rice, if you hurry. I'll get whatever I can and meet you at the table."

"Thank you, Suki." She muttered. "You're right, I didn't sleep much. I keep having nightmares about Orochi. I'll tell you about it later. I'm sorry I kept you. I'll hurry as fast as I can."

Suki was waiting at a table in the dining hall when Emiko finished dressing. By the time Suki made it to the serving line, there was but one serving of rice remaining. She asked that it be split between two bowls, the extra for her friend who overslept. Suki's cough surfaced again as she waited for the elderly woman to find a second bowl and split the serving in half.

Emiko seated herself across from Suki, who had already started to eat her meager ration when the serving lady walked over to them. She looked at Emiko.

"Has your sister been to see the nurse? I've noticed her before, when you've come through the line, and she seems to be getting worse."

The two girls stole a quick glance at one another and grinned slightly. It was not the first time they had been mistaken for sisters, even though they didn't look that much alike. It was probably because they were usually seen together, and always in a protective sort of way.

"Yes, I've been to see the nurse," replied Suki. "But she wasn't able to do much for me. She said it was probably just a cold and would eventually go away."

The serving woman, who faintly reminded Suki of her grandmother, and perhaps the reverse was also true, frowned as if in disbelief before she said. "You wait here; let me see if I can find something more to eat. It's a disgrace the way they feed you young people. I don't know how they expect you to do any work at all when you're practically starving to death." She abruptly turned and headed back in the direction of the kitchen.

The two girls tried to quickly eat what little portions of rice they had in front of them. They knew the whistle was about to sound and could not risk being late. The supervisor loved to punish anyone who arrived late at their machine.

Just as they were finishing their last bites, the woman returned. She presented a small bag to Suki. "Here, take this with you so you won't be late. I found a slice of bread that is still soft enough to eat, a little cheese, and two carrots. That's all I could find. I wanted to get you an egg. We have plenty of eggs, but only the men and the supervisors are supposed to have them. Watch for me when you come through the line, and I'll give you a signal when I have something extra for you. We have to keep it between us, though. Do you understand?"

Suki was shocked by her kindness. Her eyes blinked as she tried to comprehend her meaning. Emiko understood and replied for her. "Yes, we understand. And we cannot thank you enough for your kindness. We'll watch for your signal."

Then the whistle sounded, which meant they were supposed to be settling at their machines.

The factory floor was adjacent to the dining hall, designed for that very reason: so workers would not waste valuable time coming and going to meals. There were eight rows of machines, and each row contained twelve reelers. Emiko was assigned the first machine in the first row, and Suki the first machine in the second row.

Emiko and Suki settled in, after their abbreviated breakfast. Both girls thought about the serving woman as they worked.

Suki was thinking mostly about how she could eat the bread and cheese without detection. Of course, she would share it with Emiko, but where could they eat it without creating a problem? Their hands were too busy to eat as they worked. If they waited and ate it with their noon meal, everyone would wonder where they got the extra food. And bread, cheese, and vegetables besides! Then it occurred to her the kindly woman might be trying to get them in trouble. She must have known there was no place she could safely eat her contraband. Maybe she planned to report that Suki had stolen it from the kitchen.

Emiko was stuck on something the woman said. She, too, had noticed Suki's cough getting worse. Emiko knew deep down that it was, but kept telling herself that it wasn't. She started counting in her mind the girls who had started out healthy, then, after months of breathing the dust-filled air of the factory, began to cough, and eventually were forced to leave. She hoped they recovered once they left this unhealthy place, but there wasn't any way of knowing.

Eventually Emiko forced her thoughts back to the factory floor and carefully wound another filament around the thread.

When she heard Suki cough louder and longer than normal, it pulled her back to the moment. Was she having a more serious attack? She looked over at Suki, who was watching her from the corner of her eye.

When she saw Emiko looking over at her, Suki tilted her head with slight jerks toward the end of her row.

Emiko caught her meaning and turned in that direction. She took a breath. Her entire body, only moments ago weary from exhaustion, sprang to life. Orochi was coming her way and this time it was not a dream.

Emiko tried to collect her thoughts while pretending not to notice Orochi as he drew near. She adjusted the filaments and swirled the cocoons in her basin while watching him from the corner of her eye. He was standing at the fifth station in row two, pretending to observe a worker there. After watching the terrified girl a few minutes, he slowly moved on to station four, three stations away from Suki. Occasionally he would steal a look to the end of the row, looking first at Suki, then over at Emiko, before turning his attention back to the girl at station four.

Minutes later Emiko jumped, as a large hand, warm and sweaty, placed itself on the back of her neck. It was exactly like the nightmare dream she'd had two nights before. Having seen it in her dream, she tensed her legs in anticipation of another large and sweaty hand grasping at her thigh. She held her breath waiting for the hand to land. When nothing happened, she turned her head slightly in the direction of Orochi, standing at her left, next to the hot water basin filled with cocoons.

When he saw her turn slightly toward him, he leaned down close so only she could hear as he said, "Thank you for being one of our best workers. I have seen how good you are. Please accept this flower as a gift for being a good and productive reeler." He then pulled a twig of plum blossom from his pocket and offered it out to her. "This time of year I couldn't find much to choose from, but I hope you enjoy it. It has a very nice fragrance when you smell it."

He smiled at her as he retreated. Then, almost as an afterthought, he added. "I'm sorry if I frightened you, and also that my hand might be sweaty. I was nervous about bringing you the flower."

Then he moved quickly over to the third row and ambled off toward the other end of the factory.

Emiko lifted the blossom to her face and inhaled a long, deep breath. Then she closed her eyes and found herself seated along the bank of the Kitakami River, at home on the farm. The plum thicket she knew so well would be in full bloom, and its imagined fragrance filled the air around her. The sun felt warm on her back, and she could almost taste the ripened fruit that was sure to follow. Her father and brothers were busy planting rice in the field. The potatoes were beginning to break through the ground in evenly spaced mounds. Her stomach was full, and although she was thin from working in the fields, she was healthy and nourished. She could be happy along that riverbank for the rest of her life.

When she opened her eyes and looked at the single twig of flowers, held by hands attached to arms not much bigger than the twig, her eyes began to water. And when she heard her stomach growl in search of even a single plum, it was more than she could bear. She closed her eyes again to keep the tears from flowing down her cheeks.

She opened them only at the sound of Suki's coughing, one aisle over. She looked at Suki to see if she needed help, only to be met with a look of concern and confusion. Suki seemed upset with her; for what reason she didn't know. She wiped her still teary eyes with the backs of her hands, and when she could see again, well enough to find the filaments, slowly began to pedal the reel that created the silky thread.

When the whistle blew for a thirty-minute lunch break, Suki rushed over to her, still wearing a rigid look of contempt as she said, "Emiko, please don't tell me you're falling for his tricks! You know how evil he is. All he wants is to make you his girlfriend for long enough to sleep with you. We've watched him do that since the first day we got here. You've got to find a way to put him off. Maybe we should tell the owner what he does. Maybe they will listen if we both go together."

Emiko looked at her as she tried to formulate a response. Finally, she said, "No, I'm not planning to fall for him. The plum blossoms reminded me of home and how much I wish we were there instead of here. But I don't know how to get rid of him. I've tried to make myself as homely as possible, but it doesn't seem to bother him. Look at my hair. Who would want to sleep with a girl with hair so tangled that mice could hide in it? And my uniform is so worn and dirty, who would want to touch it? I can barely stand to wear it. And look at my fingernails. The few I have left are filled with dirt. And you know how bad we smell. He has to be a crazy person to want to get close to me."

She stopped for a minute before continuing, "As long as I'm his target, there is nothing I can do. He's the one with all the power. If I don't succumb to him, he will make my life miserable. He can withhold my wages, or extend my contract, make me work longer hours, or whatever else his evil mind dreams up for me. There is no way I can win unless he decides to move on to someone else. I'm afraid to talk to the owner. It would be my word against his. It would probably only get worse if we complained."

That night, Emiko barely slept at all. Between trying to think of a way to get rid of Orochi and the ever-increasing coughing spells of Suki, sleep avoided her. When morning came, she and Suki were the last to dress and head for the cafeteria. When they arrived, they hurried to the line, grabbed their small bowl of rice and a cup of water, and found a place at a far table where there was space for two.

They had just begun to eat when the elderly serving woman approached from the kitchen and addressed Suki, saying, "I think you left this yesterday. We found it at the table where you were sitting." When she tossed it on the table in front of Suki, they could plainly see it was empty, which puzzled them both. The woman had hinted she would try to smuggle extra food to Suki, but this was obviously not a part of the plan.

Chapter 43

Orochi

With broad shoulders and a stout frame, Orochi was an anomaly on the factory floor. He was the only person there not malnourished. The reelers considered him lazy, and rumors arose from time to time suggesting that his parents had sent him packing. It was general knowledge he only worked at the factory because his uncle was the owner.

Sitting alone at the table reserved for supervisors, he savored his breakfast of rice, eggs, and freshly baked buns covered with honey. The table itself was located along one wall of the cafeteria, where the floor was elevated by one step. The meaning was clear. Supervisors were above the general workforce. A railing around the raised floor further signified the barrier between supervisors and their workers. An added benefit was that it allowed supervisors to view the rest of the cafeteria, thereby keeping a constant watch on everything they did.

Often, Orochi skipped breakfast because he had eaten his fill the night before and preferred the extra sleep. But this morning was special. He had been waiting nearly two years, since the day worker number 8-8-0 and the girl he assumed to be her younger sister, number 8-8-1, walked through the cafeteria on their orientation tour. Employee 8-8-0 was striking, with her natural and unpretentious beauty. She was the most attractive girl to work at the factory in his three years' time. He had judged her to be about fifteen and the younger sister to be eleven or twelve.

Orochi was living proof that if one desired something badly enough, one could overcome one's shortcomings in order to prevail. Even though Orochi was not particularly bright, he did have certain powers of observation. As early as his first year at the factory, he watched as young girls began their contracts filled with self-confidence and enthusiasm.

Over time, they settled into a state of resignation. For the first few months they kept their bonds with parents and siblings alive by writing letters often. Some, as often as three times a week in those first few months. But with the passing of time and only occasional letters received in return, they gradually fell into a condition of loneliness, and eventually, despair.

The girls had no way of knowing their letters were intercepted by supervisors, particularly the letters from home. Isolation helped to loosen their bonds with family.

As Orochi watched the girls become more and more lonely over time, he found that given the slightest bit of attention, they almost always countered with a positive and immediate response. If he told even the most unattractive girl she was beautiful, she reciprocated with a blush and a smile each time he crossed her path thereafter. If he followed up with a hand on her shoulder and another compliment, no matter how phony, she would likely return the favor with the touch of her hand on his arm. The trajectory had begun.

In a cruel act of irony for employee 8-8-0, nature gifted Orochi with the season's very first plum blossom. It had more meaning to Emiko than it might have, had she known there was a plum thicket just meters from the factory, growing right along the path Orochi took to work each day. Still, it had the desired effect, if only temporary, that Orochi had hoped. He was quite sure he had seen a smile form on her lips. And he was just as certain that her thin cheeks had turned slightly red. Later, when he turned from the end of the aisle for one last look, he was pretty sure he had seen a tear run down her cheek.

By now, Orochi had forgotten about breakfast altogether, as he anticipated their first night together. He could hardly wait to remove the buttons from her uniform and lift it slowly above her head. He would step back without speaking and admire the beauty of her body, from her face, which was itself heavenly, to her neck, her shoulders, her small and beautiful breasts, her slender waist, her perfectly proportioned thighs, down to the toes on her feet. He imagined her standing before him, two meters away, smiling faintly as she anticipated their coming embrace. *Would she be holding her arms at her sides,* he wondered? *Or would she delicately try to cover her privates in a display of modesty?*

His standard formula called for the first date to be an invitation to his hut for an evening meal, following the end of her long day at work. Usually, Orochi could find a reason to get the worker excused early, which, of course, they readily accepted. Once there, he offered them enough saké to put their inhibitions at ease. Although he hated to cook and was not particularly good at it, he managed to feed them well, but not enough to make them sleepy or sick. He had learned from experience that since they were unaccustomed to eating a full meal, they would often gorge themselves, only to later throw up their meal and make a mess. Not to mention ruin his plans for a lengthy dessert.

His plan for number 8-8-0 would contain something special in recognition of her undeniable beauty. He would offer her a hot bath, for as long as she wanted. That should not only soften her defenses, but it would also make her even more attractive. He rightly guessed she would relish being clean again, particularly in the privacy of his little house, where she wouldn't have to wait in line or bathe in water already used by a dozen other girls. It would be the crowning touch. She would be like putty in his hands after a light meal and a hot bath.

He would offer her saké, just like all the others, but this time he would dilute it with water to keep her from getting drunk. For some girls, he didn't mind them drunk. They often startled him with their aggressive lovemaking when they were a little too tipsy, and that could be fun. But it was too much work to get them up the next morning and back to the factory. He could cover for them to some degree, but not entirely. He did not want them getting sick when back at work, or falling asleep at their reeling machine. It could lead to questions from the higher-ups that he preferred not to answer.

His uncle had given Orochi almost free rein on the factory floor, which he appreciated. He dared not jeopardize what he considered the best job in all Japan. His primary responsibility was simply to maintain the status quo, and never draw attention to the girls or their work. If his uncle periodically noticed his infatuation with some of the workers, then so be it. Boys would be boys.

He wondered how long his affair with number 8-8-0 might last. Usually, he tired of a girl after several weeks, though sometimes it could last for months. It would start with the initial dinner invitation. Occasionally, it would take a second or even a third invitation before he persuaded his date to spend the night. Then she would come for dinner every three or four days for a few weeks, followed by a week or two of nightly encounters where he skipped formalities altogether and led her straight to the bedroom. Then, as his interest turned to boredom, they would taper off to weekly visits, then biweekly, and eventually, just an occasional tryst when both were feeling lonely.

Orochi was hoping for a longer-term relationship with worker 8-8-0. Six months seemed a good target. He would move slower with her because of her almost haunting beauty. He wanted to savor every minute, not only their lovemaking, but the anticipation in between. What if he even fell in love with her? That had never occurred to him before. But he could almost see her as his wife in the little hut close to the factory. He could come home to sleep with her every night. But even worker 8-8-0 might grow tiresome after a year or two. He decided not to think about it now.

Then, as if to confirm he was not a man worthy of marriage, another thought came to mind. He wondered what her sister might be like. He had never slept with sisters before. Would they behave differently from one another, he wondered? What an interesting possibility. Would one be more passionate than the other? Would they feel the same, as they rocked in unison in the intimate act of love? His imagination ran wild with thoughts of upcoming conquests. By now, number 8-8-1 must be almost fifteen years old. A little young for his taste, but still, for this experiment, it might be worth the effort.

Perhaps he could even create a jealous tension between the two. If he started dating her sister, would 8-8-0 become even more passionate in a fight to keep him to herself? The more he thought about the possibility, the more intrigued he became. He would begin to take more notice of the little sister from now on. She was not the beauty her older sister was, but there was a faint resemblance, and he had frequently noticed mannerisms that caught his fancy. Like the way she tossed her hair to keep it from her eyes, or the way she stretched her body sometimes, with arms extended toward the ceiling. It made her tiny frame look most tantalizing. He remembered watching once, wondering how her body would look naked in a pose like that. But at the time, he had many other, more eligible numbers listed in his diary.

Finishing the last of his second cup of tea, Orochi watched the two sisters as they entered late for breakfast. But he was particularly interested in their encounter with the serving lady. This might be just the opportunity he'd been waiting for. Food smuggling was an egregious offense at the factory. Unless, of course, it was done by a supervisor. Hoping to catch the offenders in the act, or at the very least, to get them to confess to a crime, he jumped from the table, leaving part of his second bowl of rice unfinished.

Approaching their table, he greeted them with a smile: "Good morning, girls." Facing Emiko, he said, "You're looking especially nice this morning. I hope you had a pleasant evening and a good night's sleep."

When neither girl replied, he tried again. "Are you still hungry? Did you get enough to eat? I have influence with the kitchen, you know. If you're not getting enough to eat, let me know, and I will use my influence." He turned slightly, to stare at the sack on the table, then at the older woman who had brought it there.

Pausing while she chose her words, Emiko replied to him in a voice loud enough for the adjacent tables to hear. "Yes, I am still hungry—in fact, we are all still hungry. We're all hungry because we never get enough to eat. Look at us. We're practically skin and bones, all of us. Why wouldn't we be hungry when we're expected to work every daylight hour on a meager ration of rice and watered soup?"

Before he could think of a reply to what he had expected would be a polite and gracious answer, she continued, "And we are all grateful that you have special influence with the kitchen. Whatever you can do to improve the size of our portions will be truly appreciated by all of us. It was kind of you to make the offer." Then she forced the sincerest smile she could, leaving him to wonder if she was thanking him or mocking him.

The dining hall had gone completely quiet when they saw Orochi approaching Emiko's table, hoping for something new to gossip about. So almost everyone in the cafeteria heard the exchange. They cheered in silence when they heard Emiko's surprising reply. She had called his bluff in front of the entire hall, in such a way he didn't know if he was being portrayed as a caring supervisor or a foolish blowhard. Unable to contain themselves, the entire dining hall began to clap in a spontaneous outburst of applause for the seventeen-year-old with matted hair. She had shown the courage to stand her ground and tell the supervisor face-to-face, what every last one of them wished they could.

They watched eagerly while they awaited his response. He seemed totally lost for words as he realized the predicament he had brought upon himself. Finally, as his face flushed red and tiny dots of perspiration formed across his forehead, the whistle began its wailing sound, calling all workers to the factory floor. Suki deftly grabbed the empty sack and stuck it in the pocket of her uniform as they rushed toward the door.

Orochi sensed the looming potential for disaster. Luckily, most of the girls had already left the cafeteria and headed to work when he was rebuffed by number 8-8-0. But if word spread to the other workers about her standing up to him, who knew how bold the entire group might become? What if they managed to go on strike for better food? He would be the first to catch the wrath of his uncle. His job might even be in jeopardy. Only minutes ago, he was dreaming of his first nightly encounter with worker 8-8-0, and now he might end up humiliated, maybe even sacked. If he lost this job, who would even consider hiring him? His life would be in shambles.

As he hurried to the reeling floor, a plan began to emerge. He pushed himself to the front of the group in order to make himself first to the door as the whistle wound down to an empty sound. It was the signal all workers should be seated at their stations and beginning their day.

Orochi abruptly stopped just inside the doorway and barred entry to everyone following behind. He stared directly into the eyes of the first poor girl behind him and announced in a stern and steely voice, "Remain exactly where you are until I get back."

Looking at the first worker in the line, he saw her shake uncontrollably. He knew she would obey, from fear alone. He turned and rushed to the far end of the factory and pulled something from a shelf. As he hurried back, almost at a run, Emiko could see the writing pad he carried, along with a sharpened pencil.

"Didn't you hear the whistle?" he boomed. "Anyone not seated at their station when the whistle ends, is tardy. Obviously, anyone in this line was not at their station when the whistle ended. You will all be charged with one count of tardiness. If you choose to dally in the cafeteria and collaborate to criticize the hard-working women in the kitchen, you can expect to be punished."

Orochi recorded each worker's number in his tablet as the stranded girls filed, one by one, through the door and to their station. When Emiko and Suki passed through in their turn, Orochi gave them faint smiles, as if trying to say he didn't want to do it. He even paused for several seconds before writing down the numbers 8-8-0 and 8-8-1 on his pad. But he did write them down.

***

Emiko didn't know if she had won or lost the battle. At first, she was exalted by the support of the other girls. But when it resulted in penalties for many of them, her spirits plunged. It was a vivid reminder of who held power at the factory, and it was not the workers. Even with odds of eighty to one, or whatever it happened to be, the *one* held the power. Any ideas she had about uniting the workers had been dashed in minutes. Now, perhaps even worse, she knew Orochi would be watching her every move. She knew he could make her life unbearable even if he didn't manage to get her to bed, and it bothered her too, that he seemed to have taken interest in Suki. Surely he would not use her in his depraved use of force. Her health was bad enough as it was. Emiko didn't think Suki could withstand more penalty hours, or less food. She saw tinges of red sometimes, after Suki's coughing spells. It was one more thing to worry about.

Later that night, still puzzled by the empty sack the kitchen worker left at their table, Suki pulled it from her pocket, loosened the drawstrings, and looked inside. There was a note. Looking around to make sure no one was watching, she slipped it out and held it up to an oil lamp.

There is a shelf at the far end of the dining hall which contains cleaning supplies. Behind the supplies I will leave an identical sack whenever I can. Make sure no one is watching you, then swap your empty bag for the one on the shelf. Please destroy this note. A friend.

Whatever the note was meant to disclose, Suki would never know. She showed it to Emiko, and together they traced the letters with their fingers, but without the skill required, neither girl could read the words.

Chapter 44

Orochi Exposed

OSAKI SILK FACTORY - APRIL 1881

Eight magnificent horses headed south from Kitakami on a crisp, clear April morning. Six carried riders. Two did not. Leading the group was Gordo, longtime friend and confidant of the Empress. He rode a dusty-white gelding with a gray face. He would be their guide for the trip to Osaki.

Following close behind was the Empress, riding the blood bay owned by Kazuo. He remembered how much she admired the animal that first time they met. Seated erect in the saddle, back straight, chin high, limbs held close and taut, she was the picture of determination.

Behind the Empress followed Jun, riding her own black mare. Like the Empress, Jun was a samurai, even larger in stature than the Empress, but with a more relaxed demeanor.

Next came Toshi and Haruki, riding two gray mares that belonged to Kazuo.

Kazuo brought up the rear. Two spare horses followed without need of a tether. Both horses carried small bundles of supplies on this leg of the journey. On the return, if all went well, they would each carry a rider. Emiko on one, Suki on the other.

At the end of the second day, Gordo, still in the lead, stopped and turned to converse with the Empress. After a few minutes, he signaled the rest of them. This would be their campsite for tonight. Osaki was five kilometers farther south.

Kazuo, Gordo, and Jun took care of the horses while Toshi started a fire and Haruki assembled tents for the travelers. Jun and the Empress heated tea and warmed fish and bread. The group took turns selecting cheese and carrots from a bowl as it passed from hand to hand.

When they finished eating, Gordo refilled their cups, and the Empress began. "We will breakfast at eight and break camp at nine. Gordo said we should reach the factory before ten o'clock. I don't know if the workers get a morning break or not. They are supposed to, but my informant said they usually don't. I'm hopeful we can tour the factory floor soon after our arrival, to identify Emiko and Suki, and find out what condition they're in.

"Then we'll ask to see the cafeteria during their noon meal. Our official mission is to make sure the factory is living up to proper standards of the emperor. If they accept that, a tour of the factory as well as the cafeteria would be a natural request."

Kazuo darted a puzzled look at the Empress when she mentioned the emperor. "We're on a mission for the emperor?"

"That's our ploy," she replied. "That is what we want them to think."

"What if they don't believe it?" Toshi asked.

"I've been thinking about that," the Empress said. "Toshi and Haruki, I want you to stay here at the camp. If something goes wrong and we fail, we might need to use force. I don't want family members involved. Not only that, if Emiko would happen to realize who you are while we're in the factory, she might accidentally give us away. I'm sorry, but you will need to wait here for us."

Toshi looked at Haruki, hoping he might intervene, but Haruki did not return his look.

The Empress continued, shifting her gaze to Kazuo and Jun. "Only Gordo or I will do the talking. If someone asks you a question, try to re-direct it to Gordo or me. The first thing we have to do is identify the girls."

Turning back to Toshi and Haruki, she said, "What can you tell us about the girls?"

Anxious to be helpful, Toshi answered quickly, "Ayami said she was considered one of the prettiest girls in Hanamaki, and that she was slender with black hair."

The Empress held a straight face, knowing he was trying to help. "That's a start," she said. "What else?"

"How tall is she?" Jun asked.

"Oh… Ayami said she was about a hundred and forty centimeters when she left home two years ago, and she weighed about fifty kilograms."

"How old was she then?"

"Fifteen," Toshi replied.

"So, she is seventeen, a little taller than one-forty, probably gained a few kilos in two years, in spite of the work, attractive, with black hair," the Empress summarized. "There must be something else."

"Ayami said she hurt her left hand when she was young and has a slight scar just above her left wrist. She thought it would be visible unless she was wearing a long sleeve."

"Well, that's something, at least. What about Suki?"

"Ayami said she was twelve when she left home and was a friend of Emiko, so they will probably stay close together at the factory."

"That's not much to go on," the Empress replied, "but it's all we have. Once we get past the owner and into the factory, we'll separate and scan the work floor, pretending to take note of the machinery and how productive the factory is. Whoever spots Emiko should make their way to me, trying not to be conspicuous. If I spot her first, I'll make my way to Kazuo. That will be the signal that we've found her.

She stopped talking after several minutes, giving time for the others to understand her plan, then she continued. "My hope is to rescue both girls along with their employment records, to make it harder for them to track down their families. If the owner has any suspicion we're not who we pretend to be, the rescue could turn bad.

"One last thing," she added. "We should not use our real names in case they try to track us down later. I will be *Mei*. Gordo will be *Gaku*. Jun will be *Fuyumi,* and Kazuo, you will be *Riku*. Memorize those names before tomorrow. Mei is my real name, but hardly anyone knows that. Everyone calls me the Empress. Do you have any questions?"

The three met her intense eyes and shook their heads.

"Now, let's get some sleep. We'll need to be one step ahead of them all day tomorrow. It starts with a good night's sleep." Then she headed for her tent.

All of them were awake and ready before nine o'clock. They loaded gear and supplies on the two unridden horses to make them look like pack animals, in case someone at the factory studied their arrival.

"Wait for us here," the Empress instructed Toshi and Haruki. "We should be back by three o'clock. If we're not, head for the factory, but don't come in. Stay far enough away to observe, but do not come in, no matter what."

"Okay," Toshi replied. "But where is the factory? Is it on this road?"

Gordo answered for her. "Yes, it's about four kilometers ahead on this road. A big building all by itself, surrounded by a high fence. It's before the Eai River. If you get to the river, you've gone too far."

"Okay," Toshi said. "Good luck. We'll see you this afternoon."

***

The four liberators climbed down from their mounts at nine-thirty. Had Gordo not known where they were going, the others would not have stopped. With its high perimeter fence encasing all the buildings, it looked more like a prison than a factory.

The Empress led the way to a solitary door marked 'office.' As they approached, she turned to Gordo, directly behind her, and asked, "Do you have the documents?"

Gordo nodded. The Empress opened the door and the four impersonators walked in.

A young-looking woman sat at the desk reviewing some papers. She was an attractive woman, or could have been. Her face was striking because of the Western-style cosmetics that covered much of her skin. The Empress had once considered selling it in her emporium, but decided against it. It was one more example of the many unintended effects of the Meiji Revolution. A silk factory seemed an odd place to wear such coloring. And the Empress knew it to be an expensive luxury. The woman must have been well paid for her work.

The Empress walked boldly up to her and spoke in a tone that indicated it was not negotiable.

"We are from the Ministry of Labor. We have been instructed to inspect this factory on behalf of the emperor." She bowed as she referenced his title to ensure there was no misunderstanding. "Please summon the owner and tell him we bring the emperor's gratitude and seek his approval to conduct our business."

The woman responded with a look of surprise. She looked down at a paper briefly and then replied. "You're not supposed to be here until tomorrow. Come back tomorrow."

The Empress had rehearsed several responses in her head during the long ride here, but not once had she considered being expected.

"What?"

"Come back tomorrow. We weren't expecting you until tomorrow. We're not ready today."

The Empress was so surprised that she hesitated less than a second, but it was long enough for the woman to wonder if she really was from the Ministry of Labor.

"The letter said tomorrow. Why are you here early?"

"We finished our last inspection early. There was no reason to wait a day. We try to be as efficient as we can for the ministry."

The woman pulled open one of the drawers at her table and rifled through papers until she found the one she wanted. Placing it squarely in front of her, she scanned the words. "It says here, there will be two of you." She looked at the other three impostors standing behind the Empress. "How come there are four of you?"

The Empress was beginning to recover from her initial surprise. She had to regain the upper hand if the ploy was going to work. She glared at the woman behind the table and replied. "The reason we were able to finish our last inspection early was because we had more help. It's not a difficult concept."

She nodded to Gordo (Gaku), who pulled a parchment letter from his ornate leather pouch and handed it to the woman.

"As you can see," the Empress said, "we are from the Ministry of Labor, and we are here to perform our duties. Please alert the owner we are here to begin the inspection."

The woman looked closely at the document and then, as the impostors watched in horror, compared it to the letter she had pulled from her drawer. She studied them carefully, side by side, and then held them up to the light, shining brightly through the window. Every breath in the room but hers was still. She laid the letters down and gazed at the four unexpected visitors.

"The letter seems to be in order," she admitted.

"Thank you," the Empress replied. "Now if you will kindly alert the owner that we're here, we'll begin our work."

"I can't do that," the woman said with a stubborn look. "The letter says you will arrive tomorrow. That's when we have you scheduled."

The Empress was out of patience. "Do I look like a ghost to you?"

"A ghost? No. Why?"

She tilted her head at her three companions behind her. "Do these people look like ghosts to you?"

"No, of course they don't."

"Good. Then we must be here today."

She stared down on the woman, half her size, with the same eyes that were the last living things ever seen by at least a dozen courageous warriors from her past. "Now, if you will please alert the owner, we would like to begin our work."

The woman rose slowly from her station and headed for the stairs. "Wait here," she said. "I'll see if he has time for you."

The Empress darted looks at her fellow impersonators. They stared back in return.

"How can that be?" Jun hissed under her breath. "Why were they expecting us?"

"A real inspector must be coming," the Empress whispered back.

Jun looked at Gordo, then back to the Empress. "We have to get out of here!" she whispered loudly.

The others stared at the Empress, looking for guidance. She glanced at the stairway and turned back to her friends. "We can't leave now. If we do, we'll never get another chance. We have to keep going. Maybe we'll be gone before..."

She did not have time to finish. The woman was coming down the steps with an older man close behind. He was lean of stature, with serious features and dark penetrating eyes. Her first impression was that the owner was not a man easily duped.

All four visitors bowed to the man. Then the Empress took control before he had a chance to gather himself.

"I am Mei. This is Fuyumi-san, Gaku-san, and Riku-san." She tilted her head toward each member as she named them. We're from the Ministry of Labor and have been instructed to inspect your fine factory. I am sure it will prove satisfactory, but the emperor is very concerned about the health and working conditions of his subjects."

She halted long enough for the owner to grasp her introduction, and then asked. "And, if I may be so bold, who do we have the honor of greeting on this fine April morning?"

"My name is Cho. I am the owner of this factory. I was expecting you. But not until tomorrow. Why are you here early? We were expecting you tomorrow. I was planning to give you the tour tomorrow. Our tour isn't ready yet…that is to say, our cafeteria was expecting you tomorrow…the supervisors, that is. The supervisors were expecting you tomorrow. We aren't exactly staffed to show you around on short notice. If you come back tomorrow, we can provide a much better tour."

Bowing again, the Empress addressed him, "Cho-san, that is most generous and thoughtful. However, we do not wish to intrude upon you or your fine factory more than absolutely necessary. In order to cause as little imposition as possible, we would like to start immediately. We have been instructed to inspect, first of all, the factory itself. We need to assure the emperor that your equipment and work spaces are safe and healthy for the reelers. Secondly, we wish to inspect the dormitory space, to make sure it is quite safe and comfortable for your workers. And finally, we will need to inspect the cafeteria. We can do that during the regularly scheduled lunch period so as not to interfere with your normal routine. Will that be acceptable?"

She then looked directly at the owner, using the piercing stare she had perfected during her samurai years. He looked away and responded. "Yes, that is acceptable. My assistant will show you to the factory. I will be with you shortly." Looking at the woman, he nodded for her to lead them to the factory floor.

As soon as she led them away from the office and toward the factory, Cho made a dash to the cafeteria. He had to alert them about a morning break for the workers and make sure they had enough tea, and hopefully, some kind of snack to feed them. He burst into the cafeteria and, seeing no one there, pressed on to the kitchen. He could see and hear several workers starting to prepare for the midday meal at one o'clock.

He grabbed the first person he could find and blurted out, "Quick, the inspectors are a day early. We need to prepare for a morning break at ten-thirty. Do you have enough tea made? What can we give them to eat? Do you have any rolls and honey? We don't have much time. What about for lunch? Today we need to serve double the normal portion! Inspectors are here, and we need to serve a bigger meal today!"

The kitchen helper, who by coincidence was the elderly woman who had conspired to help Suki gain a few extra scraps, summoned up courage to look Cho in the eye as she replied, "We can have tea ready in thirty minutes, but I don't know what we can manage for snacks on short notice."

"We must have plenty of food in the pantry. Take me to the pantry and I'll find something myself. We've got to show the inspectors we're feeding the workers even more than they need."

The two of them headed to the back of the kitchen where the pantry was located. A single door provided entry, and it would normally be locked to prevent pilferage by either the staff or the workers.

Orochi, as it turned out, was already in the pantry. He often used it for pillage of a different sort. Located away from normal activity, particularly while the reelers were hard at work in the factory, and the kitchen help was busy preparing the next meager meal, the small room provided perfect seclusion when he felt the need for his favorite dessert during working hours.

He had, in fact, visited the storeroom so often that most of the kitchen help would avoid the area whenever Orochi came near. Workers were well aware that Orochi was a nephew of the owner, and not a single employee had enough courage to snitch to the higher-ups regarding the nephew's egregious behavior.

And so it was, that over time Orochi let down his guard at hearing voices, footsteps, or any other noises emanating from the area behind the kitchen. He was confident he would not be disturbed while visiting his private sanctuary.

But his overconfidence was now his pivotal mistake.

Hearing two voices above any others, and even a slight rustling, as the door to the pantry opened with a start, he had no time to rise from atop the bed of flour sacks and pull down his uniform. And lying as he was atop one of the younger serving maids, she herself was even less able to pull her uniform down across her neck, waist, and tender, shapely legs.

"Orochi!" One of the voices blared. "What is going on? Is this what I pay you for? You're an embarrassment, not only to my brother, you're an embarrassment to me, as well! Get dressed and get out! You are no longer employed here. Do not cross my path again!"

Then he looked at the hapless girl, still trying to cover her young body while shaking uncontrollably. He almost felt sorry for her, caught like a mouse in a trap, and facing her accuser without an ounce of defense. "You," he sputtered, "you may stay and work in the kitchen, but your every move will be watched by this poor woman beside me."

He turned his head toward the woman. "I'm sorry you had to witness this despicable scene. If you're willing, please watch over this poor harlot. Without my good-for-nothing nephew around, maybe she can redeem herself. As much as I hate to admit it, I'm sure it was Orochi who orchestrated this little rendezvous, and I'm trusting she might turn into a decent girl if given a chance.

"Now, what can we find to feed the reelers? We've only got thirty minutes to get something prepared. And don't forget, at one o'clock, everyone is to receive double the normal portion. The inspectors will be here watching."

Next, Cho headed to his office. He needed to alert the operations foreman to sound the whistle at ten-thirty.

Having taken care of the tea, the snacks, the whistle, and lunch, Cho made a hasty return to the factory. Who knew what might go wrong on the reeling floor after what he had just encountered in the kitchen?

Cho was beginning to perspire, and the inspectors had only just arrived.

***

Toshi and Haruki watched forlornly as the Empress and her troupe rode away. "Now I know how a child feels when a teacher won't let them play with the other kids," Toshi said. "I'm not afraid of the factory owner, and I can't believe he would follow us all the way back to Kamaishi, even if he did find out who we were."

"That may be," Haruki replied, "but I don't want to get on the bad side of the Empress. She's only trying to protect us."

"What if something happens to them? I would feel terrible if something bad happened. We're the ones who got them into this."

"I think she knows what she's doing. She's been through worse, I'm sure. Remember that *naginata* hanging on her wall? I'm pretty sure she can handle herself."

Toshi paced back and forth across their small camp trying to hurry time along. First, he studied a cluster of bushes on one side, smelling their flowers, then a small stand of trees on the opposite side.

Haruki watched him pace. "Bring a little more wood, and I'll heat up the tea," he finally said.

An hour later, they sat together on a long-fallen log and finished their third cup.

"I've got a bad feeling," Toshi said. "Something is not going right. I haven't felt like this before. Something isn't right."

"The Empress told us to stay here," Haruki replied. "We better stay here and wait. She said if they're not back by three o'clock we could go check on them. What else can we do?"

"I don't know… Nothing, I guess. But I'm worried."

Around ten o'clock Haruki offered to make more tea. "Maybe we should eat something. It will help pass the time. Besides, they were planning to eat at the factory, so we might as well eat, too. Then we'll be ready to go when they get here."

Eating didn't help. Toshi was even more restless after rice cake and an apple. He paced again, from the bushes to the trees and back to the bushes. There was not much to see or do at this small camp, and he had already seen and done it, at least three times.

Haruki watched him for another half hour, first one way and then the other.

Starting to get nervous himself, Haruki stood up and gazed to the south. Then he saw it. Low on the horizon several kilometers away, a column of smoke. He jumped up on the long-fallen log, shielded his eyes from the sun, and stared to the south.

"Come and look!" he shouted to Toshi. "Smoke!"

***

Hurrying through the main door to the factory, Cho glanced around to see where his assistant had taken the inspectors. She was sticking close to the woman, whose name, if he heard it correctly, was Fuyumi. Cho presumed it was because, of the four of them, Fuyumi seemed the least intimidating. Certainly, no one would want to hover near Mei. She seemed easily capable of swallowing up anyone she came in contact with. Cho decided it was up to him to stick with her, as she went about her official inspection.

Rushing to catch up to her, he said, "Do you have any questions? Is there anything I can get for you, or show you about our operation?"

Mei looked at him with the face of a smile but one that left no doubt who was in charge, as she replied, "You are most gracious to ask, but no, we need nothing except quiet privacy in order to carry out our inspection. We will come for you when we're finished here." Then she turned away and continued her sweep of rows seven and eight.

Who was the most attractive girl in the factory? That was the object of her search. Her first impression was that none of the girls were attractive. And how could they be, as malnourished and exhausted as they were? Most of the girls had obviously not bathed or washed their hair for weeks. Her cheeks began to flush at the sight of them. The arms on some of the girls were barely more than bamboo sticks. She could see the red in their eyes as they fought, some of them, just to stay awake. The Empress began to anger. She had to remind herself to stay calm and find Emiko and Suki. But in the back of her mind, she wondered how she could help the rest of these poor creatures as well.

Occasionally, she glanced around the floor to locate her other inspectors. Had they spotted either of the girls? She looked for a sign but received empty stares in return. She traveled the length of her two rows along this side of the floor. Jun was moving through rows five and six, Gordo in rows three and four. Kazuo was taking rows one and two. For some reason he had started at the far end of the rows.

The Empress turned around and retraced her steps through rows seven and eight. Maybe the girls would look different from the opposite direction. Periodically, she stopped, pretending to study this machine or that bowl of heated cocoons. She had hoped not to have to speak to any of the girls for fear of arousing suspicion. But if they didn't find them soon, she was prepared to ask if one or another of the reelers knew a girl named Emiko. She decided she would ask one of the few male workers as she encountered them. That might throw off any onlookers as to their true purpose.

Kazuo had just reached the end of his rows, and looked over at the Empress with a look that implied 'maybe.' She was encouraged by his expression and making plans to saunter in his direction when suddenly her ears began to pierce. A whistle sounded somewhere in the factory that felt like it was right inside her head. Once she realized what it was, she noticed the look of shock on the faces of the reelers closest to her. At first, they lurched in their seats, then they looked around at one another as if wondering what to do. It had quite obviously caught the workers off guard. The Empress considered whether this was an emergency drill and should they exit the building. Then a few smiles crossed the worker's faces and they jumped from their machines and bolted toward the cafeteria.

Whatever signal Kazuo had tried to send was lost in the throng of bustling workers. It did not take long for the Empress to figure out it was the signal for a rest break, and only a moment longer to realize the workers were not accustomed to hearing it. The break today was obviously for show. The owner was trying to convince her team of impersonators that he took good care of the workers.

This planted an idea in her head. *Maybe she could improve the lives of more than just Emiko and Suki.*

Letting the workers exit first, as it was obvious they were excited at the prospect of an unexpected snack, the Empress followed them to where Kazuo stood, at the end of row one. Gordo and Jun likewise made their way to the end of row one for a short conversation.

"I think it could be Emiko at this machine," Kazuo began. "I didn't get a chance to look at her wrist, but she would definitely be a beautiful girl if she had a chance to clean up and gain some weight. I noticed she waited for a younger girl across the aisle in row two. Unfortunately, that girl was coughing so much I didn't get a good look at her face. She seemed attractive and would be about the right age for Suki."

The Empress replied, "Cho obviously thinks we're real inspectors. Otherwise, he would not have staged this break period for the workers. They were as surprised as we were when that awful whistle sounded. I'm surprised they're all not deaf by now."

"What about the real inspectors?" Gordo asked. "What if they come while we're still here? I don't like it."

"I don't like it either," the Empress replied. "But we can't quit now. Cho was expecting them tomorrow. Hopefully, they won't come until then. If they don't come until tomorrow, we'll be fine."

Kazuo was nervous. He kept scanning the factory in search of other visitors. "There aren't any windows here. We can't tell if anyone else has arrived or not. If we had windows, at least we would know when they arrived."

"We have to stay calm," the Empress said. "If the real inspectors come, we'll have to find the girls and get them out of here. This is our only chance."

"I could wait outside and watch for them," Kazuo said.

The Empress considered his suggestion. "What would be our excuse for you standing guard out front? I'm afraid it would only make them suspicious. And if they came—could you convince them they were at the wrong place? Would you shoot them with your chassepot—I wouldn't want you to end up in prison for shooting someone."

"I don't know what I would do," he said quietly.

"I admire your courage, but we have to stick with our plan—find the girls and get them out. If the inspectors come, the rest of you get the girls and go. Even if you have to ask for them by name. Find them and get them away from here. Get them on the horses and go. I'll take care of the rest."

She locked eyes with Kazuo to make sure he understood. She didn't need to look at Gordo or Jun. They were samurai; they understood.

"Good, let's check out the cafeteria and see what tasty morsels they're having this morning. I'm willing to bet whatever it is, was hatched up after we arrived."

As the four of them headed to the cafeteria, the Empress said, "Let's spread out again and pretend to admire the food, if we can keep from laughing, that is. Kazuo, try to find your girls again, then give us a signal and move on. We'll each take a turn getting close enough to get a look. When the break is over, I'll move to row one and try to get a look at her wrist. If nothing else, I'll have to ask if her name is Emiko. We don't have time to snoop around, and the more we delay, the more chance they have to get suspicious."

They headed to the cafeteria, arriving to find eighty excited young workers in one or another step toward satisfying their chronic hunger. The later ones, who also tended to be the younger and less aggressive ones, were still waiting to receive their ration from the serving woman. Those quicker to equate the shrill of the whistle to a snack in the cafeteria were already seated at one of the tables, eating a small rice cake or hard roll left over from a previous meal.

By the time the Empress and her conspirators had positioned themselves to survey the short rest break, the whistle sounded again, signaling time for the workers to head back to the factory. The latecomers were forced to shove the last few bites in their mouths as they made their way back to the machines.

***

Toshi, who was smelling the still odorless flowers from a nearby bush for the fourth time, craned his neck to look over at Haruki and ran to the log.

"What do you think it is—is it the factory?"

"I don't know," Haruki replied. "But it looks like the right location for the factory."

Toshi looked, then jumped down from the log. "We better go check!" he shouted. He grabbed his saddle and with a single move, swung it atop the plain gray mare with a grace even Kazuo would have admired. He reached under the horse for the girth and tightened it with the cinch so fast that Haruki had only placed the saddle atop his horse by the time Toshi climbed aboard. Their bags of gear and supplies remained behind, fully visible, easy prey for any passing traveler. The campfire still snapped and popped as they galloped off toward the smoke.

The column rose higher in the sky as they rode. Not only because they were drawing closer, but because it was growing in size. Toshi squeezed his legs against the horse's flanks and the horse picked up speed. He had never ridden this fast before and it was frightening. Together, the two men chased toward the column as it grew taller and darker in the April sky. So intent were they on the ominous cloud that neither man gave a second look at the large wooden building enclosed by a high wire fence when they passed it by.

Ten minutes later they came to a river and slowed to a stop. "Gordo said if we came to a river, we've gone too far," Toshi said.

"We must have gone by it," Haruki replied. "He said the factory was close to the road."

"The smoke is too far away from the road to be the factory," Toshi said, as he watched the dwindling plume.

"You're right...thank goodness it wasn't the factory," Haruki replied. "I was afraid something went wrong and they started the factory on fire to get the girls out."

Relieved to learn it was not the factory, the two men rested their horses and panned the horizon. Osaki was vastly different than the rocky coastline of Kamaishi. "The landscape is so much different here," Haruki said as he looked around.

"That must be Osaki just across the river," Toshi replied. He pointed to a cluster of rooftops just beyond. Further away, he saw the steeple of a church and smoke from several chimneys rising upward. "It looks like a nice village," he continued. "Probably a nice place to live, aside from the factory. I suppose the owner lives in a nice house somewhere over there."

"Not only the factory," Haruki pointed out, "but also the prison. I don't think I'd want to live this close to a prison."

"I don't see a prison," Toshi said. "Where is it?"

"We passed by it about a kilometer back," he said. "That building with the fence…"

They turned to each other with a look of alarm. "Gordo said the factory was a large building with a tall fence around it."

They were just about to turn and gallop back when two riders approached from the south. One of the riders was waving.

"It would be rude to ride off in front of them. We better see what they want," Haruki said.

When the strangers drew alongside, the first man called out, "Can you help us?"

"What do you need?" Toshi asked.

"We're trying to find the Osaki Silk Factory. It is supposed to be somewhere along this road."

Toshi stole a glance at Haruki and his face began to pale.

"Uh—we're not from this area, but maybe we can help," Toshi said. "Why are you looking for the silk factory?"

"We're from the Ministry of Labor, and we're on our way to perform an inspection."

Chapter 45

Back at the Factory

The short rest break provided just enough time for the Empress to adjust her plan. It occurred to her the real inspection team would be asking questions of the workers about their machinery, their working conditions, and about their treatment.

But it also provided just enough time for Cho's assistant to follow him to his office and complain. "I don't trust them," she barked to her older husband. "I saw her wince when I told her we were not expecting them until tomorrow. She had a panicked look on her face. I saw it."

Cho asked her to sit down. "You saw her wince?"

"Yes, she had no idea we were expecting someone. I think they're here to spy on us."

"Spy on us? What on earth do we have worth spying on? We're a factory, just like a hundred others in Japan. We have nothing to hide."

"I don't know," she said, her voice beginning to calm. "But something is fishy. Maybe they're planning to start a factory of their own and take our business. Or steal our reelers."

"But didn't they show you a letter from the ministry?"

"Yes. They did. It looked real but I don't trust them. Especially Mei. She looks mean. I don't like how she looks at me."

"Did they act strange when they inspected the reelers?"

"No. At least I didn't notice anything. But I was only there for a few minutes to show them where it was. That big woman I was with said they needed to be alone for their inspection."

"I think you're worrying for nothing," Cho said. "But keep an eye on them, just in case."

***

"When we go back to the factory," the Empress continued, "I think we should talk to some of the workers and pretend we're trying to gather information about their working conditions. We don't have to talk to all of them, but we should single out one or two and ask whatever questions you think an inspector would ask. I'll start with the girl Kazuo thinks might be Emiko. The rest of you split up like we were before. Let's plan on a half hour in the factory and then ask to see the dormitory. After that, we'll try to catch them during the meal break. If we're lucky, we can leave right after that."

Watching Emiko for a few moments, the Empress became concerned about the girl in the next row, who she suspected might be Suki. She was coughing almost constantly. It gave her the opening she needed.

Looking at Emiko, she asked, "The girl next to you, I've noticed she coughs a lot. Do you think she is okay?"

Emiko replied, "I'm not sure… I worry about her too, but there's not much I can do."

She could have said she worked extra penalty hours for her young friend not long ago, but didn't see the point of it.

"How long has it been going on?"

"About six months. I first noticed it last autumn. It seems to be getting worse."

"Can you tell me her name?"

"Yes, her name is Suki. Her family lives close to mine, near Hanamaki."

Emiko lifted her left arm up for just a moment to reach for the next cocoon, floating in the heated bowl. The Empress spotted a slight scar just above her wrist.

"I see. Thank you."

She knew before seeing the scar these were the girls she wanted. She debated briefly in her mind whether to reveal their mission, and decided not to play her hand quite yet. She studied the faces of both girls as best she could before making her way to Kazuo. Gordo and Jun saw the silent signal and made their way to the exit door.

The four of them headed to the front office, which had a window, and when they entered, found the owner's assistant gazing intently at the six horses tied just beyond. A feeling of panic swept through the four of them when she mused aloud, "Those certainly are beautiful horses. Especially that reddish one. It must be worth a fortune. Does the ministry provide them?"

The Empress tried to remain calm. "You are an astute woman to notice such things. No, the ministry does not provide them. We have to furnish our own horses."

"I'm surprised working for the ministry pays that well. I'm not sure even Cho could afford a horse like that red one. It's beautiful."

The Empress darted a look at Kazuo, who looked stricken with fear. She tried to turn the corners of her mouth up enough to resemble a smile of encouragement, then turned back to the assistant. "Yes, it is a beautiful horse, isn't it? And you're right, it's an expensive horse. However, it does not belong to me. You're also right about our wages. We don't get paid enough to own a horse like that. I borrowed this horse from a friend. I have to return her when we get back."

"She must be a really good friend…to trust you with a horse like that."

The Empress smiled. "Yes, a good friend." She smiled at Kazuo while the assistant gazed at the bay.

"Cho would love to see them up close. He loves horses. I'm sure he would like a closer look."

"If we have time we'll be happy to show him, but at the moment, duty calls, and we need to inspect the dormitory. If you would be so kind as to lead us, we would like to see the sleeping rooms before the meal break." She started walking as soon as she finished speaking, hoping to distract the assistant and move them on their way.

The woman continued to gaze out the window at the horses until the Empress finally had to ask, "Can you show us the way to the dormitory?"

But the assistant was not yet satisfied. On the way to the dormitory she asked, "How far can you travel in a day?"

Whether she was suspicious or simply nosey, the Empress didn't know, but it was beginning to test her patience. She answered with as many words as possible while providing the least amount of information that she could.

"It all depends on the terrain," the Empress replied. "And how far it is between factories. Some days we have to travel after dark. We prefer not to do that, but if it's a long way between assignments, we have to keep going."

"I noticed that all of the horses have a saddle. Is that normal? For horses to have a saddle with no one using it?"

"It may not be normal, but neither is it uncommon," the Empress replied. "As I said, sometimes we rotate horses to keep them fresh. This way, we don't have to take the extra time to switch saddles. It is especially helpful on those days when we have a long distance to travel."

"Where was your last assignment?" the assistant asked as they approached the dormitory.

"Oh, are these the sleeping rooms?" the Empress exclaimed, louder than she needed. She shot a look at Gordo to see if he was alarmed. Beads of sweat formed across his forehead.

***

Toshi looked over at Haruki astride the other gray mare. The two strangers held back the reins to hold their horses in place.

"Where did you say you were from?" Toshi asked.

"The Ministry of Labor."

"And you're looking for the silk factory?"

"Yes, we're on our way for an inspection."

Toshi felt weak. He held to the saddle with both hands, trying to keep from shaking. All he could think to do was stall for time. "I see," he said. "Where are you coming from?"

"Our office is in Tokyo, but we're coming from Sendai. We've had a long trip and would like to finish our route so we can return home. Osaki is the last factory on our schedule."

Toshi pictured his friends at the silk factory, pretending to be from the Ministry of Labor. He tried to remember the steps the

Empress laid out before they rode off: inspect the reeling room, inspect the dormitory, inspect the cafeteria. How long would it take for each one? She said if they were not back by three o'clock… that means they would likely be at the factory until two o'clock, maybe later. It was barely one o'clock now…they would probably be in the cafeteria.

They were less than ten minutes away from the factory. He had to do something, and with no time to think, blurted out the first thing that came to mind. "I am sorry to bear bad news," he said to the stranger across from him.

"Bad news?"

"I'm afraid so." He pointed to the column of smoke two kilometers to the west.

The stranger and the man with him scanned the western horizon. The column was smaller now, but still prominent in the afternoon sky.

"The silk factory?"

"We were looking for it ourselves, but decided to turn back. From the looks of the smoke, there can't be much left—and even if there is, I don't think it will need an inspection. You should probably come back another time."

The man looked at his friend. Toshi heard them talking softly between themselves until the man turned back to Toshi.

"Have you been there to see it?"

"No, we came from the north. When we got this far and saw the smoke, we decided to turn back."

Haruki spoke up. "I'm not sure you could even get to it by the looks of the smoke. The road is probably blocked off to keep people away."

The first inspector stood in his saddle and squinted west. "It's too far away to see the fire. All I can see is smoke."

"The column is getting smaller," Haruki said. "There must not be much left to fuel the fire. The building is probably gone by now."

The inspector's partner spoke up. "I think we should turn back. We've been gone long enough. Like the man said, if they've had a fire, they won't want to deal with us, and there is probably not much left to inspect anyway."

The inspector looked at his partner. "What if it's not the factory? We'll look pretty foolish when we get home if we tell them we couldn't do the inspection because of a fire, and it turns out there wasn't any fire."

"I think the factory is the only building around here," Toshi said. He neglected to say the building was north of there, not west.

"I suppose so," the inspector said.

Toshi and Haruki both bowed lightly from their horses, turned, and headed north.

When they passed by the large building with a tall fence, Toshi pointed to the six waiting horses tied out front. There was no sign of the Empress or their friends.

Chapter 46

Emancipation

The tour of the dormitory was equally as disheartening as the factory floor and the cafeteria food. There were no windows. There was no heat. The rooms were stuffy and either hot or cold, depending on the season. There was no furniture, only a few pegs on the wall to hang either their uniforms or their nightclothes.

Ten identical rooms could accommodate up to a hundred workers, but with the factory short of its total capacity, there were only eight girls assigned to a room. Each girl was allotted a tatami mat measuring one-half meter wide by one and one-half meters long. The mats butted against one another so that, in reality, all the girls were sleeping side by side in two rows of four girls each. Everything at the factory seemed to be either rows or numbers.

"Next, we will need to see the washrooms," the Empress said as they started back to the front office.

Jun clamped her nose for the brief time they were able to poke their heads through the door. At one end of the room was a single tub and a pair of small basins. Even Gordo had trouble picturing eighty girls waiting in line for two wash basins. Along the wall opposite the washbasins was a long bench with small holes cut at intervals. Below it was a wooden trough that sloped the length of the bench and exited through a hole at the side of the building.

"Now I understand why you didn't want an inspection until tomorrow," the Empress panned, looking directly at the assistant.

The assistant turned red, but the impostors didn't know if it was from anger or embarrassment.

Abruptly, the Empress turned to the assistant. "I believe we've gathered enough information for the emperor. Now, if you would be kind enough to lead us to Cho-san, we have important matters to discuss with him in private and will soon be on our way."

The four impostors entered the office of Cho, which was startling in its splendor compared to the facilities for the workers. It took all the self-restraint she could muster not to tell him what she thought of his factory, but the mission was to retrieve Emiko and Suki. That had to remain her focus. Maybe she could instigate a larger change eventually. But for now, it was Emiko and Suki.

The four of them bowed to Cho.

"Cho-san,' she began. "Thank you for the gracious hospitality shown by you and your honorable assistant. That you are able to produce such large quantities of high-quality silk for our country is indeed an enviable achievement. The emperor would be delighted to have a hundred more of yourself—no, make that a thousand more."

She stopped talking to watch his reaction. This was a risky maneuver, and she understood that. The truth of it was, she was trying to appeal to his ego. If, by chance, he was a humble man, this line of conversation might well turn out the opposite of her intent.

When she caught a slight smile cross his face at the pompous flattery, she felt sure she had taken the right approach. If only she could keep it moving.

"We have observed any number of silk factories, and dare I also say, a few cotton factories, which I fully understand are not of the same importance as silk, other than that they also produce revenue for the emperor and our beloved country. Only a select few factories could match the productivity of the Osaki Silk Factory."

She paused again to see if she still had his attention. Then she continued, "Although my assistants and I can easily tell you needn't seek outside guidance to improve your production, to show our appreciation of your excellent hospitality, there are one or two suggestions we are compelled to leave with you."

By now, Cho was too far into the exchange to decline an offer of improvement. It would be rude to do so after the many nice words the Empress had showered on him. "Of course, we would be delighted to hear advice from such obvious experts as yourselves. Please continue," Cho responded.

The Empress bowed slightly once again and pushed forward. "We have noticed that a few of the workers—well, many of them—actually most of them, if I may be so bold—appear to be undernourished. I know you have only their well-being at heart, so I'm sure it is mere oversight, and perhaps the fault of the kitchen, that so many workers appear to be underfed. But perhaps more importantly, if I may once again be so bold, is that it is quite obvious from our observation at other factories that workers who are well fed and well rested produce a much better result than those who are not so well provided. Wouldn't you agree?"

Cho hardly had much choice, looking at the determined face of the woman across the desk from him. "You are absolutely correct that the well-being of our workers is most important. And it only makes logical sense that a healthy worker will provide more silk, and higher quality silk, if I may state it in such a way." He paused, then added, "As a matter of fact, only minutes ago I found it necessary to sack one of our supervisors. I suspect he was the one responsible for shorting the worker's food portions."

"You are indeed, a wise and honorable man, Cho-san. It is no surprise to me that you quickly see the value in improving the quality of nourishment coming from your fine kitchen. And of course, it is important to increase the portions, as well. If you find you cannot do these two things adequately, it might be acceptable to eliminate *one* of the daily breaks. But only so long as you provide a nutritious snack during the break that remains.

"My suggestion would be to eliminate the morning break, as they will have had a full and nutritious breakfast. You could schedule the midday meal at eleven-thirty so it would not be too long between meals, and the afternoon break could be held around three o'clock. That would help balance the time between each meal and make the workers more productive throughout the entire day. Does that seem a logical plan to you?"

Again, Cho was so far down the path he was being led there was little choice but to agree. And he had to admit, explained this way, it did seem a worthwhile improvement for his factory. "Yes. Yes, I believe that is a very good suggestion, and we will make every effort to try it out."

"Excellent, Cho-san, you are a man above many others in your grasp of the future. Someday, all factories will emulate your practices.

"There is only one additional matter we must bring to your attention, and then we'll be on our way and let you get back to more important matters. Well, make that two. First of all, the washroom needs…it needs to be cleaned more often. A dirty washroom is the doorway to sick workers. That leads me to the other matter. It is with unpleasant surprise that during our tour, we chanced upon a young girl who seems quite ill. We observed her coughing, both frequently and somewhat violently. I am certain the matter had not come to your attention, or you would have seen to it that she received medical treatment."

Once more, she waited to see his reaction. His face turned just red enough to give away that he was well aware of Suki's condition, and probably those of a number of workers before her. Not wanting him to feel backed into a corner, she continued.

"If I might offer one possibility regarding the future of this poor girl. I confess we have assisted a special few factory owners in the past, even though it is not a thing I wish to have commonly known. If you can provide the location of her family, we would try our utmost to deliver her safely home. Would it be possible for your assistant to learn of her homeland? Then we can decide if our offer might be feasible. I believe she said her name was Suki. She was seated in row…" Turning toward Kazuo, she continued, "Riku, which row was she seated in? Do you remember?"

"I believe it was row number two, and I think it was the first station in that row."

"Excellent. Can your assistant find that information for us now? I don't need to remind you that if word gets out your factory is not a healthy place to work, recruiting workers will become even more difficult than it is at present. I assure you we will remain discreet in this matter."

Hearing that, Cho jumped up and left the room to find his assistant. He soon returned with word she was looking up the information. Not more than three minutes later, she knocked lightly at the door before entering.

She glared at the Empress for an instant before she spoke. She seemed to take any criticism of the factory as a personal affront. "Her name is Suki Ishii. She lives near Hanamaki, about a hundred kilometers north of here."

The Empress attempted a frown as she turned to Gordo. "Unfortunately, that is not exactly convenient for our travels." She knew she was going out on another limb but could think of no other solution. "We were planning to continue south toward Tokyo. That's where most of the factories are located."

Then she turned back to Cho. "I suppose we could rearrange our schedule. There is a small factory to the north, but I don't recall exactly where at the moment. We could inspect that facility first, then head back south." She looked at Gordo, then at Kazuo, as if to get their approval.

"For you, Cho-san, we would be happy to alter our plans. But we have a favor of you as well. Is it possible Suki has a friend working here who might travel with us? I'm not sure we're equipped to care for a young girl as ill as Suki. It is most fortunate that we have two additional horses, but who knows if Suki knows how to ride, or what kind of care she might need?"

Turning to the assistant, still standing in Cho's office, the Empress now circumvented Cho altogether. "Can you find out if Suki has someone close to her who would be willing to accompany her back to her family? I think she was talking to the girl in the next row over, right across from her. Maybe they are friends."

The assistant looked at Cho. She tried to shake her head just enough to tell him no, but with the four impostors watching, it was either too subtle for him to see, or he decided to override her request. Cho gave a slight nod. She would have to find Suki's friend.

Soon after she left, the whistle sounded once more. This time, the travelers, though not expecting it, were at least not startled by the piercing sound in their ears. They looked at Cho. "It's time for the workers' lunch," he said. "You must be sure to visit the cafeteria again before you leave. I believe you'll find we've already started to improve their portions. Things should go smoother now with Orochi out of the picture."

A few minutes later, the assistant appeared back at the doorway. "The other girl is Emiko Matsumoto. She lives in the same village." Her eyes were narrowed, and the skin on her face was tight and flushed. It was obvious she did not agree with Cho about the two girls.

"Excellent work," the Empress said. Her voice came out sharper than she intended. Something about the assistant grated on her. Instinct told her to get the girls and get out.

Looking at Cho, she said, "Then it's settled. We'll take the girls with us and deposit them with their families. We can only hope Suki will survive the trip. Then we'll continue our journey south once more." She wanted to remind Cho they were doing him a favor by going out of their way to deliver Suki home.

Then she looked at the assistant and said, "Would you be kind enough to take Fuyumi to the cafeteria and retrieve the girls, then collect their things? If you need something to put them in, we have an empty sack they can use."

The assistant glared at Cho momentarily to gain his approval. When he nodded again, she moved her glare to Fuyumi (Jun) and walked coldly to the door.

Looking next at Cho, the Empress said, "I'm sure you will want to send the girls' wages with them?" and held his gaze long enough to catch the flicker of a grimace, confirming his hope she might overlook that particular detail.

Something about the way she said it gave him little room to negotiate, and he replied, "Of course. That is the honorable thing to do."

"It is up to you," she continued, "but if I were you, I would destroy all records that link them to the Osaki Silk Factory. You never know when someone might try to hold you responsible for her illness. Gaku, (Gordo) go with Cho-san to collect the wages for both girls. I will meet you at the front office.

"Oh—one more thing before we go. Gaku, do you have the certificate of merit from the emperor? We must make sure to leave it with Cho-san, to thank him for his contributions toward the building of Japan."

With that, Cho's countenance elevated noticeably. The frown from having to pay two workers about to leave against his wishes faded away as he turned his thoughts to the most dignified location to display his certificate from the emperor.

Emiko and Suki waited in the small office, afraid to speak. Never had anyone been removed from the cafeteria without warning. Every eye watched as Cho's assistant found and led them out. Orochi must somehow have found a way to get them in trouble.

Jun held the sack of belongings and led them out to the horses. Gordo carried their pay envelopes in his pocket. Not ten minutes ago, they were sitting down to lunch. Now, they were ushered from the building to six waiting horses and four unlikely strangers who appeared from almost nowhere.

Standing next to Cho, the Empress smiled, this time with a look of gratitude, if not an appropriate amount of guilt. Bowing, she said, "May the peace of Confucius and the Emperor be with you and remain with you, all of your days on earth. We will meet again, not long from now, and I look forward to seeing your well-fed and rested workers."

Then, not allowing time for accidental betrayal by words or actions, she bowed one last time and hurried toward the waiting blood bay. Kazuo helped the girls on the smallest of the six horses, instructing them in a voice barely louder than a whisper, how to hang on and what to do.

"I'll hold the reins," he told them. "Just keep your feet in the stirrups to help keep your balance, and hold on to the saddle with both hands. Look straight ahead. And don't talk unless you absolutely have to. As soon as we're safely away from here, we'll stop and help you get settled. Everything is going to be fine. Toshi and Ayami sent us. We're taking you home."

Chapter 47

Heartbreak

Tears ran down the cheeks of both girls as they listened to instructions from Kazuo. He turned his head away from the girls to prevent them seeing tears form on his own. But when he turned away, he found himself looking toward Jun and Gordo. Both were blinking their eyelids rapidly until they, too, turned away. Kazuo looked then at the Empress, intending to decipher what place in line she wanted him to be when he saw, without any doubt, moisture on each cheek of the legendary samurai warrior.

She turned, and with a slight twitch from both feet, signaled the blood bay to begin the long march home. Gordo led the group as before, with the Empress second in line, followed by Kazuo leading the two girls' horses by the reins. Jun brought up the rear. They left the factory and headed north. From her position at the end of the line, Jun watched as Emiko turned in her saddle and gazed at the slowly receding landscape.

Northward they went, but before three kilometers had passed, the extra pair of reins Kazuo held in his right hand began to falter. Turning to see what caused Suki's horse to pull up, he looked at the horse's face, and big brown eyes stared back. He shouted ahead for the Empress to hold up while he checked Suki's horse.

Dismounting, he walked back for a closer look. Just as he drew beside the animal, he saw movement atop the horse. Raising his arms in a reflexive move, he realized it was Suki, and she was falling from the saddle. He caught her in his outstretched arms and was about to tease her about her horsemanship when he saw her eyes go closed.

"Hurry!" he shouted. "Something is wrong with Suki!" He laid her on a nearby bed of grass.

The others quickly dismounted and rushed to her side. Emiko was first to arrive. She bent down and gently rubbed Suki's cheeks. "Suki? Suki—can you hear me? Suki, wake up."

Suki moaned just enough to let them know she was alive. Jun knelt down and took Suki's tiny hand in hers and began to massage it. She watched her chest, hoping to see it move lightly up and down.

Kazuo pulled the leather bag of water from his saddle and handed it to Jun. She poured a little in her palm and rubbed it across Suki's forehead. Then another splash on each cheek. Instinctively, she opened Suki's mouth slightly with two fingers and tried to dribble a swallow down her throat.

As the five of them stared down at her, motionless on the first green grass of spring, Suki took her final breath.

Unable to believe their eyes, they kept watching, hoping to see two eyes flutter and open to gaze up at them, hoping to see an arm or a hand slowly spring back to life. A full minute passed. Not a muscle of the fifteen-year-old girl moved. Jun put her ear to Suki's mouth, listening for even the tiniest breath. Desperation growing, she took hold of her wrist and felt for signs of a beating pulse. There were none.

Suki was dead.

For the second time today, tears formed on the cheeks of three hardened samurai warriors.

Emiko was less familiar with death, and whether that made it more difficult or less difficult than for the others, she did not know. Exhausted and emaciated herself, her tears transformed into uncontrollable sobs. The Empress wrapped her in her powerful arms and held her so tight she could no longer tremble. They stood that way for many minutes.

It was Kazuo, perhaps taking an unwitting cue from Toshi or Haruki, after working beside them for years, who took charge of the moment.

"Form a circle around her and take each other's hands. We need to show Suki how much we love her. Perhaps she can take it with her to the next world."

Everyone closed ranks to form a circle around the lifeless girl.

"Let us send our peace to Suki," Kazuo struggled to say.

After a few moments, spontaneously, yet almost as one, they bent down to the child and gently took hold of a hand, an arm, a leg, whatever they could reach, and let their tears flow. Their implausible victory to recover the girls now rang hollow. *Why had they waited so long? What should they have done differently? Did they overtax her poor body by forcing her to ride this far on her own?*

Then more pragmatic questions began to emerge. *Should they bury her body at a pleasant spot along the way? Should they take her home? Would her body survive the trip?* It would be more merciful to give her a proper burial along the way. But not in this place, not near the factory that took her life.

Turning to the others, Kazuo listed the options. "We have to decide the best way for Suki to be remembered," he began. "Should we try to get her home to her family so they can have one last goodbye? How much would her body deteriorate by the time we got her there? Should we bury her in the mountains along the way? Or, should we travel day and night? That would get us there tomorrow night. Could we even do it? Emiko, are you strong enough to ride twenty-four hours straight? The last thing we need is another casualty."

He turned away from Suki to consider all that happened. *Am I up to the challenge of an all-night ride?* Maybe that is not an option after all. *Am I thinking clearly?* he wondered.

The others were silent as they weighed the choices. None seemed desirable, or even real. But one was necessary.

Then the Empress took the lead. "Emiko, what do you think? If I'd been through everything you have, I don't think I could travel all night and another day without rest. If you fall asleep on the trail, you could easily break an arm or leg, or even worse. What do you think we should do?"

With hardly a delay, she replied, "If it were me instead of Suki, I'm sure my mother would want to see me one last time, even if I were dead. I can make it, if that's what we decide."

The Empress continued. "It's settled then. Kazuo, use our tents to build a sling. Jun and I will wrap Suki in our blankets. Gordo, get our food sack and give Emiko something to eat, and make sure she has plenty of water to drink."

They tied Suki's body snugly along one side of her horse and balanced it with their camping supplies on the other. Kazuo outlined a plan to alternate horses to keep them fresh. They would stop for thirty minutes every three hours.

Kazuo was the last to mount. After one last check of Suki and the remaining supplies, he placed one foot in the stirrup and was lifting himself into the saddle when two riders bore down from the north. When they waved, he recognized Toshi and Haruki. He climbed on the chestnut and waited.

Toshi slowed to a stop beside the Empress and looked around. He counted five riders. "We were getting worried about you," he said. "You said if you weren't back by three o'clock to come looking."

The Empress stared back without speaking.

She must have somehow figured out we left camp earlier, he thought. *She is upset with us.*

Toshi tried to smile, but even he knew it was fake. He had let the Empress down and there was no making up for it. Then he looked around and counted again. Six horses, five riders. He gathered his courage and faced the Empress. "Did you only get one girl?"

Without changing expression, the Empress replied, "We got both girls."

Toshi counted the riders again.

"We got both girls, but only one survived."

This time, Toshi searched their faces as he panned the group. Every face reflected the loss. One face was new. He stared at the girl, not sure if it was Emiko or Suki. He had never seen either one. *It could not be Emiko,* he thought; *Ayami had called her beautiful.* This girl was frail; her cheeks were sunken, and dark circles surrounded her eyes. Her hair was a dirty, tangled mess. It must be Suki.

"Oh no!" he wailed. "What happened? How did she die?"

"We didn't realize she was so sick, or we would have stopped sooner. Her horse pulled up and when Kazuo went back to check on her, Suki fell off the horse. We tried to save her, but she died…just now…minutes ago. We tried to help her, but there was nothing we could do."

"Suki?" Toshi asked.

"Yes, Suki." She pointed to Emiko, sitting on the horse between Kazuo and Juno. "Emiko is with us. We've decided to travel all night. We want to get Suki's body home."

Toshi looked at Emiko and tried his best not to stare. "Hello, Emiko. I'm glad to meet you. Ayami has been worried about you."

She smiled at him in return, but was too drained to speak.

"We need to get going," the Empress said. "We need to get her home."

Toshi and Haruki fell in behind the others, and together eight horses and seven riders headed for Hanamaki.

The quarter moon above only added to their grief. The light it provided was too little to see by, but enough to cast murky shadows across the unfamiliar trail. Several times Kazuo felt a sudden change of rhythm as his horse stumbled on a hidden rock or a fallen branch. *What if Suki's horse stumbled and fell? What if Emiko's horse stumbled and fell?*

As the band of emancipators made their way slowly north, their temperament began to shift, particularly the Empress. Her feelings of grief and sorrow for Suki slowly turned to anger. Each hour that passed brought the pendulum closer to a state of rage. By sun-up, at one of their scheduled rest breaks, she approached Kazuo.

"I'm so angry at that place. I'm thinking about taking Gordo and going back. The two of us could easily intercept that tight-fisted scoundrel on his way home from the factory and cause him to disappear from the earth for good. While we're at it, we might even burn the factory down. Vermin like him do not deserve to live. When I was an active samurai, we had to kill people because they were enemies. Most of them were not as vile as the cowardly Cho. He is a disgrace to our country and does not deserve to live."

Kazuo listened intently, if only to assure her he valued her opinion. When she eventually came to a pause, he screwed up his face as if deep in thought and responded, "You're right. Cho is an evil man for the way he treated his workers."

Her face lightened somewhat as she anticipated his forthcoming agreement.

When he did continue, he said, "But what if you got caught? A man like that is certain to have plenty of people watching out for him. He's not worth putting your emporium at risk. Think about all the people who depend on you. Toshi and I, for example. If it weren't for you, we wouldn't be able to trade for fish and rice."

He let her think about it for a minute, and then he said, "Even though it would be sweet revenge to burn the factory down, we have to remember it *does* provide wages for eighty or more girls."

He waited again. "I think maybe you've already taken the right step by pressuring him to feed the workers better. We should give him a chance to make amends. If he doesn't do what he promised, we can come up with another plan."

Her body muscles loosened ever so slightly as he talked. When he was done, he simply stood and looked at her, hoping she had vented enough to think more clearly again.

She did not speak, or look at him directly. She simply stared off into the distance at the rising sun.

Jun broke the silence. "Emiko, did you get something to eat?" she asked. "You're looking a bit weary, if you don't mind my saying it." She smiled to show Emiko she was only trying to cheer her up. "We must be halfway home by now. Can you make it the rest of the way?"

"I can make it. I'm too tired to be hungry, but I'll try a little more fish. I don't remember when I've tasted anything so good. Maybe before I left home, but definitely not since I started at the factory."

The Empress watched as Emiko ate several bites of fish and rice cake, followed by a cup of hot tea made over their small fire. "This will be our last break using a fire. From now on, we'll make do with a brief stop and water to drink," she told the others.

When they mounted up, Kazuo kept a close watch on Emiko. She could barely keep her eyes open. She had eaten more since they left Osaki than she would normally eat in two days' time. He could hardly blame the young woman for feeling sleepy. Looking around, he asked, "Jun, do you think Emiko could ride double with you? I'm afraid she's going to fall asleep and off the horse. We can all take turns until we get to Suki's farm."

It did not go unnoticed by the Empress how Kazuo stole frequent glances at Emiko. It caused her anger to subside further, as she wondered if Emiko had somehow become more than simply a safe delivery to Kazuo. *She is young,* she thought, *but even so, a match with the handsome bachelor might well be possible.*

***

Reaching Hanamaki, Emiko directed them to the farm of Suki's parents. She had been there several times before their factory life, and she filled with emotion as the farm came into view. It felt good to be home. If only Suki were still alive and riding beside her. She tensed with every jog and bounce of the horse as they turned in the lane to Suki's home.

The Empress came to a halt three hundred meters away. She looked around at the surrounding fields to see if Suki's father might be working in the fields. She saw no one. It was almost dusk, which added to the weight on her shoulders.

Turning to the others behind her, she said, "I think you should wait here. I'll ride ahead and see if they're home. I'll tell them we rescued their daughter from the factory but were too late to save her. When I give the signal, bring Suki."

But Emiko was not too exhausted to speak her mind. "I'll go with you. I'm the one who lived with her. It will be some comfort if I'm the one to bring the news."

"Are you sure you're strong enough? You've been through so much already. I don't think you should have to be the one."

"I'm strong enough. And I have to be the one. She was my friend, and she looked up to me for protection. But I failed. I'm the one who has to bring the news."

"There was not one thing you could have done to save her, Emiko. And I will not hear you speak of that again—ever! Do you understand me? If anyone is to blame, it was us, for not coming sooner."

Emiko nodded but did not face her directly. She walked over to the Empress and waited for someone to help her climb on the resplendent bay.

Together, the Empress and Emiko rode slowly toward the tidy little house. Drawing up short, the Empress dismounted, then helped Emiko down. They started together toward the door until Emiko held her arm out, palm facing the Empress. Emiko would go to the door alone.

She lifted her right hand and knocked as forcibly as she could, but it was not very loud. Even from several meters away, the Empress could see the tremble in her arm. When she looked closer, she saw it was more than her arm; her entire body was shaking.

Emiko took a deep breath and knocked again. This time, it was loud enough for the Empress to hear. They both waited. Finally, the door opened and a short figure appeared in its wake. Getting closer to dusk now, the Empress could barely make out the silhouette. It did not speak; it merely stared at Emiko, still standing at the entrance. The figure seemed not to know her. It looked beyond her to the Empress who seemed to baffle her even more. The Empress watched as she peered into the distance at the rest of their party, still waiting near the end of the lane for the signal to approach.

Turning back to Emiko, the figure stared at the girl for what seemed many minutes. As she stared, she saw tears begin to trail down the young girl's face. By the time they reached her chin and dripped to the ground, the figure understood their meaning. She wailed aloud in a heart-wrenching voice. A second figure appeared. This time, a man. He looked at the woman and then at Emiko, then called her by name.

"Emiko…what's happened?" he uttered. "What's happened to Suki? Please don't tell me she's…" He saw his wife begin to fall, from the corner of his eye and grabbed her with one arm as she slumped to the floor.

Emiko was too spent to move, or even to reply. She simply stared at the two people just inside the doorway and let her tears continue to flow.

The Empress stepped forward then, and put a protective arm around Emiko, helping her through the door.

"They call me the Empress," she said. "Toshi and Ayami sent me to Osaki, to retrieve Emiko and your daughter. I am so sorry. We were too late to help. She died shortly after we left the factory. I can't tell you how sorry we are for what's happened."

She helped Emiko sit on a nearby mat, then helped Rikuto situate his wife. At first, the Empress thought she had fainted, but saw now that her eyes were open and she was watching Emiko. A third person entered the room from the rear of the house. It was Suki's younger sister, Chiyo.

"Please, do you have any spirits of ammonia? Get it quickly if you do."

The girl disappeared toward the kitchen and soon appeared with a small jar. The Empress removed the lid and held the jar under the woman's nose. When she responded with several shallow coughs, the Empress passed the jar to Emiko. Then she looked at Rikuto to see if he needed a sniff, but he shook his head.

"We rode through the night to bring your daughter home. Emiko thought you would want to see her one last time. Our friends are waiting in the lane. Would you like them to bring her to you?"

The woman wailed again. Rikuto looked at her and nodded.

The Empress returned to the doorway and stepped out far enough to wave her powerful arm from side to side above her head.

A figure in the lane, some distance away, returned the wave. It was too dark to determine which of the travelers it was. Most likely, Kazuo, she thought. Then she watched as the riders mounted their steeds and slowly headed toward the house.

The group stopped twenty meters away and climbed down from their horses. Toshi and Kazuo untied their precious cargo and laid it softly on the ground while Haruki worked diligently with material from one of the tents. They lifted Suki's body to the makeshift litter and carried it forward.

Tears welled again as the Empress watched them bring Suki as far as the doorstep. "Wait here," she said, and entered the house to announce their arrival.

As Kazuo, Toshi, Haruki, and Gordo stood straight and still, each holding tightly to a corner of the fabric, her family emerged from the house. Her father and mother came first, his arm still wrapped around her torso and under her arm. Chiyo followed close behind, and once outside, came to stand beside her mother. She placed an arm around her from the opposite side. The three of them stared at the lifeless bundle, wrapped in a plain cotton blanket.

Finally, Rikuto said, "Bring her inside. We'll put her in her bed." He turned and led them to a room at the rear of the house. "Please lay her there," he told them in a voice softer than a whisper. "We'll uncover her when you've gone."

The Empress replied in a voice almost as subdued, "Of course…just remember, time is important. She has been gone for twenty-four hours." She did not feel the need to elaborate further.

When Suki's body was settled, her mother turned her gaze to Emiko. "You poor child," she said. "I'm sorry I didn't recognize you when you came to the door. You hardly look at all like the girl I remembered. Does your mother know you're back? She'll be so happy to see you again. I hope she can put some weight on you. I'm sorry to say it, but you look terrible." She tried to smile, but it was of little use. When that failed, she pulled Emiko into her small body and squeezed her as if she were her own.

"We've not been home yet." Emiko whispered in her ear. "We had to come here first. We're going to my house now. I don't think they're expecting me."

Having done everything they could for Suki, the Empress began to assemble their troupe. "Suki's family needs time alone. And it's time to get Emiko home."

They retreated to the horses, still waiting obediently, exactly where they'd been left more than an hour before. Emiko's house was seven kilometers away and it was almost dark. They would need moonlight to guide them.

In this part of Hanamaki, there were a number of farms, and the roads were easier to follow. Still, it would not be easy, some thirty-six hours since last they'd slept. The Empress had already decided they would stop along the way, to feed Emiko as well as themselves. Arriving unannounced as they were, her parents would not be prepared to feed any extra mouths. Not even if one of them belonged to their daughter.

Chapter 48

Homecoming

Following the delivery of Suki to her family, the travelers now had an extra horse. Even with the supplies attached to one, a mount was available to Emiko. But the Empress would take no chance with her. "You will double up with Kazuo this time," she instructed Emiko. It was too dark to fully see the reaction on Kazuo's face, but she was pretty sure she saw him smile.

Kazuo carefully lifted her to the saddle and deftly climbed on behind. The others were mounted and ready. "I'm going to put my arms around you, one on each side, so you can't fall off. I'll be holding the reins in the middle, in front of you. Will that be okay?"

He kept his voice low, careful not to let the others think he was doing anything other than providing protection. In truth, he was also trying to convince himself that he was only trying to protect the little sister of his good friend's wife. When he became conscious of the thought in his head, he mentally made sure to emphasize the descriptive *'little'* in the sentence. She must be ten years younger than him. Besides, she was in a precarious state of health, both physically and emotionally. What kind of man would allow feelings for a young woman in such a situation?

Then he realized he was also referring to her in his mind as a young woman. *Which is it? He questioned. She must be one or the other.*

As the dilemma fermented in his mind, he thought he heard someone call out. He listened more carefully.

"Are you coming, Kazuo? Or are you going to spend the night here without us?" The rest of them were already down the lane.

Kazuo could hardly concentrate on guiding his horse. He was grateful it knew him so well that he needn't, anyway, particularly with the others leading the way ahead. Kazuo had never been so self-conscious about touching a person in his life. *Was he holding her too tightly between his arms?* But he did not want her to fall. He could sense when she was falling asleep, and it began almost as soon as they left Suki's farm. *Did that mean she trusted him entirely? That she knew he would not let her fall? Or simply that she was so exhausted she couldn't help herself.*

After riding an hour or more, the Empress signaled to stop and rest. She quickly began to pull fish and cakes from their remaining sack of supplies. Hoping Emiko's parents would at least have a stove for hot tea, she handed around a flask of water for them to drink. Food was the most important thing, especially for Emiko. After a twenty-minute stop, she signaled it was time to leave. "Emiko, you stay with Kazuo the rest of the way. He got off easy on the way from Osaki."

He gingerly helped her mount again, possibly for the last time. Then he climbed up behind her and this time was not as worried about touching her, as he held her firmly in the saddle. But he made sure they were not the last to leave.

Emiko had perked up considerably by now. He could almost feel her excitement at returning home after nearly two years away. And he could tell the snacks were starting to rebuild her stamina. It was an easy progression, then, for him to wonder how attractive she would be after a hot bath, a long rest, and adequate food.

Beginning to feel uncomfortable riding in silence, now that she was more alert, he tried to think of something meaningful to say. Because of darkness it would be hard to comment on the rice or potato crops. Or the tree leaves, or the wildflowers.

Then he remembered something Cho had said. It might only bring bad memories, but thinking of nothing else to talk about, he ventured, "Did you know the supervisor who was sacked the day we found you? Cho seemed pretty upset with him. He blamed him for the lack of better food in the cafeteria."

Emiko was silent for a moment before answering. "I didn't hear about a supervisor being sacked. Do you know his name?"

"I'm afraid I've forgotten it with certainty, but I think it was something like Onofre, or Orrick, or something like that. He only mentioned it once, and I have to admit, I was more concerned about how we were going to get you out of there than I was about the name of the supervisor. Were there a lot of supervisors?"

"No, not many. Do you think his name might have been Orochi?

"Orochi? Orochi… Yes, I think that *was* the name. I'm pretty sure that was the name. Did you know him?"

It was dark, and Emiko was facing the same direction as Kazuo, so it was not possible to see her face for either reason. If he had, he would have seen Emiko smile for the first time in many months.

"Yes," she said. "I knew him. We all knew him. He was not a nice person. I'm not sad he was sacked."

She fell silent again as they traveled on. Finally, she said, "I very much doubt Orochi had enough authority to control food in the kitchen. That would have to come from the owner. Everyone said Orochi was a nephew of the owner. I wonder what he did that upset his uncle so much. Or maybe it's a case of what he did that his uncle found out about. The girls at the factory will be glad he's gone."

Before Kazuo had a chance to ponder her replies, he heard the Empress exclaim in a tone of relief. "We're here. I see light in the windows."

The Empress was leading the group, with Toshi and Haruki close behind to guide the way. She halted the bay and turned in the saddle. Looking at Toshi she said, "Do you want to go first and tell them we brought Emiko home early, or should Emiko go to the door alone?"

"Kunio might not be happy to have her home," Toshi replied. "It's our doing that brought her here. Haruki and I should go first."

Haruki nodded. The two of them climbed down from their mounts and walked to the door. "He won't try anything with all of us here, but I don't know about after we've gone."

"Maybe Fujita still has her spunk, like the last trip," Toshi replied. "Why does it feel like we've been in this predicament before?"

"You mean when we brought fish instead of money?" Haruki responded. "Hopefully, he'll be happier to see his daughter than he was the fish."

Toshi arrived first and knocked on the door. He was ready to knock again when he noticed several scales of paint still missing. He trembled at the memory of their last visit.

He turned to look at Emiko, standing a meter behind them. This was the closest he had been to her since leaving Osaki. They were on different horses, and during the few short breaks, the Empress and Jun stuck close to her. When he looked at her face—the matted hair, the drawn cheeks, the darkened eyes—his courage began to rise. He turned back to the door and soundly knocked again. He almost smiled when three more flakes of paint drifted to the ground.

The door cracked open and Fujita peeked through. "Toshi!" she cried. She looked at the man beside him. "Haruki!" Then, instinctively, she shot a look between them. Whether she had received their letter Toshi didn't know, but either way, she was desperate to see her daughter again.

"Mama!" Emiko cried, and rushed between the men to reach her mother. It was quiet then. No words—only the sound of sobs.

Toshi and Haruki stepped aside to let them be.

Then from behind the door, a familiar voice. "Who was it? What did they want?"

"It's Emiko," Fujita said. She was sobbing and it was hard to understand her words.

"Who?"

"Emiko. She's home!"

"Emiko? What's she doing here? How come she's not at the factory? Did she get sacked?"

Fujita pulled Emiko through the door and motioned Toshi and Haruki to follow. The Empress stayed behind with the others. Just before the door swung closed, she heard Kunio's voice once more. "How am I going to pay the taxes if she's not at the factory?"

When Shoji saw who it was, he hurried over to Emiko and threw his arms around her in a long embrace. "I'm glad you're home," he said. "Mama has been worried sick about you. Are you alright?"

The twins watched in silence from across the room.

When Kunio saw Toshi and Haruki his face went cold. "I should have known you were behind this," he said. "What gives you the right to interfere in our family affairs?"

Fujita was quick with a reply. "They are family, in case you've forgotten. And a good thing they are, too." She turned to Toshi. "Are there more of you? Ask them to come in. I don't have much food, but I can make a fresh pot of tea."

Haruki stepped out and motioned the others in.

"Suki died!" Emiko suddenly burst out.

The room went quiet.

Fujita darted a look at Emiko, then Toshi, then Haruki, and finally settled on Kunio. "Suki? she whispered, almost under her breath. "Suki died?" Her face began to flush. "It could have been Emiko," she said as her voice returned. "What then? Would you be happy then? How could you!"

Kunio shifted his gaze to the floor. The only sound was that of Emiko sobbing.

The Empress looked over at Kunio, staring at the floor as if it might bring Suki back to life.

"Did you know Suki?" she asked Kunio.

"No, I didn't know her," he said in a muffled voice. "But it's too bad what happened to her."

"Yes, it is too bad. Someone should have warned her parents about the silk factories. I'm sure they would not have let her go if they'd only known how difficult they are."

Fujita turned to Haruki with a sudden look of panic. Then she turned to Kunio to see if he had seen it. He was still staring at the floor, but the Empress saw it.

"What?" She said.

Fujita glanced again at Haruki and then stared at her husband.

The Empress picked up on it immediately, without any words needed. Looking at Kunio, she said in a level voice, "Did you know about the silk factories?"

Kunio continued to stare at the floor.

"Haruki tried to tell him they were bad places to work," Fujita said, raising her voice. "But you didn't listen. You only thought about the money. It could have been Emiko. Then what? Would it have been worth it then?" Her voice rose with every word she spoke. Months of misgiving and guilt welled up from deep within, and now with the sudden return of her daughter, she could hide it no longer.

Then the Empress spoke up. She looked him in the eyes and spoke in a firm and level voice, and there was no doubt about her feelings. "In that case, Kunio, I have no sympathy for you. In fact, my sympathy has changed to disgust."

It was the first time in many years Fujita saw Kunio show remorse. He excused himself, saying he needed to check something in the barn, and left the room.

No one spoke for several minutes.

When the tension eased, it was Shoji who asked, "How were you able to get Emiko released before her contract was up?"

Kazuo turned to the Empress and asked her to tell the story.

"How on earth were you able to get letters from the Labor Ministry?" Kazuo asked. "And how did you know Cho would let Emiko accompany Suki?"

"My samurai friends have many other loyal friends," she replied. "It happens that one of them is good at making documents. But the truth is, I didn't know how it was going to work. I made up the plan as we went along. We were lucky the way it worked out."

"Yes, especially about the fire," Toshi said. "I wonder what the fire was."

"Fire?" the Empress said. "What fire?"

"When we were waiting at the camp," Toshi replied, "we saw smoke and thought it might be the factory. I know you told us to wait until three o'clock, but when we saw the smoke, we rode down to see what it was."

The Empress looked at Toshi and then at Haruki. When neither of them responded, she said, "What was it?"

"That's the thing," Toshi said. "We couldn't tell. But we rode past the factory while you were inside. When we got to the river, we realized we had gone too far. That's when we met the inspectors."

"Inspectors?"

"Yes, I meant to tell you about them, but when we found you with Suki…"

"What about the inspectors?"

"They were looking for the silk factory. They said they were supposed to do an inspection there."

It was the first time Toshi had seen the Empress unable to speak. She stared at Toshi and then at Haruki. Finally, she said, "What did you do?"

"Well," Toshi began, "we may have misled them a little... I didn't want to, but we were desperate and didn't know what else to do. We pointed to the smoke and let them think it was the factory. They talked it over and decided to turn back."

The Empress smiled. "Uwa! Cho was expecting them the next day. They would have come while we were there. I had no idea what we were going to do if that happened."

"We were afraid you'd be upset with us for leaving the camp."

The Empress laughed. "I suppose I would have," she said. "But I'm glad you did."

Fujita watched her youngest daughter all the while, as the Empress told their story. It was clear Emiko was fighting to stay awake and hear the story herself. She knew nothing of the days her rescuers had needed to make it possible.

"Emiko, shall I heat water for a bath before you go to bed? Or are you too tired to bathe?"

"I would love a bath. I can hardly keep my eyes open, but the first hot bath in months is enough to keep me awake."

Fujita headed to the stove to warm several pans of hot water. "I can fix you a nice bowl of our home-grown rice while the water warms, if you like."

"I can't believe I'm home," was all she said.

Later, when Emiko was soaking in a tub of hot, clean water, the Empress said to Fujita:

"Emiko needs time to rest and regain her health. But when she's ready, I'd like her to come and work for me at the Emporium. She can live with me above the store, and I'll pay her as much as she was making at the factory. And I promise to take good care of her."

Chapter 49

Return To Osaki

OSAKI SILK FACTORY - JUNE 1881

Kazuo hoped it was not a coincidence that Emiko was sweeping the boards in front of the Emporium when he rode up. He had been watching for her since the Emporium came into view.

She had been watching, too, and waved when she saw him.

Kazuo waved back. He had been thinking about her since he left Kamaishi the day before.

"How is the new shopkeeper?" Kazuo called out when he was close enough. "Did you take over the Empress's job yet?"

"She only lets me use the broom," Emiko shouted back with a laugh. "And she said I'm not to go near any display of thread or silk!" This time, Kazuo laughed.

Kazuo dismounted and smiled. "Your new life must agree with you."

"I love it here," she replied. "The Empress treats me like a daughter. It's nothing like the factory. And I never dreamed there were so many things you could buy. At home, we made everything ourselves. You should see the things you can buy here."

"I have seen them," Kazuo replied. "I come here every two weeks, remember?"

"Get the mules unloaded and put away," the Empress called to Kazuo. "We'll leave early in the morning. I want to arrive at the factory in time for their noon meal. Tomorrow will be a long day."

It was not easy to argue with the Empress. Kazuo did as he was told.

The Empress and Kazuo met at six o'clock the next morning in front of the Emporium. Gordo was already waiting when Kazuo brought his horses around. The three of them rode until dark. Stopping only to rest and water the animals, they camped a half-day's ride from Osaki.

Well before noon on the following day, the Empress pulled up near a copse of oak trees, two kilometers from the factory. "This will be a good place to camp while you wait for us," she said to Kazuo. I don't want them to see you again. They'll never be able to find Gordo, and if they do find me at the Emporium, I can take care of myself. But I can't put you in danger."

Gordo and the Empress rode off together. "Wish us luck," she called back. "If we're not back in three hours, make yourself scarce, and we'll meet you back at last night's camp. Keep your eyes and ears open, and be suspicious of everybody."

***

"This is it," she declared to Gordo when they approached the factory. "Time to check on the girls."

The two dismounted and walked to the front office. Gordo went through first, followed by the Empress. Cho's assistant was at her place at a table facing the doorway. When she looked up, her face went pale. "What brings you here? Wait here, and I'll get Cho."

The Empress and Gordo looked at one another when she left. Something wasn't right. "Stay calm," the Empress whispered to Gordo. "We've been in worse spots before."

Sooner than expected, the assistant returned with Cho close behind. "Come up to my office," he said, without any greeting. Then he turned and motioned for them to follow.

I wonder if this is a trap, thought the Empress, but they had no other choice.

Once inside his office, Cho turned to them and said, "How many times are we to be inspected? Have we done something wrong? And how can I be sure you really are inspectors? Not three weeks after you left, another inspector was here. He claimed he didn't know anything about you. He and his assistant were here for the entire day. I'm trying to run a factory here. I don't have time to give total strangers tours of my factory, hoping they won't force me to make expensive changes or shut us down."

The Empress watched his cheeks turn red and listened to his voice escalate with every word. Somehow, she had to turn it around. Then she remembered Toshi's story about the inspection team the day they took the girls. They must have come back later.

She started with a formal greeting, which Cho had skipped over entirely. Bowing, she began, "Cho-san, a thousand pardons for our inconvenience. Can you tell me who was here? Do you remember his name?"

While Cho took a moment trying to recall the name he'd been given, the Empress began to think about how to defend their fabricated story.

"What did he look like?" she continued. "Was he tall or short? Was he alone? Are you sure he was from the Ministry of Labor?"

"He was alone. Well, he had an assistant, but it was just the two of them. Yes, he said he was from the Labor Ministry. When I told him you had just been here, he said that was not possible. He said he would know if there had been a previous inspection. Then I pointed to the two certificates you left with me, the ones from the Ministry of Labor. I took them off the wall and showed him."

Both Gordo and the Empress held their breath. A real inspector might realize they were fake.

"He studied them carefully and finally decided they were authentic. But he insisted he should have known about any previous inspection."

The Empress looked at Gordo and asked, "Do you think he could have been from the *special enforcement* unit?"

Gordo had worked with the Empress enough to know when to play along. "Yes, that's possible," he replied. "Can you remember his name?" he asked Cho.

"I think it was Katsu, or something like that."

"I think there might be a Katsuo at the ministry who is assigned to do special investigations at times."

Turning back to Cho, the Empress pressed on, "Cho-san, you say the man was satisfied our documents were real. At any time during our inspection did we behave in a manner contrary to what you would expect from the ministry?"

"No," he conceded, "you behaved as I suspect your superior would want."

"Thank you, Cho-san. At any time, did we interfere with the operation of your fine factory?"

"No," he replied again.

"Thank you, Cho-san."

"Did we inspect each of the primary aspects of your fine factory? The reeling floor, the cafeteria, and the dormitory?"

"Yes, you inspected each of those areas."

"Did we also offer advice, based on our years of experience inspecting factories of various types?"

"Yes, you did offer recommendations to us. Thank you for that."

"Is it also true that we relieved you of a very sick worker, even though it took us days away from our schedule?"

"Yes, you did remove a worker who seemed rather ill, but it is also true you took with her one of our very best reelers."

"We did—and it was a very good thing—because we needed her to show us the way home for the other girl. Our inspection party is not familiar with the region to the north of here." The Empress was proud of herself for that last comment, as she hoped it would send a message they were from the south, not the north.

"Did the young woman not know the way to her own home? Surely, she could have guided you."

"She could have," the Empress replied coldly, "if she had been alive to tell us." She looked at Cho, her eyes boring directly into his.

Cho flinched and his face began to pale. Cho was greedy, but not without a heart. Finally, he said, "I am sorry to hear that."

"She died two hours from here. Now you understand why I'm back today. I want to make sure your workers are safe and well provided. I won't leave you alone until they are." She held her gaze to reassure him she meant what she said.

"When we were here on our previous inspection, do I remember correctly that you sacked a supervisor earlier that morning?"

"Yes, that was Orochi. Good riddance, if you ask me. I think things have been running better now that he's gone."

"Is it possible this 'Orochi' might have had ill feelings towards either you or the factory when he left?"

"Oh, I think it's more than possible. He was my nephew, and I haven't heard the end of it since, from my brother."

The Empress remained silent for a few moments, hoping Cho would connect the dots himself. When he did not respond, she dropped another hint. "Do you think either one of them might have contacted the Ministry and filed a complaint?"

"Yes, I suppose it's possible one of them did," he said, as he began to see the connection.

Suddenly, the whistle let out its shrieking sound, announcing time for the noontime meal.

"Oh, that reminds me. We haven't eaten since last night. Would you mind if we joined you for lunch? I can't wait to see if the workers have gained weight since our last visit."

Cho had little choice. "Of course, how thoughtless of me not to ask earlier. Please join me for something to eat."

When the three of them entered the cafeteria, most of the workers had already been through the serving line and were seated at benches in groups of four or five. All eyes turned to the trio as they fell in line at the serving counter. One by one, they began to recognize the Empress and her companion.

As they received their bowls from the server and walked toward an empty bench in the far corner of the cafeteria, the Empress was dismayed to hear a scattering of coughing, coming from a few of the tables. As the other workers looked around to see what was happening, there soon became a litany of coughing from nearly every table. The Empress smiled back at the workers in acknowledgement, but there was nothing more she could do.

They followed Cho to a bench and sat across from him as they looked carefully at the serving in front of them, and then at the appearance of the workers throughout the cafeteria. They did show signs of better health. Mostly it was their eyes. Their eyes were brighter. And their cheeks not quite as drawn.

Turning to the bowl in front of her, the Empress took one small bite, interested in the flavor and the texture. She could see even without tasting that it was inferior grade, and definitely mixed with a cheaper grain. After several bites, she looked over at Cho, trying to read his reaction. He seemed to be playing with his food more than eating it. "You don't seem very hungry, Cho-san. Did you have a late breakfast?"

"I don't usually eat lunch," he replied. "Yes, I had a late breakfast, and we have our primary meal in the evening when I get home."

"I'm glad to see you're giving the workers larger portions. And I can see they've gained weight since our first visit. We'll be sure to report those improvements in our next report."

"Thank you, Mei," he replied.

"May I ask how much you pay for the rice?" she boldly inquired. "I have to wonder if you're being overcharged. It has definitely been mixed with something cheaper."

"I'd have to check our records to be certain, but I believe we pay about ninety *yen* for a hundred kilos."

She pretended to think that over in her mind for a short time, then responded. "That seems plenty high to me, based on what I've seen at other factories. If I were you, I would look at other vendors when you get a chance. There might be too many 'mark-up fees' with your current one. That seems to be a common practice these days. But not all vendors have them."

Having seen the workers and planted the seed for Toshi, she was anxious to be underway. Kazuo would worry if they lingered too long. In order to make their story look good, she diligently finished her bowl of rice, and with facial signals, implored Gordo to do the same. Since they 'hadn't eaten since last night,' it would hardly do to walk away with food left in their bowls.

After finishing their meal, the three of them returned to Cho's office. "We will not interrupt your day further," the Empress told Cho. She bowed and continued, "You have been a most pleasant host once again. The next time we come, I'm sure your workers will be even stronger and healthier. And our best wishes for finding a more honorable rice dealer."

Cho bowed back to the Empress. "It has been my honor to receive you once again, Mei-san. And thank you for illuminating me regarding the reason for our last inspection. I have ways of dealing with scoundrels like him."

When the two of them mounted the black mares, a quiet sigh of relief escaped her lips. "I think we did it," the Empress said as the horses began to walk.

***

Kazuo paced back and forth with his eyes scanning the horizon. He already had the horses loaded and the campfire extinguished. It was after lunchtime, and the Empress should be coming. *Why does everything take longer when you're waiting?* He wondered. Then he spotted two riders in the distance.

"I was going to give you another half-hour before leaving," he said when they pulled up. "How was the inspection?"

"I was shaking the whole time," Gordo replied, "but the Empress covered our tracks. In fact, she covered them so well we may have started a reprisal against Emiko's boyfriend."

Kazuo was all ears. "Emiko had a boyfriend at the factory?"

"We'll tell you about it on the trip home," the Empress replied.

Chapter 50

Epilogue

"I'm happy to see you brought the mules," the Empress said. "When you go to Osaki, you can't be riding one of the horses we've already used. I'm afraid you're stuck with a mule." She waited to see if Toshi would smile or frown.

He seemed to take it in stride. "I can barely ride a horse," he said, "so I guess it doesn't matter much either way. I'm sure it won't be any harder on me than it is on the mule."

"With an attitude like that, you're sure to make the sale," she retorted. "This could be just the break we needed. If Cho agrees to buy rice from you and then smoked fish, who can imagine what else? Have you thought how much food it takes to feed eighty workers, even half-rations like they do at the factory? Kazuo will be coming here every week instead of every other week." She looked over at Emiko, standing next to her and smiling at Kazuo. "You might even get tired of seeing him here so often," she chided Emiko.

Emiko smiled. She knew it was impossible to top the Empress.

"Come and get something to eat while Enji unloads the fish. Then you need to get started for Osaki. I don't want anyone else to get there ahead of you. It would ruin everything. Enji, leave one sack of fish on the mule. And along with it, load two bags of rice.

"When you get there, Toshi, give him the items for free, and make sure he uses them both before you leave. If he actually feeds your rice to his workers, they won't stand for anything less after that. And the fish will be a bonus. He may not share any with the workers, but even if he only keeps it for himself, that's a start. Now let's eat and get you on your way."

Two hours later, Toshi and Kazuo were on their way once more. This was the third trip for Kazuo, and he had no trouble finding the route. Tomorrow night they would use the same camp Kazuo had used on his previous trip. He would be waiting again, but this time, while Toshi made his very first sales call.

*****

"Do you have any last-minute questions before you go?" Kazuo asked. "I'll wait here until you get back. You'll probably have to leave the food with him today and go back tomorrow to see what he thinks. I'd give anything to see their faces when they dish out real rice for a change. If Cho allows that, he has sealed his own fate. The workers will refuse to work if he doesn't keep it up."

Toshi sat on one mule, looking down at Kazuo. The other mule carried two bags of rice and one sack of fish.

"I hope so… Right now I wish we were both back at the foundry where we knew what we were doing. My biggest fear is that I'll let down the workers. Wish me luck. I'll see you this afternoon."

*****

Toshi dismounted the mule he was riding and tied them both to a post in front of the factory. *Riding a mule is not so bad,* he thought. *The pace and rhythm are actually more peaceful than a horse.*

Breathing deep several times, he opened the door and let his eyes adjust to the light. The woman seated opposite the door looked up when it opened. She stared at him without a hint of welcome.

"May I help you?" She intoned.

"Good morning," he bowed. "My name is Toshi Ozawa. Please forgive the intrusion. I seek a brief appointment with the manager in charge of purchasing food for your kitchen. Might that be you?" He was quite sure the responsibilities of purchasing were beyond her authority but hoped it might flatter her ego to ask.

"No, that would be the owner," she said, her tone lightening somewhat. "May I ask what, in particular, you are selling? I'll check with the owner to see if he wishes to make time for you."

"I represent the Kamaishi Trading Company. We supply several fine factories, such as yours, with farm-fresh rice, as well as many varieties of ocean fish. I have samples of our products just outside. May I bring some in for you to see?"

"No, not unless the owner requests it. Wait here and I'll see if he is interested."

"You are most kind. Thank you," he said with a bow.

She soon returned with the older man Toshi already knew was Cho.

Toshi bowed to Cho as he said, "Good morning. My name is Toshi Ozawa. I represent the Kamaishi Trading Company. I am traveling the country, hoping to introduce many fine businesses such as yours, to our very fine rice and fish." Toshi didn't want Cho to think he had been singled out by the Ministry of Labor. It was important to make this encounter seem a coincidence, in case Cho someday learned the Empress was an imposter.

Cho's face brightened slightly at the greeting from Toshi. Bowing in return, he replied, "I am Cho. This is my factory. We already have an outstanding supplier of rice, but since you've traveled all the way from Kamaishi, I'll listen to your story. Only for a short time, however, as I must get back to my other duties." Cho had already begun his bargaining strategy. "Come with me to my office." He turned and headed to the stairway from which he'd come.

Toshi bowed to the assistant, an expression of thanks for her role in getting him the audition. It was hard not to dwell on her face. It was certainly an attractive face, but he had never seen colors applied to a face quite like that before. They seemed to cover areas of perfectly beautiful skin.

When they reached Cho's office, Cho closed the door as a signal he was not to be disturbed. "My assistant tells me you have rice to sell. Is it good rice, and what is your price?"

"Oh, yes, it is very good rice. We buy directly from several farmers throughout the northern valley. We guarantee it to be fresh and pure. We do not mix it with oats, or rye, or any other grain. We also guarantee it to be free of rodents and insects at the time of delivery. Of course, we cannot control what happens after that."

"What is your price?"

"Our price is eighty *yen* per hundred kilograms. That includes delivery to your factory. It's a very fair price."

Cho frowned at hearing the price. He pretended to ponder it for a moment before replying. "I'm afraid your price is too high to be of use to us. Since we buy a lot of rice, we're able to get it for sixty yen per hundred."

Toshi was prepared for this, thanks to the efforts of the Empress two weeks ago. He recognized it as the bargaining ploy that it was, but pretended to appear dejected at the news. "I'm sorry we can't meet that price, even for large shipments. But I'm confident our rice is the finest quality you will find anywhere. And rest assured, there are no additional fees or commissions required. We buy directly from the farmers, and we sell directly to the buyers, such as yourself. We do not require or accept hidden payments in the form of taxes, or commissions, or anything of the sort." He could not think of any additional ways to say 'bribe' or 'kickback' without actually using the words.

Toshi watched the face of Cho for some sign of interest, even the slightest flinch of a movement to indicate interest in Toshi's rather amateurish sales pitch. But Cho was far more experienced than Toshi at buying and selling. He gave away nothing but a rigid face.

"We might be able to pay as much as seventy yen if the quality is as good as you say," Cho said.

"I'm afraid that is not possible," replied Toshi, looking directly at him. "As much as we would like to have you as a customer, we must still make enough profit to stay in business." His chest was pounding, and he struggled to prevent his voice from breaking. "I'm sure you understand that as well as anyone."

Both men avoided eye contact for the next minute. They each pretended to be thinking of a way to accommodate the other without actually doing so. Then Toshi spoke again. "I have a proposal. I have two hundred kilos of fresh rice, in addition to several kilos of our very popular smoked fish, with me today. The fish, by the way, is not only delicious but also very nutritious. It would make an outstanding supplement for your workers. I would even venture to say it would pay for itself in the form of additional production. If you promise to use it right away, I will give you enough rice to accommodate one meal for the entire factory. And I'll throw in the ten kilos of fish to go with it."

Toshi paused to let his offer sink in. He knew Cho would expect something in return, which there was. During the long day's travel yesterday, Toshi had time to think about how to protect the workers.

"I will give you the fish and the rice without charge—but they must all be used in one meal. It would not be fair to me if you held back part of it for later meals. Should we enter into an agreement, our contract will be for an amount equal to three meals of the same quantity, for each day, for one year. That will allow me to schedule our purchases and subsequent deliveries accordingly."

Toshi wanted to make sure Cho did not pretend to give full rations to the workers with the free rice only to starve them again once he had to pay for it.

"If you accept my offer—one complete meal for all your workers—I will deliver the fish and the rice to your kitchen before I leave today, and return tomorrow at mealtime to see what you think of our excellent quality. No doubt you already know that a happy worker is a productive worker. I would be surprised if you didn't see an increase in production immediately, once you start feeding them our rice. And if you served them fish, even small portions, along with the rice, perhaps at either the mid-day or the evening meal, you would be amazed at the improvement."

Cho was still trying to resist. His solemn face did not betray his eagerness for at least a free meal for the factory. *And even if he did have to pay eighty yen per hundred, it would be ten yen less than it cost now.*

"I don't know if we can afford to pay eighty yen," he muttered, "but we'll try your rice and fish tomorrow at noon. Then we'll decide. I'll have the cafeteria people meet you down front and help carry it in. I'll have to discuss with them the amount we need. If we commit to an amount for the entire year, we need to be sure it's the right amount."

"Thank you, Cho-San. You won't be sorry, I promise you. And your workers will be very excited once they get a taste of your new rice."

Toshi hurried down to his mules and began to untie the large sacks of rice and the smaller bag of fish. He hoped they would take at least one of the hundred kilos of rice, maybe even more. He had a hunch Cho would not be willing to pay for the added extravagance of fish, but there was always a chance.

Cho soon followed, with one of the kitchen helpers pulling a cart. "We've decided sixty kilos should be plenty for one meal. Ten kilos of fish will be enough to give everyone a few bites. We normally don't provide fish in addition to rice, but since you've made the offer, we'll pass it along to the workers."

Toshi was disappointed they weren't taking a full hundred-kilo bag but was encouraged by Cho's willingness to take some of the fish. He had a feeling that once teased by a nutritious meal, the workers would not return to the previous rations without a fight.

"I'll help carry this to the kitchen," offered Toshi.

Together, he and the kitchen helper loaded tomorrow's meal onto a cart and pulled it as close as they could to the kitchen doorway. Together, they carried the large sack of rice to a pantry, just off the kitchen.

Toshi noticed an elderly woman busy cleaning and organizing. She was also tending a fire in the stove in preparation for today's noon meal. She smiled at Toshi as he brought in the bag of fish and asked where she would like to have it placed. Toshi was taken by her kind and gentle eyes. She looked like a person he could trust. Approaching her cautiously, he greeted her, speaking softly so others wouldn't hear.

"My agreement with the owner is that two-thirds of the rice and all of the fish is to be served at lunchtime tomorrow. I want this food to go to the workers, not to his personal use. Would you be able to help make sure that happens?"

The kitchen worker felt a pang of emotion, knowing this stranger had the interests of the workers at heart. She thought back to the poor girl a few months ago who looked so frail. She still regretted not being able to help. Almost every day she wondered what had become of her. Even if it was too late to help that girl, she might be able to help the girls who still worked there. "I'll do whatever I can," she murmured back. "But of course, the owner will do what he wants." She thought for a moment. "I do know a place in the back of the pantry where I could hide the rice we don't use. And I think I can make sure we serve everything we prepare."

Toshi smiled at her and nodded inconspicuously, then moved to join Cho and the others.

Having delivered the food, Toshi followed Cho to the exit. "Thank you, Cho-san, for the opportunity to present our merchandise." He bowed respectfully to the owner. What time will you be serving tomorrow? I would like to be here to see for myself how your workers respond. I'm certain you will see an improvement in their demeanor."

Cho replied, "If you are here at half past eleven, we can go together and see if they notice a difference."

As he mounted the mule and headed back to camp, Toshi relaxed slightly, but something still nagged at him. This was only the first step. Giving away a free meal was the easy part. Whether Cho would sign a contract was the real question. And of course, his current supplier would surely make a counteroffer of his own. Toshi might have to drop his price to seventy-five *yen* to get their business.

Kazuo was watching for him from behind a large plum thicket. He emerged when he saw the two plucky mules plodding toward their camp. "It looks like your load is lighter. Did you make a sale?" he shouted.

"Cho agreed to try our food for their noon meal tomorrow. I'm to meet him then. I'm certain the workers will be happy, but I don't know if Cho will agree to change to a new company. He's probably buying from a friend, and may not be willing to switch."

***

After a restless night, Kazuo waved goodbye to Toshi as he headed to the factory for the second time. "Wish me luck. I should be back around two o'clock."

Toshi arrived at the factory shortly after eleven o'clock. The assistant met him at the door and led him upstairs to Cho's office. Cho sat across from him, and with a somber expression, began. "As luck would have it, our current supplier stopped by late yesterday afternoon. When he saw your rice in the pantry, I had no choice but to tell him we were thinking about a change. When he heard that, of course, he was not happy. He offered to drop their price to seventy *yen* per hundred. So now I have to decide what to do."

Toshi looked him in the eye, not with a look of disdain but simply a look of quiet confidence. Then he smiled. "I can see why he would drop his price. Even at seventy yen, it's a high price for what you're getting." Toshi thought there was an almost zero percent chance the supplier had dropped by, but he was willing to engage in the charade. Not only would this be a good contract for them, but more importantly, it would make a difference in the lives of the workers.

Toshi jumped as the shrill of the whistle shook the factory. Kazuo had not thought to mention the whistle, and it made his ears hurt. When Cho could see he was settled again, he said, "That's the signal for lunch. Shall we go see how they like your rice?"

"Yes. And fish," Toshi added. He really wanted to find a new outlet for the fish.

Cho tended to a few papers on the top of his desk and then called down to his assistant to ask if she would like to join them.

By the time the three of them entered the cafeteria, most of the workers were already seated at the tables. The cafeteria was quiet as workers stared at their bowls with dumbfounded looks. The first ones to enter the cafeteria had already begun to eat.

Cho went through first in the serving line, followed by Toshi, and then the assistant. He noticed his bowl was filled higher than normal, even for him. The servers knew to always give more to supervisors, and particularly the owner.

Toshi did not miss the guarded smile and sparkle in the eyes of the elderly kitchen worker as he took his turn through the line.

Cho was often arrogant and self-indulgent, but he had been raised by his parents to be polite. So even though he was first through the line, he waited for Toshi and his assistant to receive their meals before leading them to his favorite bench in the far corner.

As they made their way to the table, something strange happened. The workers began to clap their hands. It was slow at first, from only one bench with three occupants. Then the neighboring table joined in. Then another, and before long the entire cafeteria came alive with the clapping of hands. When Cho looked around, he witnessed not only hands clapping, but faces filled with smiles. Never, since the factory opened, had he witnessed such a demonstration.

Toshi was standing behind him, or he might have noticed the slightest bit of moisture forming in Cho's eyes. Cho made sure to face away from his two guests, even as he seated himself on the bench. He started to acknowledge the demonstration, but his voice betrayed his emotion. "It…it…it looks like…they approve," was all he could get out.

The pressure was full force on Cho when they returned to his office. Toshi sensed a small change of heart from this normally solemn and obsessive owner. He seemed somehow more relaxed than when they had met prior to lunch.

"I'd like to be around to see how they perform this afternoon, but it's time to head back to Kamaishi. I'm willing to bet it will be your best afternoon ever. Did you see the excitement in their eyes when they left the cafeteria?"

"I'm quite amazed at their reaction to something as mundane as a little extra food," Cho said. "But I have to agree, they seemed excited by it."

"Someone told me once that 'happy workers are productive workers'," replied Toshi. "I think there is something to that. Are you ready to make the switch?"

"I hate to spend the extra money," Cho lied, "but I can see it made the workers happier. Maybe it would be worth a change."

Toshi left the remaining one-third sack as well as the other full sack of rice with Cho. The only load the mules had to return with, was Toshi.

Thank you for reading my story. If you enjoyed this book, please take time to leave a review to help others find it. Even better, tell a friend.

Look for the next book in the Kamaishi Heritage Series.

The Difficult Years of Toshi Ozawa – Book 2

Author's Note

This is a work of fiction. It is centered around actual events of the time, but the actions and conversations of all characters in the story are fictional.

When I set out to write this story, I had planned to profile one or two families who were victims of internment in 1942, following the Japanese invasion of Pearl Harbor. It was a dark chapter in our history that many Americans might not be aware of. The concept of forced roundup and encampment certainly held many possibilities for human interest stories. But when I began to write, the first questions that came to mind were: what kind of people were they, and where did they come from?

Reaching back in their history I learned of a small fishing village on the northeast coast of Japan. Kamaishi was home to an emerging iron foundry in the newly awakened environment of the Meiji Revolution. The Japanese industrial revolution had just begun, and changes were taking place in every segment of life. But the intriguing part was that by 1945, the Kamaishi Iron Works had become a leading provider of munitions for the Japanese war effort. It found itself high on the list of targets for Allied forces, specifically, the U.S. Navy. In July of that year, three battleships paced just beyond the harbor, lobbing round after round of sixteen-inch shells on the foundry... a complete circle.

Kamaishi was the perfect place to begin the story.

The smelting furnace, a cornerstone in the story, was loosely based on the Hashino Iron Works, a primitive smelting operation later recognized as the birthplace of Japan's modern iron industry. It utilized a simple procedure for blending charcoal with magnetite to produce iron.

I have simplified the foundry for this story to give the workers a more personal voice. The actual foundry was much larger and operated around the clock. But it was real, and plagued by charcoal shortages as depicted in the story, shutting down more than once until it finally found permanent footing by switching from charcoal to coal. *Takato Oshima* founded the blast furnace, but was later replaced by a German, brought in to help modernize the facility. Why Takato was ousted is not determined, but it is easy to speculate a difference in personality or management style. That is why I characterized the director in the story as a rigid and demanding leader.

The events in the story regarding the furnace and its shutdown periods are pure speculation based on what was likely happening at the time. I found no record of the foundry paying partial wages during the shutdown periods, but many Japanese companies have reputations for taking care of their workers, and it seemed a realistic possibility.

Yamagata Aritomo was a Japanese statesman and military commander, sometimes considered the father of Japanese militarism. Whether there was actually an open house to reveal the new blast furnaces is not known, but given their importance to the nation, it seemed likely. And whether Yamagata Aritomo was present for it is another question, but it also seemed plausible. The words attributed to him are pure speculation based on how he might have felt at that moment in time. They were also intended as a harbinger of what was yet to come in 1945. (book four)

Whether foundry workers tried their hand at fishing is another unknown, but it seems likely, since Kamaishi was primarily a fishing village. Toshi and Haruki would certainly have done whatever they could to provide for their families. This is reaffirmed by their willingness to transport rice from Hanamaki to Kamaishi as a supplemental business venture.

Fr. Henri Lispard was an actual person who lived in Kamaishi at the time. He was a Catholic missionary in a country only recently open to Christianity. It had been banned for over two hundred years prior to the Meiji Revolution. Japan was predominately Shinto, Confucian, or Buddhist. Fr. Lispard, at first an interesting historical figure for me, grew in importance as the story progressed. He carries a larger role in book two.

The thread factories were one of Japan's more promising industries following the Meiji Revolution, helped by a downturn in silk production in China. It became a leading export for Japan, and production was encouraged by the government. Workers in the thread factories were frequently the daughters of poor peasant farmers, and conditions in many of the mills were as bad as characterized in the story. For more information on the thread mills, I recommend *Factory Girls*, referenced below.

Toshi was not able to pursue his dream of emigrating to America in this segment, but the dream is not dead. Follow the story in book two to see what becomes of Toshi, his family, and Fr. Lispard.

THANK YOU to…

 My mother, Mary Esther Davenport, who taught in country schools throughout her long career, and always championed proper use of the language.

My English and writing teachers along the way, including Dr. Jean Pettit at UNK, Jack E. Nellson at Shelton Public High School, and Liz Kay at MCC in Omaha.

Kirsten Bublitz, who inspired me to write this book, having written two of her own before she graduated college at UNA, and to her mother and family, who went out of their way to help support this project.

To my friends, when asked how the book was coming, listened patiently through a longer response than they thought necessary.

To Petra Jacobsen, my pen pal research assistant, for her help in language translation with the Kamaishi Iron Museum as well as her first-hand images from Japan.

To my beta readers at *fiverr.com*. The story improved because of their candid suggestions.

Daniel Pugsley
Robert Marshall
Sasha Pinto-Jayawardena

Cover art depicting Ayami and Toshi on a mountain trail:
Rob Williams @ ilovemycover.com

To learn more about the early Meiji period in Japan, and the fictional account of Emiko at the thread factory, read:

Inventing Japan, by Ian Buruma
Factory Girls, by E. Patricia Tsurumi

Other Books in the Kamaishi Heritage Series:

Kamaishi Heritage Book 2 – *The Difficult Years of Toshi Ozawa*
Kamaishi Heritage Book 3 – *Isamu's American Dream*
Kamaishi Heritage Book 4 – *Isamu's Broken Dream*

About the author

Don was born in Custer County, Nebraska, attended public schools in Callaway, and later graduated from Shelton High School and the University of Nebraska at Kearney. A lifelong learner, he also continued his studies at the University of Nebraska at Omaha, and the Metropolitan Community College of Omaha.

During his career as an IT specialist, Don commuted for extended periods to Worcester, MA, Houston, TX, and San Antonio, TX. He currently resides in Omaha with his wife, Marian.

The story of Toshi's family was seven years in the making. It is a story for the 'everyman,' which reflects the difficulties each of us encounters at times in our lives.

You can reach the author at dddavenport.author@gmail.com for comments.